French
Modernist   Series Editors: Mary Ann Caws, Richard Howard, Patricia Terry
Library

Louis-Ferdinand Céline able for Another Time

University of Nebraska Press : Lincoln and London

(Féerie pour une autre fois I)

With explanatory notes

and a new preface by Henri Godard

Translated and with an

introduction by Mary Hudson

Publication of this translation was assisted by grants from the French Ministry of Culture – National Center for the Book, and the National Endowment for the Arts.

Féerie pour une autre fois 1 copyright © Editions Gallimard, 1952. Translation, preface, and translator's introduction copyright © 2003 by the Board of Regents of the University of Nebraska. The notes to this English edition are based on those by Henri Godard, originally published in *Romans*, vol. 4: *Féerie pour une autre fois 1*, Plèiade ed. copyright © Editions Gallimard, 1974. All rights reserved. Manufactured in the United States of America. Designed and typeset by Richard Eckersley, in Monotype Bulmer. ∞

Cataloging-in-Publication Data available
Library of Congress Control Number: 2002026720
ISBN 0-8032-1520-7 (cl.: alkaline paper)
ISBN 0-8032-6424-0 (pa.: alkaline paper)

For animals, for the sick, for prisoners

Contents

Preface ix

Translator's Introduction xvii

Fable for Another Time 1

Notes 221

P REFACE *Fable for Another Time* in Céline's Opus

MORE THAN FORTY YEARS after his death, Louis-Ferdinand Céline's work cannot be ignored – in France or throughout twentieth-century literature. Because of its polemical aspect, it still presents its readers with the same literary and moral problems. But his novelistic writings made a unique contribution in terms of both their vision and their language. As writers and readers, we are still feeling the aftershocks of the literary bombshell that was the publication in 1932 of his first novel, *Journey to the End of the Night.* Its reverberations were amplified as the years progressed by the seven succeeding novels, which developed according to a rigorous internal logic. The one that remains the least well known, even in France, *Fable for Another Time*, represents a key moment in this overall development. It is the first of this novel's two parts (published separately) that Mary Hudson reveals today in translation for an English-speaking public, fifty years after its original publication in 1952.

The four preceding novels, *Journey to the End of the Night*, *Death on the Installment Plan*, *Casse-pipe*, and *Guignol's Band*, had for their center of gravity the experience of the First World War, where Céline had been wounded and which decided his fate, both as a man and as a writer. In 1937 he started writing a series of nonfiction books known as "pamphlets." Their primary purpose was to combat the threat of a new war, but this purpose was overshadowed by the racial hatred of the Jews unleashed in them. War broke out. France was defeated by Germany in June 1940, then occupied for four years. In the spring of 1944, Allied bombing of strategic sites was a forewarning of the coming offensive and liberation. One of those bombings, meant to destroy a sorting station not far from Céline's Montmartre apartment, would be the subject of the second part of *Fable for Another Time*. Two years later, while he was being held prisoner in Copenhagen, waiting for the Danish authorities to decide what to do about France's extradition request, Céline undertook to turn into novel form what he had lived through since that bombing, which for him had been the sign that he should seek exile.

But before doing so, he was aware that he also had to renew contact with his audience. He knew perfectly well that in the years following the liberation, he'd become a literary outcast. Whatever it cost, he had to tear down the wall of this hostility or, as he wrote in a letter, "blast a second hole through the ceiling" (the first being *Journey to the End of the Night*). Once again he went about it scandalously, by evoking both his situation in Montmartre in the spring of 1944 and his detention two years later. The two became the subject of this first part of *Fable for Another Time*, in which he takes the opportunity whenever the whim strikes him to recall the positions he had taken, thereby provoking his readership. But he also imposes himself on us through his comic genius and the novelty of his prose. He forces us to read him, like it or not.

Fable for Another Time thus appears as a decisive step in the development of Céline's work. It is in this novel that the narrative and polemical veins meet. At the same time, Céline virtually reaches a culminating point from the narrative, stylistic, and thematic points of view (he will hardly go any further in the last novels).

Already with *Journey to the End of the Night* he dug deep into his own experience to write the story of his protagonist. But by giving him the fictional name of Bardamu, he kept within a form that from the point of view of novelistic narrative was not at all groundbreaking. In the next three novels, he drops this name. The protagonist-narrator is now called only by his first name, Ferdinand, which suggests a possible identification with the author, whose pen name is Louis-Ferdinand Céline. In *Fable for Another Time* a new step is taken: here the one who says "I" is sometimes called Ferdinand but at other times is referred to as Céline. At other times he is called by his real as well as his professional name, Dr. Destouches, and even sometimes by the name used only by his intimates, Louis. Thus, everything necessary for an autobiographical work is brought together and forthwith confirmed, it would seem, since the events written about, starting with his incarceration in Copenhagen, were all well known to the public as events in Céline's life.

But who would even think of taking as literal truth his interpretation of these events? The detailing of the facts and circumstances is so obviously exaggerated, the characters so patently caricatured, the general tone so cavalierly indifferent to verisimilitude, that the reader always senses the role of invention and the imaginary. Part of the reader agrees with the words "novel" and "imaginary" intentionally used by Céline in his opening statement. But at the same time, the reader cannot forget that the historical background to this work was actually lived. With this book, at the beginning of the 1950s, Céline was the first to perfect a new novelistic formula destined for a great future in France and elsewhere: a novel in which invention is grafted onto a presumed autobiography.

The step forward is no less evident in his treatment of the language, that is, in the ever more insistent assertion of a personal style. The use of French as spoken by the people in *Journey to the End of the Night* was only a beginning. Already with *Death on the Installment Plan*, Céline had begun to reap the consequences of this initial choice: everyday spoken French was just that, merely spoken. To adopt it implies finding a way to express it in writing. The very nature of the written word comes up against the principles of how oral discourse works: it cannot follow for long a conceived order; it breaks the sentence up into segments; these segments are linked according to all sorts of associations that have nothing to do with pure logic; they happen linearly, in the ever present. To indicate the silences between these segments, Céline came up with the idea of usurping the normal function of suspension points. But this simulation of speech had itself a consequence, which would become one of the great strengths of Céline's style: since the spoken word is inevitably linked to our experience of the present, the overall result of Céline's method tends to render these sentence fragments present for us, even though they were written consecutively on a day well in the past. *Fable for Another Time* is also the novel in which Céline becomes fully conscious of the possibilities offered by this spontaneous choice of a discourse that is supposed to be oral. In particular, he realized that the more a fragment carries the weight of emotion, the more it will have the ring of the present.

Toward that end, one emotion serves as well as another, but there is one type that Céline adds to the others in *Fable*, exemplified in the aggressive give and take between the author and the reader. Here Céline turns upside down what authors of every epoch have done when they seek to reconcile the reader to him, to make him a friend. Céline treats the reader as an adversary, and vice versa. For him, the important thing is that there should be between him and the reader an emotional link. For that, hostility will do just as well as complicity (athletes and soldiers speak of "seeking contact"). Given the state of public opinion toward him at the time, Céline in any case has no choice. But he plays the hand he's been dealt for all it is worth, by taking it as the source of the emotion while at the same time making sport of it.

The game, however, is ambiguous. Céline has found a new way to attack the reader. In his previous novels, the aggression took the form of destroying our illusions. Sometimes it is those concerning our feelings ("love is the infinite placed within the reach of poodles" at the beginning of *Journey to the End of the Night*); sometimes it is those by which we try to deny the reality of death ("I haven't always been a doctor ... crummy trade," on the first page of *Death on the Installment Plan*). While he was writing *Fable for Another Time*, immediately after the Second World War, Céline knew that nothing would shock the reader more than distancing himself from the general feeling about the Nazi camps whose existence was just being revealed, and from the tone everyone was using in speaking about them. So he lost no time doing just that, through little touches here and there throughout the text. He could hardly have thought at the time that this was the way to win readers over to his point of view. But he was certain that by touching this most sensitive spot, he would provoke a reaction, even if it was one of rejection: one of his poetic principles was always and everywhere to hover right at the brink of the abyss.

Even though the violence done to the reader is inflicted playfully, it still adds to the thematic role of violence and its imagery throughout the work. This presence has the effect of making *Fable for Another Time* a quintessence of Céline's writing. From beginning to end, this novel conjures up acts of corporal violence, first the tortures that would have awaited him had he stayed in Paris, and then those of the prison, whose echoes reach him in his cell. These images will be replaced, in the second part, by the apocalyptic violence of the bombing, which is the sole subject of this narrative – if we can still call it a narrative – through all of its three hundred some pages. It is no doubt Céline's singular contribution to world literature to have bared man's innate violence, demonstrating it in ever better ways, in all its forms, and furiously tearing off the veils with which we try to cover it. *Fable* constitutes one of the strongest segments of this trajectory.

After the "overture" afforded by *Féerie pour une autre fois I*, Céline plunges his reader into the story, transposed in his inveterate way, of what he saw and lived through between the spring of 1944 and that of 1946. (The story is recorded in *Féerie pour une autre fois II*, the one Céline novel that remains unpublished in English.) During this period, after the bombing of Montmartre, he crossed Germany during the last year of the war and found himself under other bombs and in the midst of many other mad escapades. These are the volumes that the English-speaking readers already know: *Castle to Castle*, *North*, and *Rigodoon*. In bringing out *Fable for Another Time*, Mary Hudson puts into place for them a missing piece of the puzzle, thus helping readers to form a view of all eight novels that make up Céline's opus and grasp their dynamic unity. Without that unity, it is not possible to get the true measure of Céline.

Henri Godard,
*editor of the Plёïade edition
of Céline's novels*

Translator's Introduction

LOUIS-FERDINAND CÉLINE (27 May 1894–1 July 1961) was the most controversial French writer of the twentieth century. To this day, there are many in France who refuse to read his novels, or who read them with a jaundiced eye, because of his infamous prewar pamphlets that expressed pro-Nazi opinions and contained grotesque examples of the kind of antisemitic sentiment that was rife at the time. Even in this country, it can prove politically awkward to deal with Céline in academic circles, where his association with Nazism is naturally excoriated. Those of us, however, who read him either ignorant of or despite his pamphlets find a treasure trove of the most powerful writing to come out of France in the twentieth century, writing that was to influence future generations of authors both in France and abroad.

Céline was born Louis-Ferdinand Destouches in Courbevoie, a modest suburb of Paris, to lower-middle-class parents in the very year the Dreyfus Affair broke out, 1894. His father, as depicted in *Death on the Installment Plan*, was unstable, a raving antisemite and French chauvinist. His parents' great hope for their only child was that he become a salesman in one of the new "grands magazins," or department stores, that were destroying the commerce of people like his mother, a small shopkeeper dealing in laces and bric-a-brac. To that end they sent him as a young teenager to school in England and Germany for extended periods, knowing that the acquisition of foreign languages would enhance his chances of attaining this lofty goal. He became proficient in English and German but would never use them in his professional life. Rather than fulfill his parents' ambitions, the rebellious youth enlisted in the French army on the eve of World War I. Shortly afterward he was seriously wounded, resulting in his hospitalization and eventual honorable discharge from military service. He then traveled to London (where he is said to have enjoyed a tryst with the spy Mata Hari) and to Cameroon, where he worked briefly for a logging company. Returning to France, he managed to earn a baccalaureate degree and entrance to medical school. He became a medical doctor in 1924 and worked briefly for the League of Nations, doing research on disease prevention and control.

Medicine would be his abiding vocation. By all accounts he was an excellent physician with the most gentle bedside manner, but he was incapable of asking for money in return for his services. As a result he exercised his profession in the public health sector among the poorest levels of society.

He was a restless soul, however, and traveled extensively, visiting England, Germany, and other European countries, including the new Soviet Union. He sailed a few times to the United States, once venturing as far as California in his fruitless quest to win back the affections of his American mistress, Elizabeth Craig, to whom he dedicated his first novel, *Journey to the End of the Night*.

The work was published in 1932 and became an overnight sensation. It was slated to win the coveted Goncourt prize that year but was pipped at the post by the novel *Les Loups* by Guy Mazeline, now long forgotten. This disappointment, together with the disapproval to which his second novel, *Death on the Installment Plan*, would be subjected four years later, greatly contributed to inflaming the latent paranoia of this extremely sensitive physician and author. The result would be the venting of his great resentment and sense of persecution in the three notorious "antisemitic pamphlets" published from 1937 to 1941.

Fable for Another Time was Céline's fourth novel, coming after *Journey to the End of the Night* (1932), *Death on the Installment Plan* (1936), and *Guignol's Band* (1944). *Fable* also came after the prewar pamphlets, which were to make him a postwar pariah. Through the pamphlets – *Bagatelle pour un massacre*, *École des cadavres*, and *Les beaux draps*, – he had become known as a Nazi sympathizer. *Fable* preceded the "German trilogy": *North*, *Castle to Castle*, and *Rigodoon*, in which he recounted his wanderings and misadventures in Nazi Germany as it collapsed under the combined might of the Allied forces.

All of Céline's novels are a vibrant, compelling mix of phantasmagoria and autobiography. They recount in distorted, exaggerated, and at times hallucinatory language the author's daily activities, travels, and relationships. They contain a constant stream of his mocking, often indignant, and sometimes outrageous musings on human foibles, rendered in his own singular, fierce style of lyrical yet earthy Parisian street-French. *Fable for Another Time* is all of this and more. In fact, it is unique among the author's novels. Coming midway in his literary career, it not only represented a turning point in his development, but it was also his most singular work. Like his previous and subsequent novels, it is intimately related to his personal experience and feelings. It differs from his other novels in one important point, however: when he wrote his other novels he did so as a free man, stealing time from his activities as a medical doctor or passing countless nocturnal hours depriving himself of sleep in order to pour out the tumultuous ramblings that constantly erupted from his mischievous genius. When Céline began *Fable*, by contrast, he was a prisoner. The novel thus has the peculiarity of being written at the time of his life when he was the most self-tormented, the most persecuted, the most vulnerable. This novel would be his consolation and his vindication.

Although he consistently refused during the war to collaborate in any way with the Nazi war effort, his identification with the enemy was strong enough for him to receive death threats, sometimes in the form of little replica coffins sent to him in the mail. Shortly after the Allied invasion of Normandy in June 1944, Céline fled to Germany with his young wife, the dancer Lucette Almansor, and extraordinary cat, Bébert.

On 17 June 1944 the Destouches ménage arrived in Baden-Baden, where they stayed at the Brenner's Park Hotel and where it was at first temptingly possible to make believe they were merely on vacation while the author-physician tried to plot his next move. He consistently maintained that his aim in going to Germany was to reach Denmark, where he had gold stashed away in the care of his friend Karen-Marie Jensen, another ballet dancer. That mission was much easier said than done, as the peregrinations and machinations of the next nine months would prove. By the end of August, when Philippe Pétain and other top officials of the Vichy government came streaming into Germany in the wake of the Allies' advance, the Brenner's Park Hotel was no longer a comfortable place to be. The Destouches household was shunted off to a small room on an upper floor and rations became thin. Through medical and political contacts in Berlin, Céline was able to procure a temporary home near a village in Prussia named Kraenslin not too far from the Danish border. There they remained for two months on a farm that was to become the setting for the hallucinatory and often hilarious pandemonium portrayed in *North* as Germany became squeezed in the vise created by the Russian onslaught from the east and the English and American assault from the west, and as it was pummeled from the air by the Allies' bombs. The strange trio's welcome soon wore thin in this small community where more foreign mouths to feed were not appreciated at this time of near famine, and again through contacts, Dr. Destouches got permission to join his fellow refugees in Sigmaringen, the beautiful little medieval city in the south of Germany that had become the seat of Pétain's government-in-exile. There he was able to practice medicine among this wretched, defeated band of Nazi supporters. This experience provided the material for the second novel of the trilogy, *Castle to Castle*, which would be the most successful because of the stories it contained about the doomed collaborators. However, Céline insisted on deriding and mocking any notion that a German victory was now possible, which meant that in the end he was hardly any safer in Germany than he had been in Paris.

All of the Destouches's attempts to get to neutral territory during this time failed until Céline was able to prevail upon contacts in the Danish government and the Red Cross to convince the German authorities to let them depart. After a nightmarish train journey that lasted five days (and provided the material for *Rigodoon*, the last of the German Trilogy), they finally got permission to leave for Denmark. The de Gaulle supporters, Communists, and other resisters who had come to power after France's liberation, were understandably not in a generous mood, and Céline's life was still under threat. Hoping to wait it out in Denmark until tempers cooled, the haggard and hungry trio finally arrived in Copenhagen in March 1945.

They lived there incognito until 17 December, when they were arrested and imprisoned in the Vestre Faengsel fortress, where Céline would spend most of the next eighteen months, his wife having been liberated after eleven days. He would be charged under articles 75 and 76 of the French penal code, which punished high treason and carried the death penalty. (He was eventually convicted in absentia, in February 1950, of the lesser charge of "national disgrace.") The Danish government, however, could find no substance to the accusations. Officials nevertheless held him at their discretion in the ancient fortress, where he raged and fulminated for over a year through more than four hundred letters to his lawyers, wife, and friends in which he protested his innocence and advised his lawyers. He also wrote the first drafts of *Fable for Another Time*.

The French title of the work, *Féerie pour une autre fois*, gives a better understanding of the type of book it is. Unfortunately, English has no word for *féerie* (from *fée*, meaning "fairy"). It can be translated as fairy tale, or fairyland, or enchantment, but it is not precisely any of these, rather a mixture of all three. *Féerie* also refers to a type of entertainment similar to pantomimes, popular at the turn of the twentieth century, in which a brightly lit stage threw out sparkling images of sprites, princesses, goblins, and the like to the delight of the children in the audience. The author's maternal grandmother, Céline Guillou (from whom he adopted his *nom de plume*), would bring him to see them as a boy, and he loved them. By using the word *féerie*, Céline drew attention to the magical, escapist aspect of the work: it was a life-saving flight into the enchanted world in which pleasure was still possible, in another time, another place, and which now only the imagination could recapture.

Féerie I was conceived of as a "prelude" to *Féerie pour une autre fois II*, a hallucinatory recounting of the bombing of Paris by the Allies in April 1944. However, *Fable I* is a story very much of the present. Repeatedly, the narrator complains about prison life, particularly the wails coming from his fellow prisoners, and his personal ailments exacerbated by the rigors of incarceration. He boasts, however, that he no longer hears inmates' howls because he is lost in his memories. All he hears are the sounds of his language as it was spoken by his friends and neighbors in Montmartre, to which his caged imagination relentlessly returns for its life-sustaining nourishment.

Fable very much bears the stamp of prison writing. Throughout the reader senses the frantic restlessness of the convict. The usual prisoner's preoccupations and obsessions are ever present: the inhuman conditions, the noises, the aggressive and hostile relationships with the guards and fellow prisoners, the solitude, the nostalgia for one's home and former freedom, the view of the world as divided between "them" on the outside and "us" within, even the ruminations on one's wife's infidelity. But it is much more than just a prison novel. It is a *tour de force* and requires some explication in order for the reader to enjoy it fully.

The work contains little by way of narrative. Past, present, and future are conspicuously and intentionally jumbled. It opens in the narrator's Montmartre apartment overlooking Paris as the city awaits its liberation by the Allied forces. The wife and son of an old friend and fellow World War I veteran – who now, significantly, disdains to call on him – are paying the narrator an untoward visit. He doesn't know the reason for the visit but sees it as an omen of things to come. They seem to be looking around for spoils in anticipation of the "General Sale" of his possessions once he's fled. There follows a long tirade exposing his persecution, and it is only later that we learn that the narrator is in prison.

Scenes of prison life alternate with nostalgic memories of the narrator's former life in France, with snippets of songs he shares with the readers, and diatribes against his persecution. Some episodes can be described only as paranoid hallucinations, notably that of the wheelbarrow, during which literary enemies trundle him through rocky roads to dump him into a cesspool. One of the most charming sections of the book is the Saint-Malo scene in which an eccentric *fin-de-siècle* casino represents the halcyon days of a better, bygone France. These soothing escapes into his fond memories are constantly interrupted by the screams of his fellow prisoners and interspersed with his fantasies of being vindicated by the future success of the novel, which will win him back the public's admiration and his own self-esteem.

Although the novel has its playful and humorous side, *Fable* is very much a polemical piece of writing. It is a painful and wrenching *cri du coeur*, venting as it does the author's rage over what he considered to be the tremendous injustice done to him. The book takes on the aspect of a fierce dialogue with the reader. The narrator constantly berates the reader, who in turn spits back opprobrium and insults at the ranting storyteller. When the inmates are not hurling abuse at each other, or the guards at the inmates, the caged "Ferdinand" is hurling abuse at the reader and vice versa.

It is not always clear, however, where the adversary's words end and the narrator's begin. As with the author's choice of words, which very often leaves room for multiple interpretations, there is a deliberate tactic here to blur distinctions. The hunter and the hunted, the guilty and the innocent, the powerful and the weak all become interchangeable. At one point, for example, while being roundly abused by the reader, the narrator suddenly starts defending him before the court of the "First Specters," a regiment in a ghostly French army of yesteryear, the narrator's last remaining supporter and ally.

The broken narrative at first makes for confusing reading. The novel seems to lack structure, but this is not the case. On the contrary, it eventually becomes apparent that it is as daintily crafted as a piece of lace. Céline's mother was a lace dealer, and he often referred to his work as similar to that of the lace-maker. Language no longer serves Céline's narrative; it weaves patterns that are repeated and enjoyed for their own sake. Language is no longer merely a tool for conveying a message; it has become the message. It performs virtuoso feats never before accomplished. It is not the story that is of primary interest, but the astonishing verbal and phonetic acrobatics that his French can perform.

Céline's aim in his novels was to reproduce in writing the immediate effect that the *spoken* word had on the listener, including its comic effect. In this novel he achieves that aim to the highest degree, so much so that he sacrifices coherency at the expense of the emotional impact of the sounds of the spoken word.

It is no accident that this apogee should be reached just at this juncture. Living the dire consequences of his foolhardy foray into the world of political ideas (for which he had no talent whatsoever), the author seeks consolation in doing what he does best, stretching the boundaries of French prose. But he also seeks revenge on those he sees as having wronged him. Whatever he did, he says, he did out of patriotic motives. He was a good old soldier, having only his country's interests at heart, and now his country has turned against him. His consolation and revenge, his vindication, will be *Fable*. His countrymen consider him a traitor? He will show them that no one is more French than he, for no one else can wield the French language to such effect. He may be a pariah, but he is still the master of French language and literature.

If the novel begins coherently enough with the arrival of unwanted visitors, it ends conventionally enough in a humorous, dreamlike scene in which the narrator's best friend is busy betraying him, both through seducing his wife and calling attention to his pro-German sympathies in front of an increasingly pro-Allies group of onlookers, as the first Allied bombers fly over Paris. In between, however, the text is splintered into small "sound bites." Words rather than sentences carry the thread of the narrative, which is constantly broken, only to be taken up again at a later time. Subjects are approached and abandoned, but not for long. The narrator systematically circles around each obsession in a lacelike fashion. At one point it is no longer even words that carry the narrative; the text is splintered into an explosion of syllables, rendering an astonishingly emotive "atomic" writing that is barely comprehensible. This is the scene in which a silly, sycophantic journalist visits Ferdinand in prison and commiserates on his plight while callously dismissing the fate of the Jews. Perhaps it is not an accident that the author chose this most sensitive juncture for his most virtuoso linguistic performance. Having scapegoated the Jews, he became himself a scapegoat. The irony was not lost on him, as his subsequent identification with Jews would demonstrate.

Céline's novels were revolutionary in style and have had a great impact on subsequent generations of writers. When he was seeking a publisher for his first novel, he wrote to one of them that he'd never read anything quite like it before. He felt that he was influenced by no one in particular. We do, however, see in previous authors elements of style or attitude that bear similarities to the work of Céline. In Emile Zola's work, for example, there is a tendency toward the kind of sweeping overstatement and exaggeration that will become sheer hallucination in Céline's writing, although for Zola, unlike for Céline, the narrative still retains its traditional storytelling function. Like Céline, Zola dealt with the more graphic aspects of birth, copulation, and death in a way that must have appealed to the medical man in Céline. They both wrote from firsthand experience about the underbelly of Paris, as both lived and worked among its lower classes. However, being a nineteenth-century man, Zola could still be optimistic. If Céline's writings, by contrast, had not been tempered with his often hilarious sense of the absurd and his constant self-mockery, they would make for grim reading indeed.

Having survived the traumas of World War I, read the works of Sigmund Freud (which made a deep impression on him), and seen the rise of fascism and Stalinism, Céline held a dim view of humanity's prospects for self-improvement. In some ways his stark pessimism recalls the mood of the works of the Marquis de Sade, who shares with Céline a refusal to ignore man's brutality and lust for power. Unlike Céline, however, de Sade is interested in little else. De Sade's genius focused obsessively on power and its excesses, the sexual act becoming a vehicle for cruelty and domination. Though the wickedness he portrayed contained a mischievous, and at times amusing, element, he is deadly serious. De Sade's genius is not a comic one. There is no room for court jesters in his world. And Céline is nothing if not a jester. He has a fierce sense of hilarity and the overwhelming absurdity of human pretensions and ambitions, including those that de Sade exalts.

Rabelais is perhaps the French writer with whom Céline has the most in common. Like Rabelais, Céline was a master of the phantasmagorically picaresque. In the latter's work, however, the phantasmagoria takes on a nightmarish, surreal quality befitting the monstrous nature of the times in which he lived and wrote. He shares with Rabelais an exuberant vulgarity, a penchant for gross exaggeration, and a need to poke fun at life's vanities. The two authors also shared the habit of distorting one aspect of reality to express a truth.

Céline himself felt he had much in common with Rabelais. They both managed to get themselves into "desperate situations" with the law, to make themselves "well and truly odious." More important, Céline shared with Rabelais a desire to democratize the French language, to make the vernacular acceptable in literature. This he did spectacularly well. He brought French as it was spoken by the urban proletariat to the apotheosis of literary acceptance. He did for Parisian French what James Joyce did for Dublin's English.

In fact, the two writers Céline resembles more than any others are both Irishmen, the one being Joyce and the other the eighteenth-century poet, satirist, and pamphleteer Jonathan Swift. Both Joyce and Céline were fascinated by language itself and fully explored their languages' linguistic and metaverbal possibilities, in the end, many readers would complain, to the detriment of the narrative. Céline's explorations were restricted to his native French, while Joyce drew upon his knowledge of a number of languages and played with them, finally blending them all into one stream in *Finnegans Wake*. Both of these writers would revolutionize the way their languages were perceived and used in literature, exercising enormous influence over the writers of subsequent generations.

"The horror of reality" could as easily have been the epigraph for Swift's work as it was for *Fable for Another Time*. In the same way, in Yeats's description of Swift's vision as one of "savage indignation" could equally apply to Céline's. Neither Swift nor Céline could resist exposing the contrast between the "horror of reality" (as they perceived it) and the pretensions and follies of human beings. Both deployed ferocious irony and satiric exaggeration to do so, and both exhibited a gift for the fantastic. Though misanthropic and pessimistic about human nature in general, they had tremendous compassion for the individual. The prevalence of injustice and suffering brought forth the same "savage indignation." Their pamphleteering brought them both notoriety if not infamy. (Coincidentally, they even suffered from the same inner-ear ailment known as Menière's syndrome, an affliction mentioned in *Fable for Another Time*). They also shared a conservative temperament and outlook and experienced the deep bitterness of greatly talented people who felt deprived of the honors due to them.

Many of George Orwell's observations about Swift in "Politics vs. Literature" could well apply to Céline. Politically, according to Orwell, Swift was "one of those people who are driven into a sort of perverse Toryism by the follies of the progressive party of the moment."[1] After the publication of "Voyage," Céline was embraced as a favorite son by the entire left. A number of Communist authors, including Louis Aragon and Paul Nizan, regarded him as a champion of the leftist view of life. He was embraced by the Communist Party, not only in France but in the Soviet Union, where a heavily edited version of *Journey to the End of the Night* was much admired. That all changed, however, when he published his first pamphlet, *Mea culpa* (1936), in which he expressed his outrage against Communism and the Soviet Union under Stalin.

Orwell's observation about Swift's vision also resonates for readers of Céline. Orwell wrote that Swift "did not possess ordinary wisdom, but he did possess a terrible intensity of vision, capable of picking out a single hidden truth then magnifying it and distorting it. . . . [I]f the force of belief is behind it, a world-view which only just passes the test of sanity is sufficient to produce a great work of art."[2]

Fable for Another Time represents a transition between the type of discourse found in the antisemitic pamphlets and that of the postwar works. The pamphlets were so hysterical in tone that they did not pass the test of sanity. They were beyond the pale of literature altogether, belonging instead to a peculiar genre of demented journalism. In *Fable* the hysteria, although still present, is softened, and there is a renewed bid

xxx

to achieve artistic balance. That balance is still precarious, however, and as a result, the distortions of Céline's rage continually threaten to overwhelm the novel form, making this his most quixotic work.

Céline's antisemitic writings are at the same time both representative of French antisemitism and paradoxically singular. They contained nothing new; they were a rehashing of the same hackneyed fears of Jewish conspiracy and conquest, with outrageous generalizations about a supposed Jewish physiognomy and character, not unmixed with admiration and envy. But Céline's pronouncements, as absurd as they were, were so unforgettably obsessive and grotesque that they constituted an indelible mark, so to speak, on the nation's collective psyche. Thus, it was perhaps less his antisemitism than his very linguistic genius that caused him to become such an infamous outcast; it was not *what* he said, but *how* he said it. After all, many others were spouting the same nonsense at the time. Most of the antisemitic ranting published in the prewar years has long since been forgotten. Céline's cannot be forgotten. Like the rest of his writing, it was too powerful. Many in France already recognized him as one of the greatest literary figures of the modern world. He was not to be forgiven for investing his formidable powers into such an unspeakably unworthy enterprise.

He knew perfectly well as he languished in prison that he had become a pariah to his fellow countrymen, and why. But he never, at least publicly, fully admitted his awful error in attacking the European Jewish community at the time when it was quite literally threatened by extinction. Nonetheless, it would be a mistake to say that he was a monster, an inhuman, heartless man, as is often assumed. His novels, his medicine, and many of his human relationships attest to enormous compassion and tenderness – especially with regard to the sick, the disadvantaged, women, children, and animals – that coexisted in him alongside his racism, his paranoid tendencies, and his ferocious indignation.

The old truism that things get lost in translation is more applicable to *Fable for Another Time* than to most works. Because the inspiration for this novel came from the author's desire to stretch the boundaries of literature rather than to develop a coherent narrative, translating it presents numerous peculiarities and challenges that do not exist with more straightforward material. As noted above, the author continually played in this novel on the *sounds* of French words, and more specifically on the tones and rhythms of *parigot*, the slang, accent, and syntactical peculiarities of working-class Parisian French. In short, the words' sounds, and the "music" they create, the effect they have on the ear, take precedence in this novel over the concepts contained in them. The narrative is disjointed at best, as the author free-associates pell-mell, treating the reader to one non sequitur after another. The fact that sounds transmit ideas is always overshadowed by the fact that they convey feelings.

If neither ideas nor narrative is important in this work, tone, mood, and humor certainly are. To convey these authentically requires a less strict word-for-word translation. A more supple approach is needed. One must find the sounds, phrases, and idioms in English that can best translate these qualities of the original French. There's a need for vigorous, colloquial English to express the skepticism and raw emotionalism of Céline's proletarian French. The translator must also make intuitive leaps and daring approximations that with other authors would neither be necessary nor advisable. Since the author deliberately seeks in this novel to disorient the readers, much fleshing-out and choosing among possible meanings has to be done. Translating this book is more like translating poetry than prose. Céline himself said that this book was more a work of verse than of prose. As a result, while utmost care was taken to translate the meaning as rigorously as possible, it was a matter at times more of interpretation than of pure translation.

Although what Céline said and wrote can never be taken at

face value, he often expressed disparagement of other languages, and he did not have a very high opinion of translators. In this book, in fact, he refers a few times to translators and their work. At one point, for example, he lumps translators together with those who conspire to deprive writers of their livelihood one way or another through their devotion to cinema, radio, and the like: "falsifying, deliberately destructive asshole translators." This harshness may seem unjust and even unwise in an author who was highly solicitous of his place in history – and who, in fact, collaborated with his first English translator, John Marks. But to be taken aback by this attitude toward translators and their work would be not to understand the peculiar relationship Céline had with his native language. Part of his distaste for translation no doubt sprang from his ferocious attachment to French, his quite carnal need to be surrounded by it, to be nourished by it. Never a man to shy away from contradictions, he was proud of his ability to speak English and German and often said that he spoke them "perfectly." (In fact, he overestimated his competence in English.) At the same time, he often proclaimed his aversion for other languages. In *Fable* the narrator complains that he was obliged to speak English with his wife, Arlette, when she came to visit him in prison: "I who have a horror of foreign languages! . . . feeble, screwed up gobbledigookery! . . . It's the final humiliation!"

For him French was the king of languages. Others are belittled, as people are, falling victim to his relentless mockery and aggression, which he applies indiscriminately to friend and foe alike, but especially to politicians, pedants, and the powerful. And English, at the beginning of its overwhelming worldwide predominance, was powerful, the language of the victors in the war that cost him his freedom, his readership, and his self-esteem.

But if Céline was more skeptical than most about the art and craft of translation, it was perhaps also because he was aware of the impossibility of completely rendering *his* particular French in other languages. There are many reasons for this.

For one, *Fable*'s punctuation is highly eccentric. Also, it contains a plethora of esoteric and slang words. Many unfamiliar but real events and people are continually referred to. It is full of puns and neologisms. It is repetitive and continually returns to the same obsessions. Its syntax is distorted. And willful confusion is caused by the play upon the multiple meanings of many words in the original French. These eccentricities all present unusual challenges for the reader and translator.

Because of this stretching of the language's stylistic possibilities, the loss in translation is more metaverbal than narrative in nature. What was lost was some of the poetic quality of the text. At another level, because the author played so much on multiple meanings, the English translator had often to make an educated guess as to the best translation of some words, choosing from two or more different possibilities. As well, for the text to be understood in English, more words had to be added to flesh out the ideas that the author merely sketched that were comprehensible in the context of the French language and culture, but not necessarily in an English-speaking context. As a result, the English text is more clear, or at least less ambiguous, than the French. The English is less nuanced, less mystifying, but conversely more coherent from a narrative point of view.

Thus, in *Fable for Another Time*, language play has usurped the primacy of storytelling. It has come into its own. The language has become the main protagonist, fighting the author/narrator's battle in the only arena left to him. And it is a protagonist of protean virtuosity. It can capture an enormous range of sounds that erupt in the quiet of our reading thanks to the constant barrage of hammering, screeching, and squawking that constitutes the jarring musical backdrop of this work. Language can be twisted almost out of recognition and still produce images that amuse us and cause us to reflect. It can break up the sentence structure and even word structures in ways that startle and disconcert. It can communicate impotent rage and bitter resentment at the same time that it expresses frank self-mockery and poignant regard for others. It continually blends words together to form new ones that make us laugh or muse. It repeats sound patterns for the sheer pleasure of it, without regard for semantic consistency. It can mystify and confuse but never entirely lose its focus. It can jump from one half-finished notion to another in a circular pattern with spritelike mischief and ease, each time expanding upon the point of departure. In short, the language exercises its magic on its own, as if independently of its semantic dimension.

It is for this reason, no doubt, that the novel was given the name *féerie*, a word that keeps slipping through the net of English – appropriately enough for a work whose elusive nature is captured, it is hoped, in the pages that follow.

The horror of reality!

All places, names, characters, situations set forth in this novel are imaginary! Absolutely imaginary! No relationship whatsoever with any reality whatsoever! It's only a Fable, and even at that! . . . for another time!

Fable for Another Time

SO HERE'S CLEMENCE ARLON. We're the same age, or there-
abouts. This is one strange visit! Right now . . . No, it's not
strange . . . She came in spite of the air raids, the metros not
running, the streets barricaded . . . and from such a distance!
. . . from Vanves . . . Clemence hardly ever comes to see me,
neither does her husband, Marcel . . . she didn't come alone,
her son's with her, Pierre . . . She's sitting down – there – at
my table, her son's still standing, his back to the wall. He'd
rather look at me sideways. It's an awkward visit . . . She's also
looking at me sideways, not facing me . . . neither one of
them's comfortable, people are all thinking what they're
thinking these days . . . what they're thinking, who they're
meeting, who they know. It's a good three or four months that
they've been thinking what they've been thinking, that nobody really looks me in the eye . . . because of what's happening, that's why. People behave almost all of them in the same
way at the same time . . . the same tics . . . Like ducklings
around their mother, in Daumesnil, in the Bois de Boulogne,
all at the same time, right face! . . . left face! Whether there's
ten of them or twelve or fifteen! same thing! all of them! right
face! to the split second! Clemence Arlon is looking at me out
of the corner of her eye. That's how it is these days. If she had
ten, twelve, fifteen sons, they'd all be looking at me cockeyed
the same way! For them I'm the notorious sellout traitorous
felon that they're gonna assassinate tomorrow, the next day,
next week . . . The traitor fascinates them, they gotta look at
him out of the corner of their eye . . . This Pierre, he takes
after his mother, looks and characterwise, for sure . . . but she
was better looking, finer featured, more regular . . . I'm an
Athenian. Very fussy when it comes to looks. About character, morality, God knows, I make do . . . Them, their problem

is morality, that's why they all want to do me in . . . not just Clemence! her son! all of them! . . . one reason or another, the war at the moment, the Krauts, Monsieur de Brinon[1] . . . the black-market martyrs! the defense of the Montrouge fortress![2] They always have their reasons . . .

I was saying that Clemence was really lovely looking . . . in her day . . . our youth! . . . I look at the kid again . . . I smell a sneak . . . the same instincts as his mother. He didn't want to sit down, he has his back to the wall, he doesn't like being here. He's arching back and forth, one hand in his pocket . . . They've been talking about me at home, around the table, with friends, to the neighbors . . . There again, it's the same old thing, the same stupid bullshit, all together, now, keep time . . . For months now, wherever you go they've been re-hashing all the little ins and outs of the matter. I'm good for the killing! for a laugh! for the country! Only they can't agree on how to do it – gouge out my eyes, draw and quarter 'im, bury 'im alive! Major topic of conversation at family gatherings, at the theater, in the metro corridors (those air raids) . . . So of course the Arlons, who've known me for more than thirty years, they have a little something to say about my weaknesses, my ways, my delectable disgustingness! Permanent topic of conversation at their house! Down there in Vanves. A University of my vices! The way I go nuts over things, my incredibly warped ways. Just one of my excesses deserves at least a thousand, ten thousand hangman's ropes! Friends are walking police logs, red hot, animal heat . . .

The kid there, the sneak, he's doing law . . . Maybe he'll be a judge one of these days. It's the first time he's seen a hanged man up so close . . . A hanged man of tomorrow . . . Hanged? Who knows? Radio reports are contradictory. hanged. skinned alive! . . . Drawn and quartered? In any case, judgment is nigh. A matter of hours . . . From Brazzaville, Berne, or Tobolsk,[3] by every window in the neighborhood, you can hear them bellowing, bleating, quacking. According to the valiant ones at the microphones in London he'll be "im-

2

paled"! from New York the most bloodcurdling war cries. *We'll make mincemeat of the Monster of Montmartre!*

That's why they came, both of them. Clemence and her son. It's imminent! . . . I don't listen much to the radio, but the patients keep me informed . . . For them at Vanves all day long it's "those killer waves"! And with such derring-do! With the windows wide open, there they go, "The Krauts are beaten. Draw up your lists!" Oh, those are some characters over at Vanves . . . and in Bezons![4] my practice! . . . And here in Montmartre! In my building even! I'll get back to you about that . . . They're here for the imminence of it all. To see their old pal go down for the count . . . Clemence and her son. The kid, he wouldn't dare whack it to me right there, off his own bat, just like that and *wham!* A little pistol, maybe? He's fiddling around in his pocket. Don't think so . . . He looks sneaky, but not crazy. You gotta be crazy to kill a man to his face, point blank. Requires a certain madness . . . He's not mad, I'd see it. If there were three or four of them they'd be mad. All alone he's just a jerk, that's all, a jerk.

– Acne, young man?

I go to his chin with my finger, I touch it . . . He's full of acne.

– You scratch yourself?

– Huh, wha?

He's trembling. All clammed up, over nothing.

– Goddamn clam! Shit!

I know what I'm talking about. This kid could only kill with three or four others. Okay. So why did they come so far? For the spoils? Maybe they thought I was already done in. Is that why they look so dumb? Surprised? . . . Maybe for Clemence it was out of affection? Because she used to be sweet on me? Does she want to warn me? She doesn't look full of tender concern . . . It won't be long now! Twenty radios a day tell me so . . .

Ah, dear Clemence! Ah, dear Marcel! Ah, dear young one! . . . Such memories! . . . Will they visit my grave? The thought strikes me. Maybe. unlikely. First of all, I won't have a tomb! I'll be torn limb from limb, thrown to the dogs . . . They're hungry at the moment, the dogs . . . not just the neighbors! The airwaves promise-crammed: The monster quartered at zero hour! not even the time to get a word in edgewise!

When you come down to it, they're just a little ahead of time, Clemence and the kid . . . They want to be the first to get there, before the rush . . . Otherwise what's the use of knowing him since 1914? The kid from his little corner, from the shadow, he's inspecting my books, well, what passes for my bookshelves . . . At Clemence's place all would be in order! No books everywhere, no! I never put them away. They come as "heirs in the making." At Clemence's place it's spotless! Her "interior" . . . But, damn it, this is pissing me off. I'm being too goddamn nice. The kid! The rope! Brazzaville! The guillotine! The spoils! To hell with all these nosy-bodies! I look at Clemence. I get a good look at her. Not an iota of prettiness left. She's all puffed up, wrinkled, ashen . . . I'm gonna tell her so: Sweetie-pie, you deadly bitch, you're nothing but a big fat dirty whore! Fuck off! You and your brat. Out o' here! out!

They deserve rough treatment. They came to see a soon-to-be-dead man, a tomorrow-he'll-be-hung, she, who's almost dead already herself! From seepage, shriveling, rotten menopausal horrors. The bilious bitch! Women, they deteriorate like wax, they go bad, melt, ooze, puff up, leak out right under your nose. Poisonous mutineers, rascalettes, their bleeding, their fibroids, rolls of fat, their prayers . . . When candles finish they're ghastly, women, too . . . Go, the mass is ended . . . Leave! Get out! No laughing matter.

So there they are, the two of them . . . Okay? So? Will they talk or won't they? What the hell do they want in the end after all? Out with it! They're none too brave.

– Come on, out with it! I try to get them to come clean . . . Not a word!

We've known each other a long time – Clemence and my-

4

self, I mean. It's been thirty-two years – I'm counting. Thirty-two years, makes you stop and think. A building that's thirty-two *is* somebody. The johns overflow, the elevators don't work any more, the concierge's a friggin' grandma, I'm trying to find you a comparison . . . wear and tear . . .

The first day we met is far away now. I've got quite a memory. Engraved in my mind, things are. I can't forget anything . . . It's not a sign of intelligence . . . Nothing to boast about, memory . . . that's just how it is . . . So I'll tell you the date, the month, May 1915 at Val, you know, the hospital, Val-de-Grace . . . That's going back a ways, the Val! . . . But I don't want to get you lost in my memories.

I go back to the young man there against the wall, the awkward big dope. I won't give you an in-depth picture, he's not worth it. He's fiddling around in his pocket . . . nothing to worry about . . . all the young ones fiddle around in their pockets . . . a pistol? an erection? Maybe I'll give him another talking to about his acne . . . A little lotion? Nah, to hell with it. I'd never get rid of them . . . They're Gaullists, the whole family . . . Of course they are! It's all the rage . . . Hate is all the rage . . . There's always been hate, the same hate, but now it's "in"! . . . There are four million of them in Paris boiling over with the same hate, the "in" hate . . . That's nothing to sniff at, four million hatreds. The last remaining Fritz in la Villette, and all the cutlasses come out! I swear to God! Garrotes, boners, principles, Honor, Nation! And I'm part of the mass uprising, my kidneys, my head, my aorta . . . they're promising a meter's worth of my meat at the place de la Concorde! At the public quartering of the traitors. Precisely timed work, bet your ass, it'll be bigger than the jumping around they did at the Marne! The paddling around at Verdun! The hundred-thousand-against-one hunt is on! Absolutely risk free! The dream come true for the ladies, the maidens, the big hide tanners! Your hide! National industry! The Game of Every Delight! The Hounding of the gagged and ligated beast, prey on a platter! What bliss! The Nation! Rapture!

Could he have a Browning, the kid there, that sneak? What would he be risking? Nothing at all! Fame? A medal! Point blank, *wham!* Bullet right to the heart. He hasn't got that little madness it takes. He's not six or seven at a time. He's no crowd . . . He'd like to be. It's my place Clemence has got her beady eye on, the view over Paris, the elevator, the metro right there . . . They're in a four-room place in Vanves . . . comfortable, sure, but small. She's daydreaming there, by my open window . . . then she takes another look at the furniture, the ceiling, how she'll get rid of the partition . . . How she'd fit it all out.

All the radios are making them drool over my apartment – for the taking, 18 rue Gaveneau, Montmartre, they give the floor – seventh, even which landing.

It's possible – even probable – they'll chuck me out the window, chop me up on the sidewalk . . .

Madame Esmeralde at number 15, she's always been pleasant to me, nice, she's the one who had me warned by a woman whose name I can't reveal just yet . . . Madame Esmeralde does nails, she has clients who know everything . . . Just like for when they land, they know the time, the exact spot . . . No longer any doubt about it according to the radio. So you should hear them go on about it! On the streets, wherever they mill around, the cafés! Everybody's in on the Screech-fest . . . the Krauts are fucked! We'll slaughter the rest.[5] The airwaves are going hoarse over it from Tomsk to Sydney, Australia, from Aberdeen to Chad, that it will be a giblet letting such as we haven't seen for three centuries – ooh, the way the blood will spill, flow in torrents, guts everywhere! The gooey mess, Nazi gut-heap! The whole goddamn bunch! "Draw up your lists!" Definitely a landing in the air.

Me, too, I'm fated for the air! I can see it now! I'm already sailing! Not only Madame Esmeralde! Many other quite proper persons have more than insinuated to me . . . that I was snoozing, not paying attention! . . . Aside from the radios! Every which language! As soon as the Landing is over, total nationwide bloodbath! Butcher the whole pack of whores! At least fifteen cadavers per precinct! Maybe more! One for every floor! That's what they've ordered! It's the future! Widespread rejoicing! I haven't got many hours left! France can no longer breathe! . . . for three or four months now they've been on my tail . . . Lines of the curious at my door. *Knock! Knock!*

They tumble in.

– Hello, Doctor!

They look at me out of the corner of their eyes . . . even the most determined get embarrassed when it comes down to it . . . they're all in it together. They've got butchery in their souls . . . I fascinate them from the corner of their eye. The men tremble, their voices quiver, awkward as hell. The women, they get a hard-on – shamelessly – the young ones even more so. They can already picture me hanging from the hook, torn to shreds, emasculated. "Hurry up," is what they're telling each other, "get his tongue, his eyes!" They're swaying, they climb on my knees, they kiss me with such tenderness! . . . even in the very street I'm hailed – on the sly, of course – people who hardly spoke to me any more, acquaintances . . . suddenly they all gotta tell me something. I know that certain look in their eyes . . .

The Krauts have been weakening for a long time now, but it's really only been three, four months that you can say that they're really fucked . . . and it's been three, four months that I've been treated to big tits with a hard-on.

It's amazing how they keep on coming! The *knock knock* never ends . . . My door again! Me, who isn't very welcoming, not even polite! I cut it short . . .

– The basics! fast! Goodbye! So long!

Knock, knock! Another one! And another, a woman this time.

– If you don't mind, Doctor.

The tragedy is, I'll tell you right now, I should've already been far away . . . in Lapland, Portugal, as soon as the first "voyeur" visits started happening, the first cockeyed peeps.

7

That's a sure sign. People's interest is ghastly. It's the death in you that they come to see . . . cozy up to death so it doesn't come breathing down their necks, *their* precious necks, when the time comes . . . their time . . . Get nice and cozy . . . They'll trifle with death – your death – take advantage of the fact that it's around to make nice to it . . . You can go straight to it, on the other hand. They'll recommend that it get a good grip on you, not let you slip away, make sure death knows that they're just there for what it leaves behind . . . that they and death are on the best of terms, that you're the one to swing! Just you! That they'll come to the scaffold full of verve and applaud . . . They're all for your torture, oh, yes, but please, one more hour of life for them! What you call the Pact of the Instincts.

He who doesn't fuck off soon enough is a jerk. That's the whole moral of the story! Oh, I was aware, all right, but over-wrought . . . And then there was still a lingering kindness about me from way back . . . I don't know why . . . All that's gone now! Kicked in the ass! Maybe it was self-respect. Spare me the curiosity! I shouldn't have let anyone come to see me . . . Overwrought? I've been overwrought since 1914, I've got a thousand reasons to be ungracious, unkempt, impossible. And even so, I went and opened the door to them! *Knock! Knock!* The door! Shit! My foot up their ass is what they should've got!

That would have been the wise thing to do, the only wise thing! What the hell were they all doing, coming to set me off like that? And not only at home, at the dispensary, too! In Bezons! Ten, twelve, fifteen people to see me . . . A lot of good it did to tell them: I don't give interviews! Allez hop! Who cares? they just keep on comin'. That's what you get for be-ing about to swing. They trip over each other in the rush to get a whiff of you. Just give them an opening and they talk a load o' crap . . . you gotta be discrete . . . very tactful! and pretend not to notice that they've come sniffing around to get a good whiff of your rotting flesh . . . For that, Clemence was

8

the same . . . as well as our old friendship she was supposed to want to talk to me about . . . not a peep . . . leaning sideways in her chair . . . mumbling a few words, clamming up again. I laugh . . . I would laugh.

– Come on, Clemence, out with it!

I help her. Give a little cough. What if I showed her my little birdie? Pull my drawers down, right there? *Bam!* She'd get over her bashfulness but quick. I think about it . . . but I'm too beat! limp! It'd be an effort . . . She'd go "Oh, dear!" That's all. What's the use? my goddamn foot up her ass is what she deserves! But I'm not violent enough. I was very violent once. Damn, but my character's been frayed along the route. Now I'm wary about everything . . . it's probably the lack of sleep . . . Funny that Marcel didn't come, her husband . . . He found some excuse . . . It's a tossup who's the most yellow bellied in any household.

– So I'll go myself, she says.

But what do they want from me exactly? Marcel, the son, the family, they all agree . . . She'll go, she's the daring one. Gaullists, all of them! Absolutely! Gaullist Super-resisters. Marcel took over a bistro, a Jewish one, replaced them, and not just a bistro, a depot, too! . . . He told me all about it. Two years ago, before Stalingrad[6] . . . hasn't been back to see me since . . . since Stalingrad . . . Everything's gone a bit fishy since Stalingrad . . . Not that he's got a problem with me personally . . . But since everybody knows about it in his neighborhood, he's gotta hedge his bets . . . so now he never shuts up about me . . . He's a busybody, a boozer, a braggart. He's blabbing all over Vanves what a sellout pig I am . . . Yeah, we were old pals, but since I turned "Nazi" – oh, you can bet all that's fee-neesh! finibus!

It was all flattery before the war, "Céline, he's a buddy of mine!" Now, forget about it! It's true that we've been friends for a long time . . . We were in Val together. Operated on, cited, decorated together, for real wounds in a real war, without any thought of personal gain, I can safely say, not a penny of

9

profit . . . how times have changed. Now he can't even look me in the eye. I can tell you what I think! What I feel! . . . I have as much to confide as the next guy. Simply put, what we know as France, that went from St. Genevieve on her mount to Verdun in 1917,[7] after that it's been just a bunch of odd-balls, people who're not the full deck. I look at them there, the shifty pair, the kid, the mother . . . there's an example for you . . . lousy, underhanded! With them, more than with a thousand others, I was always generous, friendly, I felt for them . . . And here they are, coming at me like grave diggers! Them and the others! I don't keep track of my good works, godfuckingdamnit, it's impossible! They've taken everything! From one end to the other, by hook or by crook. the proof: I'm skint and skinned! I'll wind up in a dungeon! That's where he belongs!

– You climaxed!

– That's possible!

– You're right!

– So what?

May it do them a lot of good. I'm thinking, the time has come, I look at them. I'm cutting my story up on you. People haven't treated me very well. What am I talking about? It was more like a bloody, frenzied whore of a manhunt! It began in '14. Any excuse at all! First it was the cannons, then the gossip, then the police! I wanted to save their goddamn necks, my fellow countrymen! their foul necks, their shit-ridden hearts, wanted to save them from the Slaughter . . . my books for that!

– Smart aleck, they carp, drop dead first!

Brothers of my flesh, I worship you! Love of my waking hours, hurrah! I got Cain's ass up against the zenith! squirt septic finger! Triumph! I can see you now! *Pro Deo!* Bash my head in and do it big! Bigger, brother, bigger! So that the whole sky fits in! Take a star for yourself! You want it? Here's my life – a gift! Can I do better than that? Would you like to give me a kiss? What if I gave the kid there a nice big hammer,

10

invite him to bash my mug in? that's right, my own face, right then and there? He wouldn't have the guts. He'd back down . . . Others will come, they'll break in and carry off the place, the library . . . I'm thinking . . . getting ahead of myself . . . So that I keep my goddamn mouth shut they'll cut my tongue out, poke my eyes out for a laugh, they'll chuck me out the window and onto the sidewalk . . . Others will get fancy . . . I'll be tied to a horse's tail and go, horsy, go! at breakneck speed! Avenue of the Opera, Concorde, like Brunehilda![8] I learned this bit of history at school in Louvois Square, public elementary school, to show you I'm from the neighborhood, got my elementary school certificate and everything!

It'll be in front of a huge crowd, the whole goddamn city celebrating! I get carried away – just the way I am. But I don't forsake my words, nor my visitors, nor you.

– This guy's going off his rocker!

If you like, but you'd upset me . . . that would be judging me very hastily . . . you'll see why. What direction shall I take? Let's get back our bearings! . . .

– Eh, you're navigating in Cloud Cuckoo Land!

– Me? No Cloud Cuckoo Land about it! I see Clemence and her son, they're sniffing around, my books, my rags, my highly saleable curiosities . . . They've already made money . . . (Detail not to be forgotten!) out of another kick in the balls before! . . . when I got screwed at Rueil![9] What a wreck that was! Ah, my nursing home! My lovely nursing home! Now they think: It's going to start again, we'll have to beat the crowds, the General Sale! . . . This is a windfall we won't see again! There'll be ten thousand of them pillaging! In a matter of hours!

– Get on with it, Clemence.

I think again about Rueil, there, thinking about it again . . . the beautiful trees . . . the barges all along . . . My Rest Home! what rotten luck! The kid there, he was finishing up his rhetoric . . . he got all my books, the kid . . . It's the one sure thing in my life, I can't ever keep anything, anywhere, not a single book . . . Fate plunders everything on me. The landlord was gonna sell off all my stuff, so I give them advance notice: help yourselves, friends! They carry off my entire library . . . the kid the reading matter, the mother the kitchen stuff! Marcel, the cellar!

Nothing gets me more excited than big disasters, misfortune intoxicates me. It's not that I go looking for them exactly, but they come all the same, like guests who have some sort of rights . . . So I was telling you about Rueil, when all hell broke loose! What an enterprise that was! Two bailiffs from Chatou on my ass! I call my worthy friends to help me – I mean Arlon, Clemence, the kid. The seals are already on my goddamn locks! the sale the next day! Lost no time! Anything for friendship! They go to it, these nifty-fingered devils! they even bring an aunt from Nantes, one they were putting up for a few days! they cart off all my stuff! in one night! reduced to beggary! From Rueil to their place! Ipso presto! On their backs, and then in wheelbarrows, coming and going it've filled three trucks! Aside from the library and at least twelve cases of bottles, five medicine chests, a Poupinel sterilizing chest, two other vapor baths, twenty-four entire beds, the whole kitchen . . .

I was flabbergasted . . . By daybreak all I had left was fifty *Revues des Deux Mondes*, bound, that is, in good shape, and a motorcycle with sidecar, and a "Pachon" tension meter and five syringes . . . So as not to say I left nothing . . . at least two months rent's worth. Talk about a hatchet job! But what consoled me a bit was that Marcel, his wife and kid, and the aunt had salvaged something from it! not for me! for them! Personally, I don't like relics . . . I always get the feeling they're jinxed . . . I wanted to start again at zero, confront life again from another angle . . . with more umph! . . . With real zeal! I tell you! All the little ins and outs, the imaginings! Grandiose plans! . . . Dining room, living room, twenty bedrooms, bourgeois standing, taxes! . . . Damn! Just my stethoscope, a pen, a whitewood table . . . no overhead . . . no decor!

12

Go get stuffed! Bunch o' crap! All your junk comes crashing down on you! Life catches up with you. No quarter! You get your toboggan going again, you get on with it, you get knocked around, you go head to the wind! You get clobbered, you're reduced to rags, a useless heap! One long slide downhill! Destiny is the worst with then-some added . . . the toboggan runners are greased . . .

Lower than being flung in the slammer you can't go. Not to mention being exiled! . . . The kid has it made! How much did the toboggan ride take out of me? Fifty years of blood, sweat, and tears, of horrible, superhuman effort . . . Hey, you played your cards right! Ruined, loathed everywhere, such a goddamn asshole it's a miracle I'm still bleating . . . My poor wife, there, on the other flea pit, my dancer, just had an operation . . . There was something good about the Middle Ages . . . A little trouble with the law, you could live . . . nowadays you gotta write tomes . . . You know rue Réamur, the Court of Miracles?[10] These days it's a movie house. The Age of Charity is over! Before the Era of Liberation, a word from a prince got you out of jail! or Christmas! Nowadays! Go scratch yourself! One lousy situation! King Oluf, from where I'm eating my heart out, he couldn't get me sprung with a word. The least little prank and the masses would whip his ass but good. "Grant this man his freedom!" – they'd knock him unconscious.

I'm writing you this from everywhere, by the way. from my place in Montmartre! from the depths of my Baltavian prison! and at the same time from the seaside, from our hut. Time and place all mixed up! Shit! It's a Fable, isn't it? . . . That's what a Fable is: the Future! the Past! the False! the True! Fatigue! All the same, I'm thinking something – I'm thinking that the mangiest stray dog who's wandering around there in the gutter, who's sticking his nose everywhere, let's say he's called Piram, *he's* got less to fear than yours truly here. Hounded as no dog is! Not hounded because of *his* name, Piram! You can survive that name, Piram! Piram's no walking catastrophe!

13

But my unspeakable name isn't all! There's illness! there's spite! there's spies all over the place . . . You'll see as you read each chapter[11] . . . if I managed to outsmart them! If I wandered here, there, and everywhere! We did some wandering! Lilli and Ulysses[12] . . . Without some juicy little stories, I could go scratch myself – if I weren't funny you wouldn't read me, ever! Oh, but only buy me under the counter! At the moment everything's been confiscated in advance (ruling of 23 February) and a hundred thousand worth of debt backed up![13] and other rulings and appeals and Super-Court, and so on! as well as prison! Disgrace! Stripped of civil rights! The whole lot! . . . Once the toboggan's been sucked into the abyss, at every turn you get bashed in the face, and by the time you get to the bottom you're just a ball of muck and tears.

Think about it! The centrifugation of hate!

You give up, the last gasp . . . No gettin' around it! You belch up your soul and it's curtains for you! To the winds, cutie!

But the pain is still there, piercing as ever. Gets you going again! At every corkscrew turn! You rage! You're saved! Hatred! it's not wonderful . . . it's not moral . . . but shit! to hell with my scrutations! pulsations! Let's get back to brass tacks! I was telling you that after Rueil, when everything was lost, reduced to beggary, the furniture, and all. I'd finagle things here, there, managed one way or another, cast my Science, my mind, to the wind! . . . The fill-in work, the scrimping . . . in town, in the provinces, in the fields, wandered through manys a path, climbed manys a floor, all fervent about the art of healing, bandaging, consoling, giving birth, dispensing drugs, gently stroking, too . . . Down with pain! with germs! with weariness! with death! with at least twenty-five kinds of despair! . . . What did I get for it? sweet fuck-all! tribulations! piles of shit! good God! Piddling gains out of powerful pains in the ass! My quills everywhere! . . .

Only one promising project, maybe, that would have dethroned the Bourboules, the Néris, the Cauterets! Even Enghien, its lake, its sulphurs![14] You can see it from here: at Sannnois, an Aerium for asthma! The Mont-Dore you can get to by bus! The Royal Spa for the Small-of-Purse! A mere trip to the outskirts of Paris and back! I had all the rebellious catarrhs of the "economically disadvantaged" for myself! from spring onward, they kept on comin'! spring, what am I talkin' about? all year round! the ideal place! You know those quarries above Argenteuil? sand veins, naturally dry! white as silver along the top, facing south! They'd leave their factories, their barstools to come spend a couple of hours at my place ... They'd waste no time! Right away, the natural cure: immobility in a hammock ... air heated by the sands, that's the whole secret! You won't find any asthmatics in the Sahara! Once you breathe in the air of the torrid sands, Mont-Dore can go fuck itself! For those a bit better off I had a house and a few beds, the "Night-a-Torium"! All the windows wide open, facing south! Had to be south!

For once I had something going. The venture was proving healthy. Fortune smiled on me ... And then the rains started! Floods and more floods! The sand washed down the banks! Torrents from the Sannois Heights! In one downpourous year! Once a century! The banks of the Seine ripped out! Floods in July! Three catarrh sufferers who want it all the same, who absolutely have to have their cure, get stuck halfway up Argenteuil, in the mud, the plaster! Not one who makes it to the hammocks! Desperate, lousissimus weather! Extremely rare! I waited, figured in a year I'd boom again ... You can't get the Deluge every summer! Had I ten thousand francs in my pocket, the Mont-Dore would be no more! Argenteuil-Sannois, Queen of the Bronchial Tubes! ... the "circum-urban" solution. I had to wait. Never, never have I been able to wait! Waiting is money! The "Spa of the Elite and of the People." The man who can wait is like God. He's got time in his scales. You have no time, you can go take a hike! How much Time have you got? To tell the exact truth, it've taken three years . . . But two summers in a row were wintry . . . not to mention my other medico-social ventures . . . There were some funny ones . . . some a lot less so . . .

Oh, but I'm not straying from the point! Don't think I'm blathering! Clemence is the one who makes me stop and think . . . There, precisely in the flesh . . . I want you to get a picture of the person . . . the kind of relationship we had.

Excuse me, but as I say these things, I necessarily have to get a little bit personal . . . you could say almost intimate . . . Perhaps I'm going to upset you, I don't know what line of work you're in, your tastes, your little whatnots, your place in society . . . those are whole different universes, places in society, different dispositions, health, not to mention how much money you've got socked away! and ages! And madness of cosmic proportions to boot! Mass uprisings! I know not whether you were on any of the lists . . . I know not your *pedigree*. What side you were on! Your ass on such-and-such a chopping block? On such-and-such another? Your head on yon gallows? We've seen it all! Have you been labeled, pinned down, spread out, you intergalactic horror, you hexed cow, you ogre, you *Magog*,[15] you traitorous whore, you Gestapoop, you Landruste,[16] you bag o' bowels who prevents All Honor from sleeping? The Nation, the Army, la Villette,[17] the loveliest neighborhoods right to the Flea Market, to the north the Médrano Circus, Barbès (and Trudaine Street), the southern regions down to Antibes, La Ciotat? Maybe you catch my drift . . . see it from here!

To put it succinctly, I'm the most pestilent traitor who could have had Petiot for breakfast,[18] sold off les Invalides by the pound and the Legion of Honor to Abetz,[19] traded the Arch of Triumph for a garage! the Unknown Soldier for twenty marks, the Maginot Line for a kiss! Ah, you wouldn't cry "Get the madman!" But "this guy knows what's what," Yes, siree! Had you but had the goddamn pack on *your* tail, the ladies, the damsels in heat, your old pals frothing at the mouth, necromaniacs, grave robbers already sniffing at your dead meat, you'd understand what I was talking about! wanting right now, but right now, your pecker, your balls, the last drop of your juices, wiggling, panting for you to be cut up into little pieces, losing control behind their fitting countenance . . . They're looking ahead, in paroxysms over how you're going to swing, spew up your liver! . . . how you'll be twitching all over the place as you give up the ghost . . . you'll have had your fill of jumping . . . your mucus, your guts all over the sidewalk . . . do we go for it? You get my drift? It'll be magic! boiling over! divine! and I'm only talking about the men, here! There's the ladies to consider, and the youth!

I knew at least a dozen marvelous, sinewy virgins and high-school Apollos who had to have me in ecstasy, who wanted me to do all sorts of dirty business with them before they did me in. I'd have found over a thousand of them if I'd put an ad in the paper . . . so goes the world, fads. You have a Coliseum right in your own home, you're a martyr, you're modest, you say, "But my place is so small" . . . Ten million starving people who come sniffing at you right through your walls! Once they're on your ass, funny things happen.

– Oh yes, but they do. Such a twisted mind you have. Vice-ridden pig!

– Not at the moment. In any case!

Amorous, religious, curious, voyeurous, discutatious, whatever, I don't like visits. In truth I could never stomach them! So a propos! I tell ya, I'd rather see twenty patients than have one friendly visit. How I hate all the blatherbroth! Especially along with all this coveting of my few rags! . . .

I was forgetting you there! I wasn't including the sound effects for you. The distant cannons' roar! The tambourines . . . It had been relentless for two weeks . . . I, who've traveled through Africa, have seen them make a meal out of a man to tam-tam accompaniment. Every bit! I was forgetting to give you the cannons roaring in the distance, the southwestern suburbs! I'm a po-it, agreed! I have noisy memories, and then irritation, fatigue, and my personal buzzings . . . but all the

17

same I didn't dream it all up! . . . I knew from Pamela, my housekeeper, about how the precinct was preparing, the whole of Montmartre even . . . how they'd fix my wagon . . . and then the coffins, the "death announcements." I didn't dream all that! And the solemn "death sentences," and never signed, of course. Certain individuals boasted later that they'd gone looking for me, in my cellar! . . . It's not true at all! Other people maybe! All cowards are romantic, they think they're straight out of a novel . . . they invent lives full of sparkle for themselves as they retreat. Campéadors in afterthought only![20] Crime comes to them once all risk is extinguished, the daggers at the Flea Market! I wasn't so much afraid for myself, don't believe it! I was aware of the horror of it all, that sure as shootin' everything would go to hell, that the awfulness would be worse than '14 . . . so don't talk to me about being lucid! seeing that the future was pretty damned weird, the skies, too, and the people, and the corridors . . . and the doors that were just about to close shut . . . everything was an ambush . . . Definitely, since 1914 you have to admit that men like me, we're leftovers, we had the cheek not to die . . . dubious spot to be in, all right! . . .

– Hey, you, psst! psst! you, the one that got away! cheater!

There they go, having a go at us again . . . If that's the way you want it! See ya some other time!

But Arlette is not from the class of '14![21] She had no reason to die! She had no scores to settle with the next world! On her account I refused to resign myself . . . absolutely innocent, they'd have cut her guts out just for butchery's sake. She was lovely, that's all. It's serious business, being lovely . . . And then my mother almost blind, they'd go and torture her for fun. There was a school in Toulouse for "torturing the old" . . . just let them accuse me of lying! . . . they were terrible to mothers . . . And then there's Bébert, another innocent, my cat . . . Don't tell me a cat's just something to pet. Not at all! A cat is bewitchment itself, tact emanating in waves . . . they go "grr . . . grr" and it's words . . . Bébert with his "grr . . . grr," he actually used to talk. He answered your questions . . . Nowadays he "grr-grrs" to himself . . . doesn't bother answering questions anymore . . . he monologues about himself . . . like me . . . and like me, he's finished . . . There was only one other in Montmartre, almost as outstanding as Bébert, and that's Alphonse . . . Empième's cat, Marc Empième's.[22]

Now Alphonse, where he really could bluff you was at the jump . . . as soon as the door was opened! . . . Plunk! . . . one leap onto the door handle and he was gone! But not so amazing as Bébert when it came to understanding . . . a real language, "grr . . . grr" . . . or when it came to beauty, either . . . or to whiskers . . . Was I proud of that cat! . . . The extraordinary thing about Bébert was the way he would go for a walk, a stroll, the way he'd follow us . . . but not during the day, only in the evening, and only if we talked to him . . . "You okay, Bébert?" . . . "Grr! . . ." He kept wanting to go back to those places. Place Blanche, Trinity, the Boulevards once . . . but for at least three or four months we didn't go out any more in the evening . . . after the threats . . . didn't go out after six any more . . . Bébert wasn't too happy about that! Should've heard him meow . . . all over the hallways . . . He didn't give a fuck about the reasons. He was a night wanderer . . . but never all alone solitary! . . . with us . . . only with us . . . and all talk every thirty, forty feet . . . "grr . . . grr . . ." once almost all the way to the Arch of Triumph . . . Only thing he was scared of was motorcycles. If there was one in the street, even far away, he'd come running at me all claws, jump at me as if I were a tree. Real excursions often, the Quays, right to Mahé's place,[23] not every cat goes to the Quays . . . They don't like the Seine . . . Empième, I'm getting back to him, yeah, you got it, Marc Empième, the writer, Alphonse's owner . . . He lived two streets down from us. I'll tell ya about Marc Empième . . . another little detour . . . I won't lose you, though . . . Now that's a friend! . . . and terrific! just to give you an idea of the man's tastes . . . So you get the picture . . . I don't know anyone comparable to Marc in the world of today's letters. Not a one who can compete at the ink-and-blotter stakes in all the writing bullshittery in France. Not a single rival. Prose, drama, verse, laughs! . . . Notwun! that I know of! and for the last fifty years! that's a long time to be inspired by a man! He can distill a dream as niftily as a sprite . . . there's Maupassant and then there's him. Around, before, ingainst, among? A bunch of swindlers! . . . So why shouldn't he take good care of himself, spoil, pamper himself, refuse himself nothing, yachts, hunting parties, castles? . . . I'm a bit jealous of him . . . not on account of his castles, on account of his illness . . . He's a lot sicker than I am and he produces like a bloomin' Homer! Me, my headaches, my insomnia, they're knocking me out, they're killing me; him, the less he sleeps the more he masterpieces. Okay, so we're all Sisyphus! goddamn recidivist rock scramblers! Me, the rock comes crashing down again on my schnozola! fucking screwup! Public Prosecutor's Office! Him with one foot in the grave, he goes over the top! and on the front page! He sends his rock to the top! Exactly where he wants it! Talk about ovations as far as the eye can see! The Olympic Champion of the Rock! His plays run a thousand nights at the Ambigu! Naturally! The revivals never stop! Klondykes for the movie industry! In the bookstores he sinks them all! He'd go through fifteen tax brackets with a quarter of a half-novel the way they grab everything hot off the press! By the hundred! two hundred thousand . . . four hundred! It's simple! His "rare editions," his "Japanese," the crowds tear them apart at the Auction Rooms! They go nuts over them! Off they go to the Auction Room! They say there are safes full of them! The Aga Khan would like some, can't get 'em! I get such a kick out of it! *Vanitatas! Invidivia!* Jealealous! Like Jules? Way off the mark! my ambitions do not lie in the Arts. medicine is my vocation! . . . but I couldn't make a go of it . . . I was a doctor without patients! . . . The novel came along . . . I worked at it, alas! Piddling profits in the beginning, and then handcuffs! prison cells! loathing! don't ever write!

In the beginning, in the very beginning, I was humming along . . . I figured it would be a little like an Operetta . . . Shit, that would've been a lot easier . . . but no doubt because I was apprehensive and lacked contacts, I never got further than the libretto . . . and then what with one bad blow after another, here we are at three thousand pages of sheet music that have turned into prose! And from prose work to prose work it keeps getting worse! darker! novels! You can picture the falling off! Alas, you know the rest! From uncomfortable to worse and worse, from curses to God-strike-you-dead! it turned into the Ultimate Infamy, martyrdom, baseness! . . . So there's no question that I'll ever rival Marc! Shameless puke-ball of a weirdo! What next? hanged? who cares?

It's quite natural that big deal poet laureate–type Marc de Marc should burst forth! Triumphs everywhere! I wouldn't be surprised if he lived in a frigging museum, if he had sing-ing hotplates – gold ones – I'd find it only natural! I under-stand these things.

I've often heard myself say:

– You don't amount to much! You don't know how to cre-ate a real work, a play for instance, a sonnet!

– Shit! God damn it! It's true!

– Just look at Marc!

Words that cut me to the quick! Bitter words! I know . . . I know. But all the same . . . oh, boy! the Rock crashes down on the old schnoz! . . . I don't send it over the moon, the way Marc does . . . everything comes crashing in on me, shatters all over! Avalanches everywhere! My vocation is in medicine! my talents are cockeyed, too! Even my ill health doesn't do me any good . . . it's killing me . . . Marc, he's got a direct line to the Muses, sick or not sick . . . if he had the Taj Mahal at his place, one helluva treasure trove, a chapel full of worshipers come expressly to adore in open-mouthed wonder, on their knees, it'd be terrific and that's all! There are enough belly crawlers around who triumph, make their mark, encumber Glory, crowd the stages, the Dictionary, ministers' bidets, and

21

even Prisons! At least one should be justly adulated! The top all to himself!

Him, his illness makes him toil . . . me, I've got one that's killing me . . . I lie here rotting away . . . repeating the same gibberish over and over again . . . Look at this page! With him it's Suffering-as-Goad, me, it's just another pain in the ass . . . I can just see myself on a cross – I'd bore everyone to death, on the scaffold, too, I'd maybe manage a few pathetic rude remarks, no sublime jibes! I'd be one of those martyrs they hiss at! This book, for example, lucky if it doesn't turn into a big flop . . . a disaster! You'll never pay the kind of money it'll cost, the corrections, the typing, the printing, taxes . . . lucky if war doesn't break out, if they don't screw it up out of all recognition at the press! (Talk about an obsession! fifteen times!) And all the awful things they're gonna tell you about it! It's frightening how many enemies I have, all vying to out-do each other! It's as if they've run out of spit and you know it! but I'll give them a piece of my mind! You bet I will! I may be dying but I'm still wicked! Wolves drop dead without a cry, not me![24]

You fucked it all up, imbeciles! you didn't stalk the right monster! the Céline, shit kickers! He doesn't give a fuck! Even if you were a thousand times more the vampires that you are, the stalking ghouls, jackals, condors, and dragons that you are, every kind of brute-beast herded together from Africa, Asia, and America – he'd still just get his rocks off from it all. It's Dr. Destouches who's the sensitive one! Had you so much as laid a finger on his Medical Degree, it would have been fee-neesh, dead! But about this bullying by bogey-men, this cry-for-the-kill from will-o'-the-wisps, this moon-struck butchery, I should give a fuck? If you knew how soon I'd rub your face in it! Let it keep on coming! more of it! pant-ing at the specter! piss, sweat blood, screech louder! Go on, split your spleen in your mad rush, but it ain't me! In moon-light! heinous! Make it even more vile, enraged, death rat-tling! Plunder! By the sea hag's belly! The horns! To the horns! let me sound them for you! both the trumpet and the oliphant![25]

How fine it is to hunt down the phantom. Seeing you do it is a treat, a vice, I'll catch up with you at the charnel house. I'll despoil you of your stinking hides! That'll be a show for the Odeon! for Punch and Judy! for the Casino? No! for the Chaillot![26] Even though I prefer operettas! Usually I'm light-hearted and roguish, full of verve, happy-go-lucky, a regular Vermot's Almanac, mischievous![27] With a weakness for dancers! so don't give me any of your hangman's stuff! swingin' stiff! What I like is watching those little girls dance, nice and rosy, all vigor, music, snap! such balance! Oh, fairy-childs! Calves, thighs, smiles, darting life! it takes your breath away! Joye and Joye![28] Diarrhea of the Horn! from the depth of the woods! Great birdturds! Strewn toilet paper! Owlish old buggers!

– You're gonna wind up in the clink!

– Yeah, sure, thanks a lot, you pig! spare us your wisdom!

– Oh, reader, I bow to you! forgive this moment of High Art, these noose swingers, these burdensome sorrows! . . . and this bit of licentiousness . . . I wasn't losing you, not at all! . . . you're right here with me, up here on the seventh floor, looking out on the gardens . . . my table . . . Clemence . . . my little story . . . her son . . . the pillaging about to happen . . . I was reflecting on the "double Zero" hour, oh, I wasn't imagining it, not at all! all the radios were bleating about it . . . "double Zero, double Zero"! . . . from one end of the earth to the other . . . Dead serious! not just shootin' the breeze! how the sellouts would be cut up! Cross our heart and hope to die! stiffs piled high at the place du Trône, place de la Révolte, place de la Bastille! That it was gonna be the biggest, the most flamboyous victory celebration you'd ever seen! with parades! fandaroles from the Concorde to Notre Dame, since the coronation of Louis XVI! How we'd see what stuff the People are made of, and the Avengers and the Nation! Dancing in the street that'd last for two weeks all over town, and on the roofs! A bonfire to last ten years! The sellouts' meat barbecued in a pyramid as high as the Arch of Triumph! Your spine would be tingling with anticipation! Every floor, every metro, every concierge's flat was palpitating.

That's why they came all this way, the two of them, Clemence and her son. Part of the general spine tingling.

– What about the icebox?

I'm breaking the ice. I'm not gonna waste my time.

– Has he got an *Ausweiss*, Marcel?[29]

– Yes, she sighs.

– If he had one why didn't he come?

I love touching the most exquisitely sensitive spot, it's the medical man in me . . . oh, but maybe it wasn't so easy! Maybe they had to bam-bam me first? The kid there? or another one? . . . Point blank! Assassin with a mission, this kid? He's milk-toast pale . . . God damn it, they weren't budging! Murderers or no murderers! Was I imagining it? Was I romancing? . . . Marcel had stayed home . . . what did that mean? And what about his business? his sales pitches? His "lightening carts,"[30] which are rare these days . . . other fish to fry! money transfers, maybe! atrocious worries! ball-breaking nutty stuff! Grease the palms of the Germans, the Jews, the northern French, the southern, from Vichy, the shore, the ports, plus the Majestic![31] and the Brussels Comptrollers Office! enough to make them abandon Europe! You go too far! he shouted at me! before Stalingrad . . . when we could still trust each other . . . so me with my unholy mess! my curious claims!

But still 'n all, there she was, his wife . . .

– Go ahead. Go see him. Ask him!

– What?

Ah, the B-B-B-B-C! *the question!*[32] A prescription? a kiss? a small favor?

There's something feline, fierce, prickly about friends' wives. You haven't seen anything until you've refused your friend's wife a little favor. Because then, you'd be better off with a reputation of four and twenty Blue-Beards. a crook

without a car! a defeated field marshal! your feet stink, your
fangs, your breath! I'm telling you!

Ah, refuse a friend's wife a little favor? the famous little
favor! . . . tell me about it! Orestes, the Furies, a joke in comparison! A woman "three months gone," now that's someone to reckon with! . . . You haven't known the Antique until
you've been looked over, peered at, disgusting yellow-bellied
less-than-dog! A curse on you! You'll bellow like a stag for the
rest of your life!

You don't do that little favor?

May the Erinyes descend upon you, low-down sonofabitch! May they tear you apart! You call yourself a doctor?
What nerve! Ah! Ah! Ah! She's in paroxysms of outrage!
some kind of charlatan! hen-pecked sucker! traitor! unimag-
inable she finds you! all of a sudden! Basically, women, when
you think about it, I mean when they're young, there are two
kinds, those who're dying to get a bun in the oven, and those
who're dying to get the bun out . . . You can't win . . . But
there, with Clemence, it was peculiar . . . they had other doctor friends . . . But then, if it were for that, she'd have come
alone . . . and then her "periods"? . . . could it be her periods?
. . . I was leaving out her age . . . our age! pregnancy? grandmother more like it. old and ugly! like me! the years! . . . what
breast-feeding does to your breasts . . . not an abortion? then
what? just a visit? . . . come on, screw that idea! Could it be
affection? Hadn't thought of that! A last gasp of friendship?
. . . because there I was like an idiot grinning stupidly at all the
perils breathing down my neck and I saw fuck-all of any of it?
I was sleepwalking! . . . maybe she was coming to suggest I
skip town? a little way of getting to Portugal? an "every-man-
for-himself" en route for Paraguay? . . . The Low Countries?
Guadeloupe? . . . To this day, in my cell, I wonder . . . the
events have passed now . . . long passed . . . I think about them
again . . . What the hell was she up to? Picking out a few bits
of furniture? Marcel would've come along! . . . with a truck
they coulda got everything! . . . Repeat performance of Rueil!

. . . Life's a series of repeat performances, and then you die. It brings people back to us, the same people, their "doubles" if they no longer exist, always the same gestures, the same old song . . . you screw up your entrance, your exit, and your lousy luck begins! flops! catcalls! . . . You only get one act to play! One only!

That day, if he'd've come in a truck he'd've saved me a few things, Marcel . . . Now it's fee-neesh, I'll never get any of it back . . . And since I've been "confiscated for life," my future is more than taken care of! . . . Them, they were robber-friends! . . . quick, hurry, Marcel! get into the truck! . . . Maybe I'd still have a bed somewhere . . . you realize too late . . . If you could only choose your own assassin! . . . The gods are kind to you for once and you don't comprehendo? To hell with you! knucklehead! . . . Had her visit been for the good, Clemence . . . she surely would have kept the picture of my mother for me . . . I don't have it any more.

Come to think of it, since I'm hiding nothing from you, my place, rue Gaveneau, seventh floor, fifteen gangs came one after another over let's say . . . sixteen months . . . to clean me out! . . . think of it! What a *vacuumclining* that was! Not a blade of floorboard left untouched! . . . my hidden treasure! They dug out my benches, tore the stuffin' out of the furniture, everything broken, dissected! the carpets! curtains! rage and more rage! the john torn out! What a pretty picture I make, here, pondering on the plundering . . . And not a week goes by that doesn't bring more insults! . . . I've stopped counting all the dirty tricks from the Courts . . . Five or six times they've found no grounds for prosecution! Shot down! "The time you did counts!" "The time you did doesn't count!" I know at least fifty nutcases who'd have hung themselves over a lot less than I've had to swallow by way of promises, persecutions, dejections, rejections, spit . . . They throw me in the slammer, I'm stagnating, pus covered, my pelt's dropping off . . . They get me the hell out of there, they throw me back in! . . . Back in the hole, goddamn stiff! I can hear the courtroom echoing, "The Supreme Court having reassembled . . ." It's a cross between the BBC and a fucking bitch! "Confiscate more than everything he's got, the pig! for all Eternity!" Subjected to endless privations, placed in stocks, pilloried, the nation's pile of shit! His medal of honor to the Flea Market! Let them reopen all his war wounds! disabled! Seventy-five percent! Roll your drums! . . . Let them lacerate him again, skin him alive! lard and pepper! Yo! Yo! Yo! *Yes!* ten thousand percent! Doesn't it make you stop and think? Let me spell it out for you . . . They don't even leave me a gas heater! Where will I go sterilize my syringes? I'm thinking about my practice . . .

– What about your Degree?

The bastards didn't touch that! If they took that I'd never speak to you again . . . I'd be suing this very minute! Riot Act! . . . can't you see the Shades of Honor? The French army, the great, the ruddy, the 1914! . . . If they'd inflicted the final affront on me, I'd have set Europe going again! I'd have knocked those guys on their asses! the mere sound of my voice and *poof,* everyone gone! the steppes! Moscow at hand! and preserving everything! the little bells! the Kremlin and the rest! burning nothing! everything according to tactic, down to the very pom-poms! *pomm-pomm,* the beating of the heart! the uniform! That's what you'd have seen if they'd so much as put a wrinkle in my Diploma! They can thank their lucky stars! It was their doing if I wound up with the extremists!

To each his own misfortunes, no doubt . . . to each his own Destiny . . . you got guys who shake their piggy bank, guys who shake their thing, and guys who shake the world, and you got "no grounds for prosecution." Listen to this, for example, Denoël,[33] they shot him dead and that's all there was to it! . . . Me, I shot nothing dead at all, I have no "no grounds"! Eeny, meeny, miney, mo . . . Of course, I have my own ideas about that, set and sincere . . . my idea is that they'd kill if they could! . . . But not me or my idea, madame!

Oh, but life is more than just a few pranks! I hear what you're saying! Survive? Prosper? Manage? So, Sweetie, buy three or four copies of *Fable,* it'll be double the fun – I get to survive and you get to pay! Great idea! my old bike back! my villa! You can find something funny in anything! I'm sick as a dog and falling to bits, but I'll give up joking only after I give up the ghost! my last gasp! The proof, here, with only an eighth of a glimmer of light, things oozing out of my asshole, my armpits, and the elbows, too, blood coming out of the eyes, from the soupy mess of my grave, me whistling a tune, that's what you'll hear! A regular blackbird! . . . putting on a brave face while I ham it up? Maybe you're right! So what? But you won't catch me taking it lying down! Goddamn weirdo repeating himself all the time!

And not only pellagra up the ass! Article 75 and the Public Prosecutor, too![34] Four arrest warrants canceled, reinstated! and Gaëtan Serge d'Hortensia,[35] that half-breed Underling from the Embassy, representing the Union of Diplomatic, Political, Colonial, and Ectoplasmic Madmen, who insults me as of daybreak! Obsessive! Nobody, not even someone of very high morale, could escape turning into a gibbering idiot, uncouth and shivering, hair turned white! Hortensia arrives at dawn to see me! He emerges at the cell window, he mocks me, you should see the faces he makes! in black and white! You who don't have much sense of fun, you'd shout "death rather than this!" and he emerges just at first light . . . just at the time when the guy next door is taking a break from screeching . . . when the new shift of prison guards are taking out the juices . . . when I could have a bit of time to myself . . . Am I seeing things? Hearing funny things? I'm just having a bit of fun for myself! nothing more than that! Laughter comes naturally to me . . . I see the pretty part in any petty trick . . . not everybody can do that! So go buy *Fable,* three francs! Let's say three francs! three francs before the First World War! Talk about three francs before the Great War and you're talkin' money! a gift! And if it's gifts you're talking about, I'm your man! yes, siree! I go from one little concession to another! It's not that I like you! you've hurt me far too much! you go from one felony to another, sheepish bunch of cowards! you can go drop dead! I'll tell the Koreans, "come and get 'em!"[36] all yours, from the bottom of my heart! But in the long run, the bookstore does count! You buy *Fable!* The text vexes you? Your business! I'm the one that I'm making fun of! I'm the scabby, moss-covered skeleton! a funny one, jeez, the fate that's befallen me! in fifty years of relentless labor, innovations, conscience and honor, heroic, I was decorated before Petain was, and I'm pilloried by the pillagers! shamed by the shameless, and the exodus, while we're at it – in whatever direction – Bruges, Bayonne – they had us by the pants – one endless line of us, was all it was! And then the "Caca shirts"! Holy Shit!

Forget all this pettiness! . . .

My eyes are the real problem . . .

Writing is painful, I'm bug eyed . . .

– It was darker in the mines!

You go right for the weak spot, don't you? These walls are soaking, I sponge up the puddles . . . on all fours, it's not at all easy for me to get up again . . .

– So he's complaining about being locked up? if we'd only had him at the Villa Saïd![37]

– Were *you* at Villa Saïd? on which side, may I ask?

– And what about Luppenthal?[38]

I'm upsetting you. This tiff isn't over! Choose your weapon! Go on! Hand shield! and the whole blade, and split yourself down the middle! Chest forward! where were you in August 1914? . . . I ask you again! not in Flanders? nor at Charleroi?[39] . . . Gotta know who it is you're mad at! where you loose your arrows. So you dabble in commentating, avenging? you're established? patented? puffed up? card-carrying member of six different parties? Hit the mike, avenger! Hit the mike! all the avengers are on the airwaves! in waves, in folds, curlicues, curly-heads! dimples! No one to stop the tanks, but they can sure talk a volcanic offensive! this *furia canto* all over the airwaves! billions of kilocycles of thunder! a deluge of bla-bla-bla!

Madness, mobs, the same at the Hôtel de Ville during the nationwide bloodfest! When they tore out the losers' eyes! The great orgasms of the Prudent! Sade's Army at History's Picnic! The Church that's going to get built in let's say a dozen, fifteen, twenty years! Petiot Pope! Europe-the-Glutton!

– Have you forgotten St. Martin? the saint of the Gauls?[40] not St. Martin's boulevard! not St. Martin's neighbor-whored![41] no! the saint! Can't you make use of him? Ah, the bitterness of a nation that's reverted to paganism, with no more sacred images! Go try and make them laugh at the stake! Forget about it! All the same, *Fable?* my bicycle? . . . Yeah, you'd've had a much better laugh, had one helluva kick, gone completely berserk! and gratis, too, if they'd dragged me to Blanche place, you see the grid, well, my guts'd be draped over it like the beads of a rosary, a lacework of vivisected organs . . . the little ones here, the big ones there, delicately picked apart in front of the Duquèquet Restaurant![42] How my screams would have resounded from the Enghien Heights to Port-Royal! . . . at least five million people getting all worked up, all tender hearted: psychiatric patients nobody wants, people inured to coke, kola, girly shows, the strap, urinals, croutons![43] everything! You couldn't find a more desperate bunch! . . . I'd have been the delight of five hundred thousand households! But I let them down! Not just around there, Montmartre, the slopes, Caulaincourt . . . Custine . . . Dufayel! . . . but also the inner and the outer suburbs! They still hold it against me, people who write to me furious! You fucked off, you bastard! you coward! you gonorrhea germ!

I deprived them of my stake and scalp! They'll never forgive me!

Martyrdom, the Golgothas of this world, are gifts from heaven! Never do families get it on better, never is the soul more groped, or the tits and asses either (and let me bite them again on you, remunch those toes),[44] as when a martyr gets butchered! and the bloodier it gets the more the fuck juices gush out! and the knout to boot! *Bam! Plop!* the more they're in seventh heaven! the more they get their rocks off!

– Program, darling?

Ah, coming in neon lights! the ultimate frolic! Ah, honeybunch, love me, baby, love me! Ah, take all of me! in love me! in love me! in! in! in! you've got four of them! ten! twenty! a hundred! big ones! Oh! Ooo! Whooo! in! all of it!

Just imagine from Enghien to Marcadet! the bastions! Pantin! Saint-Michel! . . . and still others! . . . brothers by the wagonload! marching! . . . tipcarts full of victims with their guts torn out and still hot! . . . The more innocent the victims, the more you get their stink, the happier you are! Cut up every goddamn Jasus! The more they pierce the air with their cries the more Juliette gasps, writhes, climaxes, the more Romeo rams it in! Gallop in there and grab those buttocks. Charge! Ah, milove! some love! in, love! be mine! fire me up! juice me, I'm coming! Oh my God! Oh, oh! Stay! Come, come! Fucking hell, what a load of crap!

– This wise guy is going too far!

– Yeah, forget about him! but the fact remains, the promise has been signed, notarized, heard on radios all over the place! at xyz hour my balls will be hanging from the neck of the most renowned purgative avenger from the Porte d'Alfort to the Flanders Bridge! . . . the Eastern Sector – from the Goutte-d'Or to the Great Quarries! Judge the extent of it for yourself! the networks! Oh, but those times have passed! all those carcassfests down the drain! I'm splitting hairs! Those quickie Saint-Bartholemews with no clarions sounding, no Paternosters, no trumpets!

These times call for other ways to make 'em laugh! To wow the readers now, you gotta get hippos to hop! Here's to you, Bozo! So goddamn many murderers around that as long as it's not them, they'll just yawn! . . . If they saw the Daumesnil Lake piled high with the bodies from the night before, from a hundred guillotines from the various Parties, they'd say: Gee, it stinks! That's all! total disregard! . . . So don't even mention buying my books! . . . me and my pathetic little problems . . . mere fables . . . and they got to grip their shaking bellies, uncontrollable fits of hilarity, shitting, pissing all over the place, can't take it any more, in their parlors, the train stations, under the watchful eyes of the Tax Collector. Betcha you'll laugh so hard they'll have to lock you up! That you'll be in convulsions of hee-hee-haw-haw over my nonsense, all over the Tuileries! . . . That they'll arrest you for public obscenity and ask you what it's all about!

– It's *Fa!* . . . *Fa!* . . . *Fa!*

You drop down dead from laughing right on my book!

Reuters reports it . . . And there's a mad rush to buy it! The bookstores are sacked! . . .

– Gimme, gimme more! Anything for *Fa! Fa!* My daughter, my cows! the Brooklyn Bridge! My credit's good anywhere! They print me on toilet paper! On the priciest paper, on rice paper! Affluence abounds around me! my pride returns! my self-respect . . . a government minister arrives at my door, I kick him where he chucks a moon! *Whap!* Whopping good time! Maybe I can even buy back my bike! Picture that! and two villas in Saint-Malo! And while you're at it! two maids to open the doors! A great big Pachon to take pressure readings! fourteen thermometers in gold cases! twenty-five masses a year for me alone! for my soul and for come what may! In church, where Heaven, the rain through the holes, the sun but less, and God not at all, they come in, don't come in, as the case may be.[45] Shittin' shindig! only one mass for my assassins! And one not at all for Fartre![46] A hundred for all the animals that are lost, as many for the men in prison, all you want for Aunt Amelie and my friend Mr. Verdot,[47] and other people, too, some more serious than others . . . Their names, blabbers? You'd like them, wouldn't you? But you're not gonna get them!

I'm showing off! I'm intoxicating myself with my own thoughts! I'm chasing rainbows. I, who never touch a drop of alcohol, I'm forgetting myself! I'm forgetting you! and my story! and the episode! the kid in my house there, with his pimples, his mother! with Marcel! No, not Marcel! . . . their cockeyed ways . . . I never finish anything for you . . . back to the drawing board, reader! Hey, you, reader! my place, rue Gaveneau! Seventh floor! I was about to tell you about our exodus! . . . well, you know, when we flew the coop . . . We had to . . . three months before all the others! . . . Should've seen us shifting all our gear! Winfling-Oder . . . Blaringhem . . . Neurupin . . . Rostock[48] . . .

– He's got the audacity to complain? Gas-off artist has no shame! He took all of Europe for a ride! . . . (So what are you gonna do the day the tanks arrive and Ivan the Terrible's in the Tuileries?) They were waiting for me at Stake place – I mean the Blanche place . . . and at Pigalle . . . and Monceau! . . . you'd have tripped over all the experts! panting! . . . the animal who flees from the Arena, what's he worth? manages to sidestep the pickaxes, the pitchforks, the voyeurs, the Carmens, the Josés, and the Alcades all together?[49] It isn't even worth the sawdust anymore, a trip to the Circus Maximus, guts everywhere! If you don't believe me just look at the state I'm in, flayed alive, rotting in this hole . . . Eh, leave me alone . . .

If it weren't for that weedy black Hortensia, the Underling from the Embassy, coming again to lay more abuse on me first thing in the morning, through my cell window . . . the faces he makes! the threats! I'd think oblivion had totally engulfed me! long live the Abyss! But no, the Hortensia reemerges! Can't with him around!

– I'm Louis XV! I'm Louis XV, rogue!

That's the way he berates me from up there!

– Come give me a kiss!

And his voice is hoarse and greasy! I'd call it common! takes himself for Louis XV, no less! . . . Louis XV!

– I am France! I am the colonies!

If I didn't have Hortensia I'd think everybody was abandoning me ... There's also the guard sometimes ... With his finger he makes like he's going to shoot me, but he does it ten times a day! ... real funny ...

But I know what's what! Avenging reader, you have might on your side! You say, "This show-off is taking us for a ride!" Well, I'm going to show you my posterior! I told you, "I'm rotting!" ... Your eyes are better than mine! even here in the dark you probably see! ... the bright red is the pellagra ... next to it, forming like a fringe, the grayish yellow: that's mold! This is not a common occurrence! ... oozing pimply little eruptions! I think I caught it back in Blaringhem. Down there I had at least fifteen ... sixteen cases! and scabies! ... at least a thousand! And now they've decided my ass is the occupied zone! not to mention the elbows! and the back of the neck!

– Yeah, but in Augsbourg! it wasn't just pus-filled scabs! there it was total butchery! all those hides for AA lanterns! Scrotum-skin lamp shades and bookbindings, little flutes, Walkyries, Odin's sabbath, and gas ovens![50]

I declare that I had nothing to do with it! neither with my ass nor with Augsbourg! I didn't go and declare war, I declared nothing at all, except "Long live France and Courbevoie![51] Down with the Slaughter!"

Volunteered for service twice, 75 percent disabled, I swore nothing to Pétain, nor to von Choltniz,[52] nor to the pope! Nor to that other guy, Hortensia there, who haunts me through the cell window ... nor to the lunatic across the way ... nor to the "yep yep" in 73! Putain,[53] let them cut his goddamn throat! ... Are you K wing or are you not K wing?[54] ... "Death row," it's actually written there!

They don't kill them all! You might be surprised to learn, you who like a good laugh, that at the bottom of the ditch, the body is overrun by mold, I mean the limbs, the torso, the

34

epidermis, the eyes, alas! But the heart, excuse me! cast iron, the heart! the 1914 heart!

– So where were you in '14? Am I wasting my time? you weren't there . . . you were under other skies! With other feelings, other legends . . . Hateful old man, oozing, bitching, I'm not going to amuse you a helluva lot! Why not, here, I leave you my eyelids! they're bleeding and gummy . . . I'm bug eyed . . . all the rage to donate your eyes these days . . .

– Yeah, and what about Cassel? on shaky ground there!

– You weren't there either, Petunia! You can't talk to anybody about torture! Just wait your little turn! The times we live in are generous in nothing, except in butcher blocks, burnings, hangings, you'll always find something! . . . at least wait for the handcuffs! . . . Haste makes waste! . . . Don't jump the gun, when the garrote's around your neck you'll be whistling a different tune! Oh, a different tune altogether! Youyou, Gertrude!

– Hey, this jailbird's really having us on! God damn it, he's whipping us up, the caustic little bastard! The vault he's buried in! His posterior! His dreams! Extradite the bastard! Outta here! cut 'im up! riddle 'im! skin 'im! two stakes! outta here! twelve stakes, sixteen!

– Program, darling?

I hear you.

– You got ants in your pants, buddy! What about the Satory Camp? and Cadoudal? and la Roquette? and Gambetta in his air balloon? And Sarah Bernhardt up there on one leg? Were those not sublime and surprising exploits?[55] doubly exalting to the soul? centubly rousing for the Nation? If you had even the shadow of an atom's worth of their stuff, the billionth of a crumb, everything would have turned out all right! From Quimper-on-Odet to the Bering Straits! to the last miserable Alution-louse-of-an-Island, down there, in the sea, a mere drop of earth. It's very simple – three continents! The heart is everything! How many times do I have to tell you?

Do you count all that as nothing? Would you doubt?

– He's having us on . . .

Let me call to mind Gambetta, la Roquette, let me call to mind Landru, let me call to mind Pétain-living-off-Verdun, Petiot, the Grandeurs of Fontenoy, the Marne, the great deeds of Rambouillet, President Galoubet bringing Hitler to lunch with Gallieni in a taxi, plus Lartron! his wife on the Isle of Yeu! Odes everywhere![56]

– This stuff is mental anarchy!

– I've got no position in society to maintain! I've no air balloon! I've got no sky for Chrissake! No one will stand and cheer and hoist me to their shoulders! I had to bleed for my standard! the most glorious one! the Seventh Infantry Division! They brought it back to the Invalides, torn to bits, like me, they tore my medal off me, they left me with only the bullet in the brain and the buzzing[57] . . . No one will stand and hoist me to their shoulders! And on my belly in the dugout trenches, I don't even have a stove to fry the goddamn iguanas, salamanders slandering me in a thousand languages! I haven't got a guillotine either! . . . I've got an ass that sticks, that's all . . . I entertain you with the little bees in my bonnet . . . if it were only just the daytime it would be all right . . . Jailbirds, cells, handcuffs, that's the bottom of any human community . . . you have to see it from the inside! . . . hospitals, diseases, I know all about them . . . and war, too . . . you gotta do everything once before you croak . . . not a single regret! . . . Ah, this self-respect that we carry, exaltedly, to the grave! Vercingetorix! Pétain! Voltaire! Blanqui! Oscar Wilde! Lecoin! Jaurès! Thorez! Mr. Braguet! Francis the First! Sacco! they're kinda like predecessors! and others! and Latude![58] He who hasn't been in prison is just a silly pansy . . . a crummy little windbag . . . he goes "Gad-thookth,"[59] what does he know? and he doesn't wanna know, the jerk. Gabbing, fibbing, that's all he knows! . . . that's why the world stays so fucking stupid . . .

I was saying that if it was just the day, it'd be okay . . . but

36

you got the night, too! The night screamers, they're stark raving out of their skulls! Jailed sea lions! The sound goes right through you! Think about it! prisons are mostly hollow! You should hear the echoes! And then there's their huge fuckin' watchdogs outside! Ah! Chenier with his "Captive"![60] If he could hear mine over there! Number 92! She'd put a stop to a verse or two! "Yeee! Yeee!" as if her throat were being cut . . . You see Muses all right! . . . and "ruff ruff" the dogs! Ah, yes, I dread the night . . . About four in the afternoon the screaming calms down . . . four little rings . . . chow time . . . the peephole, the screw comes in,[61] he takes away my papers, my writing tablets, pencil, everything! he turns the lock again, *crr! crr! crank!* you'd think he was closing Vincennes! . . . three Mont Saint-Michels! a Creusot of locks![62] . . . by Judas he calls me every name in the book . . . it's his way of saying "good evening to you" in Baltavian . . . that I'm loathsome! that I stink! . . . Oh, when it comes to foreign idiom, it's the intonation that counts! . . . a man in a moment of despondency, he doesn't give a fuck about understanding . . . everything goes straight to the heart! that's nature! . . . insults, lies, kindness . . . the animal instinct . . . the flan of words goes flat . . .

I tell you, at four o'clock, it's finished . . . night, real night, descends . . . I can still see a little red, and then some gray and then black . . . I drop off my stool! if it sticks to my ass I go down with it . . . Have to be careful how I go down! . . . the mattress! a cover! Okay! I wait . . . It's the darkness of dreams . . . let the poetry begin! pain's lonely pleasure? I wouldn't come? Fuck! Me, who's so good at it? But, you know, I'm going to sue! I'm sick and tired of these "arrest warrants" for me alone! sonofabitch for sonofabitch, I know a few others! mobitudes of them, a hell of a lot more gangrenous, degraded felons, plagues of shame, playing a double game, triple game, forty games! Pimps! Fuck them, with their "warrants" for me alone! . . . I never was anything at all, now that I think about it, here on my straw . . . not ambassador, not minister, not participator, not celebrity, not with Vichy, not with Leahy,[63] nor the

Little-Swiss,[64] and not with the next guy that's gonna come along, either! None of 'em! and not a deserter to the enemy!

– That's exactly what your trouble is, knucklehead!

I never sold any concrete, my word of honor, nor the Pyramid, nor Napoleon's coffin, nor Argenteuil's wooden bridge, nor Madame Tabois's antenna, nor Toulon's flooded harbor, nor Darlan's fleet full of holes![65] *Nix!* I'm getting down to details again . . . the Iconoclasts made a mad rush, drunk with their own Virtue, Truth, convinced that the monster up there in my place on the seventh floor was a typhus plague . . . Yeah, burn 'im at the stake! petrol and sulfur or nothing!

They stole everything they could, shattered anything that was too heavy! . . . they burnt my manuscripts . . . into the garbage also *Guignol's, Krogold, Casse-Pipe!* my offerings![66]

That's what excites them, what's excited them for centuries! Burnings at the stake, massacres, trash! Even more than thievery! Islam, Port-Royal, the Guillotine, Genghis Khan, the atom, phosphorous bombs, now that's somebody! Never any problem to torch prayer books, feed the *Iliad* to the pigs, stick a tongue up the Virgin's vagina, a pecker up Petrarch's ass! No sooner said than done! Crusade? Let's crusade! The bastards should be hung? Let's hang! Anyone scared shitless is a sissy! Take me, for instance, here in my hole, the taxmen are still taxing me! The twenty-second arrondissement! The Tithe! The Internal Revenue! millions! on all my so vanished works! "That they're gonna sentence me to three life sentences if I don't come back and execute myself" and that afterward they'll cut my head off! That's what they're like!

And the best proof that they're not fooling around is that they're already auctioning off my mother's bed!

They're selling air, phantoms . . . If I sent them my Hortensia, they'd sell him off cheap, Louis XV! . . . Ah, the mammoth complexity of it all! have your cake and burn it, too! But don't go thinking there's nothing they bow before! It's their Almighty Position they worship! their supreme Goddess! They never stop assassinating the core of their soul! Nation, I have not a centime to send you! Taxman my heart! (They claim I have debts to Pétain!) I'm dead broke! Bébert's hide's not worth two bits! Two bits? I'm thinking big! I'm thinking '14!

The man of today is a crime! The way it is nowadays, the Bastille, they'd leave it standing, they'd lock all the filth up in it, in chains, just like that! all you pig-headed writers, get to work! under the knout, twenty masterpieces a day! and get the line right, and make it anonymous! There'd be no dozing! Clang-bam à la '89 into the dungeon, the tower, house arrest![67] Don't think they're not thinking about it! . . . It's maybe even been done already! . . . Here where I am, the cop who's got me cornered is the ultimate yokel! He'll never read any manuscript of mine! The Baltavian Brute! in the morning he brings me back my bundle of papers, throws it right at my head . . . flies all over the place! he gets a real chuckle out of seeing me on all fours . . . sign-languages that he's gonna blow me away . . . they all do it . . . on account of their papers, my photos, my heinous crimes, with a hundred details . . . I'm the one who sold the Devil's Own Plan, the Kookie Fortress, the Pas-de-Calais, the Eiffel Tower . . . and Gamelin's ulterior motives[68] . . .

Now they see me here! . . . So, of course! . . . The truth of the matter lies there: in prison! "He's in prison!" . . . There's your proof!

Couldn't give a fuck about their gut feelings! but the pain in the ass in 73, trumpets like a goddamn elephant! a hundred donkeys! that one adds to my misery, all right! I could have his guts for garters! And the shrill dame in 48! I hear the blows, the punch-up twice a day . . . at the shift change . . . afterward an hour or two of calm and then it starts up again, only worse . . . women scream at such a high pitch! . . . men gasp . . . I know the "hitmen," there are three of them, three bare-assed Hercules, in white smocks, they came to see me one evening, one night . . . they made me get up . . . they kicked the shit out of my mattress! straw, my rags everywhere! That sent me back a few years, you know the kind of thing,

39

haze the greenhorn there in number 12! What a bunch of kids! Baltavians don't make good soldiers! . . . They know nothing of the military arts . . . They go to it! . . . just kids! . . . they do it all wrong! . . . now me, I know how to kick the shit out of a mattress. These guys kinda make you feel sorry for them! . . .

They insult me! "They'd be back." They were having a good go at me! . . . But I hear them at it . . . here . . . there . . . one floor . . . another . . . the sound the digs make . . . the shrieking! and then nothing at all . . . calm through force! they go from one landing to another . . . the funny part's the suicides . . . what an avalanche that is! all the guards! You should see them skedaddle! all five floors! . . . the whole horde! . . . prison rattles with their footsteps! and the ten buildings full of cages! "A suicide!" And they come baradabooming down! get to the schnook's cell! Swinging there in his cell, you bet he gets a visit or two! the band strikes up! Sirens! whistles! mutts! It's a goddamn Opera!

– And you, my fine Lyric Poet, what hope keeps you alive? Haven't seen enough misery yet? Duke Ayer of Vendôme waiting for you to snuff it?[69] you think you'll wind up on the rue du Repos?[70] . . . you're nuts! asshole! Go on, do the right thing! They left you your belt! . . . the bar up there! a noose! end of story! . . . You can't even be sure for Chrissake they'll make fast work of you down on rue du Repos the way they did Denoël at the Invalides! . . . that'd be doing you a favor! . . . Maybe it will happen at the Concorde in front of five hundred thousand onlookers! . . . Ah, nostalgia! homesickness! choke back those sighs! Next year in Paris! bite the bullet, poet, insanity reigns in Paris, and insanity, now that's something to reckon with! if only you showed up already dead! that'd be the most useful, the greatest good will have been served! . . . Your country of fellow Frenchmen, your only one, is Père-Lachaise . . . they're the only ones who won't do you any harm . . .

– Oh, don't worry, they'll inspect the coffin, they'll check out your remains! gotta be sure it's really you! and then there'll be peace, the real thing . . .

So if I get you right, in your opinion, good sense, reason would dictate that my days are numbered and should end here? Ah, my days! half a day! quarter of a day! . . . Fuck you! I'm gonna face it down! Have a look – this is open rebellion! my responsibilities, my duty? I've got Bébert, I've got Arlette on the outside! I've got five grandchildren in the Wood![71] I've got my mom that I never saw again and my father Fernand next to her, I abandon nothing on the way, Sir! not a soldier, not a patient, alive or dead, not a mistress, not a care! Never! and not thirty-six thousand feet itching for me to kick your butt!

– Equivocator! Scaredy-cat! Alibiber! stinker! pig!

– Go easy, sweetie! Come over here with your baloney and we'll blow holes through each other at twenty-five paces! Twenty-five paces? I'd have to have room for them first! Where would I get twenty-five paces? in my little cage? more like four!

Okay, so I blow you to kingdom come! so long, pal! God-damn bitchery! they'll all drop dead from it! I've been subjected to it all! but while we're on the subject! I argue with Hortensia when he emerges at my cell window! I argue with the bellower, their "appeals reject" in 26! with that lunatic she-spy in 32! and the one in 64! my contiguous sea lion! who comes right through the wall at me, damn sure!

– Into the sewer! I scream at him! I mean he's stopping me from working! He won't shut up? I sweet-talk him! I turn on the charm! . . . well, I try . . . I whip out my song . . . I got you wondering there, a bit earlier . . . I let it slip about my songs . . . (all copyrighted!), here, take this number:

JUST BETWEEN US
Ill find you some foul night
Dead meat in my rifle's sight!
Your dumb cow of a soul'll be gone in a glance

To the Heavenly Choirs –
You'll see how they dance!
In the Good Children's Bone-Palace in the skies!

Is it too aggressive for these parts? . . . okay, so it's too aggressive . . . but what about the refrain? pure charm! almost seductive! . . . you should hear it . . . with the music! . . .

(and right at this very moment – the artist caught unawares! . . . the scene changes! . . . he sees others arrive on the set!)

But here come Auntie Estreme and her little Leo! . . .
And here Clementine and the valiant Toto!
Shall we tell our friends every party ends?

(the scene changes again: Eh, he should go get fucked, the ugly son of a bitch!)

To the devil your kind!
Be gone with the wind!
Adieu, dead leaves! antics
And cares!

the last bit sweeps you away, doesn't it? lighthearted! dizzying!

I'd promised it to Revol[72] . . . it's a classy number, I can tell you . . . full of tact! . . . finesse! . . . not the gravelly street song you can get anywhere! He was supposed to sing it for me in Bécon at a benefit concert![73] "Donations to prisoners of modest circumstance!" . . . and then, of course, events took over! . . . There were six other verses . . . spicy ones, I can assure you! For me, to be sung at The European, now that was fame![74]

It could have happened!

I belted my whole song out at him, at my howler, from down there in my hole, the contiguous one! . . . Once in a while that puts a stop to him . . . a quarter of an hour . . . an

42

hour . . . and then he rehowls! Only more so! Oh, but excuse me, I can drown them all out! quite a resource, the thorax! when I really can't take it any more, when I'm in too much pain, when I haven't for example been to the john in ten, twelve days . . . thirteen days . . . all of a sudden! when they don't want to give me my enema, I let out a bark!

They give it to me hotter than hot, almost 130 degrees! on purpose! I don't give a fuck! it's an enema, isn't it? . . . When they hear the barking I know they'll come running! . . . I drown out all the howlers! I'm a shock-trooper mastiff in the barking department! . . . the watchdogs answer me . . . three or four packs of them . . . the din that makes, by your leave! "Whaa! Whaa! Whaa!" The guards burst in, four machine guns, I make sign language at them: I stick! no can get up any more! . . . no can turn over, either! . . . fee-neesh! they leave again, they're gonna look for clamps . . . a stretcher! And that's it! . . . Reminds me of Africa, and of Flanders . . . Ypres 1914 . . . you gotta manage somehow . . . And Bezons, too, the R.A.F. . . . I was the one wielding the instruments there! who was sticking the bits back, the arms, the genitals, the heads! . . . "sworn in" medical man, and still am! Argenteuil Township![75] Mr. Death Certificate, that's me! Faultless! conscience! character!

Life is some panorama! You picture yourself . . . against such backdrops! . . . Up there in the prisoners' infirmary my case is well known, all right . . . I'm treated with a certain regard . . . except for the water, which is too hot! . . . the doctors are less dumb than the others, that helps lighten the burden a bit, the despondency, the harsh reality . . . not that they ever speak to me, but they see . . . I'm allowed three days, fifteen phials, two more enemas, seven bottles of strong beer, and the swabbing of my scabs with "violet crystal" solution . . . If they have a nut job they send him to me, bed next to mine, there's two of us . . . so I can get him to eat, keep him amused . . . that's esteem for you, trust, the doctors know what's what . . . For example, there was this enormous Russian, a desperate case named Barrabas, a shoemaker by trade, I can safely say I saved his life . . . He was gouging out his forearm by the forkfuls . . . and then he had a go at his thigh, under the covers . . . he was making fast work of himself . . . I tell you, this guy! his resolve! Had he found his femoral, the artery, he'd've been done for! . . . Two days later he was on the mend . . . purely thanks to my influence! the convincing show I put on! I tell you, the morale that I emanate! . . . he was taking his grub again . . . but I hear he commited suicide two weeks later . . . threw himself under a train . . . in the tunnel . . . he'd broken out of his handcuffs . . . they were escorting him . . .

You should've seen me back in the can! real umpf! hope! completely revitaminized! the belly pliant! enema! youth! I churn out marvels! I don't even hear the sea lion any more! . . .

Hortensia comes out at me . . .

– Out of here! carpetbagger! I shout at him . . . Epileptic! Hysteric! Official, my ass!

Jeez, the insults I spit at him!

– Vichy-boy! Nigeria! Cigar! Cart hauler! Go get your ass shined! Caribbean! Bum-boy! . . . ill-mannered lout! Jazz-band!

That's what vitamins will do for you! I completely floor 'im . . . all ecto that he is . . . plasm! His Louis XIV and so forth! Apparitions like him! I know how to deal with them!

– Article 75! I insult him.

That's the last word!

He disappears . . .

Can you picture the sangfroid, the energy? five, six days I stay in this state! exhilarated! crackling! the pages I cover! . . . the magic pencil, there you go! and then things go a bit less well . . . and then worse . . . my eyes haze up again . . . I see fuzzy . . . everything's vague . . . don't see anything any more . . . I bark, they hoist me up to the sick bay again . . . Stretcher! . . . If I were in Fresnes,[76] wouldn't it be worse? . . . A hundred times worse!

44

– And at Wuppertal,[77] ham artist?

– And your pussy, sweetie pie? Listen here, I knew "What's-his-face," since you're so goddamn punctilious, a Londoner, he did thirty years' worth of "inside"! Twelve convictions! He came out each time so bleedin' pale, so transparent that everybody could see through him! . . . called himself the "gadfly" for a gas! in person! Talk about sweet natures, and optimism! fourteen times they nabbed him! twelve times he got done! Kept coming back for more, on purpose!

– He's an angel! they'd say . . . everyone looked up to 'im . . .

He finally took wing . . . damn sure . . . They found him one morning stone cold . . . nothing left of him . . . flimsy excuse for a corpse . . . you couldn't call that a corpse . . . talk about skin 'n' bones . . . they buried him with his all clothes on, old coat, cap, shoes, his few rags, the whole kit 'n' caboodle! . . . a very special favor . . . the chaplain didn't want him naked . . . I'm skinny, too – and I don't even know the chaplain! . . . I lost forty-eight kilos! he never came to see me, the bitch! the Lutheran on call! the Papist one, either! No one . . .

Let's get serious here, let's tell it like it is, twenty months in a cell, thirty months, thirty years, what's it to you? . . . You're outside! . . . it's the elixir of the gods, being outside! . . . They all have a very high opinion of themselves outside! no point talking to any "outside-the-wallers." They all have a little amulet inside that tells them that *they'll* never fall! . . . Go ahead, get drunk on it! Prayers and all! May Lourdes endure! . . . It's the stars that are holding up the sky, without them it would fall down! . . . you'd need nails everywhere! Catch a hold of yourself! The little Theresa of Lisieux is still churning out the miracles! . . . And Beelzebub at the other end! Undaunted, the pair of them! as long as everything polkas along! double game! Me, I don't have your ambitions, I'd be happy just to see a bit more clearly, be a little less dizzy . . . or even a bit less pellagra . . . doesn't look like much, pellagra . . . Philippe-Auguste, he had it, too . . . when he left for the Crusades he was a good-looking kid, he came back downright ghastly, wrinkled, all bent out of shape, his neck one big ball of pus. Me, too, when I get back, they won't be able to look at me either! . . . That'll make Jules happy! . . . Jules is my own personal jealous rival, gotta laugh at him . . . the idea that I could be good looking makes him foam at the mouth, turns his stomach, "Yeah, you've got a point, Ferdie's good looking," and there he goes! his teeth rattle, he loses control . . . if he had a knife he'd kill me! high dudgeon! he has a huge fit! turns purple! Loses it . . . He'd be happy to see me lose all my teeth . . . every morning three . . . four teeth I pull out! . . . I'm getting there, I tell you . . . they're very shaky . . . Oh, of course, there are worse cases! . . . Stylishness, respect for one's body, you, what would you care? Of course you can live without teeth, that's what you think! Especially in prison! For thousands of years prisoners have been losing their teeth! that's the way it goes! . . . Nothing ever to chew in the food, everything's mushy! broth and that kind of stuff . . . mushy . . . mushy . . . everything mushy . . .

– But where do you think you are, my good man, what stone are you burrowed under after all?

I hear your question . . . but I ain't talkin'! . . . all the papers claimed, even the telegrams, even the so-called detectives, that I was on such-and-such a latitude, in such-and-such a country, such-and-such prison fortress! . . . Hogwash! . . .

I'm up north, that's all I'm sayin'! . . . Even farther! Neither the city nor the place! If I so much as gave you a tiny inkling of my whereabouts, the smallest idea of where the most insignificant outlying chimney was, a branch of the wood . . . that'd be the end of it! my end! the busybody loses no time. He takes off! reporter, porter, tale bearer, blithering blatherer! My goose is cooked![78]

Oh, such a miserable state he finds me in! . . . He stops at nothing, spouts such a line! the injustice I'm subjected to!

– Ah, my dear Maestro, France has gone mad! . . . the infernal *quid pro quo!* . . . the irradiating genius of Europe! . . . the

46

Bikikini of the Novel![79] . . . Ah, if you only knew, Maestro, how we're bominating the Berbers this year! Aa, bom! bom! bom! dear Maestro! Ah! it's horrible! Hold on while I bo . . . boke! Min! min! minate! Bombom! nable! . . . This hole! this hole! holy smoke! where you're ho! ho! holed up! What if we imp . . . skew . . . skew . . . imp . . . impaled your enemies? . . . Ah, speak to me, Maestro! speak to me! Ba! ba! Bastille! I no longer know what I'm saying! badmoon! I'm all choked up, Maestro! All choked up! Tell me that you're confident! It's nothing, prison, nothing! Have hope! Think of freedom! Tell me you're not going to repudiate anything! Ah, I knew I could cheer you up! Panache! Fame! Honor! Victory! Rabble! Yi! yi! Envy! Rabble! everything! You! You! . . . This hole, here! you! you! you're holed up in! neither here nor there! your poor face! ah yi . . . yi . . . yi! . . . What if we skew . . . skew . . . ered them? imp . . . imp . . . pal . . . ed them? Do but speak to me, Maestro! Ah! I would have brought my tape recorder! you realize? your voice! . . . a record . . . speak! speak to me! chin up! not a single Frenchman left who sheds a tear over them! . . . the state they've reduced you to! . . . Choked up, Maestro, oh, Maestro cho! . . . your poor eyes! . . . to the ovens, all of them! all of it! a thousand ovens! ugly mugs! moch![80] mugs! . . . here, tell me, tell me . . . shout it out! that you're stronger than all of them! swear to me, Maestro! Oh, it's over! Not one Cassel do we have qualms about! ten thousand! a hundred thousand! two hundred thousand grills! You should see France now! You show up at le Bourget! forty thousand bouquets! little girls will be carrying them! hands clasped together and all! If you only knew how highly everyone everywhere is speaking of you! The Greatest Writer of the Century! and not just filler, either! on the front page! Full-page spread, *with* picture! your cat! your good lady! your poor face! your hair all long! and in court, too! and at Fresnes! *and how,* they're thinking of you! France can't sleep, you've been outraged so! Spoliated! slandered! spat upon! Brasillach,[81] nobody gives a shit about him, he's dead! What people want is pictures! records! words! They want meat and photos! Show me your ass where it's bleeding! Move over here, Maestro! Maestro! your drawers! Get on your knees! ... On your knees, that's right! There, where there's a shaft of sunlight let me get it ... that's right ... that's right ... so I can get it all in! your face, too, Maestro! Let's see you weep now! get the stool in, too! good! your little table! your eye! ... rub! ... till it bleeds! ... the cockroach, too ... there you go, your photo! are they going to let you out soon? don't you think so? Why, of course! ... repeat after me: "I hate them!" ... with feeling, dear Maestro, with feeling! ... and now weep! weep! ... Ah, dear Maestro, they're all waiting for you! Your pecker's drooped? ... Can I write that? It's the illness? The gloom? Your mother's dead? your daughter, too? your grandchildren? your wife? weep! weep! There, now I've got it! Ah, the supreme reparation! Ah yes, it will be yours! the Pantheon for you alone! We'll pitch the rest of them out for you! Wouldn't you like that? your head at the Bouffes Theater! your feet at the Backo'beyond! your brow at the Sainte-Chapelle! how handsome you are, how truly fine looking! ... your coccyx at the Sorbonne! ... Ah, how your enemies admire you! ... Just see the amnesty you're going to get! Right? ... Right? ... You have misgivanderings? But Madame Abetz is in on it![82] and the count Atamule of Ayer! and Mr. Abbess-My-Uncle! and the archpatriarch of Arsol! you'll see, it was all just a nightmare! I'll send you vitamins! three tablets a day! and drops! may I? you promise? you'll take them? the Pinpin drops? you know them? Pinpin? you don't know Pinpin? you, a doctor? And what about your novel? *Fable? Fable*, heh? You'll see! Get a hold of yourself! Enjoy yourself! You're young, Maestro! You're still so young! Long live everything! The plaque! you'll see! I guarantee you'll get your plaque! you'll see! didn't I read it all to you? ... and the other thing, right? I'll bring you the record! the sound! such a voice! Let me embrace you! I idolize you, Maestro! I'm in tears here! I idolize you! Work on this for us! Work hard! Enjoy life. Maestro, Enjoy life!

The screw's had enough . . . he comes in, chucks 'im out. Here I am on my own again.

Jeez, have I been reduced to confiding in you? I have my little secrets, believe me! . . . The devil didn't come into the world on his own, he was born of an indiscreet remark! . . . All the world's ills come out of one word too many! . . . I tell you the temperature, even the humidity of my ditch here, there you go! ten . . . twelve . . . twenty lice slip under the door . . . I'm fucked! . . . no locks against lice . . . make themselves right at home!

I'm pissing in my pants, *Phew!* I was holding it in . . . Get a hold of yourself, he tells me . . . Enjoy life! . . . Little ones! little ones do pee pee in their pants!

And here I am on my own again.

It's the pal across the way, in 17, the goddamn pain in the ass I'd like to kill! . . . "Yowl! Yowl!" he won't stop! . . . It'd be good if I just go over there and strangle the guy . . . but where would I find the strength? . . . First I'd have to get up! . . . And rip three or four strips of scabs off my ass while I'm at it . . . and the screw'd have to let me . . . he'll never let me! . . . a savage! . . . that poor reporter! who was already so fond of me! my face! my burning behind! my eyes! my tears! he was fond of everything!

All things considered, when I really think about it, not a single word, you'll get nothing out of me! neither the city, nor the vague whereabouts, nothing! . . . not even all the sounds in the air . . . the rustling on the treetops . . . the squawking of the gulls in the wind . . . the sound of the snowflakes that strike . . . noisy devils, snowflakes! . . . nothing, I tell you! . . . not the *ting! ting!* of the burials . . . the cemetery bells . . . the little bells . . . I'm not talking about cemeteries for effect . . . the hooting of the owls . . . I'm not doing the owls for effect . . . it's the forest all around . . . and very far, really far, the ships . . . I'm not doing the ships for effect . . . and the sirens night and day . . . Oh, I'm not going for the novelistic touch . . . If you came here you'd say, "No, he didn't lie." No, he is not

49

lying! He's telling the truth! Lucky son of a bitch! They're turning him into Jesus Christ! martyr! and music! And he dares complain! . . . I'm getting on your nerves!

– Impale the sonofabitch!

That's the only thing you know! . . .

– That may be so! but just a wee word first, Your Honor! the floor! I'm having a word with His Honor, I ain't talkin' to you! I spoke with Laval![83] He was a patient of mine! I know how to talk to officials! Presidents! Any president! You can never go too high! My mother died of a broken heart all alone on a bench on avenue de Clichy while you were out killing everything[84] . . . what do you make of that? I have nothing left to go back to at all . . . my apartment rue Gaveneau, they've had sixteen different tenants . . . I told you that on page Y! H! Z! Seventh floor! . . . they carted everything off, go see for yourself! Snuffed out! such a way! the inside gutted! sacked! Those are dastardly deeds you don't forget! And hold on, it's not finished! History, I'm now talking about History! I'm tallying up the horrors! I don't give a shit about the Gaveneau apartment and I never did give a shit! It's just to get your goat! because you're a goddamn bunch of thieves! singly or in bunches! the proof, that I've been "confiscated for life"! to death I love you! like the other one was saying who maybe didn't come at all, my so-called purger, all spruced out with his machine gun, the brat drunk on "no risk whatsoever," champion at "Old Maid" who'd've had my buffed boot up his butt if I'd met up with him: there are still scores to settle![85]

My mother had her place on rue Thérèse, 14, that she'd been in for forty years, I made a few inquiries . . . Oh, la, la, they tell me, people you can depend on . . . "the less said the better!" and then maybe two weeks later: "Well, it was like this . . . your mother died on a bench . . . ! and you can shut your mouth about it!" . . . just like that, from a long distance this news . . . the mysteries that await you . . . gotta wait a hundred years, and Lenôtre,[86] and for everyone who knows me to be dead . . .

Shit, I ain't gonna wait a hundred years!

I'll spill it all out now! like it or lump it! I'm a child of the Passage Choiseul, where I was schooled! of Puteaux thanks to my wet nurse Mme Jouhaux (Shepherdess Way),[87] and of Courbevoie, where I was born. She was innocent at heart, my mother, no doubt about it, wouldn't harm a fly, like me! If you please! I fled, I had to, the avengers were all prepared, gathering, nosying around beneath my window . . . they came a hundred at a time! a thousand! they were burning the place, they were tearing the neighbors apart! just for being there! for seeing! that's fury for you! take no bloody chances! the floor, the whole building was in for it! They were blowing up half of Montmartre! It'd all been got ready in the basement! like goddamn moles, the avengers! kegs! plastics! Bickford![88] and oop! They were gonna assassinate Arlette, they were gonna assassinate Bébert, they were gonna assassinate Jules The-strider,[89] so he'd shut his mouth once and for all . . . they were gonna assassinate the concierge . . .

It would've been some orgy, admit it! Blood! kiloliters of it! If I'd've stayed I'd've unleashed bedlam! The number of lives I saved by getting my tail out of there! . . . When madness fills the skies (should've heard those planes!) you can be damn sure it will fill the earth and below, too! into the depths and the sewers! and into minds! you couldn't even call them aircraft any more! more like metro cars loaded with bombs! All in an uproar, rage, metal! and more! much more! "Flying fortresses" they called them . . . are they not portents of the end of the world, "flying fortresses"? They were thrilled with their "fortresses"! A hundred times a hundred devils' castanets letting it rip, crackling, through the air!

– He was a coward, so they said, so they wrote, the audacity of them!

– I saved 220 people by fucking off! (Yeah, and they wouldn't be yelping now!) Besides all the other statues in the squares they wanna tear down, I should get one, place

Dereure, modest of tone, not gilded, but serious all the same, touching.

He left, we lived
Ferdinand-the-Tactful.

– He didn't want us to draw his blood! that's their big gripe . . . he was alone, there were a thousand of us! (besides the "Old Maid" Avenging Angel). Had we caught up with him in Vauvenart Square we'd've made mincemeat out of him by the time we got him to rue Féval!

Hey! easy does it! . . . Two sides to every coin! . . . People in heat for atrocities are the only Communists there ever were! The "All Believing"! mirages, bowels, bones, they swallow it all! Communion, not bread, hot and meaty! There you are! Long live Jesus! two thousand years!

– He didn't want us to! wouldn't cooperate!

I left out of pure kindness, chivalry, love-thy-neighborliness! that's the whole truth! the proof: the statue! nobody was nailed on my account! mashed to a pulp! God knows what! It was a beau jeste, no doubt about it! This thing was bigger than all of us, no mistake! If I'd've stayed another week there'd've been a thousand assassins: three hundred thousand! so they'd've decided to go for it. They'd've come charging up my stairs . . . smash down the door . . . overpower me, tie me up . . . bring me down to where they're gonna torture me . . . impale me, maybe? sure, that's nothing to you! being slashed into strips, either! . . . why not the rack? . . . the scaffold! Coo-coo! Gallows? The high jump! The swing! I see you, knocked for a loop, me! up there wriggling in hysterics!

Oh, compete with you? Who could possibly be up to it? I'll never be able to come close to your valorous deeds! My trials have broken me, I admit it . . . while we're at it, getting back to my mother . . . I can't come to terms with this grief . . . they buried her in Père-Lachaise, lane fourteen, division twenty . . . how I'd love a compassionate leave . . . just time enough to go see the slab . . .

It all happened in such a way . . . she never found out how I wound up . . . I'd bring her a jar of daisies . . . that was her flower, the daisy . . . Marguerite Louise Céline Guillou . . . She died of a broken heart over me, and from exhaustion from too much stress on the heart . . . palpitations, worries . . . of what everyone was saying . . . just imagine the people on the avenue de Clichy . . . a bench . . . what must they have thought? . . .

She never found out what had become of me . . . we watched her leave one evening, she took rue Durantin and then went down toward Lamarck . . . and then that was it, forever . . . she hadn't been sleeping for months . . . She never slept much . . . now she's sleeping . . . She was like me, anxious, too conscientious . . . She had a little bit of laughter inside her all the same, there's an awful lot of it in me . . . To show you, at the bottom of this hole, I can laugh when I want to, I think about you – magic – how you're gonna be doubled over, laughing your leg off, when the flute starts to play, the little tune I mentioned above that you don't yet know . . . If there's no laughter inside you there's nothing . . . I saw her laugh over her laces, my mother, on the "Malines," the "Bruges," spider fine, little knots, the links, edgings so fine she was ruining her eyes . . . they'd turn into these huge bedspreads, a vamp's paradise, such graciousness of design . . . filigrees of daintiness . . . that nobody nowadays understands! . . . it went out with the Epoch . . . it was too light . . . the Belle! . . . it was music without notes, without sound, for the lace worker, it was her eyes . . . that's how it was with my mother . . . she wound up blind . . . sixty years in lace! . . . I inherited her poor eyesight, everything makes me cry, gray, red, the cold . . . I write with great difficulty . . . oh, but I, too, will sleep! it will come, my moment of rest! . . . I'll have earned it . . . "Disgrace!" more than a disgrace! a traitor! a this and a that! no one will deprive me of my death! Confiscated! everything! Beddy-byes! I win!

How I'd like a compassionate leave for Père-Lachaise, to go see the slab, the name . . . The impertinence of it! let them choke! Excrement! they howl, get out of the country! . . . At me? From Courbevoie? they, who come out of the back end of a dung heap, who'll never put any place on a map! from the most deserted goddamn prairies that don't even have a post! a pisshole! a pond! a notion of grammar! it's the presumptuousness that'll kill me! you'll see! see the cruelty of these rejects! I'll be flabbergasted to death! . . . because anything goes! . . . yesterday's doormats! . . .

All they have is harsh words.

I've had enough of Hortensia, I tell you! and his indecent proposals through my bars, there! at dawn!

– I'm Louis XV! I'm Louis XV! come, make nice to me, grand-daddy!

These are amazing things to say.

Come kiss me, you bandit! The lily! France and her Colonies! Dubois is in command![90]

His exact words.

That's the kind of madness he subjects me to! They sent him just for the purpose from Jittery Quay in Paris.[91]

– And after that you'll be decapitated!

At least he's not trying to sweeten the pill, he wants my anu, and then my head! . . .

This is the type of person they send me, Pansy underlings from Jittery Quay in Paris! . . . to get the Saints in prison going! And in ectoplasmic form! only in the most troubled of times!

– I chant! I cry! I pray!

I make the sign of the cross . . . *Vade! Vade!*[92]

He bursts out laughing.

I remake the sign of the cross.

– In the name of the Great Can-Can! I scream . . . Who is mightier than God!

That shut him up . . . he disappears for three, four minutes . . .

– And Brasillach, hold your tirades! didn't he suffer a bit more?

54

– Don't give me any shit about Brasillach! He didn't have the time to catch a cold, they shot him still hot! with me it's rotting away for years here in this hole with the sea lions on my right, left, in front that I can't bear! the marshals with their whistles, either! Plus Hortensia and his wisecracks! and the walls full of howling! the sirens, the cemetery bells! Even as debased here as I am, it's not bearable, there are no words for it! only laughter, of course!

And André Weathervane,[93] that handsome charmer, now he was another valorous one! victim! walled in! and so on! operettas or no operettas! and Mr. Ayer of the Government Seals![94]

Oh, they were on the up-and-up again! Honor and Justice at the Ritz and place Vendôme! Let's have a drink! Let's have two! the column is high and in bronze, won't ever catch them throwing themselves off it!

– I'll never be minister!

– And Cardinal La Balue?[95] And Blanqui at Mont Saint-Michel?[96]

Well, if you're going to drag History into this! you'll always find someone who's been chucked in a cage! heaven's sake! lordy be! one beautiful fuckup after another! And Barbès?[97] And what about Latude? and Rip Van Winkle and his beard? And Mr. Capet?[98] Paris has always had its executioners! always somebody with his head cut off, his limbs wrenched from their sockets, strappadoed, boiled! just need to know what sect you're in! to which persuasion you belong! three-quarter? full-time, part-time pimp? vaseline? borderline? cross-eyed? fence-sitter? Shinola! Twisted tastes? . . .

Here, a very friendly word in your ear . . . the thing to point out at the moment . . . look at the cages! . . . thousands, right! millions of people have been in cages all this time . . . millions more will follow! . . . You'd think they'd be used to it by now . . . But not at all! Screeching like ospreys they are on the inside! yelping! terrible pain! Such catastrophes!

– Absurd! On all fours, squirts! And no arguments! All

fours! Sighs? The Animal Era has arrived! Come on! Zoology to the People! Get down there and crawl or die!

History is the memory of facts! Now 1914, that's a date! The Flat Stone Age, the Bone Age, the Herring Age, the Age on its Knees, the Age of the Cathedral, the Age of Gunpowder, the Age of the Tank, the Age of the Hole, the Age of Belly Crawling, and the Age of the Cage!

This is the end of the Age of 1914!

The entire human family at the Zoo! the Flood without an Ark, some other animal's turn to be martyred, let's flay the educated!

The Great Moral Revolution? . . . The Dove![99] we'll see! . . .

Look, I'm not just shooting the breeze, here, it's the perfect modern regime . . . Ten minutes a day in the fresh air, twenty-three hours and fifty minutes confined . . . not just a little, really in the dark . . . that bit of air lies in wait for you! one mouthful . . . you're knocked out! three sheets to the wind! through the chicken wire, the sky, the gulls gliding way up there! in the blue! you cry out, "Long live the Creator." But they don't like you getting carried away one bit! The sniper up there with his machine gun comes rushing to his peephole: "Hey, you down there, yeah, you, the one who takes it up the ass!" he shouts (it's not true at all!). *Maul!* . . . *Maul!* . . . (that's German for "kisser") furious in his tower . . . he lets you know how he feels about such things! . . . to not understand is human . . . All the same, in summer the sky, the gulls . . . who cares about insults? . . . the caged-in yard is pure delight, if you please! In winter it's foul, I admit . . . the kind of cyclone-tornado that grabs you, spins you around, knocks you from one end to the other, it's altogether too beastly! . . . even worse than the cop! . . . Would be nothing for someone sturdy, but a scrawny, skinny guy like me, just skin and bones, it clobbers you! *boing! bang!* the band strikes up! your kisser! the bars! it's bloody unpleasant! Down you get! up again! catch up! the jerk up there in his tower, he's busting his sides! A dozen guys he can laugh at from on high! guys caged in in the yard! A dozen of them tee-tering around, a dozen guys in the grill all crashing into each other, all twirling around as fiercely as the next guy! all strung out on all fours, crawling, squawking . . . True, you stop feel-ing much after they've roughed you up fifteen, twenty times . . . It's like the snow goes right inside you, you're a mass of shivers and fissures! Wind, sleet . . . It would be fun in the Tuileries, a snowman all pirouetting round! but there, com-ing through the bars there, three meters by three, it's just dumb! the whole Baltavian winter is dumb! first and fore-most! It's the huge tragedic black ogre! the All Engulfing One! Flowers, wee birds, summer, autumn! everything! spring! . . . Dirty show-off of a screaming hoodlum! Good-ness gracious! I tell you, it's BAD! Not to belabor the point! Goodness gracious! BAD! Enough! I've had my bellyful of it! *Profundis!*

Who'll strangle the bellowing monster? Screecher! Bal-tavian winter! ferocious masked ogre who splits your soul in two!

You being whacked and knocked around like a pinball (I'm telling you about the yard – the cage), the cop's had enough! . . . the ten minutes are up! he blows his whistle! fun's over! The guards charge, round up everything! the ones who are crouching, collapsed, hanging on, clutching on! Allez-up! up against the wall! The twisted ones go shuffling back! . . . all along . . . the whole way! and *crrrank!* . . . your cell door! *crrrank!* home sweet home! sitting down! behaving, melting . . . Oh, no atrocities here, no inhuman intentions! Load of crap! Violence is the winter wind! the climate that's barbaric by nature! it's not the cage that's on trial here. What I'm com-plaining about is my pellagra, the buzzings, the dizziness, and the lump in my right arm[100] . . . kind of mostly from the '14 war! That's why I got all in an uproar! that I had a fit! for God's sake that it shouldn't start again! I wanted to prevent another Slaughter! Holy Shit, was I in for it! I was gonna find out what lumber the Slaughterhouse used for heat! How the gospel writers would stand up and be counted! My subversive little pen! Oh, boy! witchcraft! my brimstone! rope! firewood! pitch! And it's not over yet! so I'm not gonna complain about the regime, austere to be sure! cell window, bars, Hortensia, when he comes at me all salacious . . . but there were intermissions, too, that I'm not leaving out! I bark! Bark some more! and they come running! they pick me up! a stretcher and that's me away! Is it not a blessing? . . . prison is finishing me off . . . hey, it's only natural! fifty-seven years of heroism! of the sublimities of war and peace . . . why shouldn't it kill me?

– Nobody asked you, you stinking kook!

– True, true, to the letter! . . .

I have no business complaining about the conditions! . . . if it weren't for the cage I wouldn't be breathing! . . . I'd be dead right now! . . . Thanks to the ten minutes in the cage that I didn't mold away completely! . . . I was falling to bits! . . . altogether worse than the wind! and my little head-spins! . . . The guards saved my skin! . . . They forced me to go out . . . come back in . . . Hooray for the ten minutes of cage!

– Oh, but enthusiasm keeps you warm! Maybe you have the calling? I can see you now! You're in Siberia! physician! missionary! polar bear! stiff!

– Ah, you're showing me an Ideal World! How happy we'll be together! thousands and thousands of us up there! speaking French together! Joye! Joye! Joye! we'll be all so lovey-dovey! my vice, I have to admit it, my only vice: speaking French!

An executioner who spoke French to me, I'd forgive him almost everything . . . boy, do I hate foreign languages! the incredible gobbledygook that exists! the bullshit!

– You really get a kick out of this Siberia thing! It's not only Hortensia you're fixated on! Siberia this! Siberia that!

– But if it was up to you you'd send the whole frigging world up to Siberia! Who knows who'll wind up in Siberia! First of all! Montandon,[101] who traveled all over the place up there, he told me that when there were storms, the sleighs, the whole frigging sleigh would up and leave the snow, fly right off into space! whole kit and caboodle! the men! everything! crack through the air and go sailing for fifty . . . two hundred versts! come to a graceful landing right on track . . . so me with my pathetic little flakes, my silly scamperings in the yard cage! . . . so they sock it to me at the drop of a hat . . . the stretcher! sick bay! be quick about it! the fruit is perishing . . . I shouldn't talk . . . There's a thin line between unhappiness and ingratitude . . . I won't cross it! . . . Good care, enemas, medication, I give due thanks! . . . but morale to fall back on? I supply my own morale! They all know me up in the infirmary! . . . gaiety personified! the optimist! anyone on hunger strike? they send 'em to me! . . . the ones who want to hang themselves, the ones who cut their veins, those who are so down on their asses that they can only stare off senseless into space: I get them! medicine comes naturally to me! . . . psychotherapy is my forte! . . . two or three words of German and some pantomime! . . . no lie: I've grabbed from the brink guys who were really suffering atrociously, ready to do anything, to do themselves in! . . . beds packed in side by side . . . absolutely no way of getting out of there . . . really stark raving ones, quite the cases! . . . no letup – night and day . . . got them to eat again, give that old razor a shake now and then! got them to listen! jolly them along! . . . I'm all for the Party of Life! sometimes singing, too . . . real tunes! . . . I can boast of playing the piano with my mouth, and that's with no teeth! . . . It's my innate gaiety! All gifts that character bestows! Humanity! Medicine! Descartes said it! Kruschen, too![102]

They told me how much a prisoner like me costs . . . almost two hundred dinars a day! . . . you wouldn't cost two hundred dinars in Siberia! . . . you wouldn't have any caged-in yards, either! . . . Did I say there'd be lots of us up there? I'm overstating! . . . maybe there'd only be a dozen of us . . . max! . . . ten? . . . five? . . . maybe there'd be only two of us . . . maybe just Remire and me[103] . . . who's Remire? . . . now

59

there's a dedicated man! . . . Doctor Remire . . . dedicated, it's like the fingers on your hand . . . you know workers' fingers, right? . . . by the time they're forty they have no fingers left . . . two, three torn off each hand . . . lost here or there, what with saws, drills . . .

Those who don't apply themselves, who do fuck all, they keep their hands, they keep their fingers, they keep every goddamn thing . . .

Oh, but there are those who are real diehard fans of penal colonies! I know, I admit it . . . Maybe you'd have a wonderful time in Siberia, you! . . . there's no accounting for tastes . . . Dostoyevsky couldn't get enough of it, always scribbling letters to the czar *Little Grand-daddy! Little Papa!* that he owed him so much, that he couldn't get over it how wonderful it was! the revelation! soul! the knout! the rotten potatoes! epilepsy! parricides! scurvy! everything! the lice! the chains . . . Maybe you'd be the same? "Little Grandpa! Little Papa! lay on some more!" For instance, Montandon, dead man and buddy, who'd explored all these places, Siberia, far and wide, he was smitten by it! . . . oh, the Tundra! he used to sigh to me . . . it was a fairyland according to him . . . blizzards where everything was blown clear away! just sailed right through space! sleighs! crews! travelers! . . . for 150, 200 versts! . . . came back on track! . . . All they saw was white! Montandon the anthropologist . . . There's such a thing as guys who are suckers for the steppes! . . . He'd have trekked all the way to Tomsk, Montandon the anthropologist, on foot, just to see the farthest reaches of the ass end of nowhere . . . Did he miss his little suburb, Clamart? imagine . . . In any case his time of touristing about the horizons that go on forever ran out . . . his number was up! . . . I loved Montandon! . . . what a beautiful scientific mind! . . . (except for his obsession with the Tundra!) . . . He died in Fulda, Germany, in a particularly cruel way . . . He was really killed twice, first at Clamart, point blank, then trundle-bumped over to Germany, such pain! . . . his train dynamited en route, and then in Fulda of cancer! . . .

What a clutter of scalpels! incompetent killers! Red Cross! med students! derailings! . . . and his hospital burned down!

Vicissitudes of the Times! . . .

– Yes, but, you know, you're avoiding the issue!

Not at all! . . . It's the web of Time . . . Time! the embroidery of Time! . . . blood, music, and lace! . . . I'm spreading it out for you, unfurling it, laying it all before you . . . Clamart! . . . Fulda! . . . don't you see! look! the web of Time! . . . if you knew the spinning wheel, the spot where two and two make three, you'd be less astounded . . . and then four! and then seven, depends! . . . you'd say "ah, yes" . . . you'd see into the designs of this world, the embroidery of the waves . . . maybe? . . . not even! . . . no longer even a little motif do you notice! . . . modulated . . . never a fragment of time without its note . . . Time's embroidery is music . . . deaf perhaps . . . quick and ever so delicate, and then nothing at all . . . little cuckoo, clock that beats, your heart, the wave on the shore, the child who's crying . . . Sieyès's harp[104] . . . midnight, the clock strikes twelve . . . twelve bullets . . . the firing squad! the adventure ended! the farrier you no longer hear? . . . what luck! . . . the horseshoe's gone out with the horse! . . . galley slaves plying their oars! . . . sounds that have disappeared and ghosts who no longer dare to haunt . . . not even a "boo" out of them! . . . watermills . . . remember? *whoosh!* . . . *whoosh!* . . . all of them gone out with the Merovingians! . . . Rhythms that are no longer? . . . as if you gave a fuck . . . you're no mystic, no nothing! . . . a follower of neither Papus nor Encausse?[105] . . . you didn't know Delâtre?[106] . . . his workshop in Path des Cloys? . . . "The Esoteric Press of the Sâr"?[107] . . . the place is nothing anymore . . . rubble . . . brambles . . . Montmartre . . . even if you heard the nightingale, the blackbird, the flies, the boule players, it wouldn't bring anything back for you at all! . . .

"Scoundrel," you'd yell! . . . he's having us on! the little creep is leading us astray . . . him and his web! his neck is more like it! the rope! and out with him! to his balcony! he must be kidding! such a place! on the seventh floor! . . . you mean he used to live there? . . . the nerve! and they didn't suspend him from it? terrible . . . chuck 'im out there with the birdies! with the crows! vultures! to perish, to rot, to swing, to stink! why, it's downright indecent! nightingales? the cheek of him talking about nightingales! . . . I mean that was The View! he's really rubbing our noses in it!

Looking out over everything, the view all over Paris, that's what you'll never forgive me for!

– The arch traitor! it's not even worth trying him! the ultimate, overwhelming evidence! a view like that! He deprived himself of nothing! To think they didn't hang the bastard!

It's monstrous! the unbelievable villain! you can't imagine! . . . his horizon was the hills of Mantes . . . Drancy to the south . . . the whole city all to himself! . . . the slopes like a fairy's wedding train! all the rooftops, thousands and thousands of them . . . red, black! . . . soft gray . . . the Seine, the light shimmering on it, rippling mauve and rose . . . Notre Dame! . . . oh, the pig! . . . the Pantheon! . . . the pimp! what a bitter pill! . . . the Invalides . . . you forgot the Arch of Triumph! . . . it's horrible! . . . he lived *there*?

I give up.

I was telling you about that other guy, the one with the afterthoughts, the threats, about my snot-nosed killer! . . . the *Old Maid* superhero . . . ah, but you don't hate the snot-nosed killer! . . . you're scared of the snot-nosed killer . . . he's got contacts, a party behind him[108] . . . me, I'm all alone . . . so you can really get your rocks off over me . . . I've really got you panting! . . . bumping me off is a cinch! . . . a giveaway! . . . that's why they're all so titillated, panting, the perfect target! . . .

To make a long story short, you're all vile, dangerous, cowardly . . . Okay! I won't go back there again! Promise! I won't go like a living reproach, sniffing around, taking stock of how much I've been dirtied, robbed, disgustingly betrayed, vilified! . . . first of all I'd recognize fuck-all . . . what do you

expect with these "shock squads"! . . . twenty . . . a hundred
. . . two hundred of them! who shat all over everything! and
that was just the taxmen, who're still after my tail . . . then
there was the public prosecutor, the cops . . . my shade is their
reason for living, their very breath, their Almighty Position!
. . . they send papers flying into empty rooms . . . they're hoping for something to sprout? . . . I don't know . . . let it sprout!

I'm of an entirely different character altogether. I've got
a whole new life ahead of me! start building all over again!
home, furniture, patients, appliances! . . . I've got my woes!
. . . and Arlette's life! How I've made a mess of her life! her
students! her dance classes!

And Bébert, who has no more teeth, or whiskers! . . . (like
me!) . . . we'll have to get youth to flower again! . . . I was
talking to you about the web of Time! . . . You should see how
I look!

– So publish, go ahead!

– And you buy it! and die laughing! . . . but just take a look
at the vultures around to see how hateful, jealous they are . . .
maybe they'll say, "He's on his deathbed!" and you add, "He
may be on his deathbed, but he's still funny!" . . . "He's the
Funny Man of the Century!" . . . not of the half century![109] . . .
faint praise, "the half century"! . . . it's like "a demigod" . . .
what the hell is that? . . . and don't talk to me about genius!
. . . geniuses are a dime a dozen! . . . you'd wrong me! . . . "Buy
it!" that's all . . . no ifs, ands, or buts, you have my undying
gratitude. The hordes make a mad rush for the bookstores
. . . attack the wholesalers, carry them off . . . I'm booming
again! . . . my ass heals, and my elbow, too! . . . *Fable!* . . . *Fable!*
. . . the lump in my arm? Yeah, that's the hitch, all right! But
Tailhefer operates on me[110] . . . I get a clean bill of health . . . I
can see again, they let me out of this hole, I'm fawned over
. . . I buy myself a bicycle, a cottage, a maid to open the door
. . . no more talk of going to Siberia! . . . I set up practice again
on the Emerald Coast! And you say it all when you just say,
"Gotta hand it to him, he makes you laugh!" Tough luck for

Montandon, the bullet in him, his cancer, Clamart-les-Asies, fucking off to Tundraland! Fulda! damn! Zazov! let him stay there!

He didn't know how to laugh, Montandon, he was gray – had a gray face, gray collar, raincoat, shoes, everything . . . but what a fine mind! entirely gray, admittedly! never a word spoken above a whisper! . . . but such admirably precise details! . . . He came up to see us so I could check his heartbeat. No sooner was his satchel on the floor than Bébert would jump on his lap and "purr . . . purr, I adore you!" . . . Bébert, who, all the same, is not your nice cat! the scratcher, the wolf-it-down made cat! . . . he understood that Montandon charm! . . . Wouldn't be surprised if his ghost or something was up there in the outer reaches of the steppes! . . . don't give a fuck! let him stay there! I ain't goin'! I'm gonna set myself up where I told you! Excuse me! but I've had enough suffering! I want a place with camellias, mimosas, carnations in every season! . . . ah, the ideal place! it's very simple! Between Tho Briand and la Douane![111] . . . has it been chosen? you picture the place I'm talking about? Rocchabe . . . the reefs . . . les Bée . . . St. Vincent's Gate . . . Quiquengrogne! . . . the tramway kiosk . . . the yacht basin[112] . . . the climate! . . . the bathing beauties! . . . the sands! . . . the golden crescent all the way up to Cancale . . . or just about . . . gold on emerald! . . . really incredibly beautiful! . . . and what about the Casino? . . . astonishment itself in monumental form! . . . malgamated armoric-metro, granite, arabesques, little gargoyles, menhirs, brick, slate! . . . and a thousand gabled windows, crenellated edgings, openings . . . There it stands over the Ocean, Epoch Pyramid, a mausoleum of the Black Stocking Queens![113] Veritable Cleopatras they were . . . I knew them from Passage Choiseul, those Black Stocking Queens! . . . they'd get their petit-fours at Charvin's . . . then their novels at Lemerre's . . . and then their lace at my mother's[114] . . . What a casino! You should go there! granite, knobs jutting out, little gargoyles, it was really a sight to behold, all decked out in gold, and the waltzes! . . . the gypsies, the Transylvanian princes! . . . you didn't know Rigo?[115] . . . other epochs, like aromas from the kitchen, fixed forever, making the head swim . . . Ah, dear friends, loved ones, you won't be sniffing around any more, either! and your demise is not all that far off! . . . You have nothing to sneer at! . . . you gotta have azaleas, hydrangeas, and roses! . . . the least little cemetery! . . . won't be there to boast! every day that passes, another one carried off! . . . so more roses, more beautiful ones! . . . and fast! . . . wreathes! . . . leave nothing out! . . . we must hurry! neglect nothing! gay forget-me-nots!

Hey, I don't want to make you sad! I was telling you about the Casino, misshapen, funny place . . . a whole world! . . . and from 1900! . . . shoulda seen its cloakroom! . . . parasols everywhere! . . . all forgotten now! . . . and the lorgnettes and the spyglasses! . . . real eye-catchers! . . . skeletons of "lost children" . . . little flags from the "Russian Alliance"! all over the place! . . . paper streamers as far as the eye could see . . . all kinds of mustaches . . . gaulois, "William," Chaplinesque, what a fandango that was! two white burnous, three soutanes, four nannies! . . .

Gone, long gone, the enchantment, the tziganes, the gypsies, even the roulette wheel! . . . all's left are the geraniums and the nasturtiums, growing higher all the time . . . climbing . . . all over the columns . . . and lanterns that imitate tulips . . . it's all imitation, nothing real left . . . just a few roses maybe, admirable roses, "dancing tea" roses . . . I've seen manys a beautiful thing all over the world, but no roses quite so beautiful as the roses in the heart of that monster casino . . . kissed by the soft winds of the gulf stream . . . the mellow clemency of the climate, the bay . . . the rose is surely the supreme flower . . . a few roses, whether it's in baskets or wreathes, you can't get around it, from the cradle to the *Profundis* the rose answers to the heavens for you . . . No question about it, you shivering, mincing mummies! . . . wherever there are the most beautiful roses people come, go, love, expire . . . Casino, pagoda, menhir, dolmen, "Comfort Stations," twenty roses are

their salvation! Pyramid of the Black Stocking Queens! . . .
there hasn't been a tzigane in Brittany for fifty years . . . Bad-
Fairy Casino full of bumps! Mammoth, Popatamus, how I
love the eternally lovely! . . . and the arc of waves, gold on
emerald right up to Cancale . . . as far as the eye can see, farther still the dunes and the storms that make everything rattle
around you! . . . the swathes of crashing sea! le Sillon and la
Chaussée, holding fast![116] . . . tramways anny over teakettle!
. . . so furious that the granite would tremble! crack open! . . .
coming in the middle of a raging storm, from Cézembre and
even farther west . . . gales to the north! . . . the ramparts awash
with the Minquier reefs! . . . they pound the jetties . . . crackle
into lacework! hailstorms of foam all over the streets, the trol-
leys, the roofs! . . . the atrocious Casino goes ash white, all
froth, all its knobby outcroppings, its crockery, its roof like a
plesiosaurus's spine, its "bite-me" arches, its plaster busts . . .
behold the miracle of passion! oceanic orgy! . . . all these hideous things, little menhirs, topped off by a squid, would you
believe! dome full of eyes! "Monumental portal," monstrous
latrine, there it is, standing up to a hurricane all pleased with
itself, quivering with foam, clear out of time, pulsing . . . dripping with a thousand thousand pearls . . . sparkly things,
fireflies, diamonds, emeralds! . . . if you saw that! . . . Of
course, it had its share of cuckolded husbands . . . and jazz
bands . . . Everything . . . but it's the memories that count . . .
the designs of the gods . . . what a place for a Casino! . . .
oriental, marmoric, Berber temple, ugly, not ugly, misshapen,
ruined, and the roses! you please! . . . inside! . . . garlands . . .
all over the place! gobs of them! strewn everywhere! . . . and
cloakrooms full of parasols . . . and lorgnettes and the spyglasses! . . . and Panama hats . . . and baby bottles for the skeleton . . . It's a place that'll move you to tears, you'll weep,
yearn, just like that, poets, poetesses, and centuries! and
that's how it is! and even Briand's "Albatross," he was the
editor! . . . and Arlette Dorgeres and Lantelme (on the jury)
and the ghost La Cerisaye, bishop of old![117] . . .

66

And the murmurs and the violins, and the people from farther afield, from Cornwall, from Léon, Bocage, and as far away as Nantes who come all the way to vacation here . . . would they be wanting in soul? . . . what about the drunken stupors? . . . Doesn't cost much to drink.

– Crazy! here? with all the people? all the roses?

Let me tell you, I lived right up against it, kinda hung over its dome, you picture the old depot? "Merlin and Sons"? . . . a three-room place under the roof beams, my old pal Miss Marie sublet it to me[118] . . . I heard a thing or two coming from that place, let me tell you! Tura-luras and the blood running high! and the squawks of the seagulls during the storms . . .

Summers rife with romance! Such equinoxes! . . . the glass roof right below my window! . . .

Won't you come home?

One little squall and off you go!

Without you I'm undone!

Excuse me while I get lost in my memories . . . What can I say? They were happy times . . .

At night, here, where I'm talking to you from, here in the hole, it all comes back, I hear it all again . . . listen! . . . the v-I-I-I-olins are sobbing! they're mewling at me! . . . and the fog-horns *huuuuunk! huuuuunk!* from the quays! and *cheuf-cheuf,* as if they had asthma! . . . the Cancale race! . . . the cheers! the crowds . . . film rushes of days gone by! . . . news-reels from the Past . . . the jerky projector! . . . make believe! . . . and the piano! . . . and the tunes everybody was singing at the time . . .

The times you lived through never leave you . . . nor do roses . . . I can tell because right now I'm sure they're scream-ing their lungs out all around me . . . both the watchdogs and the poor bastards in solitary . . . and the three on death row, in 14, 16, and 32 . . . but I don't give a fuck! . . . the violins and the sobbings fill my head, and the way the piano is playing . . . Now I'm not given over to just any old kind of nostalgia! no Tundra for me! no prison colony, either! heavens! Just happy

I hightailed it out of Montmartre before it turned into nothing but the vampires . . . who won't let go with their fangs till they bleed me white . . . I'll go wait it out in Saint-Malo! . . . They want no more of me on avenue Gaveneau? or rue Contrescarpe? I won't get worked up over so little! I have my mission in life! my art! my arts! . . . Nobody treats bronchitis like I do! . . . not to mention sciatica! so painful! They'll appreciate me up in the Emerald Coast! Specially seeing as I have my villa! . . . I won't let the Casino out of my sight! . . . everything that goes in, comes out . . . my patients! . . . specters with bones, without bones . . . or live ones! . . . with hurdy-gurdies! with lutes! with owls! everything! . . . with a villa, I'm a somebody! . . . Specters have a sense of decorum! Just take the Opera! they don't only just haunt ruins! . . . I myself have heard rappings, me, I tell you . . . like some huge piece of furniture crashing down! Right before I got arrested . . . before my Fate went to hell with itself . . . to give you an idea of their tastes . . . ghosts don't like pitch pine one bit . . . they go for the grand style, massive structures! . . .

I'm all for style! that's my fixation! So the Casino next door, that was just my thing! it was a kind of mammoth and octopus and menhirs all rolled into one! . . . Granite, slate, brick! . . . you're thinking "God awful!" excuse me! in comes the storm and out goes everything with it! the years gone by, the passions, the roses . . . the rooftops, the turrets, everything vibrates! sings! . . . the windows bending and buckling! drainpipes, oboes! the hurricane whips up streams of foam! . . . bagpipes . . . guitars . . . lorgnettes! . . . Botrel! . . . crepes . . . Paimpolaises . . . Fragson[119] . . . they all come gushing out . . . you can just about make out the Jersey ferry on the horizon . . . brushes up against the buoy, the whistling one . . . takes an oncoming wave head on . . . gets bigger, now you can see it clearly over by Cézembre . . . there's foam shavings everywhere . . . a thousand reefs and Fort-Royal! . . . the majestic skiff's sails stand stiffly to the wind . . . a thousand misses lift up their skirts, skip, run off, scatter! . . . laughing . . . chirping!

68

. . . from some boarding school someplace? . . . detained by Time somewhere! . . . two Negroes gambol around them! mandolining minstrels! . . . nothing new with that . . . mere girls out of some boarding school! . . .

Don't know if you get the picture . . . it's a Bay of Enchantment . . .

The old *Terreneuva* that's there rotting on the wharf[120] . . . that has its boom falling onto the deck, buffeted by the wind . . . has packed it in . . . its holds all empty, the bowsprit broken . . . you'd never know it, but it's full of people . . .

Yes, it's a place you remember . . . here, the *Ville d'Ys* grocery shop and the Le Coz sisters, a fairy's touch with the mussels . . . those peppery delights they grilled so very lightly! . . . and old René?[121] his little coffin? his big rock for all to see? and his cradle a hundred meters farther down . . . for real! . . . the pains he took, old René! . . . a hundred meters! . . .

Every bit of that bay is dear to me, the bells and the ruins, and the belfry that's gone now and the Corsairs' palaces . . . Ah, I suspected as much, all right . . . we all did . . . things of such grandeur are jinxed . . . I can still hear the *"Achtung"* alerts![122] . . . a sort of giant phonograph. We had one of them on our roof . . . never stopped, night or day . . . Bébert spent hours under it . . . he wanted to figure it out . . . of course it happened finally! everything was blasted, crushed to bits, in flames sky high! . . . I'd be surprised if old René, his coffin, his cradle, his cherished memories, didn't all go crackling up in smoke! passed into dust!

Everything has to pass!

I was pleased with my little place . . . people talk about places to live . . . mine was a veritable lantern! I saw everything that came in and out of town! from the Dinan side! the Saint-Vincent side! when you think of it! and flea-free lodgings! flea-free lodgings in Saint-Malo! *that's* a miracle! . . . no one escapes the emerald bay's magic! . . . sovereign stupor! . . . and such a climate! such colors! . . . the sea's violence! . . . but you pay for it in flea bites! . . . three days at the beach and you're one big blister, you die! I have a friend, for example, Rebelle, Prince Rebelle![123] I can tell you I've never seen such a pretty jewel box of a holiday home anywhere . . . four stylish rooms . . . pure Empire style! Seaside Empire! encased like a gem in the ramparts! . . . it looked out on Fort-National . . . could see everything from there: la Rance . . . the horizon . . . Saint-Cast . . . Fréhel! . . .

But you should've seen him go at himself! because of the fleas! . . . his flanks, calves, crotch, he wound up all infected! 'cause he didn't want to leave his view! . . . more and more horrible abscesses . . . people would laugh at him when they saw him . . . the way he was scratching himself! boy, did he go at it! Oh, but not once did he ever drop his monocle . . . the dignity of the man! one must keep up appearances, after all! strolling up and down that one street, Saint-Vincent . . . he finally died in September at the equinox . . . from blood poisoning . . . from his scabs . . . I used to tell him:

– Get out of there, Prince!

– They don't bother me anymore! . . .

The fleas got him! The prince was infested, all right, but so is every creature! what about birds? I used to see a gull scratching himself at the top of the long hangars there under our window, for hours on end! . . . the noble fowl! and from the other side of the Casino! he paced up and down like Rebelle, only on his little claws . . . didn't fish at all any more . . . he'd pounce on bits of fish, leftovers from the crates, the garbage . . . what you'd call a retired seagull . . . at night you'd see him climb up again, very, very laboriously . . . he'd perch on a fake windowsill in one of the Casino's trompe-l'oeil paintings! . . . way up on top . . . he'd sleep there . . .

When I think of the total hammering! those last days, under the phosphorous bombs! . . . This birdie was not about to fly away! he no doubt ended his days there, such as he was . . . it've taken a phoenix! . . . a phoenix, what am I talkin' about? . . . no such thing as a phoenix anymore . . . or a Saint-

Malo, either! . . . or Todt, who'd paved the way![124] Ah, that was another sad little story! . . . I'm liable to upset you! better not . . . I'll tell you another one . . . make you laugh this one . . . His Excellency La Cerisaye returning home from the Council of Bishops . . . detained a very long time in Rome . . . Oh, how happy he was to be home! He stands up in his carriage . . . he can't contain himself with glee: "Ah, thanks be to God! Thanks be to heaven! Oh, such happiness! Ah, Malo! I see you again at long last, my beloved city!"

And *flop!* He collapses, overcome! drops down dead flat!

Just to give you an idea of its uncanny attraction . . . You wouldn't see him dropping dead of apoplexy now, His Excellency La Cerisaye if he came back all of a sudden these days! . . . he wouldn't see anything again at long last, at all!

– Everything has to be rebuilt! that's what they're all claiming . . . Anyone who gives in to defeat is a traitor! The building tradesmen, the Public Brick Committees, the ones that build the forts, the ones who were setting fire everywhere! they all agree! I'm with them! Let's build again, build, for God's sake! I'm on the side of those who are building things up again, making everything boom again, the Old Quarters, the ramparts, habitacles, chicken coops, quarry stones, bricks, millstone, sand castles . . . All kinds of Work! I'll shirk from no effort! I don't ask whose hand I'm shaking! "He collaborates! I'll collaborate!" Long live agreement! ceramics and tiles! millstones! tar! mud! even those who ransacked my place and took everything, I'll even let them in on it! That's the kind of reconstructor I am! But I've got the goddamn arrest warrant up the ass! . . . That'll be taken care of! . . . as long as you build my fame up again! . . . "Ferdinand the Convulsor!" . . . such rocketing sales it will raise inflation! the waltz of the millions! I come bouncing back with oodles of dough! the bookstores are in a tizzy . . . all forty million Frenchmen (plus the eighty overseas) demand two . . . three *Fables* each! . . . (like cars in America) . . . Here's where Isaiah shows up again

. . . he's got four books in his satchel . . . four *Fables!* . . . here, in prison . . . he begs me to write a dedication in them . . . it can wait no longer! . . .

– My plane! your plane! is what he cries.

He gets right to the point.

– Ah, dear Maestro, let me embrace you! . . . Here's your laissez-passer.

– And my warrant? . . . What about my warrant? . . .

I'm quibbling.

– But who gives a shit? I'll wipe myself with it!

No sooner said than done, he drops his drawers and there he goes! and in deep, too!

– Long live Ferdinand! Long live the Vendôme Column! Long live all the Great Seals! Long live lanterns![125]

Those were his exact words!

– Long live street lamps! my turn now! Long live Love! Liberty!

He's a scrupulous guy, he gets me out of there! . . . no bail, nothing! . . . no killer phone call! . . . no lousy setup at Le Bourget for my "homecoming"! . . . flowers! . . . But I do not go back to Montmartre! I skedaddle right off to Rennes, Saint-Malo . . . I find Eynard in tears, as much as to say washed out from weeping[126] . . . crawling about in his rubble . . . he's turning over the ashes . . . he's been hoeing at it now for a good few years . . . digging . . . he finds a thing here, a thing there . . . a bit of a bottle, a table leg . . . What's left of his "Museum and Bistro" . . . one piano key! . . . a watering hole worthy of Surcouf![127] on a sea of flames it was gone! . . . Eynard in tears will never get over it! . . . I give him a few swift kicks to jolt him back to reason! . . .

– A manor house, and fast! I order from him! right on the water! You can't just go mucking around in the rubble all the time! Let's do some rebuilding around here!

I need a place to live – at all costs!

He's busy with the ass-ends of his bottles! he extirpates them from the heaps of rubbish . . . he looks as if he's putting

72

them away in an imaginary wine rack . . . the ass-ends of bottle fall off it . . . Oh no! he groans, my "Beaune," my "Mum," my last "St. Georges"! Ah, and here's a "nuit," it was a "nuit."

– Come on! I prod him, stop dithering! two gas stoves! two porcelain bathtubs! two maids to open my doors! . . .

I'm getting bigger and bigger ideas!

– Two garages for my four bikes! Keys in hand by Easter! You hear me? Twelve million a day in back money and no fleas!

Now we're cookin'!

All in granite! I add, are you an architect or are you a ruin?

And don't forget the furniture! the consoles and the "day-time delights"!

I haven't a scrap of furniture left! I can't tell you the number of chairs that all evaporated on me thanks to them! chests! baldachins! . . . the bailiffs, the rioters, and people with a sentimental attachment, too, the ones enamored of mementos . . . the beds, the sheets, it was awful! . . . three massive Henry I tables that would have gone through the roof at the Auction Rooms! . . . The amount of stuff that they inherited from me before I'm even dead . . . Yes! dead, after all . . . the race is on for my inheritance . . . it's written in the "personals" . . . my mother Marguerite's bed that they grabbed and sold on the cheap . . . the audacity of them!

That's one way to wind up: I drop dead in the street . . .

But I hoist myself back up on the merry-go-round! and off we go again! more music! I deal the cards, and three aces turn up! the next time I'll have a bed made like a brick shithouse! it'll be walled in! it'll be a goddamn lead coffin . . . in cement or brick? We'll see! Nobody'll be able to uproot that goddamn bed! let the tax boys come and try to tear it out then! I'll come back to haunt the sonsabitches! . . .

Like with my medal of honor, speaking about insults and gendarmes, shit kickers and blabbers . . . the one who came to officially inform my uncle Arthur (seventy-eight years old) that "I may no longer wear it"! . . . that he be sure to write to

73

me and let me know that I'm a "disgrace," worse than a stinking pig of a hero, '14 and '39, an embarrassment to the chancellor, a blight on the Flag, that I've sullied my wounds, that they're taking away my pension, stripping me of everything!
...

The public's hatred is no joke! such vigilance that even in this hole here, which is after all fifteen hundred kilometers away, they see me with my little green and yellow ribbon! ... like one little kitty should meow, they're all in an uproar! He saw a shadow! mine!

– That's him! ... go git 'em, doggies! ... cops! lunacy! Papal bulls! excommunications! after the Specter!

They've all moved themselves up a notch – veritable Guillotins,[128] hangmen, ambassadors, chargers, liars, and with such panache! the arrogance! Henry IV! eight, twelve Hercules at the mikes! steel-trap voices! ... They fear nothing but the astro-bomb! Oh, but do they ever think ahead! nobody can bolt like they can! say you're on top of them like this, strangling them! ... they're already in New Mexico! ... Zebras in the stratosphere!

This deserter hops on a Comet and zoom,[129] he lands in Labrador for you, savior of Bécon-les-Bruyères, of Ciborium's Gram and Brôme factories, of the "Code of Honors," of the "We're Patriots but You Wouldn't Know It" Network ... And the "Lists" that he keeps in his munitions kit! the plans for a new Arch of Triumph![130] ... a huge fucking cleaver hanging from its vault ... two thousand heads roll at a time! *Plop!* we've made progress since the Terror! Hey, you, you can't keep up with the times? Tough luck for you!

I'm having fun here, I'm telling you tales, I'm embroidering a little ... the guy next door ... in my wall, he's not what you'd call a laugh a minute! ... the convict next door! ... simple, he throws himself at it head first! *Va-va-va-vroom!* and there he goes again! he starts bellowing again! and boom-booming again! ... What a head! this is one helluva fixation! ... the walls are shaking, just listen to that! Maybe he finds me

74

suspicious? a spy? a low-down sonofabitch? . . . it's terrible the hatred you find . . . just an example, aside from that black Underling Hortensia from the Embassy, I've got another one who hates me . . . the one for the high jump in 16 . . . "Fuck all you fucking French!" he hollers . . . he was in the NKK, Goering's army[131] . . . got his knuckles rapped somewhere near Bourges . . . so he's got it in for me personally! . . . the locals, they condemned him to death, he'll be shot soon . . . that'll shut him up . . . don't give a fuck who he hates! . . . it's the hate coming from France that kills me . . . If they saw me burning at the stake in France, not only the Palestinians,[132] the native French, the centuries-old, the Farigoux, the Dondurands, the Dumaines! Me *and* my books! . . . people who live the good life, polished, who do well for themselves . . . they'd be thrilled! beside themselves, the native French! setting their brothers on fire . . . for the wonderment of the Tourists, to titillate the foreigners, so that they really have a good time, make pigs of themselves, come in their pants all the more! so they never go away again! "Duck cooked in its blood," you've heard of that, what about "The Frenchman cooked in his blood"? they do it the same way! the press! flames! Miss Joan of Arc went through it! They're still talking about it! licking their chops! Rouen Duck![133]

– Yes, but you have your adepts! ones all in palpitations over your sufferings!

– Don't even mention them! they're the worst, the ones you gotta beware of! see you crucified is what they want! trussed up! castrated alive, guts spilled out! . . . Just look at what they call me! the letters I get: "Yellow-bellied! Fraud!" they call me . . . how I made them suffer, my admirers! compromised them, etc.

So many pals I've driven to desperation! doesn't bear thinking about! and *similis* . . . and as many of them as there are assassins! not over yet, the grievances!

Ministers, bailiffs, tax collectors, erotomaniacs, dunces, nuns, I've got them all in my walls! . . . the repercussions! . . .

75

Thinking about it all here in my dungeon . . . the crimes
. . . the accusations . . . God, the bitterness! . . . I go over and
over it again! . . . How did it ever come to this, my friend? Tell
me . . . you played that flute all wrong! . . . you beguiled the
wrong rats . . . had you modulated your tones right you'd
have attracted the right people, intoxicated the elite, the pure
of heart . . . thrown all of them in the path of the tanks, into the
slaughterhouse, to the phosphorous, the giant gut-lacerating
barbecue, the Rights of Man and company! you'd have your
fill of rosettes, insignias, contracts, and confections! . . . you'd
have your own hole in the Iron Curtain! come and go as you
please! . . . no, you didn't hit the right tones!

While I'm thinking of it, remembering . . . they grabbed
my medal off me . . . three magic words! "no more medal!"
had they taken a pop at my head wounds the same way. . .
yeah, I wouldn't be horsing around right now . . . I wouldn't
be seeing anybody all over my walls . . . or that other one
come out at me, either, Hortensia, to offer me his Louis XV
ass fucking! I'd be on target, doing the right thing, old boy!
. . . I'd be writing Odes like Ciborium, I'd be signing over big
engines to Stupnagel, too, and lots of little satin slippers[134]
. . . I'd be one of those prison "popovers" like Sasa[135] . . . one
of Philippe's old guard like Auduc[136] . . . maybe I'd be a Swiss
Guard? . . . who knows, own stocks in Le Figaro? like Saint
Francis the Immaterial![137] What couldn't I lay claim to? . . .
take Pétain's place on the Ile Ré,[138] live a hundred years like
him? . . . All you have to do is toot the flute right! . . . I'd be
cock 'n' bulling it over cocktails at Levy's place[139] . . . nobody
would've stole my beds, the final manuscripts of five novels,
or the esteem of General Ben Chancellor of the Legion of
Honor[140] – how sweet it is to dream – or the key to my coal
shed . . . yes, rue Gaveneau, I'll tell you the whole truth, I had
more than a thousand kilos of it stockpiled . . . or the kind of
genuine affection that there was between us, me and Madame
Toiselle[141] . . . Me, go back up there? why? it'd only be awkward for everyone. More than one would have to examine his

conscience . . . friends' consciences are full of "flagrants dél-
its" . . . they'd kill me . . . And what about my appliances? . . .
I wouldn't find the least little gadget left! . . . not a mattress
cover . . . not a spirit stove . . . not a single saucepan left . . .
Imagine what it'd be like!

– Him and his pots! He can't think of anything else!

– No, not so! it's for my art! syringes have to be boiled! For
instance, at Blaringhem,[142] no reason to hide Blaringhem,
they all would have liked to be there! it's killing them! they
don't know what it was like! What the fuck do they care about
exercising the old noodle? they go into epileptic convulsions
and still get it all assways for Sunday! I used to receive patients in my hotel room in Blaringhem. Stinking dump of a
place that was! the toilet right next door, overflowing, gushing out all over the corridor! You couldn't live in it any longer
. . . "For refugees," they said . . . "Refugees" wherever you go
are pigs! No pigsty is too filthy! Black, yellow, blue nations! so
what if you're a physician! nothing is too sordid for what you
are . . . "Refugee!" . . . evil eye, stinking breath! whatcha got
dead in there? . . . a bunch of wily clowns! "Refugee!"

So, as I was saying, I'd see patients in my room, they had
to sit on the floor, no matter how exhausted they were – no
chairs! . . . the air raids! . . . (nights spent in the woods outside
of town) . . . the worst off were in my beds . . . should've seen
those beds! beds you'd see in a circus, no more than springs!
shot to hell! talk about bounce!

Who comes at me but this dame! Ah, the great Red Cross!
You know, the immense cape! And the white hair! the grand
entrance! tony broad! you picture the way they move! a sovereign!

– Doctor Céline? Doctor? is that you? ask anything you
like of me! such misery I find you in! how dreadful! frightful! I have the power to do anything I like! anything! Go
ahead! Mademoiselle Goering![143] Let me introduce myself!
. . . the marshal's sister! . . . Go ahead! Don't be shy! Whatever
you like!

– Mademoiselle, I'd love a saucepan!

– Oh, I'll run get you one right away!

She skedaddles . . . that's the last I see of her . . .

It'd be the same in Montmartre . . . in Sartrouville . . . Pierrefitte or Houilles . . . just say I get home . . .

– A saucepan!

That'd be the end of it! . . . (I'm talking to you after the atomic blast.)

– I'm Julius Caesar himself! the Queen Mother with my little hat . . . what is your pleasure?

– A saucepan!

– Has he lost his mind? . . . right away outraged! . . . why not? "My kingdom for a horse!" that sounded good . . . but "Europe for a saucepan"?

And for an enema? . . . when I've gone two weeks without a bowel movement I'd give the world for an enema. That's egotism for you! . . .

These are not just asides! little anecdotes! . . .

– And at Lunebourg,[144] you punk, how would they have treated you?

– Were you there in Lunebourg, yourself? they're all dead in Lunebourg! was it you who took over their jobs? . . . avengers, job takers, they're one and the same! . . . History's tricksters! . . . that guy over there escaped the draft (wonder how) Category 2 before the war, puking up his guts in '39 in his haste to flee, whinging for mercy, look at him now, thundering in court, expediting you, the sniveling creep, *ad patres!* to the penal colony! etcetera! . . . thanks to his goddamn cheek, that's how he got to the bench! . . . No arguing with that! . . . the luck of the draw! . . .

Lunebourg, I'll tell you about Lunebourg! there were cathouses in Lunebourg! not just charnel houses![145]

Therein lies the complete horror of it! . . . During the whole of the fucking Middle Ages, the place where they had it off most of all was the cemeteries! . . . people don't face up to these odd little sides of things, leave a lot of naughty little

facts in the dark out of human decency! A mistake! wrong!
... human decency never holds up! ... with me it's my enemas! the toilet! after two weeks without an enema I have
nothing against dying ... and they give it to me so hot that I
scream ...

– And in Claunau?[146]

– You're right, you're right! I whimper, but I'm spoiled!
but were you there, in Claunau? ... My ass you were! doesn't
stop you from screeching your fucking lungs out as if you
were the first one in and the last one out!

– And in Brazzaville? And Chad? you weren't there slog-
ging away? and with such mosquitoes buzzing around, madame! the lepers! the amoeba! the tsetse flies! buffalo everywhere! crocodiles! and vampires! ... While we're at it, I
didn't see you in Cameroon! What would you know, sweetie,
of such prodigious acts of valor? and not of recent date! donkeys years! you have no idea! You weren't even born yet! '17!
Ha! it was us booted out the Krauts that time! in 120 degrees
in the shade! oh, la, la and in white helmets! Bobillot was my
hero![147] Savorgnan! Chanoine! Rescue! My honor! the Rio
Cribi mine, not yours! Bikobimbo![148] If you had the tiniest
idea of all my military honors you'd die, you'd bury your
head in shame! not to mention getting smacked in the jaw
with the seltzer bottle! there goes your skull! I smash everything you have! your goddamn café table, marble and all! I
destroy your *Café du Commerce* on you! sheer fucking atone-
ment-for-everything fury! for your hypocrisy! ... I'm the man
of the mystics who don't pay up! But Darius's ingrates are
everywhere![149] ... they'd never have been anything without
Darius! ... the least little shopkeeper in Nogent-sur-Lys ...
fucking hell, have they moved up in the world! ... they thunder at you from the summits of the Justice System! ... the
same guys who'd've been lucky to get grubby waiter jobs at a
sidewalk café in the old days ... or as street sweepers ... who
used to dream about selling vacuum cleaners ... or going in
for dog grooming ... they're more like the doges' fleas, my

79

good woman! You seem a little suspicious to them . . . they get all worked up! beat on the war drums! to the watchtower! . . . a thousand executioners! Darius's ingrates are everywhere! . . . the "Knights of the Candle Illustrious" . . . this cult is secret and ferocious! I know of a quarry near Montreuil where they go to burn their candles . . . pray at midnight . . . incant . . . they unveil Darius . . . just a second! . . . his bust . . . his little mustache . . . Oh, this cult is secret and ferocious! . . . It's the Knights Templar of the Half Century![150] . . . damn! I'm giving it all away! . . . now I'll never go back . . . tough shit! . . .

Perhaps a little stroll all the same? . . .

– But you'd be massacred lickety-split! . . . you maybe helped out a bit setting up the Atlantic Wall? . . . built an airstrip or two? . . . you can invoke Laval . . . but if you've sold nothing . . . not even signed a little petition . . . didn't even go in for a little *zeitung*-ing anywhere[151] . . . nobody'll save your neck!

I know, I've heard the death call, I went on hunts back when I used to serve as huntsman . . . nobody takes the deer's side . . . the more it's torn apart the more they come over it, the more a hundred dogs rip strips off it, the more its still-beating heart is exposed to the air, the more excited they get! Ah, the awesome death throes! . . .

– Would you care for some of the hoof, Duchess? Right now all of Europe for me is forest, hounds, the hunt . . . look, the proof: my walls here . . . The sobbing! . . . the hooters on them! . . . I laugh it off! I bark! . . . I send them galloping every which way . . . The sweet strains of the herdsmen's pipes! let the brass weep! I'd get the duchesses gored, all right! burn! tear apart, oh yes! saucepans! pitch! make sure it's boiling! cauldrons! the whole lot!

– The son of a bitch is insulting us! cut him up! slice him! hang him till he turns green!

I hear what you're saying.

– We wanna see his carcass out of here, fast!

How little you understand of my character! I won't go moldy as fast as all that! . . . you haven't seen how swift I am on the uptake!

The other day in the infirmary, the interns wanted to have a laugh . . . you know what it's like . . . but . . . ah, youth! . . . They examine my asshole, the anus . . . I wanted an enema . . . I was bleeding . . . eyebrows are raised . . .

– Cancer, yeah, it's cancer!

They wanted to test my mettle!

So, what I do, right away! is my finger up my ass! I remove a sample! I smear their noses in it!

– You call that cancer? Little jackasses! dunces! what does that smell like? *sui generis?* it's pellagra! knuckleheads! pellagra!

That's what you call teaching!

I help myself to some more and I smear it on them again . . . they scram!

You either know how to teach or you don't! "homicidal orderlies!" I shout after them . . . They thought they could put one over on me! me, the sensitive one, the one who veritably vibrates to the medical arts! the disciple of Dr. Follet! Who himself was the student of Brouardel, Charcot, Lapersonne[152] . . .

Little yahoos!

They're double locking my door . . . *crraa! craac! craac!*

They've seen someone in prison! I remain with my special cases, the hunger strikers! They piss, they shit in their mess tins . . . They don't want to go back to Russia . . . and they're Russian! They'd rather die! Now is that any way to behave? Do I go on that way about France? Get outta here! this can't last! One, two, three! bring on the noodles! they've gotta down those suckers! it's the Law! . . . if not, I let them know what's in store for them! . . . they'll be ligated, straight jacketed, and we'll force it down their throats! Your Fatherland is there for a reason! Michel Strogoff at the Chatelet, how did he put it?[153] "For God! For the czar! For the noodles!" It was clear sighted, it was high minded! These guys, my poor slobs lying there, I'm gonna give them back a taste for life! and some boiled noodles! . . . Jeez, in Passage Choiseul, the threats out of my mother over those goddamn noodles![154] . . .

– What do you mean, you don't want any? . . . you'll never grow! . . . and right away, a wallop! . . . Would I wallop those guys? how could I, the wretches? . . . How could I beat them? . . .

Those apprentice sawbones just now, those, on the other hand, I would have happily tanned their hides . . . the cheek of them! . . . little whippersnappers! . . . wasn't even their job! . . . sometimes someone goes too far and I just go berserk! . . . young pups! . . . teach me about pellagra? Me, the student, my God, of such teachers! of such an intellectual elite! They wound you in your most sensitive spot! It's simple! Assholes! Ah, with me, it's the masters! . . . My masters! . . . I will not forgive irreverence! . . . in the utter depths of misery it's more important than a hundred thousand diamonds! . . . the harp . . . tone . . . delicacy . . . the enlightenment others have imparted . . . an understanding of this . . . of that . . . the nuances that someone now dead revealed to you . . . whom you never really thanked sufficiently . . . We're always sabotaging people while they're alive . . . an unerring sense of life doesn't come easily . . . as I myself feel remorse about certain persons with whom I was intimate! . . . Courtial . . . Follet . . . Elisabeth . . . Edith . . . Janine[155] . . . it's worse than a hundred years of prison! . . . Bastard that I am . . . even Jules who is, God knows, a venal being, all chameleon, full of venom, I owe him a potion or two! . . . some acknowledgment! . . . I deserve to be treated terribly . . . what I've destroyed! . . . Mister Messer! . . . Charon sees me comin' in the distance: "Come over here, you," he's gonna shout . . . and as soon as I get there . . . *whaaaack!* . . . right in the kisser . . . his oar! . . . *whaaaack!* again! . . . that's for all your goddamn nonsense! . . . By Styx, I'd better hurry! . . . I don't want to die with my soul smelling bad! . . . The

carcass is nothing, it's ingratitude that's everything! . . . I want
to win back esteem! . . . my self-esteem! . . . that of my peers is
a plus! . . . a seat in the Academy! . . . At the worst! . . . doesn't
matter which one! . . . the public recognition! . . . the *Lustrum
condere*[156] . . . so my dead can be consoled a bit over my ways!
. . . my inattention . . . my mother first of all! . . . I want my dead
to see me in a different light! . . .

"He wasn't as bad as all that," they'll say . . . the others
were the real sonsabitches! . . . suffering turned him bitter . . .
a nitpicker . . . stupid . . . sour . . . the horrors rubbed off . . .

The Pantheon? So be it! I accept! . . . the official rehonor-
ing! . . . enough of the living disgrace! a street named after me!
an avenue! . . . Oh, but mind you! not for me alone! . . . My
word, Altruism is my law! I want another two million streets
for two million heroes of 1914! . . . and gay street-naming cer-
emonies! . . . Gaiety's my strength! . . . They even notice it in
prison: My strong point, gaiety! . . . in the cell, in the infirmary, when they need a specialist, they turn to me: Gaiety: in the
deepest depths of degradation . . . hilarity itself! . . . I irradi-
ate! suicidibus, right on the brinkibus, they send 'em to me!
. . . get 'em eating again! the half-dead ones! . . . pablum, mar-
garine, pickled herring! . . . they chow down once again! . . .
first rule of the psychopersuasive method: crack 'em up! I've
raised lots of dogs, cats, everything! you don't make 'em
laugh, they don't eat anymore . . . same with men . . . here
where I'm writing you from it's all guys on death row . . . The
Rule is categorical: they must get their nourishment! . . . the
Governor is pulling his hair out over it . . . the guards never let
them out of their sight . . . "We'll have no skeletons at the
execution!" . . . what with the Press, the Judges, the Pastors
. . . oh, la, la! . . . "They've got to eat!" . . . Public Opinion will
make sure that only the plump go for the high jump! . . . I
manage, I tell you . . . it's a question of patience and a good
yarn . . . *The Three Musketeers!* . . . magical *The Three Musketeers!* . . . I must've told that story a hundred times! . . . first in

German dialect . . . then in pantomime . . . There're words that are understood wherever you go . . . Cardinal! . . . Buckingham . . . d'Artagnan . . . Porthos . . . ah, Porthos! . . .

The most rebarbative, stubborn of this particular audience are the morphine, cocaine, ether addicts! . . . those guys are really obtuse, ugly, uncivilized . . . epileptics of crime! . . . they hate you for making them laugh . . . they aim for you with murder on their minds . . . the puny bastards – with the strength of Hercules – their jug right at your puss! and *craack!* smithereens! they miss you by a whisker! . . . and then later they have a go at themselves under the covers gashing away with the shards! . . . you wonder what the fuck they're fucking! . . . they're slashing their veins! . . . gluttons for funishment! . . . Their mattress a blood-soaked sponge! . . . but it's my job after all . . . an MD's an MD, after all! . . . no particular merit in that, the afflicted, the desperate, they're my vocation! . . . And besides, I'm gifted in another way, with a sort of personal blessing! . . . the kind of nervous system I got, when I'm cold, when I shiver like anybody else, I laugh! . . . I can't help it . . . it's just the way it works with me . . . I'm not bragging . . . I'm not bluffing anyone, I'm alone . . . when you're "condemned to death" you're alone . . . all in individual cells . . . they let you out ten minutes in the air, in little cages . . . you go back inside, I told you all this, you're a snowman . . . takes you an hour, an hour and a half to defrost . . . You're gonna tell me: It doesn't snow every day! . . . about like it rains in Rouen, more or less! . . . defrosting is one thing . . . but when I tremble I gotta burst out laughing . . . a little story pops into my head . . . I'm shivering, I take advantage of the situation! I imagine a *quid pro quo!* . . . a funny situation . . . if I guffaw a bit too loud, the screw comes in, he doesn't like to see me laughing . . . he gestures that he's gonna shoot me . . . so I go "shit" . . . he locks the door again . . . he doesn't get "shit" . . . that's another blessing! Besides, I can always laugh all by myself . . . even without being too cold . . . it's the screamers that stop me . . . the banshees to the right of me, banshees to the left of me! . . .

if they leave me in peace even just a tiny bit, right away an anecdote pops into my head . . . I play around with it and I have a good chuckle . . . If they just didn't howl so much all around me . . . I grab my writing stuff and get to work! . . . This *Fable* that you're gonna treat yourself to, because, you see, everything's ready! . . . printers, bookstores, wholesalers, book stands! . . . and of course my royalties, in advance! oh, implacable I am! to hell with your sweet talk! . . . dollars or rubles, depends! From now on I accept only the victors' currency! Ah, you'll see me living the *high life* again! dressed to the nines! suit jackets of such distinction! turned out like a shah! the nails done! The pirates grabbed everything I had, I was telling you, all my stuff, outfits, equipment, real estate! It was wild back then! So *Fable* has to sell! I boom again! Excuse me, a new man! the hash I made of everything? who cares? You'll be flabbergasted! on your ass! the battery of kitchen utensils! my drawing rooms! my pretty little chambermaids to open the door! and the bike that's so light it almost glides forward without me, at the mere suspicion that I might want to straddle it! . . . the brand: the "Imponder" . . . faster than Arlette in a sprint! Wait'll you see me! . . . Arlette, who's a sylph on the pedals! . . . From Trinité to Montmartre: seven strides! a breeze . . . that's her! a breath of air and she's gone! and that's uphill!

So you say, "You'll have a car!" Not so! The car is a fatso, a half-hearse for has-beens! I won't hearse around! It's the "Imponder" for me! no other! A patient phones? I fly! all reflex! calves! lungs like a forge! I care for myself while caring for others! One visit, two healthy specimens! the panacea cycle! you wouldn't believe the rheumatism I suffer from! they have no name for such pain! I won't even tell you about it! the elbows, the ankles like they were in clamps! as if they wanted to get a confession out of me . . . a super-fanatic executioner who breaks his pincers on my knees! . . . Oh, but just do a little sports! a cinch! In the open air I'm thirty years old again! and with altruistic enthusiasm!

On the bike I'm a more presentable kind of nutcase! you get a look at me, the patrician! rejuvenation through zeal! brimming with health! taking care of business! ardor! reflection! heart! a new man!

When you think about it, where they take the waters, at Ax, at Bagnoles, those old guys they wheel around, muffled up piss-dribbling bags 'o bones, arthritics on crutches, all shriveled up, knarled with the gout, sufferers all sorts, wheezing acrobats from hell, with their gargoyle faces hideous from torture, eyes popping . . . St. Vincent de Paul happens along and sees them[157] . . . "Go on, you disgusting bunch of rejects" . . . he shakes them up a bit . . . "the likes of you belong to Charity! God's sake! get goin'! and burn rubber about it!"

That's what miracles are all about! you've guessed it, deep down, you think, the core of me is altruistic! ardor! that I need no kick in the ass! my locked-down carcass if I go shooting away! Get rid of these bars for God's sake!

– Off at a sprint, you rusty, creaking old bitchcarcass!

See how hard I am on myself.

Enthusiasm! the God in us![158] What I am is but a particle of enthusiasm!

– Listen to him showboating!

That's what you're thinking.

– I care for myself in caring for others!

– He's only pretending to be nuts! He'd have been sent to La Noé![159]

– Be snide! go ahead! show your hand! spare no feelings! just so I don't forget who I am? . . .

– Now St. Vincent! of Clichy! no comparison with your ugly mugs! the guy rowed galley ships! the Deep Blue! a friend! insisted you take his pittance! that was a pal, a real pal! you and your ugly kisser! that's what they mean by delicacy! you can talk! With St. Vincent, people felt for each other! you, though, you grind everything to a pulp! sensitivity, what do you know about it? . . . all you're good for is every kind of low-down dirty piggery! and slaughter!

The archangels see you ... they shake their heads ... their wings droop ... In the prayer "our trespasses" everything is forgiven[160] ... I'm supposed to forgive you again? ... I've already wiped the slate! First pay your widow's mite, and then some! And then we'll see! ... Here I'm imagining, I'm looking ahead ... let's say that I don't croak in prison ... which would be incredible good luck, rotting away as I am ... I get out of the slammer ... I scoot over to your place! ... first visit! ... your smile! ... what are you doing? on the floor beside your sofa, in convulsions of laughter, doubled over, over *Fable!* ... tearing out pages ... rollicking wildly, rolling, choking ...

– Help! Help!

I leave you in your fit ... ranting ... wriggling! Too bad! ... I scoot over to see someone else ... Another charming individual, the "Old Maid" brat, for instance, my machine-gun packing would-be assassin ...

Just one question.

– Did you get as far as Junot Square, young fella? like hell you did!

And I smack him in the face!

End of story.

I make plans, that's how I keep up morale, but if I go completely blind, well then a thousand pardons! I suspend myself by the neck! You bet! I open my eyes again in the next world, and sonofabitch if I don't find you, right in the middle of fulfilling your wildest dreams, selling off lutes, haloes, the innocence of the Seraphim! Theresa the Little Flower and that cute little Odile![161] ... turning everything into profit! ... nothing is sacred to you! ... everything to the highest bidder! the Milky Way! the Bridge of the Stars? ... Cécile's convent![162] ... Little White Clouds Ball![163] raffle off those sweet little choir boys ... gigantic sell-off of the Supersteinian Universe curves! ... Lots of things will have happened and some funny water under the bridge before I'm caught lending you a book! ... fish will have had time to grow some outrageous hairdos –

87

long ones, I'm telling you ... from Moulineaux to la Rapée![164]
... you'll put your cash down or there'll be no belly laughs for
you! ... I was telling you about my eyes ... gloom ... two
moldy holes ... being cooped up ... the starvation diet ...
what the fuck's the Red Cross doing? ... an old man like me?
... Heh? ... I ask you! ... they're giving teas, the Red Cross!
... Long Island garden parties! ... Iniquitous! ... They don't
give a whack about the real martyrs! ... what I have to put up
with by way of mistreatment! ... picture the eye infection!
and I keep working! ... retinitis! ... the pellagra is attacking
the eyes ... not just the elbows and the behind! ... it's a prison disease, I admit, but I still have ones leftover from Africa!
... Don't think I didn't suffer there, too! ... conjunctivitis
three times in Cameroon! ... Bikobimbi, Rio Cribi, go find
out! they were some nice places! here I'm going blind 'cause
there's not enough sun, there it was too much.

– Jeez, this guy never stops bitching! let's finish him off!
make sure he never comes back! Pin him to the slab so we can
dissect him a bit!

– I see what you're driving at! So be it! Prepare for dissec-
tion! The age! The badness! The person! You'll find it all!
The autopsy? Bravo! and my lump! Long live Dupuytren![165]
And, oh yes, wars! And your nastiness!

To show you: my job is open! ... All you have to do is go to
the courthouse and ask for the "little letters" ... "Notorious
outlaw presumed dead" ... the court files ... "Condemned to
everything!" more than everything! Blind Justice does not
mince Iniquity!

– Cut him up! Bell jars! formyl!

I get on your nerves? I don't give a fuck! I howl! I bark!

– And what about amoebic dysentery? I have that, too!
Tssk! tssk! so you see I've been around! I've followed the flag
of France! to the other end of the earth! Yes, the tricolor, cutie
pie! Mine! All mine! Epic? Reversal? What do I care? Red!
White! Blue! That's all! everywhere I went I carried those
colors high! In Glory! and in less glory! In defeat I wrapped

myself in it! There are wrinkles in the tricolor, in my conscience there's not a single wrinkle! Step forward if you doubt it . . . where the hell haven't I carried that flag? my carcass? . . . my diplomas? . . . Sincerity, kindness! Lift up your hearts! . . . Cathouse! . . . Nowadays a good laugh *extremis!* . . . me, wounded, decorated long before Pétain, I say go fuck yourselves!

– Heh, thrust him through, lickety-split! Tear him from limb to limb!

– What about my pension? I'll send you that attorney Catlacomb, Hell's Key Keeper! . . . you'll see what you'll have to deal with! . . . When you've got business with him, you'll screech like ten dungeons! . . . By Elzebub! . . . you'll drown out the screams coming from 30! . . . from 48! . . . from 73! . . . the ones driving me nuts! . . . you'd be knocking your head against the wall, too! . . . and there you'd go again! . . . and *vroooomb!* enough to split the building in half! . . . to send all the catwalks teetering! . . . And not only for a day or two! . . . for centuries! . . . from all the wrong you've done me! . . . maybe if you buy *Fable,* I'll get the hell out of here and put a wee word in the devil's ear for you . . . so you'll be spared twenty, fifty years of breaking and rebreaking your skull! . . . Think about it!

– Oh, the little creep is putting us down! show-off! cuckold! jerk! it's his own fault for enlisting in the first place! what could he have been thinking of in 1914? Uckle-ned ay-head! nobody forced him to be a hero! . . . he just had to look in front of him! . . . and away you go! He could've trafficked with the enemy – bargains galore for the Krauts! sold off even his outfit, plume, breastplate, the lot! didn't he have any imagination? . . . had he deserted everything would have been perfect! . . . one good deed entails another . . . back in civilian life he'd've got a couple of broads to put some steak on his plate for him . . . he had what it takes for that, the eyes, no limp fist, knew just how to sweet-talk 'em, too . . . plenty of dough! . . . He'd be a king today! . . . a manor house full of gables in So-

logne! The minks on his Lady Stalkers! . . . two private helicopters! . . .

Thus speaks the voice of conscience . . . the slammer
makes you think, all right! . . . if the guy weren't bellowing
next door! . . . the torture victim from I forget where . . .
"Yiaaoow! Yiaoow!" . . . they don't even finish him off! . . .
He's worse at night! . . . they're all worse after the night shift
starts . . . 6:00 P.M. . . . the buzzers, the barking of the dogs on
wall patrol, the cemetery that's closing, the screws, the five
steel floorsful handing over their keys, the clanging! two
times two times three thousand doors, three turns! right up to
the top! *creak crreak!* the sixteen catwalks! I'm not doing this
on purpose for effect! the cemetery locked down, us too! her-
metically sealed, the ship goes into the night . . . A prison is a
kind of ship, it travels . . . and the night is not some two-bit
broad . . . she's got class, she speaks to you only in the third
person . . .

– He'd be a pimp today . . .

You hear that and you say: she's right, that's me! especially
around midnight . . . You know, almost every midnight my
sister-in-law comes back to mind . . . what happened . . .
what's hard in life is figuring things out, untangling things . . .
I hadn't seen my sister-in-law for years . . . and a few days
before we left, that makes it the beginning of June, the Allies
already in Rouen . . . '44 . . . you picture the atmosphere! . . .
the killers were everywhere! . . . I mean mine, my killers! . . . in
all the streets around us . . . set up as kind of sentinels . . . they
relayed one another . . . a couple here, a couple there! . . .
should've seen 'em go! . . . At the corner of Hermette Street
I see a bunch of Arabs in double-breasted coats . . . Imagine
. . . with burnous over them! and spurs! and high turbans! . . .
When I passed by they'd be all touching themselves – those
Arab dresses are full of folds! . . . I didn't have to go see for
myself . . . but I went anyway on a whim . . . I went down as far
as Abbesses . . . my beat . . . made as if I was inspecting my
outposts . . . only it was me the one being tailed . . . the enemy

. . . it makes you sad, I admit . . . Another one, this one was weird, place Vintimille, was waiting for me for hours . . . hours on end . . . my route . . . place Vintimille . . . all around it on motorbike . . . the AJ bus route[166] . . . he was on the lookout for me from inside the pissoir . . . I slowed down . . . he scrammed! I caught up with him one afternoon . . . he was wearing a yellow satin half-mask . . . he got swallowed up by a door and I lost him! . . . it's strange to realize you're the enemy . . . in your own home! . . . it's awful . . . you can't believe it . . . I'd pass by to make sure it was true . . . that they were watching me from all angles . . . they saw me and they'd be all touching themselves . . . from one group to the other . . . foreigners, most of them, looked like they just got dredged out of the Danube, or the gutter of some goddamn Arabian bazaar . . . women, too, and madmen . . . the eyes of madmen . . . that's the Triad of the Times, the one who's judging you, the one who's shooting you, the one who's mutilating you: a woman, a madman, a foreigner . . . what the hell, everything's ass-ways . . . dream on that one!

Jeez, I was forgetting my story! . . . I'm dreaming! I was telling you about my sister-in-law! . . . I was going back up rue Ravignan, and I was not in a good mood, let me tell you . . . sullen, we'll say . . . so I'm going back up rue Ravignan and I hear someone calling me, hailing me! . . . I don't like when this happens! . . . I turn around.

– Marie-Louise!

"Jeez," I go, "is that you?" we hug each other . . . I hug her . . . I'd like you to have heard her! it was coming from the heart! . . . right to the point! like anxious to tell me what she had to say . . . she knew a bit of what was going on . . . well, the basics, anyway.

– If only you'd stayed with us! . . .

She was talking about London at the end of 1917.

– If only you'd stayed, Louis! . . .

Chiding . . . and tears . . . the name only my intimates use, Louis.

– Oh, no, Janine wouldn't have died?

Her sister, Janine . . . It was long ago when we'd bid each other adieu . . . I'd left them in Leicester Square, abandoned them, her and her sister . . . I can still see the tree, the bench, the flowers . . . the sparrows . . . the forget-me-nots, the geraniums . . . it's in the middle of London, do you know it? . . . in distress they were, orphaned by a man . . . I'm not an artist but I can recall flowers . . . Janine . . . Marie-Louise . . . and women, too, in fact . . . I can see it all . . . the lawn . . . and the surroundings also, the traffic, those huge scarlet buses, and the "recruiters" they were red, too! the sergeants! . . . everything is turning around! and around! . . . and the music . . . life is a filigree, what is spelled out doesn't amount to much . . . transparency is what counts . . . Time's Lacework, as they say . . . the "blond," in sum, the lace they call blond, you know it?[167] lace so fine, so fine! on the spindle so delicate, you touch it, you tear it all apart! . . . no repairing it . . . like youth! . . . forget-me-nots, geraniums, a bench, it's all over . . . fly away, sparrows! . . . lace so fine . . .

I tore myself away, it seemed the rational thing, a sort of act of conscience, so to speak, a fit of honesty and moral fiber, I saw my future elsewhere! . . . a real future! . . .

Heh, fathead! muck-crawling numbskull, to hell with rationality! We always got on together, that was enough! Janine, Marie-Louise, and me! That's all you need – get on well together! It's worth more than the Earth and the Angels and the billions of shooting, twinkling stars, don't give a fuck! . . . poor is our heart . . . what do we care about the Firmament? . . . whereas Marie-Louise, Janine . . . I've commit only one crime in my life, only one real one . . . seeing as I left my little sisters-in-law, poor little girls, in November '17 . . . and they weren't dandy-chasers either, no little businettes these girls! . . . not at all! doll-like, they were, like flowers! the most delicate faces! . . . sparkling! fresh! saucy! . . . the one a brunette, and such lips! . . . Marie-Louise! supple and alert, the shoulder, everything! a gypsy almost . . . knockout hips I dare to say

. . . Janine, a redhead . . . when they danced at Ciros, they would waltz together, no kidding, the whole room would rotate, tables, everything . . . the guys in the club got so worked up! all the glasses glittered! . . . and the bottles! later they started calling it *sex appeal,* this thrill . . . what the fuck do they know? they never saw any of it! . . . women don't raise anything nowadays! Tables no longer turn, heads, either . . . worries have taken over everything, gathered up everything! . . . smiles, frotti-frotta, twaddle!

Oh, such remorse! Such memories!

– Heh, you're half dead anyway! finish yourself off! they left you your belt! Take it off! Hang yourself! the bar up there!

Perhaps you're right, I'd have enough time . . .

The guards no longer fiddle with my peephole . . . they spied on me for weeks . . . weeks on end . . . I killed them . . . nothing they could catch me at . . . I don't smoke, I don't move . . . I just stay there, rigid, the ass all gone to shit . . . winter, summer . . . I'd be "the model prisoner" except that I sing a little, I curse, I insult the fanatic in the wall . . . he'll never smash his goddamn block in . . . Only for the enemas I bark at them! . . . so, of course, the pack loses no time echoing back to me! "Woouff! Woouff!" and the whole bloody bunch! and the machine guns! and the stretcher! I win! . . . but if I don't bark I might as well go and hang myself! . . . nobody comes looking . . . eternities, I tell ya! So I think . . . I have to admit . . . I've seen my share of hangings . . . I've touched upon the subject with you already . . . you have no idea of the time it takes people, the show they put on, to go and unhang a hanged man! . . . Such a fuss! . . . Part of my functions, since I'm telling you about it . . . I worked for the coroner's office, and boy did I verify a hanging or two! and they could perfectly well have been saved, if the people around weren't so fucking stupid, if they could bother their ass . . . the neighbors upstairs . . . downstairs . . . it's well known! I already told you . . . I'm not going to go back and reread! . . . Public-health

93

doctor in Houilles, La Garenne, Carrières . . . Argenteuil township, part of Versailles . . . *I, Doctor X, do hereby attest that I verified this day the death by strangulation of Mr. So and So* . . . usually hanging there since the day before! two days before even! You know the song?

A young man had just hung himself!
. . . young man tender of heart! . . .

Load o' crap! No "had just" about it! . . .

In the forest of Saint-Germain!

Hours! days he was hanging there!

People never arrive on the scene right away. It's one hell of a belch, the hanged man's last gasp . . . you're in the vicinity, you're all taken aback . . . disquieted . . . you say "must be a sink, some gutter chugging stuff back up . . . A huge greasy sound, grotesque . . . you gotta hear it! . . . I've heard it . . . I won't say where . . . So people explain it away . . . the neighbors think, "Somebody's flushing something" . . . they don't admit what they're feeling . . . think about it later! . . . they're chicken . . . it takes them hours to make up their mind . . . at first they knock . . . then they hammer . . . then they knock it down . . . they come in, it's all over! . . . You come on the scene, all greenhorn, to certify the guy's hanging there . . . you find his head double, triple black, purple! . . . and in his mouth like somebody stuffed an arm in it . . . red . . . green! his tongue hanging out! . . . the thickness of it! . . . It's been curtains for hours! . . . So when you think about it, me, in my hole, with the bellowings from 16, and 74, and 24! . . . I'd have ample time! . . . even with just the head basher there, my neighbor, he'd cover any gasps I'd make! . . . and his head doesn't even split in two! kick the bucket, my ass! but stentorian voice! banshees! donkeys! rams! excuse me! And the "discipline cell"! number 12! when they have a killer . . . a rapist . . . then, I swear, there's some shindig! You could have four or five guys hanging themselves, it'd be drowned,

94

snuffed out but good! nothing! blood-curdling howls! me, myself, I could be squealing like a pig with his throat cut and the screws wouldn't come trooping back for so little . . . the time it takes to wake up the guards! the ambulance! . . . you bet I'd have enough time! and even to come back! (a joke!)

– But Arlette? . . . Bébert? . . . Janine? . . . my soul's charges?

– He's trying to weasel out of this one! Two-faced son of a bitch! Stooge!

– I'm immune to your invectives! . . . with what I've been through! . . . I don't even hear them any more! you won't demoralize me! I love you! . . . I want to see you again! . . . I want to bear my heart to you . . . you'll listen . . . it's rather delicate . . . it's a secret . . . in your ear . . . a few words . . . I must! . . . I'll die otherwise . . . oh, poor people! you won't be able to figure it out for centuries . . . was it all just a hoax? not a hoax? was he being funny? beguiling? what? pranks? all just a farce? whereas now if I were to meet you I'd murmur a little funny one . . . Yeah, I'd like to see you when it's just the two of us! . . . I'd like a wee laugh myself . . . it's my turn now! . . . like in the prison yard! . . . not always yours!

But here come Aunt Estreme and her little Leo!
Here come Clementine and the valiant Toto!

Honest! I'll come after you! word of honor! even if nothing more than a rotten ripped-apart piece of crap! gut-buster doesn't know his ass from his elbow! laughable hunk of rancid meat! I'll find you! once the tanks have laminated you, chopped you up, napalm glop, I'll find you! none so true to his feelings! . . . even disintegrated somewhere, your building collapsed, you under it, I'll fiddle through your ashes for you, like Eynard and his ex-bistro! . . . Dead determined, no idea how I am! I'll have just the right stick for the occasion: the kind the bishop has . . . the hook at the end . . . only for garbage . . . I'll muck about and I'll find you . . . I'll put your ashes through a sifter if I have to! . . . I'll stop at nothing! let's even say you survive, funny as hell, legless drunk . . . had one too many ions . . . I go right to it, I identify you! . . . I take a whiff: yeah, it's you! . . . your pelt! the smell of singed hair! . . . and that's your grin, all right! . . . scoffing! . . . no other like it! . . . for ten years it's got on my nerves, that grin! I'll fix it to your face for you! . . . Forget about anyone else, it's you I'll kiss! . . . your grin! . . . and put you back together! . . . the reunion brings such joy! you get the picture! . . . and a lot of water'll have gone under the bridge! Ah, Triboulet![168] . . . I'm not kidding myself! . . . to find such infinity in each other again! . . . miracle! this mutual intensity of feeling! . . .

> *Must we tell our friends*
> *Every party ends?*

I'm joking! . . . I'm feeling impish! . . . Oh, but seriousness never abandons me! . . . I dwell in seriousness! . . . so here and there I confide a bit of the future to you . . . my two chambermaids . . . my bikes . . .

The critics'll tear my work apart? No importance whatsoever! . . . They'll snub it? Even less! . . . They've spewed so much of the worst hatred they could for so many months now, days, every minute, that it's as if they'd dried up their poison glands . . . And just what I'd like them to excrete, and how! a hundred times over! . . . torrents! . . . I float on hatred! whether or not the floods of hatred stir things up, my ship sails on! the main thing is that all the juice gushes out! all squirts out! . . . it's ill will that I go for! I'm the most stubborn, persistent bitch of a customer in the world . . . can't get enough of it! . . . the darling of the crazed whores of hatred: Me, me, me . . . of those stiletto-toting she-assassins! grenades! curare! and prick-teasers and tittle-tattlers and goodtime gals! . . . big stores! silly saphists! . . .

– You gotta read this guy in a strait jacket! Public scourge! let's commit him! commit him! shock treatment! Cardiazol! padded cell! Let's adore him! let's kill him! let's glug-glugglug 'im! suck on him! buy him! . . .

So what I need: boynutjobbers, girlnutjobbers! but the

movies? Like a hole in the head! Ah! you gotta be very careful, much more than careful! Minotaur of the Murky Depths! who is it that is gobbling up our readers? who's got it all wrapped up on us? sucking us dry? wolfing us down? The Mighty Film! Already the weeklies, those monsters of the newsstands, were half-devouring a helluva lot of the dreamy gawkers, now the Mighty Film is finishing them off! Their brains, their wallets! . . .

The hypnotist of the depths! . . . it's warm, moist, plush, the organ sounds, the gilding . . . you can have a wee wank for yourself . . .

That's the competition we're facing!

You with your punishing tome, you show up! aren't you the picture! You watch as the steamed-up moviegoers emerge staggering overripe from the Depths, they can't even tell north from south any more! from west! getting everything all assways! . . . streetlamps . . . metros! . . . pants . . . slips! . . . groping around! . . . neighborhoods! . . . sexes . . . floors! . . . their ass for their elbow! . . . all they wanna do is turn around and sit back down . . . Ah! ripen some more! get even blotchier! fester more and more! . . . shit themselves . . . ripen! melt . . . it's already flowing all over the carpets . . .

And here I come along! my avenging stanzas! You get them! You judge for yourself! My bitter lyre!

Fortunately the flush of nasties, of hate-ridden hair-splitters, will never abandon me! Ah, I'll give them what they want! have to pile it on! Risette! Risette! If they get locked up I'm fucked! I'll have to grab 'em before the Asylum gets them! Just in time for them to buy *Fable!*

Then let them be shocked! countershocked! I've got bread on my table! You have to admit that I have it hard! . . . Aside from the pellagra and the anxiety! and the Banshee who's bashing down my wall! I have it all! Aside from the taxman and the revenue boys and the confiscation of "more than everything"! and national disgrace! And the pillaging and the plagiarism! and Arlette and my soul's charges . . .

If my hands weren't tied, go see if I'd give a fuck! I've weathered other storms! But here, in my condition, half blind, immobilized, the whole goddamn world barking at me, waiting outside to cut me up . . .

Oh, but I'll bark ten times worse!

Not just the guards, not just the walls I have it in for! the Classics, the Thinkers, first of all! magnificent fartbags! they've had it! Petrarch, Dantus! Homer! Prou-Prou! pooh-pooh![169] iniquity from the depths of the ages! They just imagined hell, we are living in it! and not just a little bit packed with demons! hordes, throngs, myriads! suckling hard at the sulfur! rats drop dead! . . . poor little beasts! . . . that's what happens in the gutter . . . we're in the gutter, me, Robignol,[170] and a thousand others, and another thousand more wretched, we don't even talk about any more, that nobody dares, who're dying in jails, who've paid a thousand times over in suffering for the crimes they never commit! I don't feel like thinking about it any more. Bombs for what? Fuck! How far will you let it go, air-for-brains? The rabble has the high ground and nothing happens! The demons just laugh! Heaven no longer launches its thunderbolts!

And I'm leaving some out! I'm leaving some out! There's also the falsifying, deliberately destructive asshole translators! They also have their cursed hordes! Readership thieves! Yankee novels at so much a page! Plagues in the pay of Chaos! the felonious breed! you trust those guys? they pass off rejected scraps of Zola as re-oink-oink-annointed Yankee-speak! ghastly garglings! served up in *Readers Digest!*[171] That empoisonous impostor! . . . all our rotten spineless literati with their silly waffle! Europe-a-Gogo! licking their lips, wolfing down everything! Go back to your Maupassant, you insipid jerks! Gum-cracking gangster clergyman! Saint Genevieve, motorized vamp and her sheep at home with Attila, cocktails, and the Huns! We'll have seen everything! . . . and her corset, too! . . . Rape! Manon and Joan of Arc shacking up together, neurotic, psychoanalyzed, being grilled ever so gently by Cauchon.[172]

Your mouth'll be all agape over it tomorrow! . . . and your stomach, too! the great monstrosities? It's all in Saint John![173] the Kirghizes librarians are cooking up some tricks for you! They'll pull some pride out of a hat for you! You'll be hung for your baccalaureate! that'll teach you to be cultivated and a renegade and a deserter . . . and the asshole readers of Russian, Finlandish, Engulish, Americish, plagiarish, anti-you novels! you'll puke up your dirty dealings!

Served up as Dandins![174]

French is a kingly language! around it just fucking pox-ridden, trumped-up, humpbacked gobbledygook! . . . You want it? you like it? shit, then, you'll get your bellyful of it – to bursting! I won't insist! Every crime has its time! Tomorrow! Every dumb mistake its hour! First of all my villa! what I need the most! the name's already chosen, don't you know? "Ye Olde Cathouse"! Hell, slam it up them! . . . you'll get no giggle out of God! . . . So not a single minute! I'm dragging my feet there, I'm quibbling . . . Age is catching up with me . . . I'm oozing again! . . . One small problem, no more villa, just a coffin! It's not only men at the kill! Time has quite a crack at it! . . . Ah, the months at the breast![175] . . . sometimes, I admit, grief grabs me . . . my poor little Arlette outside shivering in the cold, and no one wants to take her in! . . . a city of more than a million souls! . . . I've said it before! . . . she's jinxed, I'm jinxed! . . . All she found was a piddling attic . . . a framer's storage space . . . ice cold . . . I could bash my head against the wall! . . . *Baaaiing!* . . . the Banshee's nothing in comparison! . . . I wouldn't miss! . . . He doesn't really throw himself into it, the Banshee! he gives the wall a shake, he takes some skin off, he bleeds, but he doesn't wholeheartedly throw himself into it! . . . if he threw his heart into it he'd bust apart! . . . me, a doctor, you can imagine, I know the difference! . . . if I bashed the old kisser the bricks wouldn't have a chance to be all shook up twice! One blow! and *craapluuunk!* I know what it means to bust your cranium open! So long, old buddy! There are real heroes! there are fake ones!

The likes of him are met but once![176]

I belt it out! . . . the Baltavian, he doesn't give a fuck! A wall's one thing, not understanding each other's language is something else again! . . . If I catch up with him in the infirmary . . . I'll tell him a thing or two! . . . He's yapping? It's worse for me than it is for him! . . . article 75 up the ole dirt road! . . . Talk about a pain in the ass! . . . The article on traitors! . . . They read it out to me when I entered the prison, and the list of my treasonous acts, underlined in red . . . Jeez, the number of towns I handed over! fleets! generals! battalions! . . . the Toulon harbor! . . . the Pas-de-Calais! a little bit of the Puy-de-Dôme! . . . they brought me back in handcuffs, I crossed the capital, Baltavia! nothing but great big squares! wide avenues! and such crowds! in a wagon with bars, padlocked, at least five, ten times! to hear the indictments . . . It's truly amazing all that I committed . . . I sold journals to the enemy! . . . a hundred fifty! . . . a hundred twenty! . . . I can't even remember! . . . and the Denoël publishing company! . . . and the assassination at the Invalides of old Robert with Madame Thérèse Amirale, manageress of a house of ill repute, cunning pixie![177] . . . Jeez, by the third or fourth transfer I couldn't tell black from white, bouquets of machine guns everywhere! of every color! *tutti-frutti!* . . . fuzziness holds you in its grasp . . . "What did he say? . . . What did I say?" . . . you're nothing but a swelling hunk of remorse! swelling! remorse about who? . . . about what? . . . you don't even know any more! . . . "What did he say? . . . What did I say?" . . . here on my stool down in the hole or in the padlocked paddy wagon, haunted by remorse over nothing . . . "What did he say? . . . What did I say?" . . . you can't help it, you turn into a Slav, Slovak trial! Take me, for example, there I am, muddle headed, confused, my ass all seeping, I'd kill myself out of remorse over nothing! . . . and the other sonofabitch at the cell window, Hortensia! the one insulting me in the name of Louis

XIV! . . . you can't live like this! . . . When they kill in "1112" I'm almost relieved . . . in the "enforcer cells" I told you about . . . now those are the ultimate death cries! . . . but the sirens and the night patrol and the buzzings in my ears . . . and my buttocks being torn off in strips, two big beefsteaks, the skin green . . . I mean what does it look like? . . . and the lump in my right arm . . . and my bleeding eyes . . . is this how it will end? . . . They chucked Arlette into jail[178] . . . "Go on, into the slammer, you traitor's whore!"

The audacity of them! . . . unbelievable! An angel! . . . I tell you, an angel! . . . and their whole police force! so she'd confess!

What? Confess what?

– Don't you know? . . . the Maginot Line? . . . Puy-de-Dome? Toulon harbor! . . .

They take shifts, her in handcuffs.

– Your husband has admitted as much! has written it down! . . . your husband's not an abortionist? . . . a pederast? . . . a pimp? . . .

She has to confess!

– What? You don't know? . . . He handed over blueprints!

– Blueprints of what?

Another guy, a bit swifter:

– He handed over Frenchmen! Sign here! He had the dam blown up!

– What dam?

– The Casino! Dinard! Malo! You weren't in Dinard? Do you deny it? Don't tell me you weren't in Dinard!

No letup, until she doesn't even know where the hell she was or wasn't.

– Okay! Okay! Okay!

Yeah, we knew it all along!

– And those syringes? what about those syringes there? you deny that? Heh?

He spreads everything on the floor . . . my medicine satchel!

The swift change in tactic.

– What about this morphine? this cocaine?

He's crowing.

Of course I had morphine! and belladonna and all! and probes! and scalpels! With what would I have practiced at Blaringhem? goddamn idiot!

Fortunately, Arlette is reason itself! Always focused, never hysterical, ever! . . . The most harmonious nature, a dancer in every atom of her being, the soul of nobility! She'd rather die twenty times over than to her own self be false . . . Her nature is classical . . . There is a kind of heroism in her dance, and elegance, and kindness . . . Supreme bearing . . . She'll never be found awkward or hesitant when she's answering the sound of her heart . . .

The dumb fucks got nothing out of her.

When they'd reassured themselves after twenty interrogations, ten months hidden away in the cells, that I hadn't sold the Alps, the Eiffel Tower, Mount Valérian, Infanticides, and sneeze-gas: "Get the fuck out of here, girl," they told her, "go get yourself strung up."

You can imagine my anguish! . . . The situation! her situation! . . . no one talking to her, no one inviting her anywhere . . . all alone against the world, that's right . . . the entire world! . . . me in the hole! . . . Hexed is what she is! . . . hexed like me! lawfully wedded husband! . . . Sixteenth Arrondissement, witnesses and everything! . . . I who used to dream of operettas! You have to admit! Things are not going according to plan! . . . And all she found was the ass end of an attic . . . Bébert is coughing, she's coughing . . . she waits for Tuesdays, the visit . . . she comes with Bébert to see me . . . seven minutes . . . Bébert in a bag . . . Oh, but he can't move a whisker! . . . utter immobility . . . the guard is monitoring every word . . . and we're not allowed to speak French together, Arlette and me! . . . English only! . . . French is forbidden! . . . Us, English? . . . I mean she's French to the core, born rue Saint-Louis-en Ile! . . . me, Bridge Ramp number 11, Courbevoie! . . . Bébert at La Samaritaine![179] . . . forcing *us* to speak English! . . . I who have a horror of foreign languages! . . . feeble, screwed up gobbledygookery! . . . It's the final humiliation! We, who are native to the Seine like no other! . . . Montmartre is one thing! . . . but English! . . . first of all, Arlette doesn't speak English! . . . well, not three words that she can string together . . . them and their mewling spewing How-do-you-do-ery makes me want to puke! . . . in my state! . . . and they spit when they talk! Only traitors speak English and German, Chinese, Volskapuke, and "filmspeak," of course! . . . Holly-wowspeak! . . . why not Baltavian while they're at it? . . . So we don't talk to each other . . . we make signs . . . Arlette, now, she knows a thing or two about signs, luckily! . . . dancers, real ones, born dancers, they're made of waves, so to speak! . . . not just rosy flesh and pirouettes! . . . their arms, their fingers . . . you get the picture! . . . Comes in handy in those times of utter agony . . . no words for it . . . beyond words! Just the hands! the fingers . . . nothing but a gesture, grace . . . The flower of being . . . Your heart beats, you live again! . . . Deaf? Mute? In chains? A dancer saves you! The proof! . . . A thou-sand proofs! . . . and messages! but perhaps you're a bit thick? impervious to waves! . . . you'd rather howl like the lunatic in 14 . . . and *whoooaaam!* in my wall? Nothing but howlers around me! . . . and howleresses! . . . No doubt you, too! . . . Myself, I don't howl! . . . I bark! . . . told you already! and only for you-know-what! I'd never get an enema without "whooaaah!" I sort of imitate those huge mutts out there! I was telling you about the total mayhem, the whole pack, the guards! . . . Up the entire length of the turret! the five cat-walks! . . . hurricanes of whistles! . . . topsy-turvy floor by floor they come tumbling, crashing down . . . they hit bottom, a pile of them at the foot of the stairs! guards and guard dogs! What the hell's going on? "Woof! Woof!" The alarm! and the sirens blasting from every direction, the ramparts! as far as the railroad! . . . the firemen on duty . . . the ambulance . . . the cemetery bells . . .

Ah, sure, you're having a bit of fun with me . . . but time is of the essence! Ill fortune ages a man . . . kills him . . . I don't want to die without my villa! . . . my mind, certainly, has been profoundly shaken, but not my patriotic sense! nor the Duty to Reconstruct . . . "Ye Olde Cathouse" . . . Saint-Malo-where-currents-flow! . . . so, don't you know! To hell with piddling trifles! down to business! I must subjugate you! You'll be my best publicity ever!

Oh, the firemen! Good old firemen! I was talking about the firemen and damned if they aren't here! my head! from telling you! from getting myself all worked up! "Woof! Woof!" for Christsake! general alert! I barked! without even realizing it! all mayhem breaks loose . . . and there you go! no doubt about it, you gotta bark! not too much! easy does it! but just shouting doesn't do the trick, either! nobody listens to you! Here everybody screams! every floor, every cell! Talk about crazy! Barking like you've never heard before . . . The guards are wondering: what, he's got some kind of dog in there? . . . they come have a look-see . . . Oh, but you can't go overboard! Once a week! no more! This time it was pure inadvertence! worked myself up to fever pitch telling you all about it! . . . I'll send them away: *Nix! Nix!* . . . if I screw up I'm lost! they'll never ever give me another enema . . . once a week . . . the stretcher, the infirmary, I win again! . . . I leave them in peace the rest of the time . . . I give myself over to work! . . . if you could see me hunched over my little writing table, going blind, with my pencil[180] . . . I don't waste a moment of daylight . . . well, what you'd call quarter-light, a dirty-water kind of glimmer . . . even in summer . . . there is no summer . . . in this cesspool of a ditch, it's never summer! . . . the walls ooze a little more, a little less, that's all! Outside in the cage I don't see the sky, I just see the grill, the rain, the snow . . . once in a while a ray of sunshine . . . it's happened . . . a gull very, very high up . . . and one or two little sparrows, you have to be fair, who come in to peck about a bit . . . it's not allowed . . . little bits of bread! . . . but we still give it to them . . . the guy on surveillance in the Watchtower puts on the indignant act . . . it's an automatic reaction with those guys, they gotta put you in your place! . . . infractions of discipline! . . . I think about him, he haunts me, the son of a bitch in the Watchtower! . . . Here in my hole I think about him and then I don't think about him any more . . . I give myself over to work . . . I give myself over to work! Ciborium would talk like that! I give myself over to work! and then he'd throw himself down on his knees and pray! . . . on his knees, I can see him now! Ciborium the Motor maker! . . . beating his breast! "I won't make them any more, honest!" *mea! mea!* By the way, how does *he* do caca, Ciborium? That's the main thing: caca . . . if I ever find him I'll ask him! . . . But I can't go all obsessional about this! I've enough personal problems! I have my little problems? I bark! . . . Apparently I'm supposed to croak here . . . I'm losing swathes of skin . . . I'm losing the meat off my buttocks . . . I'm losing teeth . . . no muscles left . . . I can't do caca anymore . . . but I ain't dead yet, I tell you . . . the proof!

> *Must we tell our friends every party ends?*
> *To hell with your kind!*
> *Be gone with the wind!*
> *Farewell dead leaves, escapades, and cares!*

Will you remember this closing stanza?

> *I'll find you some foul night*
> *Dead meat in my rifle's sight!*
> *Your dumb cow of a soul'll be gone in a glance*
> *To the Heavenly Choirs – you'll see how they dance!*

I've got music at the bottom of this hole! . . . and my word, I'll dance! . . . not collapsing yet . . . I'm not heroic like Arlette, but I've got my little pride all the same:

> *To the Heavenly Choirs – you'll see how they dance!*

Yeah, with my pencil! I pencil it! and very tiny writing . . . and I scribble and I keep on scratching out!

– The notes! now for the notes! G clef! . . . hum along!

In the great cemetery of the Good Children!

What is more I notify the Banshee! goddamn would-be skull basher! won't he ever bust his goddamn block open!

– You're cheating, pimp! . . . you always cheat! . . . I shout at him . . . Up in the infirmary I'll reason with him, all right! . . . I'd like him to bash his stinking skull into the wall once and for all! He won't do it! I'll bash it into the wall for him myself, I tell you! the hero that I am!

The likes of him are met but once!

He can bray, the faker! *blood! blood!* Let him cry: Blood! I'll catch up with him in the Infirmary! I'll tell him a few home truths! . . . me, with my article 75! . . . so what if I am a bit loopy? . . . the article on traitors! . . . it had to be that one! the list of everything I sold! aside from my crimes toward my loved ones! the handing over of entire Embassies! anchored fleets! fortifications nobody could take! Cities opened up to whomever you please! . . . What is it I don't lug around with me! no end of surrenders! countless generals and their messes! and their planes! and their pianos! and how, I should bash my head in! the crimes I cart around! and *vlop* and *vlop!* but only after him! the banshee! I want him to bust open his head first! I'm fed up always being the first! Everywhere! In everything! It'd be a riot for him if I bashed mine in *first!* Fifty years I been the first to rush right in! That's enough now! Enough! him first! I egg him on! I insult him!

– Go to it, piece o' garbage! Go to it!

All he's taken off is a few bits of forehead! His head just won't give! . . . Din, uproar, is all he's good for! I can't collect my thoughts with him around, he sabotages my muse! . . . Me, whose head is brimming with innovation! All he's got to crush is his goddamn skull! And he doesn't crush it! In mine, there's ardent reflection, and laughter, a sense of fun!

– Numbskull, Sonofabitchinbastard! I shout at him . . .

Bambambang! he starts all over again. It's him, my nightmare! I wouldn't get bored here, my ass glued, composing my

106

music for books! You can imagine how much I meditate! Enough of prose! songs everywhere! like Roland! like Arisitide![181] the triumph of verse and notes!

Note that there's a little rue Aristide! . . . Aristide Bruant! but no rue Roland. That kills me! . . . I really get excited over street names! avenues, squares! . . . injustice! fame? Why Aristide and not Roland? Maybe a little matter of prison? . . . didn't do any time either one or the other! . . . I'll find out! . . . Let me think! Let me think! Jeez, if that sonofabitchin banshee wasn't braying so much! Pathetic wall trembler! He won't bust open his skull! Won't bust open anything! Goddamn stubborn sonofabitch! He goes at it with ulterior motive! Get the fuck out is what he wants! not die! His shouting matches don't impress me! I'm a medical man! I know all about hysterics! He doesn't give it his all! Me, I'd have taken care of business . . . you wouldn't hear me twice! I wouldn't tear strips off the wall! "okay, give it everything you got!" . . . I'm thinking about Roland again . . . the traitors got him, boy, finished him off! . . . He sounded the horn as he expired . . . If I can't do caca, me, I bark! I told you! That's how I do it! They don't sound the horn here, just sirens! And not often! . . . but when it comes to whistles! Jeez! Night and day, those! Shift change! Gusts! and the bells great and small! . . . and the hooting owls . . . all around the cemetery! What cemetery? I'm not just making this up! . . . It's the most amazing sound décor! . . . What décor did he have, Roland? The Roncevaux circus! . . . Roland the Furious! . . . He struck with his Durandal! Such a mighty blow that the entire Pyrenees were sundered in twain! and the traitors' heads rolled! Ganelon, Turpin, and their liege lords! It's written about all over the place! Such was Roland! Paladin of rank! Charlemagne's rear guard, 768, torn apart by the Vascons![182]

The guy next door, all show, he sunders nothin' in twain. Banshee!

The soul of the great Roland is thus not appeased?[183]

Sure as hell isn't! It's not over yet! . . . Not even a wee bit of a street, not a square! . . . lousy ingratitude of the Franks! . . . and today's valiant ones, where's their gratitude? What are they sounding, those guys? What are they sundering? What are they singing of? . . . François? Raoul? André? Canal? towering figures! They're tooting "Suez" tunes! They're tooting "Beers"! "Saint-Gobains"![184] They're singing of Swiss banks! François, Rodolphe! André! Canal! They're dancing the la-lay-yiday! Towering figures! François! Rodolphe! André! Canal! I'd like to see them practicing here in my hole . . . François! André! Rodolphe! Canal! swapping government bonds! . . . I'd give them a spanking they wouldn't soon forget, and have a damn good time at it, too! . . . don't give a shit how historic they are! Immortal Ones, Agents of the Stock Exchange, towering members of everything! I'd get them to confess their compromises, their fiddling around! I'd develop my contacts, all right, just like they do! . . . funny two-cornered hats, with feathers, swords, the whole lot![185] just like them! They manage, so will I! The Art of Succeeding? I'll succeed! And when I do, I'll give them another good spanking! They traverse The Flood, they come out the other end resplendent with gold! Some of them are lucky with the tarot cards, some of them thundering troubadours, beribboned, some of independent means . . . and some who pimp for sprites! Would you enjoy seeing me spank them? . . . You must let laughter take hold of you! . . . You ain't laughin'? I kick the bucket! The party's over!

– What a bore he is!

Alas! I go broke! Bankruptcy! All this prison time in vain! . . . Ruined retinas! Pencils! Pellagra! Frowns! Clown!

Oh, Clementine![186] but Clementine! just look at them! they're all here! André! François! Canal! Rodolphe! and all the rest from the Song! Valiant Toto! Auntie Estreme! The little Leo! They're coming at me from the walls! They're hurling themselves at me! They manage to unstick me from my stool! Ouch! Jeez! they're peeling me off it . . . they want me to stop singing!

To the Heavenly Choirs –
You'll see how they dance!

I keep at it! Keep at it! Damn! So they go into conniptions!
... They turn me into nothing but one big heap! ... my poetic
person! ... they chuck it into their wheelbarrow! ... patch it
up! ... They've got their work tools, shovels, picks, brooms!
Infernal is what they are! ... They scratch and they scrape
below the bunk, under the bedpan, in those hard-to-get-to
places ... They turn over hunks of flesh on me! They stick
me back together, reglue it all! They pile me up again! Flatten
me out again! and *plop!* back into the wheelbarrow! ... On
the road! ... They carry me off, amazing! ... Ah, but them,
they get out of prison! ... The gigantic doors open! ... Like
magic! ... The watchmen, the dogs watch them! ... Not a
"wuff," not a whistle! ... and right away the cobblestones, the
road! ... the bumps! ... every cobblestone's like a milestone!
Jeez, can they trot along on them! bump along! ... The
wheelbarrow jumps and jiggles all over the place! ... at a gallop! ... And at every jolt they double over laughing! and me,
the pile of meat at the bottom, I'm groaning! They're having
fits! They have another whacking great go at me! With the
shovel! With the pick! *Boing! Boing!* Hooligans! Canal! Auntie Estreme, Toto, and all!

– Out past Achères![187] farther you'll go!

They're shouting at me down in my wheelbarrow ... the
hub of the wheel is smoking ... I wish it would break, burn,
the bumpbarrow! The hub is creaking ... the screws are
swooping down on us, too! All of them! ...

– Out past Achères! farther you'll go!

If they torture me aside from everything else! with the
back end of the spade! *Fling! Flam!* while they hump and
bump me along!

– Out past Achères! ...

Me, my putrid meat! ... what they dragged me out of! from
my hole! me, my putrid meat, out past Archères! you realize

109

what that means? . . . what a haul! enough to make you laugh! They take turns wheeling the damn thing . . . Rodolphe, André, François, Canal . . . energumen of the world! . . . I'd rather keep quiet! . . . The race is on! . . . I hear them creaking . . .

– To the leek fields! . . . No, the turnips! . . .

They can't agree . . .

– No, the cauliflower!

They keep wanting to chuck me somewhere! . . . the wheelbarrow's smoking! the hub is in fumes! their asses are in flames, too, talk about fire under them! At such a pace! faster! faster! Good thing I'm nothing more than a mush! . . . I'm shivering at the bottom of my wheelbarrow . . . oh, I know where the Archères leeks are! . . . Out past the plains! . . .

– Get to the carrots! the carrots!

Rodolphe wants me dumped in the carrots! . . . He's yelping so loud you can't hear the creaking! The carrots also are in the plains! heaven's sake! A real conspiracy to drive out the devil! Marsh madness! I can just make it out! I'm recognizing something! I teleview! I know what I'm talking about, teleview! You couldn't tell by looking at me, but I see through walls! the future! the past! the nasties! I transmit to you! You don't believe me? my own walls! everything before it even happens! the pitiful banshee in comparison! I capture the death-throes frequency! Goddamn banshee's in no death throes! He's just showing off! faker! he's faking! He'll never break down that wall! He'll never manage to throw himself into it! He'll never know how to dance! He'll do sweet fuck all and that's it! He's nothing but a goddamn show-off from God knows where, and to boot he's in the clink! . . . He'll never know how to give up the ghost! I see it all! I see people! . . . I see the muck spreaders, all sorts! . . . I see Ciborium and his She-Pharisee! . . . I see François in satin slippers . . . that foetus Fartre and Larengon![188] . . . I see Auntie Estreme! . . . and little Leo! . . .

– Where are they, soothsayer?

110

– In the basement of the Institute! They're putting together a fake Dictionary!

– Now how about that!

No "how about that" about it! Keep your lousy jokes to yourself! You'll make damnably good use of them! Don't waste your fine pleasantries! . . . when they nail you to the cross I'll go have a look, see how funny you are then! . . . when the time comes! myself! in person! An onlooker! It's on the cards! . . . But later on! . . . for the time being I have my duties here! my sacred tasks! Roland's horn, you hear? And the screamer there full of pains, would-be head basher, who'll insult him once I'm gone? No one! And that she-spy up in 36? . . . And that abortionist woman in 72? she screeches the loudest, I can tell you, of everyone in all the K! W! Y! and U! wings put together! . . . She wails like a one-woman hospital nursery! I have the hospital nursery noises in my head along with all the string! wind instruments! and two locomotives!

– The bitter work! Phooey! you're puking! . . . tra-la-la! I'm tipping over! my way of bowing! . . . I'm going over to the "Specters"! . . . Resolve! . . . Enlistment rue Saint-Dominique![189] . . . my chains hanging out of my mouth! . . . You're warned! you shatter my dreams? . . . Okay! my bikes? . . . farewell, my villa! cow! maids! storms! Grand-Bé! So be it! Farewell, Théo! Farewell, Marie! I'm selling everything off! No one wants to trade me for anything any more! I'll have pleaded for a few lousy crumbs? and been bumped around? suffered unspeakably? wheelbarrowed, yes, wheelbarrowed! Good thing I stick to the bottom of it! with all my meat! and André! and François!, and Jules! after me! after me! all around! all of them from the French Academy, my wall lied! it's Archères they have me headed for! and here's old Auntie Estreme again! and Clemence and her little Leo! In the name of God, they're out in force! They're breaking down the door! Here they come lunging at me again! . . . It starts all over again! . . . They tear me off my stool! "Blasphemer! to the

111

endives with him! . . . into the wheelbarrow, filthy swine!"
They're having another helluva go at me! . . . *Bis repetita! Bis
repetita!* . . . Ciborium is proclaiming! *Gloria Motor! Gloria
Motor!* . . . and here we go again, and this time sing while
you're at it! my own song! that beats all!

To hell with dead leaves! To hell with your kind!

They're butchering my text on me! They keep reclean-
ing my cell! . . . yet another hunk of meat! . . . They're patch-
ing everything up again! they're re-amalgamating me! Ass!
Bones! fibers! Allez-up, here comes the wheelbarrow and
we're off again! Bring on the bumps! What madness! The
cobblestones, my God, are even fatter! They've put on
weight! more enormous jolts! mile upon mile! from the north
where I am to Gennevilliers! can you imagine? Somersaults!
and we're only talkin' cobblestones here! Counterjolts! André! François! Canal! Rodolphe! . . . and little Leo and that
Fartre brat!

– You already told us that!

It's been pages and pages! and of course I'm horsing
around, only natural . . . after the torments I've been subjected to! I won't hide it! They brutalize me and I defend myself!
Period! *Business first!* and then from only one reading you
won't retain a thing! I know what I'm talking about, believe
me! The patients! The prescriptions! a hundred times! the
same prescription a hundred times over, spelled out, they still
don't remember it! you gotta make them sing the goddamn
thing! make them learn it by heart! all together now! it's the
same with you! When it's too detailed, no instructions with it,
you get lost, your noggin's just not up to it! . . . I lose you
entirely! . . . Everything has to be sung to you! and sung over
again! So I treat you considerately, I try to make everything
understandable-like: being dragged from pillar to post, the
wheelbarrow! . . . So you can picture it! André! François! Canal! Rodolphe! . . . all members of the French Academy! and
no dillydallying, I assure you, trotting along! Giddyap, giddyap! They play obscene jokes on each other! These hot-

112

shots of high culture on the trot! And go to it, boy! what I suffer! how I'm jostled! my pile of guts, my organs flat out! my limbs I can no longer feel!

The cannibals just laugh.

– Off you go! off you go to the leeks! to the manure! swine! What a ride!

Lout! your loutish soul!
Turnips! turnips! radishes! reveries!

Their couplet for the road!

Okay, agreed! All that's left of me is a pile of glop at the bottom of the barrow! and *dong! bong!* Oh, the cobblestones! Oh, I knew it! little ones! huge ones! . . . the Lapland steppes have arrived in Arras! When you think about it! . . . the wheelbarrow rears up! the street gushes up! they make a beeline for the tram! on purpose! and *bammm!* and another heave-ho! and they take turns at the handlebars! the "get-goin'-I'll push-ya" marathons! absolutely premeditated! One hundred percent crime! If I'd knifed a rich old lady they'd have treated me better! instead of devoting myself to patriotism! bet your ass it was premeditated! I can just see the brat Bartre and little Elsa! . . . from the depths of my wheelbarrow! I see them! They're running after us! . . . very far behind! They're calling! . . . They're denouncing me to the trees! . . . They're shouting . . . they're creaking! It's me they're pointing at! me they're denouncing!

– He's being paid! he's being paid! . . .

Oh, but the guys pushing me, they don't wait around! . . . Not a single stop . . . not a breather! . . . "Push on, wheelbarrow! Go on, filthy swine!" I'm telling you they take turns at the handlebars! . . . all the while singing, creaking, galloping! . . . prestidigiously! André! Canal! Estreme! Rodolphe! all from the French Academy! . . . Go to it, ye gallant lads! . . . We make tracks, I swear to God! . . . the road from Gonesse to Paris! . . . the barrow's breathing fire! . . . Rethondes! . . . Compiègne! . . . going so fast everything shakes! . . . Everything I

113

see is shaking! . . . The knocks, the crushing! me a gloopy mess! . . . the pellagra, rottenness . . . piece o' cake! pool of raw sewage! as they say!

– Go to it! turd! turnip! your Homeland!

They sing! They're singing!

Their couplet for the road.

Ah, the Seine! Here's the Seine! . . . The bridge! . . . Here we are! . . . La Défense! . . . And the plain! . . . No, it's Neuilly! . . . no, not yet! . . . to the left! the left! water's edge . . . Go to it! To it, I say!

– You've got one shithouse of a soul!

Ah, the plain all the same! . . . All spread out before you! . . . the little paths . . . No, they haven't gone astray at all! . . . One small plank! another small plank . . . and another! . . . balance, for once! They're practically carrying my wheelbarrow! . . . they lift it ever so cautiously . . . like the cops in Washington, Auriol's car![190] . . . did you see that? just so nothing would happen to him! . . . all of them gripping on to my wheelbarrow! . . . me, too! . . . the seven! eight! . . . twelve! . . . thirty-eight hands! They're literally hoisting me up! in one go! *pllopppp!* They give me a heave! . . . into the gooey sewage and *pllopppp!* The rat bastards! The felons! That's it! that does it! drenched! drowned! I swallow the stuff! I upchuck! Wooooee! the goo rising! I see them on top of the trench! me in the cream! they're laughing their fannies off! Ciborium and his She-Pharisee! . . . They can't take it any more, they're laughing so hard! François in satin slippers! . . . the brat Bartre! . . . All looking like something out of Heidi! . . . little shorts! . . . and funny hats! . . . Funny hats I'd already seen, but the little shorts? . . . I couldn't see from the bottom of my barrow . . . not everything! . . . and they were knitting their knees at such a speed! galloping gets fuzzy! their gallop is a fuzzy gallop. Everything's fuzzy! But now I could see them just fine around the barrow! . . . They were bending over me! They were pissing on me . . . I've got incredible presence of mind . . . they were pissing on me . . . all of them! both the brat Fartre and the

Elsa girl! . . . No, not her! . . . not her! her panties! she couldn't get her panties off! they were helping her! oh, the tears from Elsa! such chagrin! they tear off her buttons! her whole fly! all berserk, the bad, bad boys! You should've seen Ciborium! François! bracing himself and Larengon! the Fartre brat not even helping her! He was too busy pissing on me! there, bending over me, I could see him just fine! in little shaking fits!

– He's being paid! He's being paid! he's shouting.[191] He was pointing his finger at me! me, there, in the middle of the cesspool, drowning! Shows you what a revolting individual he is! And all of them nowadays who want to lighten things up again! piss is what they want to do! both Estreme and her little Leo! . . . They're aiming at Elsa's panties! . . . Scandal at the cesspool! . . . They're all firing at her frillies! . . . pissing on me! . . . me, deep down in the goo, drinking it all in! . . . Elsa! Elsa in despair! . . . how can her knickers hold out against ten! twenty! thirty of them! Should've heard her bawling! They're doing it on purpose so she'll suffer, too! They're bending over six at a time! eight at a time! to grab what's between her legs! The screams out of Elsa! I'm howling along with her! I'm not dreaming! . . . The other guy's screaming, too! there, next door! not to mention the abortionist in 16! Pee pee! peeeeeee! pee peeeee! That's Baltavian! I was not dreaming! . . . Not at all! . . . I was sitting down! . . . I saw everything! . . . heard everything! . . . hey, but no wheelbarrow! . . . Screwed! Screwed I was! to my stool! Screwed! I wasn't rolling along! you think it's funny? I was screaming in chorus . . . with 16! . . . with 18 and 130! . . . I outshout the banshee . . . the wall jerker . . . *Ow love you!* . . . I shout at him! . . . that's pure Shakespeare! . . . "I love you!" why doesn't he crack it open? go to it? Goddamn banshee next door! Eh, I see them all! And how, do I see them! the kisser on François in his satin slippers, Tyrolean shorts, and wee cap! . . . And Ciborium with Stupnagel backstage at the Comédie.[192] Frivoling around, go-betweening! Pee pee! Pee pee! thoroughly hermetic mystics! . . .

all the same, bunch of bandits, they whisked me away from those Lapps! kidnapped out by Rethondes, Achères! my meat, my glop! . . . split the prison walls asunder! I, who was a bandit of some repute! archtraitor, you can rest assured about that! never raised a fuss! I, who only barked when I needed an enema, carried off through the highways and byways! what a sprint! and in such a state! The Flanders Cobblestone Scandal! escaped by force! I had asked nothing of those great big doors! . . . they just opened as if by magic! . . . the wheelbarrow and off you go! on the road! the hub on fire! and this creaking, fuming madness! the little getaway! sneaking off twelve thousand kilometers! the gall! really! no wonder the sirens were screeching! . . . and the dogs, and the harbor alert! and of course the cops are whistling all over the place! and the fire brigade rushing all over town, Baltavia, with their big ladders, their little ones! "Catch those lunatics! get them to the infirmary, quick!" and the twelve packs of hounds scurry all over the countryside! all the cemeteries! Oh, how I amuse you! . . . how I muse! . . . and Time? . . . what about Time? . . . it's catching up with me . . . misfortune ages a man, kills him . . . I don't want to die without my villa! . . . yes, my mind has been profoundly shaken, but not the sense of how things should be . . .

And the other guy with his gal Pharisee! . . . Excuse me for the details . . . I see everything, I do! . . . I see it all in the walls . . .

– Soothsayer, where are they now?

– I've already told you! I've proclaimed it! Precise detail! Everything! Don't you remember the wheelbarrow? the leeks? . . . In the muck out past Achères! on my ass, there, and up you go! all the while making the sign of the cross at me over and over again! . . . as well as pissing on me from the sides! . . . I saw them! heard them! *Profundis!* . . . in their Heidi outfits and funny hats! My walls never out of my sight again! . . . They won't get me into that whack-happy wheelbarrow another

116

time! . . . the shovel! the mad ride! I bitch! I screech! They chuck me in again, me frantic! Me! who listens to the wails coming from all around! . . . who'll listen when I'm gone? . . . Nobody! If not me, nobody! . . . Nobody gives a fuck! "Yuelp! Yuelp!" they can all go and bust their gullets! . . . all the god-damn prisoners around me! . . . the ropes! . . . screech their lungs out! . . . with me gone nobody'll listen! He can crack his noggin in two, banshee! in the daily scheme of horrors, a mere blip! . . . Nobody'll bat an eyelash! . . . You're at the bottom of the ditch, so shut your trap! . . . You're in K wing! . . . You're still this side of the tomb? . . . this side of the cemetery? . . . the magnificent buildings? . . . you see those grand buildings? . . . Seven comfy floors . . . Oh, well, excuse me! . . . You see them from your cell . . . you're not inside those grand buildings . . . you're what? three, four kilometers away . . . after the ceme-tery . . . now, that's a resplendent view! . . . I mean from the prison, from where you are . . . after the cemetery . . . in the early days I still had some strength left, I'd hoist myself up, just managed to reach the cell window, the edge, I could see them perfectly well from there . . . perfectly well those "seven floors," say, three, four kilometers away! . . . Now I wouldn't have the strength . . . and then, of course, Hortensia would emerge out of nowhere and strangle me . . . he's forever at the bars . . . I saw those buildings, I am not lying to you . . . build-ings such as I wish for you! . . . People talk about heaven! . . . whether it exists . . . doesn't exist . . . You don't need to be a genius to figure it out: heaven is houses three kilometers away, with lots of people in them, with seven floors! all the com-forts! windows! wispy curtains! elevator! seen like that by us, peeking through a cell window . . . Anyway, I couldn't hoist myself up anymore . . . My scabs are sticking too much! . . . And here I was talking a while back about hanging myself! . . . I was just showing off! . . . and what about Hortensia and the others? . . . them in their Heidi getup? . . . They'd all emerge out of nowhere and take a flying leap at me! . . . along with

Leo, Toto, Jules! . . . not to mention Estreme! . . . Where would I go? Wherever it is, they'll chuck me right back into their wheelbarrow and up! off we go!

Just my walls! . . . that's all there is! . . . Confidence only in my walls! . . . Oh, I confine myself! . . . Confine myself indeed! . . . ears ever at the listen! . . . and eyes waiting to see! . . . I pick up everything! . . . aside from my internal noises, the goods trains . . . in twos and threes! . . . anything that moves in Batignolles . . . both under the Flanders Bridge and under three adjacent tunnels . . . and I never mix up the whistles! . . . the prison ones, the railroad ones, the ones in my ear . . . the imaginary ones, the real ones . . . Never the tiniest inkling of a doubt! . . . The exquisiteness of my hearing . . . I'm like a bloody conductor! . . . not counting that ill-mannered banshee and the bleatings all-floors! . . . for example, the one above, the abortionist, she goes at it like twenty-five newborns! . . . the cries out of her! . . . in 28! Am I repeating myself? . . . so? . . . I've got the ear for it, what can I tell you? . . . Cries of all descriptions fascinate me . . . you can imagine, with all those years in Tarnier! . . . Brindeau, Lantuéjoul[193] . . . those first cries . . . the first cry! . . . all greasy and husky and full of phlegm . . . I know all about it! . . . those tiny little mugs on them, scarlet, blue, already strangulated! . . . I've helped my share of little beings into the world! . . . How they keep on coming! . . . you're bringing it all back to me! "Push, now, my good woman! Push! . . ." I've heard manys a cry . . . I'm a hearer . . . but the duo of childbirth, mama and the little guy, now there's a chord you won't soon forget . . . as soon as the mother stops shouting the little guy pipes up . . . I'm not going to go for literary effect here, "and so life goes on, et cetera" . . . I'll spare you that . . . To hell with effect! . . . Some noises I'm stingy with, others I'll give away freely . . . the noises in Cameroon, now, you can have as many as you want of them! . . . talk about forestial orchestrations! . . . at night, jeez! . . . at night . . . you've gotta hear what comes out of the throats of those enormous animal couplings! . . . it's the howling storm of the instincts down there! and the village pygmies who feast on personal meat![194] . . . hit those Tom-Toms! and up! . . . syncopations and jitterbugging . . . better not go have a look! . . . Grandma at a slow simmer . . . Those are some bawlings! . . . I'll give you twenty pygmies from my village and you get them to howl! . . . beings, beasts who worship, grab, devour each other . . . I'll sell you their great moonlight, such a giant mirror of the night that it's as if the whole forest rose to the sky! . . . and the "tom-tom" and the sixteen witch doctors . . . six or seven prison floors can't match their wailings! . . . in prison they're raucous! . . . all the catwalks . . . traitors, thieves, sex maniacs, the innocent ones, they're all harsh gurglings! . . . the banshee, too: gravelly! . . . the abortionist, she gravels in two tones: "ouch" and "ow!" . . . but those pygmies in the forest, well, at the edge, they go at it the full range! clear stentorian tones! . . . Remember the name . . . the village: Bikobimbi! . . . Rio Cribi! . . . veritable cantors! At night, of course . . . at night! . . . from nature's depths! . . . You gotta hear that! . . . You gotta hear it! . . . it's the understanding of instincts, the accompaniment, the exercise in vocalization: "Dingua! . . . bouay! . . . saoa! . . . bouay! . . . ding . . . a! . . . bouay! . . . Ding . . . a! . . . bouay!" and drummed out all natural-like! . . . sixteen drumsticks going at a hollow tree trunk! . . . talk about spellbinding! watch out! From the elemental hollow! . . . Better not get too close! Me, I was a hundred meters away, my hut, not once did I go see . . . the Echo hollow is sacred! . . . nothing like the hollow of some dumb prison! . . . Take me, I can sing that pigmy stuff . . . still, to this day! . . . "Ding . . . a! . . . bouay! . . . and sao! . . . a! . . . bouay! . . ." It carries, I can tell you . . . I never watched their little parties, that was their business . . . They liked human meat but other meats as well, I'm sure . . . deer, warthog, buffalo . . . pythons . . . I had proof! . . . You gotta mind your own business! . . . discretion! . . . and no lies . . . I'm not making any of this up . . . nothing but facts! . . . Bikobimbo 1916! . . . They ate human meat on rue Caulaincourt . . . rue Carbonnière . . . rue Claude-Bernard . . . in the middle of Paris thirty years later! . . . so go talk about primitive! . . . And don't go tutt-tutting and get all shocked-like! . . . instincts will not be denied! There, there . . . my dear! pelts don't count, it's the meat! the flesh! Tom-Tom and tap-tap! . . . I'm drifting back, I'm being funny, I'm having a laugh! . . . but it's real, it's a fact: they didn't have malaria, or yellow fever, or the tsetse fly on rue Caulaincourt! cannibalism is nothing, but the tsetse fly! . . . So long live the entire rue Caulaincourt! and human meat!

I know what you'll say: he's delirious from fever! . . . Yes! You're right! True! but there was also the Tom-Tom! . . . You never saw this instrument! . . . A hollowed-out trunk, just like that, enormous . . . a sound like a cathedral! . . . plus the choir of nighttime gourmets that in turn was drowned out by the animal bacchanal, belly-ripping, throat-cutting lovecouplings of twenty-five zoos! wild beasts, jackals, elephants, birds, in the depths of the depths of the darkness! . . . Ah, the sounds of the forest, now that's something! . . . and I've even been told that the most sonorous night creature of them all, there, was the giant snail! Picture that! . . . and here I am shivering in my hut, from fever, from three-day fever . . . rattling myself right out of the "Picot" . . . You don't know the Picot bed? . . . the Picot, the colonial cot that earned us empires![195] . . . I was one big clanking Picot! . . . it's made up of all these little jangling rods! . . . your houseboys get a good laugh out of it! . . . and you are funny! and your teeth, your knees, your carcass, everything jingles and jangles . . . and how, do your houseboys have a laugh! . . . Creak! Creak! Creak, cute! just like Ciborium's wheelbarrow! . . . another one that jingled and jangled! jingle-jangulation all over the place! The way those guys would cart me off! and those cobblestones! such cobblestones! . . . and the tornado that we're gathering! . . . I've no doubt about it! I can see the writing on the walls! . . . Little tout bastards! They subject me to more horrors! the shrieks of the pygmies with the animals, the worst kind! . . . incredible saturnalia of matings, bloodcurdling gut spilling from the

kingdom come of darkness! . . . You should see the height of
the forests! . . . Ten . . . twenty times the oaks in Vincennes!
. . . You can bet they're killing each other, and not just a little,
under them! . . . and cooing to each other . . . and wailing . . .
It's more death rattling than prison . . . much more ferocious
than Charleroi, the Marne, Saint-Gond, Nagasaki![196] . . . humans lag behind the beasts . . . I'm comparing . . . no need to
be embarrassed . . . doesn't bother me . . . the noises I have in
my head! . . . I buzz far too much! . . . I give in to it, I get dizzy,
drop! scream! . . . bearing, first and foremost, character! . . .
but the noises triumph, I'm drunk, I yield . . . You figure what
the hell, you got out of it . . . Of course! . . . but the squadron?
. . . the colonel's cry, all alone, twenty meters ahead of the
standard? . . . spreading out in battle formation! . . . raise high
the sabres!

– Chaaaarge!

Order of the squadrons! . . . "Second! First! . . . Third! . . .
Fourth! . . ."

The fanning out of the charge – grandiose! . . . everything
vibrates . . . thunders! and the three brigades! the echelons!
. . . the division! . . . the twenty thousand cavalry horses thundering forward! The entire Army Corps! . . . can you hear the
rumbling coming up from the ground? . . . like one giant
mounting groan . . . the rising whirlwind of horses' hooves
. . . a rumbling from the ground that extinguishes everything
. . . even the artillery backup, the mobile units . . . who're
shooting there, see? . . . You no longer hear anything but the
swelling rumble from the ground . . . the rumbling fills everything! . . . the echo everywhere . . . now that's something to
hear again! . . . You're carried off, squeezed in on all sides, the
charge, knee to knee! . . . open tomb! . . . the echo right up to
the sky! to the sky! *Giddyap! Giddyap!* something to hear
again! . . . I can do what I like, I can hear it all again! . . . I do
the raging tropical storms . . . I create the grand maneuver
charges! . . . I do what I like here in my cell! . . . the artillery
backup! Had enough of Ciborium's wheelbarrow! . . . the

121

loonies out of the leeks! . . . Enough of their pee pee, too! . . . the way they urinate – a whole chorus line of them! . . . *Pfoui!* Dirty little boys! Get behind me, Elsa! To the devil with you, Toto! . . . I've no shortage of raging storms! . . . A noggin full of them! . . . Even when I've run through all my buzzings and then the "Tom-Toms," I still have a huge array of blasts stored up! . . . after the storm in my ear, lots of others! . . . lots! . . . many a man's sighs . . . little sighs . . . heftier ones . . . I've got little granddaddies who give up the ghost . . . not just one . . . twenty! ten! a hundred! . . . a little death rattle, it's over, no, another! . . . gasps, I've told you already . . . And the kinds of death rattles you don't hear any more! the way they suffocated with that croup we used to have! . . . maybe . . . just maybe you'll hear it still in a few children's hospitals . . . those sounds've become obsolete . . . like the watermills of a thousand years ago and the din raised by anvils . . . Museum noises! "Oh-hey, blacksmith!" . . . and *Boooom!* . . . Vulcan's dead! ironwork's dead! . . . Oh, Cavalry! the days of those deafening noises are over and that's all there is to it! . . . Museum noises! . . . Oh, but I'm retrospectiving for you! . . . mythologizing! . . . a lot, I give myself that little pleasure! . . . the one in 115 is no myth! or the one in 40, either, fiddlesticks! or the girl in 63! in chains and a strait jacket . . . but the worst, the worst of all, the "pip-cell" 17![197] In there they bark, all right! They dare! *"Waaaa! Waaaa!"* and such force! like me! No, not like me! . . . They're only copying me! I'll go cut their throats for them, that'll teach 'em! *"Meee! Meee!"* hear them? . . . I'm going over there! . . . I've got a shard from an old jug under my straw . . . *"Meee! Meee!"* I'm going to unstick my ass from this stool . . . I'll cross the corridor, I'll teach them to plagiarize me! . . . I've had too much grief from you plagiarizers already! One especially! a worse howler than all the rest! "Ooo-oww!" I cut his throat open! . . . I'll make you laugh at yourself, all right, you bloody assassin! . . . with all my might! . . . put him out of his misery there in 17! . . . but the screws will have to carry me, and the nurse! . . . they'll have to pour me on him! . . . on number 17! . . . Hurry, the stretcher! . . . all alone I'd collapse after two steps . . . they'll have to bump me along like in the wheelbarrow! . . . let them chuck me at him so I can cut his throat! . . . I'll slice open his trachea! . . . But the guards will have to help me . . . and the nurse, and two more cops . . . and then they'll have to write up a report . . . I'll teach that sonofa-bitchin' banshee how to behave, too! . . . I'll pass by his place on the way back . . . And I'll cut his goddamn throat, too! courtesy requires it! . . . I'm the only one allowed to bark, so there! just me! The Law! Me alone! . . . He'll be out of his misery! *"Waaaa! Waaaa!"* What if the dogs should get it all wrong? what if the pack starts barking with him? I'm done for! . . . They'll never give me another enema! nobody will bother to get off his ass again! . . . I can bark all I like for ten years! . . . Ah, it's incredible the nastiness, the viciousness of people, and the most pitiable rejects at that! go right ahead! they just have to do the dirty on you! Either I have exclusive barking rights, or I kick the bucket! At least I believe . . . I think . . . I want . . . but nobody'll come help me . . . I work myself up into a fury all by myself . . . I rattle the wall! . . . Doesn't do any fuckin' good! the banshee also rattles the wall! with his ugly mug, if you please! . . . he's rattling the wall on me! all I need! he interrupts my work, my train of thought . . . he warps my musings! I wish to hell he'd do his head in once and for all, the coward! . . . three big very strong bounds and *boooom!* with all his might! He could do it! He could do it, the jackass! . . . Head first! . . . his head gets in the way! The same old song! . . . millions of people, their head gets in the way . . . it's the Calamity of the World, the problem of the head! . . . so? . . . so? . . . So, nothing! . . . I'll see him again, banshee! I'll find him again! . . . I saw him once in the little alley to the cage . . . he's a kind of silly, shaggy youngish thing, but full of wrin-kles . . . I'll catch up with him in the infirmary . . . in the infir-mary I'll catch up with him . . . after he's messed up his fore-head a little bit . . . that's what he'll do to himself, scrape his skin, but no bones! . . . so? . . . he'll be bandaged and cottoned

123

up . . . if they drill his skull open that'll fix him! . . . maybe a little repair work on the head? . . . That's even worse! Worse! the hours I've lost on account of him, the fathead! . . . and Hortensia, too, his head! black libertine Louis XV king of France making every kind of proposal to me through the window . . . and if I strangled him what would he have to say? . . . I'd have to hoist myself up! . . . and what if I took advantage of the situation and hung myself while I was at it? . . . it's the right height! the bars! . . . the buildings in the distance! . . . Buildings are everything! . . . I see how real men live: like gods! . . . Oh, there's no jealousy on my part! There are those who carp! Who cares? I never utter a cry, raise a fuss, except for the enemas, of course! . . . two weeks you didn't do doo-doo, wouldn't you bark, too? . . . Oh, I'm not trying to move you! . . . saurian insensitivity! . . . just little miseries . . . okay! . . . The devil knows I'm of too noble a stripe to ask anyone to shed a tear over me . . . already with the pee pee, right? my business! . . . all you have to do is buy! . . . even-Steven and see ya later! . . . I've lost fifty-two kilos! pellagra and woes! . . . skin 'n' bones poet! . . . one breath of wind and I go flying! . . . they had to bundle me into their wheelbarrow . . . I gave them such trouble! the road, there, I saw how it was, every bump practically sent me flying! . . . They'd patch me up again . . . Therefore, all things considered, if you think about it honestly, I just can't give it all away to you . . . pellagra, legend, wheelbarrow, prison, think about it! . . . plus the song! . . . you wouldn't want to take advantage! . . . *Fable,* okay! . . . but the flower? . . . and the little stanza, hold on, the little verse!

> *I'll find you some dark night*
> *I'll show you, Estreme!*
> *Dead meat in my rifle's sight*

Pellagra is amusing, well, in a way . . .

> *Your dumb cow of a soul'll be gone in a glance!*

The word, the thing, too . . . are you of a historical bent at all?

124

pellagra, the Portsmouth prison ships?[198] The Grand Army prisoners, don't ring any bells for you? God knows they suffered, those poor bastards, and cruelly, much worse than me! . . . Pellagra killed them off, all right! . . . No cell windows for them! . . . No exercise yard! . . . No five minutes in the open air! just a little porthole for a hundred men! . . . rats had better conditions . . .

– Greetings, brave prisoners of yesteryear! Brothers in suffering! Vive la France! all forty-two kilos of meat of ya! Chaaaaarge!

I'd crack under the strain! . . . the Portsmouth prisoners, too! . . . Heavy cavalry! . . . Light artillery! . . . Eblé's Pioneers! . . . The Empress's White Dragoons![199] . . . Riflemen wasted away, so putrid they could hardly see . . . so you can imagine me as a Cuirassier! Jeez, they wouldn't even take me as a hussar any more![200] Couldn't mount the damn thing! A sorry sight! I'd fly right off the saddle! . . . the horsy goes nuts! . . . Where's my rider? . . . in the air! nobody'd have me any more! the Invalides mannequins?[201] . . . Probably wouldn't even let me into any of their crummy pictures! . . . Would the Bats have me? The Grévin?[202] . . . Nobody! The specters! . . . "The First Specters"?[203] yeah, maybe . . . What can I expect? . . . I'm fearful! . . . Session! . . . Tribunal! . . . Explanations! . . . we're dragged before the Appeals . . .

– Comeuppance! . . . What have you done with your medal? . . . Your pension? . . . Your enlistment? . . . You'd better watch yourself! . . .

It's me they're attacking!

– Enlistment year '10? . . .

This is not fun.

– Your commission? Class of '10? Show us! . . .

Not the moment for evasive replies! nothing but categorical! factual! . . . The Law! Period!

– What the fuck did ya do with your medal? . . . your rank? They're on the attack again! . . .

– Your wounds? citations? War-service chevrons? . . .

They're implacable.

They were putting on the pressure, I can tell you! just the facts! Don't be giving us any of your nonsense! . . . never mind the patients! never mind the men! the women! . . . never mind all the horrors I've been through!

They're gasping to hear. They do try my indulgence.

– Accomplice! disgusting! Coward! loafer!

Their prosecutor takes one look at me.

He shouts his lungs out in my face!

I mumble, whimper . . . Bozo! . . . whatever it takes to get you the hell out of there![204] . . . I do the dumb-ass jailbird act! . . . I play the game! . . . I try everything! . . . But the judge doesn't give a fuck! . . . I deny everything! I retract . . . I take responsibility for everything! . . . What do you expect with the likes of them as judges! . . . I infuriate them three times over! . . . Verdict and away you go! On with the sentence!

– No mercy for those who besmirch heroes! burning scabs on all Iconoclants!

That's their Sentence.

– Take pity on him! Take pity on him!

I don't abandon you, I beg for mercy!

But you're already on fire, every part of you! . . . I weep, I lament . . . you, your pores already on fire! . . . And on all fours and gagged, ligated! . . . I know what it's like, on all fours, the hide on fire! . . . me, too, I'm burning up with pellagra! to the quick! . . . My skin's being torn off me, I tell you! . . . right off me! . . . on all fours I'd clean my cell! . . . well, as well as I could . . . I'd soak my ass in the pale . . . I can't take it any more! . . . I understand your sufferings . . .

Oh, but the judge's getting impatient.

– Let's get this show on the road!

He's had enough of my ramblings . . .

And you, you see it all! look at everything! you don't miss a bit of the show . . . you can see very well on all fours! the Column unscrews from the square, lifts itself up, up! on its own!

all by itself! and *buuuump!* comes crashing down on his face!
... do you realize what that means? ... it's the cosmomediumnic storm! ... the point where the whole awful reality comes
crashing back! ... but not on my account! It wasn't my fault!
... I didn't want to unleash the forces! ... certain forces! ... I
had very kindly warned everyone, all up and down ... you'll
have to admit ... so? ... obstinacy? ... *Tic!* ... *Toc!* ... *Tic!* ...
Toc! the clock? the little ticking? ... the real clock? ... I have
no desire to unleash the forces ... certain forces ... but you!
stomping, pounding, howling, you're beyond everything! ...
you leave Time behind! ... blast through the web! ...

– Grab what's left of it! ... you shout ... the Laboratory's in
for it! ... test tubes, converters, fine crystals ... there you go
with the ax! emboldened! with the full force of your arms!
pulverizing finesse, modesty, waves! You're completely carried away! ... me, too! ... the cosmomediumnic storm groans
on ... the Column goes sky high! and *buuuump!* falls down
again! tears the asphalt asunder! ... blasts through the very
essence of everything! you're swallowed up!

All of History's catastrophes come but from the bile of the
Stubborn One! you've got the devil in you, too, no mistake!
just as stubborn! ... but not enough to knock down my wall!
... not infuriated to death! ... you'd rattle it on me like the
banshee! not any harder! You'd chip two or three bricks on
me ... that'd be it! no more! you'd knock down nothing! happy just to raise a bit of a fuss! He's only pretending, the banshee! he hurtles himself! looks as if! all the way? no! ... He
doesn't kill himself, that's always how it is! ... he doesn't kill
himself! ... You'd be the same ... if he really slammed himself
with all his strength his puss would be mush ... his goose
cooked! ... I could work away happy as can be! ... you, you
wouldn't hurtle yourself, either, out of your tree, but not
touched! ... all for a lark, but not a loon! ... a fine sly one! ...

When you come down to it, don't you know, when the time
comes, the tribunal will weigh it all up! It's not what I can or I
can't say that's gonna save you from a mug-shot number! Oh,

lordy, no! Oh, my longanimity! so I blather on to the point of bursting? . . . blather enough for a hundred years of head-aches? Won't I look great? blah-blah-blatheries over nothing, that's life! Cherished blah-blahs! It all comes down to one thing: Verdict and up! "Get 'im while he's hot!" Where will they send you in your state? . . . you're crisply sizzling, your soul's in little peaked flames on your head! . . . flickering? Don't you look terrific! Will they send you to the "*Two-Two-Four*"?[205] I wouldn't be surprised! . . . there you see some swaying and dipping that go on forever! I don't want to do anyone a disfavor, but a lot of the time you see the worst kind of felon at the "*Two-Two-Four*" . . . not to mention at the "*Be-tween-two-stools*"! that's another dance hall! . . . there you got all the dances from one century to the next . . . three, four centuries sometimes! . . . if you have the time to enjoy it!

> *Look at all those people prance!*
> *Knowing full well how to dance!* . . .

and with the flounces they used to wear! with mimes! Staged games! all those phosphorescent eyes of the dead! all the lights from the beyond! Ah, nothing's left out! the whole hog at the First Specters!

> *But here's Aunt Estreme!*
> *And her little Leo!*
> *Here's Clementine and the valiant Toto!* . . .

Remember?

> *Must we tell our friends every party ends?*

All this at a very fast beat! you take right off!

I'm singing here, but I can't take off, I'm stuck . . . but when I get out there with you, I'll twirl you round and round, mar-quis! the ass no longer glued! . . . you'll see what this dance partner can do! . . . here I'm just accompanying myself, that's all, I'm humming . . . if I could get up, I'd crash right back down again . . . the dizziness, *plop!* I stagger, I puke! . . . a good thing my ass is glued! . . . I sway, I pitch, I compose . . . see, don't even need the shivers, to be chilled to the bone, etc. song comes naturally! . . . Artist in spite of it all! I sing as they torture me! . . . Cocotte sings during torture, too! . . . not to mention Rangon! . . . and his wee woman! . . . it winds up being piggy, this "Torture Song"[206] . . . so I better not mention it here . . . especially seeing as I'm so slandered! I got word through my walls of rumors out of Batignolles that I'm a habitual drunk . . . me! who never drank anything but water! . . . goes to show you what hatred cooks up! . . . They put out that I'm a sadist or a wise aleck in prison? I'm in for ten more years with the "Specters"! good night! I'm stoical, myself, ever so agreeable! I don't howl at the pitch the banshee does! far from it! he could bring my wall down one of these days! . . . as I said . . . if he really threw himself into it! from the bottom, the very bottom of his hole! . . . and I'd say, now there's a man of integrity, all right! . . . he's sacrificing his skull! . . . fine! okay! Me, if I took a flying leap, you'd see! . . . it wouldn't be pussyfooting around! . . . It would be with a brass band! On my terms! a brass band! with 156 trumpets and horns and cymbals! kettledrums! brass band, every last instrument! . . .

– Hussars, prepare to charge! Chaaaarge! . . .

Sabres high! but who'd want me in the Hussars? . . . Nobody! . . . Not any more! . . . Maybe the Cuirassiers? That's a laugh! my rickety little bones! my rotting flesh! They send me to fry inside my cuirass! wherever I go! wherever I leave! and yet that's the soul of it, the charge is everything! "Chaaaarge!" Colonel Des Entrayes twenty lengths ahead of the squadron! standing straight up in his stirrups! sabre high! white plume! mane blowing in the wind! his one commandment: "Chaaarge!" the fourteen squadrons shudder into life . . . the tornado is launched! . . . the banshee is charging, too, next door! . . . and *va va va voom!* . . . he collapses . . . he starts again! . . . you gotta laugh at him! . . . he's shaking my wall . . . three bricks . . . he shakes them up for me . . . you gotta laugh at him! . . .

– That's right, neighbor, go right ahead!

It takes a lot of heart to knock down a wall! . . . not just a laugh! . . . everything is in the charge! . . . when you think about it . . . daydream about it . . . where was it that we charged? . . . it's forcing me! . . . it's forcing me to think, time . . . just where did we charge? where? at Longchamp, of course! at Longchamp with the trumpets and drums! as if I were there right now! at Longchamp before the great July![207] The Mill! The Mill! "Chaaarge!" Colonel Des Entrayes, as if I were there! His sword glinting! The authority of the man! "Squadrons"! the Dragoons! and the "Light Brigade"! General Des Urbales! "Seventh Independent Mobile"! takes up the entire wing at deployment! Twenty-seven squadrons flying! the entire Paris cavalry and the Guard and the eleven brass bands go right to the grandstands! "Those who are about to die salute you!" Sixteen regiments at full speed stop on a dime and face the president! Twelve thousand horses, heads tossing, neighing, send foam high into the sky . . . it comes down in a shower of white . . . it covers everything . . . flakes everywhere . . . Infantry . . . Engineer Corps! . . . even the "sausage" zeppelin – fifty strong Meudon Sappers are needed to keep it on the ground![208] All the train wagons under froth! under froth like so many tankards of beer! . . . Colonel Des Entrayes, General Des Urbales, standing erect in their stirrups, raise their swords in salute! the cannons thunder! the sun throws such blinding fire onto the steel, the breastplates, the coppers, the big crates that thirty years later your eyes are still blinking! your soul no longer knows where it is . . . has no age, nothing . . . the grandstands seem to be throbbing . . . from the ear-splitting hurrahs of the multitude! . . . and the colors! . . . the masses a blur . . . delirious tramping of patriots' feet . . . a hundred thousand maws agape . . . two hundred thousand . . . a halo of rising breath . . . I see through it! . . . I see the parasols and the plumed hats . . . I see the boas . . . floods of wafting feathers . . . blue . . . green . . . rose . . . as though cascading from the Grandstand! . . . the world of fash-

130

ion! of high fashion! chiffon everywhere . . . floods of orange
. . . mauve . . . nothing but elegance from top to bottom . . .
such fragile things . . .

"Those who are about to die salute you!" . . .

And now the "Sabre-et-Meuse"! and the Chasseurs' "Sidi-
Brahim"! . . . The giant clamor when the crowd hears those!
and now the positioning of the cannon on the move! Ah! the
Legion! Ah, the "Marsouins"![209] holy mackerel! more than
any play would ever do for you! . . . It's the entire nation united! That's ardor for you! . . . the entire Bois de Boulogne! . . .
over that way the heights of Saint-Cloud . . . the noise echoes
back to us! unfurls! farther still the echo rebounds!
. . . The horizons, the green hilltops of Enghien well up
around us! . . . perhaps we're being carried off by the force of
the tides of tumult around us! . . . astounding! . . . the skies
swell, move, here and there they break with shouts of "Vive la
France!" . . .

From his box, all alone under the red canopy way up high,
Mr. Poincaré salutes us![210]

I'm sketching for you a bit of the fervor, the perspiration,
the grandstands, the sun, the boas, the helmets, the crests,
the mounted artillery, the Dragoons, the charge . . . the "Do
You See Them?"[211] . . . the vast movement of the flanks! . . .
how engrossing it all is . . . forty squadrons acting as one!
. . . what a sprint! . . . engulfed! . . . "La Pépinière" . . . "Vincennes," "Dupleix"[212] . . . twenty regiments! . . . such escutch-
eons! . . . from the 12th, the 7th, the 102nd! glories such as
we'll never see again! two hundred trumpets! . . . and such
strident tones! Something else again than Roland's thickety-
thackety quickety-quackety horn! tubby thumpings from his
drums!

So you see I'm depicting everything for you! . . . nothing
left out . . . so you won't die without knowing what the Review of the Great Souls was all about! France! in July! and the
families of supporters gripping on to the mill, the sails, the
ivy, roaring their applause! There are sublime moments, what

can I say! . . . the weighing-in, the diplomats, you picture magnificent things! . . . all the Top Brass of Paris! . . . some memories overwhelm you . . . you recall them, you go all wonky, you're reeling with emotion! . . . I'm okay, my ass is glued! . . . I teeter, I sway! I don't fall! . . . right face! . . . about face! . . . I can't fall! . . . "Chaaaarge!" all the Top Brass of Paris! . . . high up in the stands! the little guy up there, black as a little licorice candy man, that's him! . . . that's the president! The little gray pasty-faced guy! . . . with his little high hat: The Nation personified! . . . you're gasping for breath, mad with fervor! *Chaaaarge!* . . . if you don't believe me just look at the way they surge forward! and Flanders, too! . . . *Chaaaarge!* General Des Urbales! Attention! one! two brigades! on the outer flank! . . . the plumes! . . . Entrayes! Entrayes! . . . start over again! the general's been wounded! . . . the attack on Craonne! "To your standards! Rally!" you hesitate? . . . tough luck for you! the squadrons surge forward! . . . Time . . . Time . . . the tornado envelops you, spins you around, sends you flying to the devil! . . . didn't I warn you? . . . this is your final reprieve! . . . the jury, after deliberations behind closed doors, my pains in vain! What could I do? the Verdict is everything! execution! where do I go to disinter your bones? Die, you hateful dumb fucks! you wanted a Shindig, you'll get one! Auntie Estreme and all the rest! Make up your mind, God damn it! . . . time is ticking away . . . three! . . . two . . . one! . . . like the Eiffel Tower clock![213] . . . a nod is not as good as a wink! . . . all recourse is vain! the jury members of the "First Specter" have chains for rosary beads and they're praying! . . . praying hard! . . . all the members of the public are praying! . . . each link a century more! . . . another century for you to suffer the tortures of hell! . . . the more stubborn you are the more centuries you get! . . . they need to be distracted from their duties . . . them, think about it, those ghosts, with their ball-and-chains . . . they have to get revenge, they whose sins were mere peccadilloes . . . who're doing Eternities . . . who night after night drag cartloads of metal around with them! . . . boy, are they happy to sit down for once and watch you prancing about there, trying to wriggle out of it . . . You're in a pretty fix now! . . . Quite a shroud you're wearing now! You and your usual clever antics! . . . you refuse to give in? redeem yourself in one go? . . . too bad! . . .

"All fame to Ferdinand! Buy it! *Fable! Fable!* All fame and billions to Ferdinand!"

If you shouted that out with all your heart from the depths of your chest cavity, you'd already feel a helluva lot better! Not quite saved yet! No! but you know, already, your stink . . . you'd smell a bit less . . . it's through smells that things go better . . . You still won't quite have reached Sanctity! but still 'n all . . . still 'n all . . . whereas, the state you're in at the moment . . . can you picture yourself in front of the judge? it'd be a massacre! . . . You're reduced to a bunch of slogans and blah-blah, your glottis is in your crotch, you're blabbering some dumb hunk of shit or another, cowardly nasty things, madly denouncing people, you cover yourself in more caca all the time! put more and more umph in it! really getting it off your chest! *hoc! hoc! hoc!* broken record! don't you look cute! . . . I can just see myself breaking my back pleading your cause! ghastly job! . . . tying myself in knots . . . it's your slate, honey! . . .

"Has pillaged, outraged, tracked down, imprisoned, dirtied, a hero! inflicted a thousand satanic acts on him, a thousand thousand shameful acts! appalling acts!"

Just see how the Court takes to you! How the state prosecutor shuts you up! closes your trap! muzzles you! So what am I going to contradict? They've got it all photographed in waves! Capers, somersaults, suspicions, deeds! Even your intentions! Yeah, you'd look great! . . . you're impossible to defend! . . . Not that I'd play it up, concede a point, go off on a tangent . . . oh, not at all! nothing of that! admit anything? . . . Never! on the contrary, I'd lay it on ten times thicker! play the clown! hey, I'm really enjoying this! . . . but go on, let me touch these untouchables! . . . shake up these members of the jury from the Other World! . . .

– Stay in your trance, pal, they're saying, keep fantasizing . . . we're getting a good laugh out of you!

Those who see inside you, think of the fun they're having! . . . those who have the penetrating "milli" waves! . . . I told you! . . . I can go on blabbing!

– Ah, this weirdo's something else! they're thinking as they clink and chime! . . . their bones banging into each other! . . . their way of grinning at the thought.

Especially since you're making a mess of it, of course.

– He got his medal grabbed off of him! . . .

And there you go laughing your leg off! Twisting all over! . . . you're not even aware of your crimes any more!

– Take pity on him! Pity on him!

I'm jeopardizing myself on your behalf? too bad!

It's frightful to be in your situation . . .

The presiding judge strikes his mallet, three cops emerge, great big Cyclopses . . .

– Take pity on him!

But those are my last words.

They grab a hold of you, they tie you up, they skin you thoroughly alive! your hide is steaming! . . .

It's written, in the Code . . . "Outrage against good people: *Reversal!* . . ." the "Code of the Specters" . . . not three! not ten penances! . . . just a single one! . . . and who gives a willy about the "circumstances"! . . . the Law is all! I break my back for you, I want them at least to give you back your hide! I'm sublime, you'll grant me that! . . .

Ho-hum!

– How long? how wide? Clerk, take note!

All I can get them to do is to "take note"!

And you there who's howling, steaming! and that's just for starters! . . . after the fleecing, the crunching! . . . roasting and darding! . . . they vivify your deep wounds, they powder them

134

with their own spices . . . bet your ass you jig high again after that! look at those legs go! . . . there'll be no weakening on the butcher block . . . they want none of that! They whip you up into quite a farandole! aren't you the sight! dancing like the devil! all around the Prosecutor! . . . and then a little variation on the Tarentella! . . . with very quick lively steps! . . . with other inflections! other lutes! . . . and then all of a sudden a hundred trombones! letting rip right there! thunderous rumblings! it's as if you're shot up stark naked! Spinning around like an egg on top of the water spout! . . . Whooosh! you're the egg! Devilish damnation with all kinds of laughing choral accompaniment! violet laughing! yellow! green! red! laughing on the other side of your goddamn ugly puss! piggy giggling, oinking! . . . the thigh slappers, the sillier-than-silly, can't even say it, like some dumb jack-in-the-box with the cover that keeps popping open and slamming shut: *pop! pop!* and even stupider than that! . . . so much so that you die you're so sick of the sound of it, even though you're there oozing blood, in strips of flesh, outraged at the too too stupid laughter . . . but the Clerk won't let you die . . . If he doesn't go at you again with that whip! lash! . . . it's his job! Thrasher of the Great Felons! . . . his birch is crackling, the tip all aflame! . . . He knows how to revive your zeal!

– You gonna laugh, you shredded Crybaby? Laugh yourself blue? You gonna laugh yourself green? . . . On the other side of your face?

And the strappado starts all over again! . . . your complete splintering! . . . each one of the judges takes a turn at the blazing martinet, vies with the others to plump up your zeal! . . . damn sure you spin around then! . . . you picture it? . . . special prize in the Tarentella stakes! . . . your raw ass . . .

I will not appear to be enjoying any of this . . . Oh, not at all! . . . they lard you, they sauté you . . . they interrupt their rosary, they roast you jigging alive, that's how they get their kicks . . . didn't I warn you? . . . *Extremis!*

Quick, disavow your villainies before hell engulfs you!

shout out your confession! bleat it out! that you'll never again wind up a coward, a double dealing, bile-spewing, dumb jerk of an informer . . .

But mind you! the confession can't be whispered! half farted out! Oh, no! You gotta shout it from the rooftops! Stentorian tones! so the echoes couldn't get any louder! the echoes should go on forever and ever! . . . and ever . . . and ever . . .

"Hardon renounces his Error! desists! cleanses! rights himself! Dedicates himself!"

Louder than the one in 115 I hear you! than the arsonist! . . . louder than 27! louder than the banshee!

"Hardon renounces his Error! Hardon renounces his Error! Dedicates himself! . . . Dedicates himself! . . . Dedicates himself! . . ."

And no coy disavowals, either! No, no, no, no, no! Belt it out!

"Buy *Fable!* the book that rejuvenates your soul! makes your belly belly-laugh! turns your cares to dust! . . . likewise your moods, woes, and wounds! . . . turns everything rosy, deflates spleen and bile! pocondria![214] not just any old work! not just any old words! *Fable!*"

You gotta be categorical.

No embarrassed murmurings as if you were shitting in your pants! . . . No, no, no! . . . it must be in broad daylight in a public place! vociferated! At the crossroads, in a square, at the Tuileries, for example! . . . hey, maybe at the Halles, even better! . . . where there's lots of people, at the fish market! . . . you take charge, you exalt, your voice is the only thing that can be heard . . . you cover the storm of gaping mouths, auctions, wagons, hawkers . . .

– You can go without food, but buy *Fable! Fable* of the senses and of the passions! and a laugh! He who reads *Fable* dines. He who reads *Fable* is no longer hungry. Ever! you can do without ortolan! . . . you can do without Houdan chicken, paupiettes, sweetbreads, but *Fable!* You can do without puking up your liver, your gallbladder (in such a state!), but *Fable!* Quick, go get the Little Sisters so that they can rid you of the toxins! excesses! leg of lamb! beans! truffles! partridge! at the Little Sisters of the Poor, at St. Eustache, the whole lot of it, at St. Vincent de Paul's! ortolans, bries you can't get for love nor money, benedictines, Medocs, pheasants! Sacrifice it all! Buy *Fable!*

Revolution in Les Halles! and it's not over yet! It's only just beginning! . . . a hop, a skip, and a jump! and you're at the Stock Exchange! 1 P.M.! you tootle over onto the steps! I see you camped out, screeching your lungs out!

– Fuck the stocks and bonds! fuck the "Rios" and the "Tintos"![215] Clerks, cretins, cuckolds, gogos, you go buy anything else and you're dead! Wipe out the List![216]

The Paris Stock Exchange at your mercy! All the lost souls rush hither and thither! . . . The columns curl, collapse! . . . all gone! . . . An enormous cloud rises up over Paris . . . the sky darkens all black . . . it's the Stocks! up in smoke! . . . You shed a tear, that's all. You collect your wits and off you go! your Evangelization begins! just the beginning! . . . the Champs Elysées! . . . Another multitude! The maharajahs! cocktails! . . . the trend setters . . . it's that time of day! The setters, the set, the settled, the unsettled, the senders, the sent! You go to it! port! stout! flip! . . . onto the sidewalk! . . . get me a table!

At your feet, awestruck, subdued, the most fatuous people in the world, the most het up, vainglorious people . . .

– If you haven't got *Fable* you're just a crummy bumpkin! Shit-kicking loser, ignoramus, barbarian! You've got a future in getting fucked up the ass!

That's your public confession!

Just see how things hop then! . . . you lay it on thicker! . . . you turn and chuck them your straight line! . . .

– See this? Thanks to *Fable* it's twice the size!

They've turned around.

I see you looming over these huddled masses, tongue lashing them with it! What a scene! . . .

They file out one after the other, quacking, whistling, squeaking . . .

– *Fable! Fable!* nothing else will do!

The women go nuts. The men go nuts.

They rush to lambast the Judge! shake his gates for him![217] Paris is boiling over! . . . Oh, but you're not off the hook yet! . . . Eight o'clock, the place des Ternes slot! . . . There, your final propaganda coup! swarms and swarms of people, black fever, the gorgements and disgorgements of the metro! Movies! public meetings! nudy shows, seminudy shows! . . . they go out, they go in! . . . you stop them all in their tracks! . . . I see you imposing your will on them from on high! . . . haranguing them from a bench!

– So where do you think you're going, little lad and lady bugs? . . . all you chambermaids in heat, jittery priests, lousy bookkeepers, Sapphic schoolgirls, prostatic widowers, Fualdès's sheep for the slaughter,[218] shopkeepers on the skids, peasants without eggs, snot-nosed lawyers, where do you think you're going? . . . Throw money away you don't even have to get swallowed up by fake-tit girly shows, by bogus hells, phony politicians, sham music, fake-ass fakers all sorts! Get a hold of yourself, you with your counterfeit curiosity! get a copy of *Fable!* that's all you need! Go home with just a copy of *Fable* under your arm! . . . you don't need to talk about this, about that, about the other thing! You don't need to reason! You don't need to understand anything! You can do without the Blessed Sacrament! you can do without looking up! . . . looking down! . . . sideways . . . the curvaceous legs a few feet in front of you . . . the planes thirty . . . sixty . . . three thousand feet high! . . . your goddamn nose way down at the bottom of your wallet! . . . buy *Fable!* the rest you can torch! . . . every last bit of it! What are you waiting for? Citizens! crimizens! loose little lads and lassiennes!

How your every utterance will be greeted! Such hurrahs! But just go get toppled from your high horse, oh ye mob's idol!

138

– To the cop-shop with you! you pile of shit! you liar!

See if you're not pummeled, garroted, pelted! . . . Oh, but you're as stout hearted as a lion! roaring, biting, lacerating!

– *Fable! Fable!* the Code can go fuck itself!

The cops knock out seven or eight of your pearly whites . . . the Press takes note . . . it's no longer a book launch, it's a stampede . . . I'm dragged into Civil Court again,[219] you with me! all hell breaks loose!

That's how things go with our friend Bozo, but imagine it otherwise . . . just imagine you're really not well . . . sick, bedridden, crabbed . . . you've got a right to be! . . . you've had your problems, you're worried . . . Oh, you don't feel like laughing now, do you? . . . you're in the grip of some nasty disease . . . cancer, let's say . . . don't go making out you're surprised! . . . you've been haunted by the idea for a good while now! . . . how many hours have you wasted already staring yourself cross-eyed up the ole asshole? . . . turning yourself upside down and inside out, a mirror in front of you, a mirror behind, crouched down, your arms and legs all over the place, weeping, your nose in your hemorrhoids, sniffing at yourself over and over again? . . .

No ifs, ands, or buts! I know what you're like! The one and only exercise that makes any sense when that certain uncertain moment comes is the on-your-knees! the super-bend into an O! into a Z! the entire torso arched over, like a bridge, at the hips! your head between your legs, snooping around under your testicles . . . so the entire body forms a J! a Y! your nose busy being squashed between your buttocks! Oh, my God, your schnoz is stained! right there and everything! stained how? is it caca or blood? . . . and the universal question! you start all over again! panting from the very bottom of the hole, your body inside out! sink that schnoz in! deeper! come on! . . . doubled four times over . . . six . . . seven times over . . . breathe it in . . . more! more! panting! your heart going . . . thump! thump! "to be M.D. or not to be M.D.?" what the hell do you think? nothing at all! . . . just your hole! . . .

your fartbox inside out! . . . dive back in again with gusto! . . . pyuush! . . . till your lungs can't take it any more! . . . you suffocate! and pyuush again! right to the tail end of the sono-fabitch!

– Help! Help! what? . . . what? my ass? . . . Your nose is one big clot of what? who?

– What? . . . oh, my God! Doctor! Oh, my all! What? of what?

There you are hanging there, in the vice-grip of your buttocks, inside out, stomach churned in anguish . . .

Not just one specialist . . . ten! twenty! a hundred!

"What . . . what . . . my ass?" You've already been to see the specialist . . . "Doctor! Doctor! . . . my daughter! my wife! my mother! my nephew Luke! my castles on the Loire! the contents of my twelve safes! it's all yours for a new ass! I'll give it all to you! . . ."

You've been back twenty times! They examined your ass till they were cross-eyed . . . nose out of joint, nodding . . . plugged up your asshole but good . . . stuck gauze up there ten . . . twenty times! . . . hum? . . . hum? . . . nodding again, rewhiffing . . . you only more and more confused . . . the number of times you went at it yourself, *at home!* . . .

– Get me the Larousse! Get me the Larousse![220] Help!

You've gobbled up twenty Larousses! old ones, new ones! . . . panic makes your hole so tight that you have to bust your gut getting back in there, harder! harder!

– Oh, bitchery! Ole iron behind! Back! there, where the hole is! Look, for God's sake! speak! Sphinx of a hole! Tell the whole!

And there you are again, re-redoubled four times over! eight times over! Gymnastics in the mirror! the three-quarter view below, the half behind! Damned Larousse! How divine it must be to be a gibbon! Why couldn't the goddamn gods have made you a gibbon? . . . a real gibbon! infinite flexibility! . . . A stiff neck floors you, beats you down, ranting acrobat, your nose stuck in caca and blood! no mistake! deeper! go on, deeper! . . . one cramp and you're all twisted out of shape! a dagger shoots out of your guts! . . . "owww!" you cry out . . . "owww!" you fall in an unconscious heap . . . but pain then grabs you in the lumbar! wakes you up, all right! . . . your doctor's there looking at you.

– Be brave, he tells you, be brave! . . .

Brave? Be brave? the tongs? the dagger? tearing your guts out, your kidneys raw? How come he doesn't talk to you about that? . . . how the meat inside your bones is aching . . . How come he doesn't see that? . . .

– Be brave, my friend! Up you get! A walk is what you need! Doctor's orders!

You're obedient in everything . . . on all fours at first . . . and then hunched over your two sticks . . . buckled over like a millenarian! . . . centenarian ten times over of suffering . . . weeping, blabbering, spewing . . . all tensed up over your canes . . . the people passing by wonder . . . turn around . . . not to them you're talking! to yourself! the lot! the truth! the horror of it! rumination! over and over!

– Just hemorrhoids like Grandma had?

Ah, the joy that wells up inside you all of a sudden! Jolts you! You do a flip-flop on your crutches! the joy! such joy! just little ole hemorrhoids like Grandma's? . . . oh, it would be just like a fairy tale! adorable! you swell with excitement! We've got Providence on the runs! as benign as Anselm's, Edward's cousin! why not, by the devil? why not? You can no longer contain yourself! Ah, renewal! Ah, hope breathes again!

But oh! too good to be true! Optimism skulks away! you can't breathe! too strong! the exaltation too high! You grunt . . . you're weak at the knees . . . you fall back to the bottom! the abyss! the abyss! It always comes back to Pascal!

– So the tumor is like Elvira's? Paul's sister's? . . . a huge fuckin' thing, fantastically bloody, that stuck out of her sides, out of her back, from her gaping, corroded lungs . . .

Anxiety grabs hold of you again, you topple over.

– Aaah! Aaah! The Larousse! Get me the Larousse!
You drag yourself up again, bellowing . . .
– The Larousse for God's sake!
Trot, trot to the Larousse!
And off you go again, upstream without a paddle . . .
– Home! Gotta get home!
You sink your nose into its pages again! . . . Page after page
you cut! . . . all those words! . . . deeper, come on! . . . in the
name of God! . . . deeper! . . . out of breath! . . . you'll never
find out enough! Which one of these is like my asshole? . . .
Back on all fours again! Come on! . . . geneticist! anatomist!
gymnast! comparative pathologist! A page torn out, single
handed! from the Larousse! and your whole body upside
down, your face between the crack in your ass! and now the
second step in the operation: comparison! A little clot at the
end of your nose . . . right then and there you take a sampling
in vivo . . . the truth will out! . . . wracking your brains for
precedents in the family! . . . does it look like mama's hole?
her final moments! on the torn-out page, there! . . . cross-eyed
is what you are! . . . you're cross-eyed, one eye on the page
. . . the other up your hole . . . And you can't get your uncle
out of your mind! good ole Uncle Charlie! his last days! . . . all
the sorrow and the fear welled up in the throat . . . and you
remember cousin Paul, who died in a taxi . . . now how was it
he died? . . . did they say it was an aneurysm? . . . did they ever
find out? . . . your neck bent all out of shape, in a word completely topsy-turvied under you, your nose like a fish hook up
your farter . . .

And how, do those intimate details come back to you! . . .
more and more frenetically, ferociously . . . The Family Album . . . The Album . . . the real one! . . . the only one! . . . The
Rectum Album! how? how did Leona die, anyway? the mi-
nutest details of her death throes . . . now was that mother's
sister or only half sister? . . . racist, genealogist, insatiable,
your foraging nose, infinite quests . . .

– So how did Leona die, anyway? . . . don't remember

much about that one . . . Ah, foolish youth! . . . puzzling questions! . . . Unmentionable doubts! . . . Ah, Holy Spirit! . . . Charles! . . . Mao! . . . Joseph![221] two thousand sphinxes! . . . time is no longer! . . . The Past! . . . Nothing! . . . Everything! . . . My heavenly kingdom for a hemorrhoid! . . . maybe a carcinoma like Emil? . . . Could be . . . could be after all . . . That's what his widow said: a carcinoma . . .

Ah, Holy Spirit! . . . Charles! . . . Mao! . . . Joseph! Who'd have thought it would be Emil? Emil, who was like Hercules! Jeez, what a build! . . . talk about vitality! and such a sweetheart! the shirt off his back! . . . his sister told us: it started as just a booboo! . . . *Whack!* and there you go again diving in again backward! . . . Emil, of all people! unbearable to think about! . . . Your schnoz stays way up your rectum . . . and here you were starting to hope again! Alas! Alas! all the horrors come welling up again! . . . from the depths! suffocating, praying . . .

– All-present God! Thee, God! Ass! Anus! . . .
You are heard.
– Not me, God who is good! Not me! My ass is a good boy! Pleading! your cries!
– Take any ass you like! spare mine! spare mine! my daughter! my wife! my son-in-law! spare mine! my girlfriend Primprenelle's, take hers! take hers! spare mine! spare mine! my dog! my little Andre, too! take theirs! take theirs!

The only real, serious, fervent prayer that isn't hot air in the air for the last two thousand years! . . .

If your Creator is listening!
– Twenty kingdoms for an ass in prime condition! thirty if you like! A thousand! for only a hemorrhoid! . . . Take back my turd-maker! give me a new one! give me two! anything you'd like!

Your infinite sincerity! Pascal's Spaces? . . . you're there! . . . the fright! the hole! the abyss! everything! It wouldn't take much for you to become a saint – just one less drop of blood up the anus hole!

143

Oh, but I'm a bit too graphic for you? Shame on those who skirt the issue! The statistics are there! . . . Face it! . . . Soon there'll be more cancer than warts! That's what the world's coming to! . . . the truth, period! It's an apartment you're looking for? . . . Nonsense! your heinie! your heinie first and foremost! on your knees! and down to the hole and look at it till you're cross-eyed! mirror in front! the other with a three-quarter view! the truth! the abyss! Pascal! the cancer's spreading! . . . the number of victims grows and grows . . . six, seven out of ten people die of it! . . . and mind you, not just old folks! . . . lots of infants, lots of little girls making their First Communion . . . Nature's one big tease! She's annoyed at you for something, she tickles two or three of your atoms, and there you are, all puzzlized, you don't know where the hell you are! . . . you got two spleens instead of one, three! . . . an eye in the pit of your stomach! . . . your entire sempiternal flank busted open! . . . nature mascarades you . . . from the inside . . . two porcupines take root in your pleura, make themselves at home, nibble away at your diaphragm . . . phantasmagoria triumphs! . . . a whole half of your face is bleeding, dislocated, tumefied . . . wads of stinking flesh fix a permanent smile on your face . . . nature has a laugh!

– Oh, fecund in the black arts! you sink and twist back down into your sodden turf, shivering, howling.

– Nature, you're a pile of shit!

You gotta be insulting.

So let's call off the phony cheeriness!

I can see you're getting a lot worse . . . Later on . . . you lying there motionless . . . nature works the thing very minutely for you . . . diversifies . . . the show is on the inside, in your peritoneum, not in your imagination! no more imagination! . . . the drama's in your belly and nowhere else! . . . your pancreas as big as your head . . . then what? . . .

Your relations came "from two to three" . . . visiting hours . . . they won't come back . . . they shed a tear or two . . . and you also stink too much! . . . and not, mind you, from my

144

smell, not pellagra, that's not real! No! No! No! . . . the real
one, pungent, that draws you, holds you, makes your head
swim . . . Already from "the hereafter" so to speak . . . the *sui
generis* . . . such a horrible stench that your relations' eyes are
popping out of their heads! . . . they go staggering off, reeling
. . . like this: eyes like lobsters! cousins, brothers-in-law, little
Leo, Auntie Estreme! . . . Ah, no more singing for them! No
more dancing! . . . what a party! They were supposed to come
back, they didn't. You don't expect them any more, either . . .
you don't expect anything at all any more . . . your brackish
color, the circles under your eyes are those of the end . . .
you're suffering the tortures of hell . . . and as soon as your last
gasp is uttered – you'll be the object of a lesson at the amphi-
theater, masterful! the students will be right there on your
navel . . . two of them there want to incise you this way . . . a
discussion ensues . . . two others completely disagree . . .
they'd rather incise you from the top, from the sternum . . .
from the manubrium . . . they decide on very wide cuts section by section . . . your thorax forming two flaps, all the junk
inside you out! into the formaldehyde! the good thing about
it is with your pancreas as big as it is, it can stay that way,
sticking . . . they have their techniques . . . you have no say in
the matter . . . the duty nurse gives you a dirty look . . . you're
lingering, she's thinking . . . your bed's needed by twenty-five
of the city's operable people . . . their families are prowling
around the hospital grounds . . . a whole crowd waiting for
you to fuck off! . . . your drawers have been jarred open, over-
turned, rummaged around in a hundred times over! . . . it's as
if your watch is already gone . . . you can piss in your pajamas
all you like . . . no more urinal for you! . . . they don't bother
taking your temperature any more . . . the head doctor passes
in the corridor . . . he barely touches your doorknob . . . he
doesn't come in . . . he forbids the greenhorns to enter . . .
enough's been done . . .

The bunch of jerks moves off . . . grumbling.

You wind up really pissed off! shitty goddamn mess!

145

– Pigs! Traitors! Cowards! that's what you shout at them
. . . you can't take it any more.

– Lazy bastards! Vampires!

You're drunk on morphine and pain! . . . Excruciating pain
. . . the term is no longer in the dictionary, «excruciating»[222]
. . . yet it was a rich term, it grabbed you by the gut . . . your ear
couldn't forget it . . . the conspirators suppressed it . . . they
had to! . . . it was their job! . . . to impoverish, weaken our
language! . . . so much so that pretty soon, even at the hour of
our death, you'll no longer be able to belt out a good death
rattle . . . you'll have to borrow words from Volsky, Syrioper-
sian, Angloslang.

Oh, land whose soul has been occupied! Oh, the muting of
a subject people! Oh, ignominious conditions! . . . Fine! The
historians are scratching their heads . . . getting worked up . . .
don't know what the hell end is up in France! . . . but *Fable!* on
the other hand! *Fable!*

With *Fable* everything's different! . . . the circumstances are
tragic, but you're more than equal to them! . . . your morale is
extraordinarily high! . . . Scoundrel! you heave a last gasp! joker! Death? By God's killer! . . . do it right! . . .

– Blessing! . . . Dying man's honor! the pig makes me laugh!

That's what they say, and it's true, how you react . . . joker
like no other! . . . thanks to *Fable!* . . . for only twenty bucks!
you turn into some kinda Socrates, not at all pompous, thanks
to *Fable!* . . . dying's a breeze! . . . The Ancients die, it's a goddamn pain in the ass for everybody . . . the proof: even today
you gotta read the bastards if you want a degree! . . . moral
fiber! everyone agrees, except brother François and Pierre
Laval[223] . . . Ah, give this kind of death the bum's rush! bring
on the flute! the lute! let's create! . . . so the guy on his way out
can laugh his way there! that's the idea! the guy gets to kick
the bucket of laughs! so I pray you! My Statue! My Square!
My Esplanades! My City! Célinegrad! that's it, Célinegrad!
the least they can do! Capital City! Glory, either you've got
it or you haven't got it! fourteen virtuous maidens and the

Orpheon! But you gotta do your bit right now! Help me! a bit of effort here! don't just mumble under your breath! No! out loud! louder! let the echoes resound! fracas and fricassee! clouds! storms! from the underbelly of Gonesse to Vrioshima! From Kamutchazki to Bécon!

– Don't go off and die without *Fable!*

That's the word I'm waiting for! the book is launched! I embrace you! what a heady picture! . . . activity all over the place! . . . the poles! . . . the tropics! . . . everything gives . . . readers and patients come back to me from every direction! . . . nobody wants to die any more without a good laugh! . . . the wholesalers do battle with each other over pyramids of my works! . . . blood all over what's left of my stock! . . . See if I don't make a huge comeback despite the hatred and blah-de-blahs spit out by the Artrons! . . . I'm back up there with a million copies! . . . think of all those poor sad people dying! there're plenty of them! plenty! . . . and you can't reason with them, not at all! . . . *Fable* is all they want! and music! . . . two or three singing parts! What a song! While I'm on the subject, you have to learn how to sing it! . . . Not that I can teach you here! . . . the ass glued the way it is! All I can do is hum . . . the guts all tied up in knots with hard caca . . . haven't been able to go for two weeks . . . not to mention the lunatics who've been perturbing me! . . . I mean the cells to the left, to the right . . . the cries of the encaged enraged . . . my poor old noggin! . . . on top of my own personal noises . . . the buzzings in my eardrums! . . . my ears are drums! . . . drums and lesions! . . . my microscopic inner ear! . . . it treats me to the sounds of twenty-five brass bands! . . . not to mention the train noises, of course! . . . not one train! . . . two, three, sometimes four! . . . When the banshee makes up his mind, finally, throws himself into it, bashes his head in, breaks down the wall! Oh, la, la! Marvel of marvels! relief! true banshee! have a look, the skull flattened! old banshee, real neighbor-prisoner! Show-off? No show-off nothing at all! For him to knock down my wall in all sincerity! I'd need a whole shitload of guys like him! his

147

kisser under the whole pile of them! make his head a pancake for him! . . . so we get some peace and quiet around here! . . . if the guards weren't so drunk, if they didn't blow their whistles for every goddamn piddling thing, if they'd stop fiddling with the twenty thousand latches . . . and if they poisoned the seven dog packs! . . . Ah, the seven dog packs! Seven packs of them outside barking! . . . then I could talk to you more intimately . . . not bothered by anyone! . . . because it's humiliation itself, brutal, the last straw, that you're fuckin' nuts and a thousand times worse, with the noise from the iron bars! *crrrrttt! crrrttt!* that never stops! the way the guards get their kicks, here, let me scrape the bars for you! and scrape them again for you! . . . the harp of the iron bars! they run their keys through them! *crrrrttt! crrrttt!* the whole cavernous inside of the enormous ship of flesh crackles, clanks . . . along with the whistle blasts! . . . you should hear it! . . . if they stopped banging the doors it'd be a few castanets less! . . . it's all castanets and locks around here! . . . *tac!* and *crrrrack!* hurricanes of castanets! . . . You expect me to go teaching you my notes, my little song, here in this din? . . . with the clogs tramping all over the place? . . . the endless clogs . . . I didn't tell you about those . . . one after another . . . *clomp! clomp!* . . . it's as if there were a deck up there at the very top of the prison . . . they hit the stair rungs . . . *clomp! clomp!* it's the prisoners lined up one after the other . . . like kids, their hands behind their back . . . as if there were a deck in the air, a crosswalk above the smoked glass . . . they go past my doorstep . . . right there . . . *clomp! clomp! clomp!* . . . they pass, they file up one side . . . the other! . . . they hit the stair rungs again, go down to the cages . . . *clomp!* . . . *clomp!* . . . endless . . . another line . . . another! . . . from dawn till dusk . . . it's the eternal maneuver of the vessel's hollow, the huge time-devouring ship, men inside, clogs all down the line . . . *clomp!* their hands like kids behind their backs right outside my door . . . all the door latches clanging . . . clanking . . . here they go again, once . . . twice . . . this door and others . . . always others! . . . as if they were dancing but you couldn't see! a whistle blow and they speed up! . . . a ballet of passersby . . . of kids . . . *clomp!* . . . *clomp!* . . . Oh, but I'm not going to leave out Hortensia! that libidinous ectoplasm, the Underling from the Embassy, Louis XV! he provokes me at the second bar . . . from my very own cell window:

– I'm wearing my high heels, scoundrel! see?

He's heckling me! I can't repeat it all to you . . .

– Love Louis XV! he demands of me, love Louis XV!

– Not Louis XV! you villain! you're lying!

I balk.

– Vampire! cesspool! bluffer! pig!

My exact words!

I don't care how low a spot I find myself in, whoever indulges in such defamation has to deal with me! This lustful Louis XV is one thing, but such vulgarity? Never!

He sees he's made a mistake.

– Take Louis XVI then! take Louis XVI! take Henry IV!

I absolutely have to . . . a king! he proposes Louis the Large to me! . . . Charles X! . . . he puts a ruff around his neck.

– Henry III!

As an ethereal substance, he does what he likes . . . he picks at a goatee on his chin . . . he tears it off . . .

– Dagobert, what about Dagobert?

He rests a little crown on his head.

– I don't want to stuff anybody up the ass, sonofabitch . . . Get beyond me, Satan!

That's how I show myself! Morale above all! my honor! in the worse than worst distress! . . . all right, so he is a bit of ectoplasm . . . so he has all the rights at my window . . . so? . . . a bit of decorum, please!

Even if he were Saint Louis it wouldn't change a thing! Saint Louis was the one who said "Dig it in to them deep," and so on![224] Unimpeachable, my character! period! virginal, you might say . . . he shows up on me all teary eyed the next day . . . at dawn . . .

149

– Why won't you hand yourself in? go back to France? huh?

He attacks me in my most sacred, weakest spot – patriotism – so weak I'm dying from it . . . He's heard about it, the monster! . . . my weakness for the lore of my land! . . . in tears he talks to me about Bezons! . . . he's blubbering, blubbering! a terrible sight, a black man sobbing! . . . looks like an animal being beaten . . . he's Louis XV, black man, ectoplasm . . .

– You're gonna get me fired! Boo hoo! . . . you're gonna have me lose my cushy fill-in job! . . . come on, be nice . . . go make a sacrifice of yourself!

That's the way he talks at my window . . .

– You're heartless! that's what he says I am . . .

He tries everything!

– Return to France!

He doesn't stop tormenting me, playing on my homesickness! . . . and don't think I'm not affected! . . . that I don't suffer terribly from being so far away! . . . no longer to have the gabbing, the wisecracking around me, my kind, city slickers, lowlifes, schnooks, misfits, pimps, stool pigeons . . . ah, dear Estreme!

Sorrow worse then aching in the bones, the ass sticking, the teeth dropping out, worse than the flesh melting, the eyes oozing, or the broken down trains in the tunnels that whistle and screech: longing for the old sod! That's the worst of all!

Oh, but hold on a second! while I'm thinking about it, I'm crazy! I'm supposed to deliver up to you my sufferings, the likes of such torments, for twenty bucks, you should be ashamed of yourself! with the song? the words? the music?

Nay, fifty bucks or your hide! That's my price! Think I'm crazy? fucking hell! not every day of the week you get such fabulous gifts! Take a flying leap at yourself!

Just think about what they read out there! what they're crying over, giggling over, getting their kicks from, in the railways or sitting on Juries! the Genius Prizes they're giving each other over! shit! and shit! You can't ever pay enough for the likes of my adventures here! in direct French, not translated? heavens! . . . not to mention the laughs! . . . It's not a villa I expect from it all, it's two! on the Emerald Coast! and through enthusiastic advance sales! and four maids to open the doors as well as a telephone that goes intercity and regional, and number unlisted! Not even René's tomb will do at this point, his hole in Bé . . . if it were offered to me! . . . It's my own mausoleum I want, lit night and day, at the spot, you see where I'm talking about, where they have the movies in the summer, where all the families come in chorus, and the lovers and the alcoholics, where the puppies do pee pee all over the consoles, the little round tables, the adults prefer to pee against the kiosk, where four movies do their thing at a time, so the heads turn to have a look, screw right off . . . *vrsss! vrsss!* spin around like tops . . . you can hear the necks spinning all over the sidewalk cafés, plus the cries of passion . . . I want to hear it all from my coffin! . . . I don't want to be interred beyond the walls!

That's René's trouble, he's "beyond the walls"! Me, I want laughing fits! I want it all! I want the gasps! I want the neck noises! . . . *tsss! tsss!* I want all the emotional upheaval of all four films . . . I want those slaps in the face! *clic! clac!* the whacks in the jaw! when the café-goers start clobbering each other, when it's the armed conflict of tastes! . . . the clash! . . . fever pitch! the café terraces swell and surge . . . the police blow the whistle! . . . the carafes: *plunk!* go flying! hit their mark! if it weren't for the carafes the heads would keep on spinning for years *vss! vss! vsst!* after the movies! Just one blow, look at that pitcher go! the little round tables are flung all over the place, everything in smithereens! the glass front! the gangster film fans won't tolerate the Chaplin devotees, the ones in the spell of that vamp Daisy tear down the other guys' screens, descend on those filthy fans over there! the ones obsessed by that Lee Poms girl![225] A battle royal – one for the books!

You know the Grand-Place? The one with two kiosks.

Even if the ramparts are ground to a pulp, blown to the skies, my spirit will be there and nowhere else! . . . That's the only place I want it to be, my Mausoleum! Bastille Day will have come and gone? So be it! They'll always be able to declare other holidays! and more enjoyable ones! much more lofty ones! . . . throngs you've never seen! Holidays are endless fallings in love! . . . They'll declare marvelous ones! and the dogs, their owners will come exactly where I say, to drink, to applaud, to do pee pee . . . The kiosks will have turned turtle, they'll be lying down flat, wrecked, rusted, I'll be the only one left to do it on . . . during the day I'll have the seabirds . . . ole René where he is, an isolated spot, no light, you can imagine the number of people who go on him! . . . it's a never-ending procession, "hand in hand" of the idylls, and those who prefer to do it alone . . . sullen dreamers . . . all of them go take a shit there, right on the granite! . . . I have no desire to be so sullied myself! They'll only be able to pee where I'm telling you . . .

– So you can imagine the Pantheon!

– While we're on the subject! I'm not that fond of the void and of glory! . . . the place is spotless but dismal, the Pantheon . . . bolted down, sealed, and so on . . . . Oh, such solitude among the dead! No! Heavens! I want people around!

You see, just between us, I'm letting you into my confidence, unveiling the course of things for you . . . but you're not such a brute, you wouldn't be one of those up at the Rampart? at the Kiosk? . . . waiting for me? . . . It's amazing how many people there are at the Saint-Malo gate! . . . You'll be waiting upon events . . . waiting to see me pass by on my bike! . . . the "ultrafine" bike! . . . pedaling like the devil! . . . my "Imponder"! your mouth hanging open . . . stammering! . . .

– Him? . . . Him? . . . Is it? . . . Is he? . . . dead? . . . dead? . . . alive? . . . buried? . . . Mausoleum? . . . him? . . . him?

Blotchy, your eyes popping!

Because, don't you see, I'll give nothing up! . . . Alive? . . .

Dead? . . . for me, well, absolutely not important! . . . I get out of here, *Fable* sweeps me away! . . . you'll only ever see me again on a bike . . . two, three bikes! No more wheelbarrows, no, no, no! . . . no more of Ciborium's brutal treatment! . . . no more of the Academy's henchmen! with their funny hats or without their funny hats! Odes to sell! . . . High Officials like Weathervane! Prostates like Bogmoleff's![226] Plague upon the rabble! You bet I'll get rid of Aunt Estreme and her gang! wrap the whole lot of them up in a parcel! and the songs! I'm keeping only my cycle! . . . my two cycles! . . . my maid, so there! . . . my two maids to open the doors! . . . a pot to boil my syringes in! . . . everything set up to facilitate my practice! . . . that's dedication! . . . more than dedication! . . . called out night and day! . . . all the same a little bit of travel here and there . . . I don't want to leave Montmartre just like that! . . . I've got my memories, attachments . . . I get off the train at Montparnasse I cross all of Paris by bike . . . what a feeling! . . . the rue de Rennes . . . the Samaritaine . . . swing up around the Ile Saint-Louis . . . I go back up the rue de Rivoli . . . a minute at the Palais-Royal . . . I have the dreamer's bench right there in front of the cannon . . . I'm afraid someone might recognize me . . . About face! back into the saddle! . . . Rue de Rome! . . . in a flash! . . . Rue de Rome! the Pont de l'Europe! . . . the old man on wings! . . . the ghost come back! . . . the Caulaincourt bridge! . . . I take it! . . . ole Julot hears about it . . . that does it! . . . he sees me flying from one pedal to another! . . . he's not talking to me any more! . . . he's gone all sullen on me . . . he takes himself off into his interior . . . his head just a frown sinking deeper and deeper into his neck! shriveled up by all the hate inside . . . till he's nothing but a ball of a headless monster . . . his head buried down in his belly, in his own entrails growling like mad! like some squished lump . . . in his gondola . . . propped up against the bench, clutching on to his irons to kill me with[227] . . . those goddamn legless bastard's slingshots . . . he saw me pedaling

153

... been on the lookout for me since the Pont-Neuf ... he's not talking any more ... he's growling ... growling at me ... he sees me turn at the Gaumont Theater ... he keeps growling at me ... growling ... from two kilometers away! ... Julot my brother, my heart, my weakness ... look what jealousy has reduced him to! ... he'd spend hours in his crate, propped up against the bench, right on the sidewalk, waiting for me to approach so he can wreck my bike on me and knock me out cold! rotting livid with envy is what he is! ... not only on account of the bike! ... everything! ... even my "class of 10," which he can't forgive me for! he's a "class 11" ... I got the medal before he did! okay, so they took it off me! ... you'd think that would've made him feel better ... but no! ... He got the Legion of Honor for his heroism and his wound, 130 percent, lost both legs ... That's decent compensation, I would say, wouldn't you? ... I was really happy about that ... when he got his Legion of Honor! ... I hear about it one evening on the radio ... I say, Tomorrow, son! at the crack of dawn! I was still living with my mother at the time ... at first light I go up Pigalle, I knock, I wake him up!

– Hey, what'd you say?

I congratulate him! I was moved to tears!

– Don't give a fuck about the Legion! he says, your eyes!

What the hell has that got to do with it? out of the blue! my eyes!

Then point blank:

– Did you bump into my model?

What model? which model? ... What was he talkin' about, his model? He had ten of them! thirty! Sylvine? ... Farinette? ... Manon? Here I'd come to congratulate him, and he attacks me for taking his girls! what a welcome! such bad faith! ... him who was always such a sweet talker! ... Really! well, in a certain way ... whatever he was accusing me of! ... he thought I was casting spells with my eyes! ... the women must have been talking to him about my eyes ... stupid, idle talk! ... they knew what he was like! ...

154

– Shoulda seen the way he looked at me yesterday!

That was enough! . . . he was boiling over! nuts! . . . if it wasn't my eyes it was something else! . . . if you're the jealous type any excuse will do! what? for what? . . . for nothin'! . . . because I got two legs and he doesn't! Oh, he found crimes, too! Yes, crimes! but he had his two arms, and me only one! . . . well, one that works . . . tough shit! him, his two legs sawn off, that was it! utter hatred! my eyes! my opportunities! my charms! go try to reason with him! If he saw me now in the hole, my ass one big scab, he'd say, ah, you got a booboo! You're too sensitive! your eyes! you've lost sixty pounds? you're awfully slim! too many babes!

I admit that for his art: sculpture, to work from his crate on rollers, was hard, almost impossible, he had to model with his stump right on the ground! and the clay all over his floor, a soupy mess! . . . he got it all up his nose, he'd look for shitty globs of it all over himself . . . at night the stuff smeared all over him like a mask, his hair full of the stuff, he'd make you laugh . . . the clown-in-a-crate! . . . and he'd get annoyed . . . his tastes were toward the stylish . . . he'd have got all gussied up, fussed over himself . . . he had this idea it was attractive . . . as well as the eyes, of course . . . elegance, the cut of his jacket! . . . because women fell for the male model type . . . by instinct he was a *clubman* . . . and he'd never stop looking in his mirror, his little round portable one . . . he was envious of the fact that even though I wasn't a sculptor, I got to fondle the behinds of my patients, as many vaginas as I wanted, there you go! . . . he thought all I did was touch my patients! with both hands!

– But I only have one hand, you erotomaniac!

No use talking to him! . . .

– So maybe you've been sticking your fingers in my pots? There, for instance, my clay! my oil pastes! if you didn't, how come you have red all over you, girl-gobbler? or is it come-juice? or period blood? which is it?

155

The hallucinating lunatic, he thought I had red all over my lips! He'd complain about everything, but the worst of all: soon it would be the total lack of clay! that his last pieces were all ruined ... that his vein was finished, his special tunnel, the only gypsum good for statues in all of Montmartre! he knew the crevice, the only crevice! him alone! and Pasco Rio, who was dead![228] ... the bottom of the Traînée Impasse and then left ... But he wouldn't tell me the exact spot! not even me! the entrance to his crevice! ... the only gypsum he wanted to use! ...

When all this bullshit is over with! ... and my kiln!

His kiln, the last one in Montmartre! ... not exactly the last but almost! ... in any case the only one for his gypsum ... collapsed in '39! ... and hey, what about my bricks? find bricks nowadays! bricks, kiln! you couldn't get a damn thing!

– I mold, it dries, a waste of effort!

He tried to make up for it with his gouaches, anyone that happens along ... the clients at the window ... But what he really wanted to do was fire clay! ... terra cotta! nothing but terra cotta!

– I'll be the one remaining ceramist!

He'd sculpt right on the floor ... little statues all over his floor ... he also painted just about right on the floor ... his canvasses just propped up against the wall ... how could he paint at an easel? ... and since he was in perpetual motion ... like a top! ... always chasing a bottle of rotgut! ... some varnish! ... some tube or other! ... a paintbrush! ... he knocked everything over! ... he'd crush his mock-ups ... put holes in canvasses!

When he lost his temper!

– Fuck off out of here, the whole lot of you!

If they bitched, the fight was on! everything went waltzing – irons! canes! jars! ... out the friggin' window! like slingshots! they'd have to come back laden down with presents ... so they'd be forgiven ... they'd have to find some champagne ... and *chug-a-lug!* ...

156

Chug-a-lug! . . . down-a-glass! . . .
Here comes the Parisian Lass!

So there'd be a celebration!

And he'd start his zigzagging again . . . so everyone could
see what a virtuoso he was . . .

– Make way for the gondola!

Right into their legs! bellies! right into the pots!

– Snap at my stumps!

And so he'd ram into the clients again! There'd be some
yelping then! There were also liters of turpentine! his sol-
vents! . . . since he was on the subject of fire, talk about fires! .
. . the number of liters of turpentine he broke! and smoking
pipe after pipe! cigars! he was playing with fire, all right! artists are a dangerous species, you can't predict, you think he's
wise . . . think again! . . . there he goes farting and fiddling
around again . . . he finds something under the sofa . . . a parcel . . . a letter . . . think he'd put it back where it belonged?
. . . what the hell! he says, chuck it into the sea! out the window! At night, when he'd be finished, he finished late, chameleon in his crate, yellow, orange, violet clay all over his face
. . . there was just the two of us, me, him, he'd given too many
people a hard time . . . so the place was empty . . . and in
gaslight . . . the place inside was gas lit, under the stairway, his
old kitchen . . . by gas mantle . . . hissing . . . reminded me of
the Passage Choiseul, we also had gas mantles at the Passage
Choiseul, the burners, thousands of gas mantles . . . in the
middle of Lent all the unwashed from the boulevards came to
warm up in the passage, raising a din, Pierrots, clowns, harle-
quins, marquis . . . what a bunch! and the old grannies, the
little old men, and the youth! Bet your ass it chirped! You
can't compare gas to moonlight, it's something more . . . it's
this wan greenish thing that stupefies you . . . floors you . . .
you see strange things . . . people not quite dead, not quite
alive, not quite anything . . . At the time these weird greenish
creatures gave me hallucinations . . . there were so many of

157

them! the Passage was full of them . . . you have to put yourself back then . . . middle of Lent! makeup jobs worse than Jules's! besides the wan green light from the gas . . . I was describing Jules's studio for you . . . the royal mess! . . . his own fault, too! . . . the whizzing wonder in a gondola . . . the way he'd make a mad dash for his jars! . . . the way he smashed all his clay! . . . Jeez, the figurines! his place was a goddamn mud hut! . . . not to mention the tubes . . . the turps! . . .

– All you need is a bit of confetti!

I was thinking of the Passage Choiseul.

– What do you mean, confetti? It's a kiln I need!

Besides, like I said, in his crate, his gondola, there were all sorts of jars between his stumps! . . . for his so-called convenience . . . and the way he'd lunge sideways into them, he'd come out again all yellow! all these colors! red! . . . puddles of it! . . .

– Am I a paint box or what?

– That you are!

– Rembrandt had no colors! But I have!

He had that over Rembrandt . . .

And right away his little round mirror!

– You're one good-lookin' fella! he says to himself.

He pissed right there in his crate . . . he wasn't going to go up into any john! all by himself! you had to help him, haul him out of the crate, once a day . . .

– I don't shit in my pants!

He'd pat himself on the back.

– You, you a transatlantic traveler![229]

He begrudged me my journeys, my luxuries . . . superluxuries! . . . that I was life's spoiled brat, that I'd never wanted for anything, that him, he had to pee in his pants! his crate leaked, of course . . . so it was all over his paints, the floor, the tubes.

Okay, he worked in a frenzy, the real artist, he couldn't interrupt his work, I admit! . . . to hoist himself up to the second floor! It'd have been a crime! inspiration is capricious, but

God knows it doesn't like capriciousness! . . . And on top of that there was the drink that made him stubborn, aggressive! His liver, and stomach! . . . you might as well say he had no liver left, just the place where it was, an alcohol-drenched sponge! should've seen the pain when I touched him! and the puke that came out of him! but when he really went off his head is when I talked to him about his kiln! . . . shoulda seen the artistry of his anger! He'd be bouncing up and down in his crate! his whole crate! base, box, rollers!

– I'll do it all again, my friend! just wait till I find the bricks! once they've stopped all their bullshit! clay soil, that's just the ticket! stuff you can get a grip of! clay soil!

But not just any soil, the very special clay soil, that was his alone! only his! his vein! his quarry in the Impasse Traînée, the lode he told no one about . . . he couldn't get to it at all any more . . . it was walled up in concrete! On account of the Civil Defense!

And the brick problem? . . . what about that? . . . They came from the Pas-de-Calais, his bricks . . . the ones he needed! the Krauts were occupying the bricks! not to mention the factories! . . . they were occupying everything! so he could go scratch himself till his oven fires again!

Ah, the torment of being an artist! they have only one way to forget: a good stiff one and then finish! either that or booze, booze, booze, and more booze! champagne, yes! champagne! . . . but who's been pouring champagne down their neck? . . . "They're taking everything on us!"

I couldn't say anything! me and my books! my Nostra-dameries! my acquaintances! . . . a single skeptical word? Up! I was in for it!

– Lazy sod! pimp! . . .

– Okay! Fine! See you next time! . . .

There were already lots of others at the door . . . blocking each other . . . admirers, fans, jerks, men of the world, models, merchants . . . All artist studios are a bit like that . . . the comings and goings . . . the bickering, the gossip . . . all the tittle-tattle, who's doing who, for free or for pay . . . men of the world, winos, gibes, cops, caca . . .

– This place is a pigsty, Ferdinand!

He realized that.

– A glass of white, Jules?

Right away, he refuses! he doesn't want any more wine! he charges into the heap! his rollers flying! . . . into his fans!

– Everybody out!

But there're too many of them . . . the door can't handle it . . . they're crushing each other! . . .

Every man for himself! They jump on the chairs, on the sofa . . . and on the women! the naked women! you should hear them!

He decided he wants to be alone! all alone! Because he needs time to think about things! He wants to be left alone! . . . for inspiration . . .

While I'm at it, while I'm depicting all this for you . . . while I'm guiding you through his little dwelling . . . his ceiling was something to remember . . . full of upside-down landscapes! . . . all his canvasses fastened to the ceiling . . . a review of all his "periods" . . . his concierge got them up there for him . . .

– Me, you realize, I'm a sculptor! Painting is depressing! . . . one dimension! . . . for heaven's sake! one dimension! Me, I can't live with just one dimension! you, you can live with one dimension! . . . you're the flat-as-a-cockroach kind! . . . the stripe kind! yeah! you're made for slits! I can just see you in a slit! in a cunt, a slit! . . . flat . . . nice . . .

He had fits of anger painting! being deprived of clay, of a kiln, of everything! . . .

He got all pissed off at his clients . . . he took it out on the clients! . . .

– Say, that's nice, what you're doing, Jules!

A town hall on Bastille Day, ribbons all over the place, flags, flourishes . . .

– This one's money in the bank, heh? I'll go for it!

His irons out the window! *boing!* and howling besides!

– Sonsobitches! Thieves! Assassins! Bring me back my irons!

People got hurt.

It wasn't so bad with the watercolors . . . he'd shower the stuff all over them! what a sauce! . . .

– So I shouldn't do my tones any more? . . .

The jackets got drenched with it! . . . the overcoats! . . . the sidewalk turned into a rainbow . . .

– So go buy me some Venetian blinds, then! What, do you expect me not to mix my tones?

Hanging off their hinges, his Venetian blinds . . . they dated back to the Commune . . . not only his blinds! . . . the whole kit and caboodle! . . . everything was falling down, moldy . . . the whole neighborhood was supposed to be renovated, the whole block and the Maquis behind it[230] . . . they'd been talking about it since the Commune . . . four wars had come and gone . . . four postwars.

– Why don't you buy me some blinds?

Not just the worst, not just the envy, not just that he was marinating in his crate, the Venetian blinds also pissed him off!

Rotten disposition, Jules, what else can you say? . . . I'm talking as a friend, and a faithful one! . . . the worst, sourest, poisonous old maid of a man . . . his little portable mirror, he'd look at himself in the mirror a hundred times a day . . . the dandy . . .

– I'm falling apart just like Rembrandt!

He'd get all upset.

– Pass me a drop!

Because that called for a gin! . . . a little glass or two! . . .

– I look at myself, I see myself, you, you don't see yourself at all! I see myself huge! . . . then minuscule! . . . a little pea I see myself! . . . the proof that the real artist creates himself! . . . you, you're a cockroach, the cockroach, all he sees himself as is a cockroach! . . . I will re-create myself, my friend! . . . I'll

161

find my lode! . . . my kiln! . . . Painting? water! turpentine! the cold!

Really miserable substances!

He was sneering . . .

– Ceramics, my friend! fire! . . . The only thing I paint for is the chug-a-lug! to drink! . . . the Creator's clay? On your knees! If I were Adam, I'd cast me an Eve! . . . You're not gonna find out where my vein is! . . . You'd go and tell the Krauts! . . . all you see is watercolors . . . just watery colors! that's all! Water!

He was giving me his beady-eye treatment . . .

He painted a lot of Infantas . . . everybody wanted an Infanta[231] . . . with no legs just about he'd make them . . . almost on the ground, little, and hunchbacked . . . just like him.

– If I dressed all loose like that I'd be like them! . . . my gondola wrapped in skirts!

It's true, he made them his size! . . . he gave them faces like his . . .

– Can you see me as the Infanta? Wait till I get my oven!

The bee in his bonnet! . . . he'd do Infantas in terra cotta!

– Nobody does Infantas in terra cotta!

One other month there was *Villages with Columns of Enlisted Men!* also very much sought after! . . . and the *Finishing Line at the Bicycle Races* . . . For a moment he reconsidered . . . didn't look at himself in the mirror for a while . . . he reconsidered his Periods . . . the Fortifications Period . . . his ceiling . . . how he'd tramped from one city gate to the other! how he'd find plenty of "motifs" before they took a saw to him! . . . all the gates! . . . Saint Denis! . . . la Chapelle! . . . Auteuil! . . . every slope . . . every bastion . . . and then his "sea" period . . . Le Tréport . . . the beach stones . . . the jetty . . . a few of Dieppe . . . Looking at his ceiling . . .

– Mural! I'm a mural man! I could paint you a Sistine ceiling just like that! Wouldn't that be one helluva pecker! The pope's!

And he showed me how it would be! his arm! stickin' out!

More often you could be sure, sure as shootin' there'd be little commissions ... you'd go in ... just when he was splashing paint all over the place! ... he'd be putting the finishing touches on a little town hall ... flags, pennants, lanterns! ... you got it all over your kisser! ... and your suit! You bitch? you protest? ... hell breaks loose! His irons! the broom!

No legs on him, but you could do nothing! he had the last word!

And what's more, he'd scream for help! Sex maniacs! Thieves! Assassins!

He got the whole street worked up against you!

It was too much of a scandal ... no arguing! ... we had to get the fuck out of there! ... Ah, that was one abject character! and all delighted to be horrible! ... and a sponge when it came to the old absinthe! and he could knock back the red like nobody's! ... should've heard him puking ... for hours ... not to mention all those poisons he sucked in! ... Varnish, paints, zinc paste ... Nutjob, he knocked back everything! ... He'd get the bottlenecks mixed up, he'd mistake the turpentine for white wine! ... Vouvray! the palate shot, paints, resin ... I took care of some paint poisonings in my day ... not an animal alive who would've held up to what ole Jules sucked in! ...

What is more, he'd bite his nails!

– Stop biting!

Okay! He'd start kneading his thighs again, his bits of stump that were always hurting him ... another obsession ...

– Stop flaying yourself alive! Stop it!

He'd start fiddling around at the bottom of his bucket, his clay, his piss ... he wound up ulcerating the whole lot! ... he'd get infected ... Oh, I knew his stumps, all right!

– Stop touching! Stop touching them!

– Go f ...

He was showing me! One endless laugh! What a joker, what a pig, ole Jules! The clients'd never stop busting their gut laughing! the models! his whole place shaking with laughter! Priceless ole Jules . . . They weren't the least bit scandalized . . . He was coming in his bucket . . . rascal, triumphant, glorious ole Jules!

– He'd make a dead man laugh!

Always a bunch of nosy people watching at his windows . . . mugs, walking disasters, losers, semiqueers, blow-ins, concierges . . .

Where I've seen him extremely fussy, you might even say dying over it, is when he was dead set on a gouache . . . enthralled in some artistic enigma . . . He'd have killed you! especially during a hot spell . . . in July or August, for example, July and August are awful in Montmartre! . . . You could fry an egg on Gaveneau Avenue . . . the sidewalks gave off fumes! . . .

That's when he'd have his Alpine conniption! . . . Off to the mountains! . . . the ice! . . . All he could think about was the Engandine summits . . . bluish summits . . . a whole other set of colors! . . . he'd use these terrible whites! . . . so toxic! . . . veritable "death-to-rats"! . . . he'd just suck it in! . . . soak it up! . . . Such insouciance! . . . Clutch on to his gondola! . . . grip it, bawling! . . . colic! he'd be shot through with pain all of a sudden! . . . then he'd have to have a rinse . . . and another! and another! . . . and only champagne would do for the rinsing! . . . so of course the sos! . . . and caca all over his gondola! . . .

– Champagne or I'll die!

Then everybody had to step to it, fans, pals, models, merchants, go back out into Paris! find him some "Mum"! . . . and only "Mum brut"! . . .

They'd bring it back to him! . . . the tyrant! . . . some people deprived their own, their family, their mothers! . . . that'd saved some for a special occasion . . . for a sickness . . . others robbed their friends! All for Jules! and not so much as a thank-you! nothing! He'd knock it back in one go! . . . Chug-a-lug! Burp! That was it . . . The window watchers would come up, they were thirsty, too! . . . They took the liberty of saying something . . . some remark or other . . . battle royal!

– Come in here, you lazy bastards!

Some guy who didn't know any better . . . he dared . . . a newcomer . . .

One step . . . a quick little maneuver . . . and then *plumpf! plop!* Irons! canes! bottles! the guy's kisser! Ah! Hee! Ah! Hee! Ole Jules's got no legs, but he's got arms! . . . what an aim, amazing! . . . the dexterity of a monkey! . . . terrible! . . . every projectile hits its mark! . . . He had a monkey's hearing, too, what a sense of hearing! . . . He had strength, too! . . . and guile! . . . so the guy gets clobbered! got the hell out of there fast! squealing! bleeding! . . .

– After the murderer!

Jules would be shouting after him! that they should catch him! finish him off! . . . so you can imagine if I take myself up there! Smelling sweet! . . . I think about it . . . I come out of the rue Burcq at a sprint! lithe! I mean, can you imagine, my "Imponder"? . . . he smashes it up, my two wheels! . . . veritable spider webs . . . the whole cycle only five kilos! So delicate as it soared! . . . he rams me! He catapults me! He crushes me! When he gets going on his two irons! Jeez! he'd leave a bus breathless, the strength he has! Me go and challenge him, are you kidding? It'd be the end of me!

Say I was at the "French"! He'd know about it! . . . You know the place, French Theater Square . . . the guy's got the senses of a rhesus monkey! Ultrafine hearing! . . . He was working himself up to it . . . It'd be my own fault! agreed! I mean, he's the sorcerer, after all! . . . quite ruthless, quite ferocious, crafty as bedamned, ham artist, abject, but all the same legless in his shit . . . sawed in half in 1914! . . . him who used to tramp all over the place, chasing down his "motifs" like nobody's business! . . . his easel everywhere! . . . fortifications at Robinson . . . Arpajon . . . Bougival . . . the banks . . . Suresnes . . . and now look at him, the crackpot in a crate, dribbling . . .

Very delicate task, reasoning with him.

– Okay, so you lost your legs at the Marne! . . . but 140 percent you got! you got the payoff! you got the Legion of Honor! . . .

– Shut your trap!

So I shot back at him . . .

– And what about my head wound! and my arm!

That was also true.

– You're only 75 percent! not like me, a human latrine!

The ultimate last word! . . . the kind of "Court of Miracles" thug who wouldn't've put up with anybody else parading around his turf . . . he'd've really ganged up on me! . . . let's say me next to him . . . the "Court of Miracles" all to himself! . . . because I had the plague a thousand times over, the pox a thousand times over . . . that they had to burn me and the others! . . . the "Court of Miracles" all to himself! . . . for him alone! . . . because all the others were rapists, blasphemers all around him! one hell of a sulfurous bunch! . . . one lousy rotten band of crooks! gluttonous crybaby rejects! frauds! me especially! me, his bosom buddy! You bet he'd've denounced my ass! to the pope! to the king! to the devil! He'd've broke his back to get my ass carved up!

Where he stopped being funny though – I mean not funny at all, just the same old boring rehasher, at least that's my opinion – was when he'd complain about the babes, that they were cruel to him! . . . that they were freezing him out and so on! . . . whereas, excuse me, they never left him alone! . . . they never stopped begging to pose for him! he had to turn some away! . . . and who did it for free! . . . and there were some cute numbers! . . . and well stacked! Here's to ya! Okay, so he had peculiar tastes, more toward the scrawny, so sickly you saw their ribs . . . If he had anything at all to do with your strapping great lasses, your resplendent creatures, your beautiful muscular types, it's because he knew I hung out with dancers . . . that irritated the hell out of him . . . brimming with health! . . . but all the same he got his rocks off! and not with old hookers, either, fresh young things! and from good families! . . . magnificent flesh tones . . . perfectly well nourished . . . in times of war! and not for money, I repeat, did they come to offer themselves to Jules, just for devilment . . . in the nude!

and in such poses! something else! and to hear some dirty
ones! all aroused, too! It was a change from their routine ...

– Ah, Monsieur Jules! Monsieur Jules!

They'd bring their girlfriends to him ... they'd pose two at
a time! three! ... playing hooky! ... he fascinated them, damn
sure! ...

– Talk about lady-killers, you old sorcerer of a stump!

I'd tease him.

The more he talked dirty to them the more they wiggled
with excitement, the more they clucked! He even took me
aback, the crude foul mouth on him!

– They won't come back!

My ass they wouldn't come back! Only too happy to!

And here he was begrudging me my eyes! my jerk-off
hands ... The goddamn bandit! ... his couch full of virgins,
perfectly agreeable, and perfectly naked ... and not little
snot-nosed, louse-ridden jades! Oh, not at all! ... Educated!
Good manners! With chambermaids, cars, horses! ... and in
times of war! In convulsions at ole Jules's nonsense! doubled
over! fainting! you shoulda seen some of those long waists,
supple, high strung! ... the gentle arch of the lower back! ...
as a doctor I could appreciate them! ... Impeccable cutis!
swathes of smooth, rosy flesh! ... such youth! ... Posing for
Jules at sixteen! I think every high school girl had her turn
... the attraction of the lair ... Rasputin! He'd chastise them!
because they were naughty girls!

– The next time I want my cake! my Saint-Honoré! You'll
have to do better than that, my little tarts!

Another time it was pineapples! ... Another time it was a
baba rum! and with real rum!

– I know you have some at home, sweethearts, don't tell
me you don't!

– I'm telling you, I loved the guy, what a goddamn magi-
cian!

– They just come for a laugh! to get their rocks off! silly
tarts!

167

– Of course! Of course! Proud as pussy! Of course!

Not an iota of gratitude! He had no business being annoyed, because what got him off wasn't the big healthy type, it was the transparently unwell . . . So don't go tellin' me . . .

A matter of taste.

– That one there I picture as a China doll! a Dresden figurine, doncha think? I cast her, get her started, anyway! I'll fire her! waddaya think? later on! we'll put her into the kiln!

His kiln!

– Are you spitting up, Sarcelle? red? yellow? gray? . . . will it be soon?

The question.

His favorite, Sarcelle, sickly, a cougher, a real skank . . .

– Will it be soon?

She came back, but that one was paid! Jules the buyer, for once! Three louis per pose! . . . As she lived very far away, after the Nation stop, she spent a lot of time in the metro! hours in the tunnel, ole Sarcelle! the air raids! One time a whole day! . . . well, almost . . . she showed up around midnight . . . they were sleeping together . . . I don't think he had a right to be jealous, of my eyes, of my this, of my that! . . . He was spoiled! . . . He liked tubercular types, and Sarcelle was that! And epileptic, what's more! I took care of her . . . well, more or less . . . some gardenal, a little retropituine . . . what they used at the time . . . drops . . . Did anyone ever thank me? . . . I could say she was even one of the worst harpies ever in my charge, ole Sarcelle! . . . I think she probably wanted me to knock her up! . . . That's what they can't stand, all of them! That you don't mess around with them! don't knock them up! If I'd've planted my seed at Jules's place, he'd've got in on the fun, too . . . I got broken in to that sort of thing in London. I leave the working girls alone, I'm no John . . . but when it came to other enchantresses, he had others for fuck sake, and some cute ones! I told you! and some of Arlette's dancers! he had this passionate need to take them from her! lift them off her! that they shouldn't go to class! . . . that they stop at his corner, gab, go upstairs a minute or two, pose . . . he'd wait for them, on the lookout . . . his schnoz right there . . . right on schedule . . .

– Olé! Olé!

He'd pull them in! . . . he'd watch them coming from a distance . . . and there you go! Hey, Carmen! Come'ere, Justine!

They'd pretend to be surprised.

– Oh, Jules! How are you?

As if butter wouldn't melt in their mouths! . . . all cathouse candy-sweet, hesitant, they'd cross over . . . the hips would sway like another species altogether! not ordinary women, Olympians! . . . and fine ankles, fine, fine, all sinew . . . like a little wild bird, the dancer! her little heels on the pavement! . . . And avenue Gaveneau is amply wide! . . . other women turn into cattle! cows! crossing avenue Gaveneau! Catastrophe! . . . if you're not a dancer! . . . crossing the avenue Gaveneau! . . . Oh, it's terribly hard on women, terrible surface! . . . ford of the demigoddesses! . . . the other miserable creatures! flounder about! *pflam! pflam!* their calves all stiff, they walk like sticks, hobble!

What can you say about Jules, he's got an evil mind!

– This way, my little darlings! this way!

The dancer is so lively, so lithe, that one bound and she's at Jules's place! that's her crossing! . . .

– Get your clothes off! Clothes off now! Hold on! I need a pencil!

The artful devil!

– I've been asked to do this! This is for a commission! Don't you want me to earn a living?

That was to soften them up . . . play on their good nature . . .

– Oh, Jules! Oh, Jules!

He'd put them in the right position.

– You, your leg there! You, there, your head!

He'd entwine them.

– This one's a Mythological scene, my Graces!

He didn't only model town halls, the Alps, cows, the Enghien lakes, people commissioned goddesses! He couldn't turn them into skeletons! the clients didn't want Sarcelle! the clients wanted warm views! full of verve! elegant curves to the calf, very delicate knees, and strong thighs! Cupie-dolls! Lithe of limb!

– I'm limited in my choice of bodies! All they want is flesh! . . . come to think of it, just like you! . . .

Anything to spite me!

What better than Arlette's dancers? especially seeing as these ravishing darlings asked nothing better than to be exempt from going to class! . . . their excuse! . . . that they were just coming back from the Opera . . . dead beat . . . all they wanted was to be lying down, amused, refreshed, even if it was only a coarse red wine! that old Jules was just the one for that! . . . and so funny and so wicked! . . . with all sorts of cigarettes and sweets! He had everything! . . . Arlette up there, her drills! . . . excuse me! her "bar"! "in the middle! little warm-up kicks! . . . six! seven! eight! pirouettes in the air!" . . . Oh, boy, did the demoiselles get their rest! eight flights up and no elevator! the guy had all the luck! ole Jules! the leader astray! the lady-killer! His rascally tricks! the girls were done for! laid to rest! and the way he had them lie down, spread out all the better! close their eyes! . . . Mythology! the mythological sofa! . . . the cigarettes . . . the port . . . and the poses he made them take! . . .

– Put your head here, Justine! here!

Poses, jeez, more than baroque! . . . what got into his brain, this hunchbacked legless old sonofabitch, when he went off his rocker over legs . . .

But they'd burst out laughing!

– Serious! he'd scold them. be serious! We're dealing with mythology here, not farce!

They weren't farcing around, they only wanted to breathe!

170

they were getting strangled one in the other! thighs! the positions he put them in!

Because it was a change from their routine! . . . little girls brought up strictly.

– Just wait till I get my oven! I'll do you in Tanagra, in Alban sandstone! This is the rough sketch, my darlings! only the rough sketch! now for the casting! I've got to cast you! by hand for the moment! let me get my mitts on you! I've got to do this hand modeling! Can't be done without it!

And *smack!* and *smack!* the spanking! there you go! . . . the laughs coming out of the goddesses! isn't he the cutest? from his crate he had an easy time of it, the schnozola coming just up to the edge of it! right at their asses! up to the sofa! and *smack!* and *smack!* and his hand was not dead, let me tell you!

Naughty little girls, that's all there was to it! Had to punish them!

– Oh, you brute! You cad!

But talk about lovely arched backs! sparks of life! such starts!

I'd be admiring! And *smack!* And *smack!* They didn't run away.

– You've got more buttocks than the Moulin Rouge! More thighs than the Opera!

I wanted for nothing! . . .

– You can whimper! . . . I love ya! . . .

It was true, damn it! Salty old devil! he could croon a tune!

I told you that he'd drink, that he'd knock back those tubes, turpentine! everything! heedless! not only the Bourgueil! he'd grab one bottle neck, another! get mixed up! he'd taste it . . . claim it was because the light was bad . . . wasn't enough light . . .

– You, you've got all the luck, born with a silver spoon in your mouth! in the sun! There are some people not so fortunate in life! There're people in rotten run-down shacks! And there're people of such selfishness! . . .

His shack was dark, I admit, but not as dark as where I'm writing to you from! . . . Bottom of a hole! . . . and as for humidity! hold on a second! Eh, ole Julot! . . .

They're all whores, all harlots, the people on the outside! You could hate them to death! I tell you! They deserve it a thousand times over! . . . With or without legs! with a big cross! a little one![232] they're all the same! . . . He could talk about selfishness, Jules! sonofabitchbastard! . . . like Clauriac! like Ciborium! like Larengon! Monsters! All monsters! Raving lunatics! Goddamn knee-bending fatsos! Skeletons in embroidered slippers ready to be crucified by tender-lipped underage choir boys!

Even if he lived in a dark subbasement, that didn't stop tons of people from coming to see Jules! Jules of the Seven Sorrows! It's true, I had my "seventh floor," air, a view! far and wide! a hundred kilometers! all the hills right up to Mantes! But what hate that air cost me! . . . that view! they still won't forgive me for it! . . . him, his walls were all dripping . . . humidity in streams! . . . Jeez, was that pathetic!

– You'd begrudge a dog his life!

– Hey, come on, you've got no goddamn legs! you wanna have to take on seven floors?

– You got the elevator!

– Not true! toad! Not true at all! It hasn't budged for three years!

He knew perfectly well . . . the elevator was just an excuse. He resented my building . . . my whole building! the garden out front! the "chimera" wrought-iron gate . . . the mosaic carriageway door! . . . the sumptuousness of the vault . . . flashy overdone 1900 style! with bronze iris appliqués, but he had his Bohemian ways! Didn't that count? the cachet? what he managed to pick up off the sidewalk! his place was better than the rue Taitbout! better than rue Boétie![233] for that all the schnooks who came snooping around were drooling with envy, at his place! . . . They didn't come from Kansas, from

172

the back end of nowhere for nothing! and he'd give them hell, what's more! He could've gone down to the outdoor artists market! old Jules! Jules the Gondola Man! he'd have seen the difference! His little statues! They've got three Rodins for every tree at the market! and twenty Corots! there it was just his stuff! his alone! his truly! no competition! direct auction! He'd brandish his little bit of clay . . . not even fired, still wet! . . . a thousand francs! he'd announce . . . a thousand! I'll fire it for you later on! . . . I'll take payment in gold! five louis!

And then they'd feel this big! . . . undone . . . no comeback . . .

– Don't be so goddamn picky! I've got to make a living! . . . Would you prefer a watercolor?

It was an Alpine one, a *Flower Festival* . . .

And if they dared stutter some reply:

– Ah, so that's how it is! don't be embarrassed! You're having a rough time! So am I! I'm falling apart! Look at all this stuff! my basement! my brushes! the eyes out of my head! I can't take it any more! my plinths! my clay! I can't get clay any more! I'm ruined everywhere I turn! my stewards! my cart! stick your head in, have a look for yourself! come on!

They had to have a look inside at his cart for him! dive way down! . . . from the other side of the window . . . bend themselves in half . . . take a closer look at his gondola . . . lower! lower! they had to bend their belly . . .

– Farther down! Lower!

Those who knew any better got the hell out of there! Damn quick!

– Cowards! cheapskates! thieves!

His dawn chorus!

– They're wasting my time! They're robbing my daylight! They're swiping everything on me!

I admit he was on his own territory . . . that he was born 6 rue Maubel at the corner of Ziem's place,[234] where his mother was a laundress, that he'd given everybody hell, the least you can say, the whole area, eight hundred thousand people, that had wound up going up there to peer into his shack of a place, their nose in his blinds . . .

Nowadays everything's "oh, the old neighborhood" . . . nobody in Montmartre could compete with him in the ole neighborhood stakes . . . he was the only one born there . . . nobody more ole neighborhood than him . . . and his mother, too, and his father . . . "It's my soul! Long may it live! my native piss hole! your Notre-Dame-not-from-here can go burn down!" Such is the passion of our day, the rage for one's native piss patch! Who gives a shit about heaven any more! it's all just here below! Oh, no, nobody had any feeling for the old neighborhood but him, Jules! He'd take it too far! . . . and nasty? . . . He liked to hear himself talk, his "number," how he'd turn away the nicest people . . . the most well disposed of people! . . . he made them cry! it was his vice! . . . even so, he could be charming! . . . he knew it, he was gifted . . . a real crooner, for example . . . the timber, the voice, everything! . . . He went straight for the heart! I know, I'd accompany him one-handed, the left one . . . because he had a piano at his place! . . . a rusty heap of junk . . . a few scraps of keys left . . . What a musician! . . . but where he could astonish you was the bugle! at the bugle, a real virtuoso! . . . not the little, tinny bugle . . . no! the big one! the one that makes a soft sound . . . he'd improvise just like that, on the counter beat of a siren echo . . . poignant melodies . . . a sound lost among the bells down there, in Batignolles . . . lively, gay little strains . . . and then others, melodic, dreamy . . . lullabies . . . he'd have you spellbound! You wouldn't have believed it possible! . . . the goddamn human stump, the pile of crap, you'd look at him? . . . the pain in the ass? . . . at the bugle, when he turned on charm, made you wonder! . . . I'm still wondering, here in my hole! I can hear myself accompanying him with my left hand . . . our concerts! . . .

Can't blame everything on the drink, nor on the poisoning from the paints . . . his obsession with tippling! . . . no! . . . can't blame . . .

– Look at this tongue, my friend! . . . take a look!

I had to admire the tongue on him, he stuck it out for me
. . . his tongue . . . long . . . almost as long as a hanged man's
. . . that's why he was so good at the bugle . . . so he claimed!
. . . his tongue! *The* Tongue! . . . boy, what he could do with
it! . . . He could curl it into a six! . . . into an eight! . . . curl up
the tip!

– It's all in the tongue! . . .

You can imagine how fast they turned naughty, the bugle
lessons! tongue lessons is more like it! The girls wanted to
learn the bugle! how to play the bugle, those cute little models of his!

– Your tongue like mine! here, look! Your tongue like this!

And he'd roll it around in their kissers for you, but good!
Ah, Romeo was an innocent virgin in comparison! him and
his rose-entwined ladder! but Jules, his crate, his bugle lessons! deadly skills! he had one hell of a time! That's life for
you!

– Your tongue, here! you! Come'ere!

All those sofa Juliets! and fresh! bubbling! and altogether
in the altogether! not sixteen years old! fifteen! . . . at the bugle! the tongues curling! . . . the lessons . . . *vlowww!* . . . *vloooo!*
. . . mewling!

He could play the crybaby, the dirty stump!

I admit he had his misfortunes, I recognize the fact! I admit it! . . . he had this need to be fondled . . . okay! but where
he got my goat, I can tell you, I will tell you, was that when he
wanted to do a bit of beguiling he didn't pick a beautiful big
buxom one with flesh on her! . . . oh, no! one of those that you
got so adorable, so fresh and lovely, perfect! no! it was for a
sickly spewer! . . . one just sprung from the hospital, not yet
recovered . . . Then he really made me sick! me, a medical
man, anatomist, hygienist! muscle fetishist! of course it was
none of my business! but it turned my stomach all the same.

So you can see we didn't have the same tastes!

She was a bag of bones, Sarcelle! his little Sarcelle!

– You, all you go in for is flesh! *Smack! Smack!* . . . and he'd respank the beauties for me! . . . and he wasn't kidding! . . . who took it all very well indeed! I admit! I admit! wriggling around! bursts of laughter! the rumps like sea swells! . . . the jerks and starts! . . . those vigorous little things!

He'd boast:

– Girls brought up on rue Saint-Honoré! crème de la crème! silver spoons!

He denied himself nothing, that stump Jules! Art! okay, that's understandable! the bugle! unbeatable! . . . Me, I couldn't play anything . . . everything is music! . . . Oh, the little bit of piano, my left hand . . . you couldn' even hear it . . . and then I was never rough! since we're talking about the ladies! you need more than just charm! you need blood near-by, the accordion in the Slaughterhouse, that's their taste for you . . . my tastes go toward the Operetta . . . I've done a lot of dissecting, of course, but I get no kick out of a corpse . . . I'm only happy at an operetta, lighthearted, seditious, all frou-frou, daring, but only just . . . If I was gonna be jealous of somebody it would be *The Little Duke . . . Périchole*[235] . . . If I were to go wild one day it would be over the ladies' tastes, they disgust me the way they like blood too much! . . . but until such time, here, the ass all stuck, I just try to think things out . . . in a ditch ten times darker than Jules's place! no gas here, shit! . . . not even fixtures . . . or girls! . . . And my walls all dripping! ten times worse than at Jules's place! I'd like to see him in the slammer! I dare him! bugle or no bugle! A fat lot of good blowing out his tearjerkers would do him then! . . . maybe that would close the trap on his obscenities! would he still play his melodies? would my guests come over? . . . would my guests transpierce the walls? they're supposed to be wall piercers! . . . waltzing . . . those guys! all of them! . . . my guys! . . . my stinking informers . . . polka-ing right along . . . then I'd see them all coming . . .

Ah, I'd say, Auntie Estreme!
And you! . . . my little Leo!
Bravo Clementine! Bravo valiant Toto!

In step with the beat, don't you see, with the beat! not like I am here, the ass glued . . . and not the other one, either, in his gondola!

Adieu, dead leaves! To the devil your kind!
Be gone with the wind!

These last rhymes all whirlpooled! whirlpooling! Three-quarter time, four-quarter time! *Allegro! Con brio!*

Escapades and cares!

Him, let me tell you, old Jules, since we're on the subject of the dirty little pooper, it's wounding people he enjoys! the difference in our natures! . . . two different characters! . . . If an angel came down to his place he'd have treated him worse than a fish! . . . He had to humiliate his young beauties, embarrass them . . . he'd mix a young one with an old one, this was another mythological one! . . .

– My goddesses have to be nice and relaxed! . . . Move closer together . . . nice and cozy, my little chickadees! . . .

Impossible poses!

– They're so bad I should do them in turnips, you hear me! turnips! not bronze! not in Saxon porcelain! turnips! Heh, my Olympia? how would that come out in the kiln?

All he could think about was his models in the kiln! a buyer interrupted him . . . the eye there . . . at the window . . .

– So, you, what will it be? . . . what do you want? . . . a satyr? . . . a behind? . . . the hams you want? the whole dame? no? . . . The gentleman doesn't like the sculpted form? . . . okay, no sculpted form! . . . A geranium then? . . . A gouache! The gentleman doesn't give a fuck! . . . The gentleman is troublesome . . .

And he dives back under his sofa . . . where he kept his stash of gouaches . . . he shouts from under it:

– A Red Sea crossing? . . . What subject? speak up! . . . What subject do you want? . . . Bright colors? . . . Blues? yellows? you prefer pale tones? . . . wan tones? . . . Here we go! . . . a couple of nymphs!

Ah, but you'd better not dillydally!

– Two grand! . . . You'll see how it goes once you get home! . . . you can't put a price on an artist's time! . . . you don't understand a thing! . . . if I have to be an information service as well as sell! . . . and then there'd be a fuss! can't you see these ladies have no clothes on?

Decency at all costs!

I knew buyers of his that he'd evict ten! twenty times! very worthy clients! people so kind! . . . who were really upset by the likes of Jules! . . . and when he really tied one on . . . worse! worse! he wouldn't even recognize them any longer! . . . sometimes . . . he'd really go at them with the insults! . . . and people really smitten with his artwork! . . . who had their living rooms full of him! who only had his works at home! hundreds of his little statues . . . frescoes! . . . they'd make excuses for him . . . they'd let him get away with anything, almost anything . . . I used to watch them waiting . . . not daring to go up, they'd post themselves at the corner of a street, some of them would do the tour of Montmartre three times . . . before they'd screw up the courage to peek in his window . . . a lot of his buyers knew me . . . they'd wait for me at Vintimille Square, they'd be on the lookout for me . . . I'd be coming back from the dispensary . . .

– How is he today?

– Vile!

People who worshipped him.

– He's drunk again?

– Ooh, la, la!

I always took rue Custine . . . the Pilon Impasse . . . Vintimille . . . they'd thank me . . . if they bumped into him another day, not too loaded . . . in one of his good moods:

– Come up, ladies and gentlemen! By all means! Come up!

Let me offer you some coffee! the filtered kind, not even Abetz has this one! a real treat!

And it was true! Mocha! . . . but people were a bit wary . . . Jules being nice? . . . they preferred to stay at the window . . . a tasting on their toes . . .

– Oh, it's perfect, Mr. Jules!

– I'm glad you're enjoying it!

All polish and refinement.

But they'd better be quick about it!

– Okay, let's go! this little Tanagra! I'll fire it for you after the war! Take it as is! It hasn't hardened? . . . mushy, you say? what do you mean mushy? I suppose you're hard your-self! . . . what's mushy is your dough! . . . think your money's hard? . . .

They'd better pay up and get the hell out of there! Off you go! No more bullshit!

Here in my hole I reflect. That's what prison is all about: reflection . . . What if I have bitter memories? . . . Yes, I've got plenty of them! . . . but when it comes to Jules? I keep think-ing about it over and over again! . . . I'm not sure he hated me . . . he was just jealous, that's all! Absolutely! . . . and at times with the worst hatred . . . he'd have eaten me alive . . . he de-tested me, and everything about me . . . my medal! my eyes! my "seventh floor"! so you can imagine Arlette! and her dancers! he had to sabotage her classes . . . to debauch her students . . . from his casement window there, his schnoz, he'd be on the lookout when the time came . . .

– Psst! Psst!

. . . that they should cross the street by his place . . . not go up . . .

– Come this way, this way, my cuties, I've got candy for you! I've got sweet things for you! I've got gold-tipped ciga-rettes! I've got Valence oranges! I've got coffee! You're tired, little darlings! You need a rest!

They'd cross over, come to talk to him.

– Just a word . . . a quick word!

179

They had come all the way from the Opera! Arlette up there? still at the bar! "One! Two! Ladies! Now . . . Pliez! . . . Pirouettes! Pirouettes! Tendez! Tendez! Arabesque! two turns! in the air! There you go! Three turns . . . Attitude! There you go!"

And don't think they didn't let themselves get sidetracked, the little darlings! . . . ole Jules . . . the sofa! . . . the meringues . . . the spells he'd cast! . . . and how, he got what he wanted! One leap! two leaps! up! . . . his window! . . . his little casement window . . . because he did have meringues, the devil! the real ones stuffed with cream!

– Come lie down, young ladies! You're not going to go up to that studio! the shape you're in? all out of breath! Make yourselves comfy! just let me get a little pencil! Get your clothes off! It'll only take a minute! A second! A quick sketch!

He got what he wanted.

He even had babas! babas with rum! . . .

Arlette could go pull her root up there! they'd cut class! her lessons! her balance! her points!

The worst is that he'd take me aside and accuse me of being a sex maniac! an ass shafter! a tutu piercer! of sowing my seed!

– They come up for Arlette, for heaven's sake!

I'd try to exculpate myself.

I'd try to reason with him, to show him how things really were.

– You ogle them, you lying weasel! The gentleman can't keep his eyes off them!

– I don't ogle them, liar! vampire! you're the one who gobbles them up!

I knew what I was talking about! . . . but you think you'd get him to admit it? . . . honesty and Jules! . . . It's true that I watched dancing, I've always loved dancers . . . so? . . . their form beyond the flesh, the mirages they create, not creatures made only of flesh! . . . not just any old bodies that come and go! . . . want to make something of it? . . . nothing wrong with it! . . . all above board! Am I not a poet? Yes-or-go-fuck-off? okay, so I'm not an artist like Jules! models with his hands, and so on! . . . okay, so I don't finger as a poet, but as a doctor I do a little bit, I'm also a doctor . . . a doctor probes, a doctor has to finger! I didn't take advantage! They came for Arlette, not for me! . . . they came for the art of dancing, for highly complicated choreography! sophisticated, if you please! . . . not for piddling little exercises! no! incredibly balanced extensions! relevés in the fifth position! . . . highly developed "second positions" on points! the little dears would be trembling from their exertions, sweating . . . the hour of torments! . . .

He had his wiles, all right, ole Jules!

Me, I understand the purity of dance . . . a pig at heart, of course, like him, like Jules, like everybody and his uncle, but my little religion – the dance! where would you go when you're dead, without dance? Me, who has twenty ballets unproduced! that'll never be! and for the pure spirituality of it! absolutely beyond lucre, beyond glory, I am! Who can deny it? maybe ole Jules denies it? Slovenly, gluttonous lowlife! Destroyer of grace! That, too! Oh, the brute! Wait! the worst! I'm getting all worked up about it, sitting here on my scabs thinking about it again! when you think about it again! the worst! the very worst! the camel's back! the straw! the dirty low-down trick! Lili! Ole Arlette! Ah, when you think about these dastardly deeds! it was an ambush! the vice of the man! but I have to face it! Honesty above all! the facts! just the facts! and with Arlette, of all people! Maybe you think I'm being unfair! Anyway, so he goes after Arlette! that's the hottest one of all! all of a sudden! too bad, I'll tell the whole story! Arlette, who saw him every day! who was like a sister, really, my wife, who was no tease, no hussy, heartbreaker, no nothing! . . . Not a bit! just nice to him, always very nice.

– Poor Jules! Poor ole Jules!

She was fond of him . . . his misfortune gave him a terrific advantage! . . . poor Jules, my ass! she was more tolerant than

me, that's for sure! . . . maternal! in a way . . . Sisterly! A sister!
She'd stop by to see him on her way somewhere . . . pure
charity . . .

– So how's it going, Jules?

And the little reproach:

– Jules, you're stealing my students! . . . she was talking
about Micheline . . . about Mireille . . . he kidnapped them on
her, I swear! on the hop! . . . with his "psst! psst!"

She'd find them posing in the altogether, smoking gold-
tipped cigarettes.

– We're on our way, Arlette! . . . we'll be right up! . . .

They promised.

– Jules, you ogre, you! . . .

Every day . . .

– Yes, I am an ogre! . . . You said it!

And he'd go at her legs! his cart a mile a minute! brandish-
ing his irons!

– I'm a naughty boy! A very naughty boy!

And he'd grab her right in the thighs! going under her
skirt!

– Let me sink my teeth into you! Wait'll I sink my teeth in!

For a laugh! always for a laugh! and then one fine day . . .

– I love you! I love you! Don't leave me, Arlette! Don't
leave! I worship you!

The declaration.

He envelops her, wraps her in his arms . . . this was on the
sidewalk . . . you can picture it! . . .

– Wait, my darling! Wait for me! Wait!

A nice thing for the people on the avenue to see! Luckily
they were looking up, aerial combat was going on just then!
Well, that's what they thought, anyway . . . they were straining
their eyes! All the schnozolas in the air! There it is! There!
They were pointing to a corner of a cloud . . . nothing at all!
. . . shouting . . . so here comes me, make a beeline through the
gathering! . . . I was coming out of the metro! . . . allez-up! they
all wanted to climb farther up and see what was happening!

all of them! . . . all the pilgrims! to Sacré-Coeur! to Sacré-Coeur! quick! quick! to get a better look! . . . others were coming down . . . from the Holy Bell! . . . the two surging crowds confront each other! . . . the ones hurrying to climb! the ones rushing to the metro! . . . knocking into each other! yelping, the pigs! up! and Jules, who's bawling:

– I worship you! I worship the ground you dance on! clutching Arlette's thighs! under her skirt! I can hear him! . . . Me! I hear him! I get down . . . I see him! He's clutching on under the surge of pilgrims . . . his head under Arlette's skirt.

– I worship you, so I do!

In his cart, clutching! Luckily the people aren't watching! They're looking at the sky! and they're insulting each other! Calling each other shitheads! what are you, blind? deaf? you don't let anyone pass! it's a disgrace! unspeakable!

– I adore you! Do you hear? ole Jules is crying . . . under the skirt . . . between her thighs . . . he was all worked up! kissing her all over! all over the place! I see this! . . . I get down . . . Arlette can't move, an inch . . . not that she isn't capable of it! . . . she could! . . . she's got quite a pair of thighs on her! . . . she could crush his face between them, no problem! the crowd is no longer budging! . . . the opposing swells . . . it's the lines at the moment! . . . the furrows in the sky! all over the sky! giant Ss! . . . Os . . . Zs! . . . "Those planes, whose are they?" Heh? Heh? . . . between the clouds . . . the crowd is now squeezed tight . . . "Whose are they, those planes?" Big argument! Whose planes they are! . . . the trajectories of frozen vapor! at phenomenal speeds! . . . They were doing Zs! . . . Os! . . . Us! . . . oh, that meant this, that . . . messages! They knew all about it, they did! They knew! . . . just had to decipher! . . . have a good look! . . . The O! the Z! . . . that the English were in Nice! that the Russians were within a dice's throw of Potsdam! . . . that's what was written in the skies! . . . all of them with their schnoz in the air! . . . "What do you know! . . . you don't know anything! . . ." They got all fired up! "They're coming! . . . They're coming!" No question! I look up in the sky . . . I look down on the ground . . . I look under the people . . . I see ole Jules hanging on for dear life under Arlette's skirt . . . Still stuck to her! . . . he's squeezing her! his nose deep between her thighs . . . he's crying "I worship you! Do you hear? . . ." The others are shouting "They're at Forges! They're at Eaux! here they come! in Meaux! they're on their way! You're a jerk, look higher! They're in Garches! Give me some elbow room, God damn it! Look over there!" They were crushing each other, all scrunched up . . . They were packed tight around Jules and Arlette . . . I couldn't get to Jules . . . grab him by the throat!

– Here come the Tommies! and Uncle Sam's boys!

And now from the windows screeching louder! louder than the throng! it's the radios in the basements . . . "They're in Lô! They're in Lô-la-Manche!²³⁶ They're everywhere! . . . They're in the air! Look! They're in the air! . . . They're in tanks! They're coming in trainloads! . . . Mont Saint-Michel has been blown up! . . . Radio divisions are coming up the Seine! They're at Forges! They're at M'lun!'"

Enough monkeying around! I wanted to get to Arlette! I move three people aside . . . twelve come piling back in! . . . twenty! . . . a hundred! . . . I have a look from down below . . . still at it! . . . I see ole Jules! in Lili's crotch! clutching on between her thighs! Jules and Lili, they're packed in I said by the crowd, compact! . . . Her standing straight up . . . him in his gondola . . .

– I love you, kid! I worship you! He's howling . . . howling! . . . she could've split his nose open on him! crush it on him! bust his kisser on him! one swift blow from the knee! the pig's knocked out! . . . she had some strength in those thighs! You know how you get when you're desperate? . . . so here's me, I elbow people aside! . . . push them apart! I come right up against Lili! right up against her! I grab a hold of Jules in his crate! God damn it, stuck! glued! Everybody's watching! I pull him! I grab him out of there! I want to grab him out of there!

– Be careful, Louis! Be careful!

Right away, that's what Arlette comes up with! Jules first of all! Jules!

I was about to wring his neck for him, so I was! and just then, a surge forward! another surge forward! a veritable charge of pilgrims! Coming out of the bottom of the rue Burcq and yelping! . . . "They're in Eaux! . . . They're in Forges!" . . . on to Sacré-Coeur! they took the shortest route! by the rue Burcq! They knock into us, our throng! surprise! turn over! they topple us! part us! "You brutes!" to Sacré-Coeur by the shortest route!

Others are coming out of the rue Durante! even more ferocious! "They're in Bruges! . . . They're in Mers! . . . the Arromanches army! They saw it all, those guys! all! Up there! from up there! from the place du Tertre! They're screaming! They saw houses up in smoke! They saw the tanks! the infantry! the airplanes above! They saw the Cliffs in cinders! The sidewalks buckle, heave with people . . . all the avenue Gaveneau! a torrent going back up stream is a funny thing to see! They all want to get to place du Tertre before everyone else! The others don't want any view any more! want no more Tertre! they want the metro! Rushing all over the place! Bumping into each other! They confront each other, the hordes! horde against horde! "Dumbbell! Lazy ass! Traitor! . . ." Shreds of clothing fly every which way! "Cannibals! Scoundrels! Numbskulls!" Jules, Arlette get detached by the force of the crowd! Jules torn away from under Arlette! . . . from under her skirt! . . . ditches his gondola! . . . goes off on his stump! . . . rolls backward! . . . somersaults backward to his place! . . . shoulda seen him go! . . . the human conveyance! right back into his clays! his statuettes! sent flying backward into his window! the crush of people! no dawdler! right into his dump! his stump this way! his crate that way! He got himself unhitched! again! he's under the sofa . . . the goddamn stump . . . he's bellowing!

185

– Help me! Arlette! Darling! My darling! Arlette! Lili! Help! I adore you! I worship you!

I spring to the rescue! should've seen the movement on my part! I drag ten! fifteen of the thieving drifters along with me! . . . there are thirty of us administering first aid! . . . we gotta shake him loose from under the sofa . . .

– Are you hurt? Where? Talk to us, Jules! Jules? . . .

Got to get his braces done back up . . . what a rigmarole! . . . put his stumps back in the right direction for him . . . because there's the right direction! His crate isn't square: it comes to a point! like a ship's prow . . . what do the Good Samaritans know? there around him . . . they hurt him getting him laced up again.

– Arlette, you know how to do it!

She's gotta show the others! . . . how to anchor him down . . . the straps . . . the twine . . .

– Stay and pose for me, Lili! Stay and pose!

Right away, there you go! his demands! the bee in his bonnet! and in front of all those people! all those dimwits! his shack full of them! and at the windows!

– The end of my rope! there! that's what he does to me! The end of my rope! Damn!

– Go ahead! Help yourself!

I no longer have any say! Shit!

Never had this many people in his cradle before! Tourists! Pilgrims! Nuns! Concierges! Soldiers! Germans!

– Pose for him! Go ahead! Go on! Pose!

I can see she's hesitating to take her clothes off . . . they're off already anyway! all in tatters! . . .

– Go on!

Since somebody has to be in charge, I take charge! I bellow! Why wouldn't I?

So then he goes at it! the whole cart! fury! I grab the whole kit and caboodle! One heave-ho and I send it flying as far as it can go! to the devil! sonofabitchbastard! let him roll! let him roll! right into his paint jars! Shame, shame, everybody

knows your name! He gets unhinged again! braces! laces! everything busts out! the stump, the head in the paint jars! . . .
there were plenty of them! . . . What a smeary mess! . . . toad
landed on his side! . . . He's screaming! Goes at it again!

– Give me Lili! Please, give me Lili!

He's asking me this! the lunatic! in front of all these
schnooks! . . . his windows full of bumpkins! Jeez!

– Take her, you pig, take her!

He's pushing me over the edge.

That's when he whispers to me, Kraut! Kraut! from under
the sofa! just like that, wallowing in clay, the shit! he shows me
the door!

The cheek!

– Fuck off!

He's ordering me!

– You others, too, scram! out!

He's liquidating. He wants his room emptied!

He shouts orders just like that! from under the sofa!

– Everybody out!

Furious!

– Out, I say!

It was such . . . It was thusly . . . exactly! I see it all again!
. . . how he was rubbing my nose in it in public! I see everything again just as it happened! . . .

Was I going to get all indignant? Jump on the lump of
lard? . . . the pack I was surrounded by . . . the bloodthirsty
mob . . . they'd have my guts!

He knew perfectly well, the Pernicious Trunk! the lying,
cheating stump! He knew what he'd said! that he'd pointed
me out as a traitor! handed me over! I could see the fangs
come out! snarling! their lips raised to expose their fangs! one
more word and they'd tear me from limb to limb! . . . more
than willing! and others arriving from the lookout post! . . .
from up there! the highest steps of Sacré-Coeur! the horizon!
. . . from seeing Sens up in smoke! Think about it! the mood
they were in! Makes sense! they'd seen homes go up in smoke

. . . houses in Fontainebleau, too! . . . and the tanks! and the bombs! and everything! Yeah, those guys were in a rage, all right! . . . one more word out of Jules that I was a Kraut lover and they'd lynch me right on the spot! You could tell the way their fangs were hanging out! their dribble! . . . They were like wild animals! Ole Jules call me a traitor one more time! It was curtains! . . . Never had I seen such a nasty bunch of pilgrims! those who were coming back down from the lookout post!

So you can imagine the relief I felt when he told them all to scram.

– Fuck away out of here! Fuck away off, the whole pack of you!

They inched back, growling, ranting . . . the fangs! . . . they felt cheated!

– Go on! Scram! Beat it!

He was commanding from his gondola! I'd laced him up again, anchored him down good! . . .

– You fuck off, too! Hit the road! I'm tired!

The cynical sonofabitch! Every name in the book!

I looked at him there, human latrine, trunkman, gremlin! I could have bashed his head in, the Sculptor! I could have jumped on him with both feet! *Plop!* toad!

– Fuck away off with you!

Beside himself at this point! Off his rocker! If he'd called for help, the whole avenue, the whole goddamn tribe would have come trooping back! The civic mood was going in his direction! All the pilgrims! All the tourists! All the house-wives! The turning point for the English! . . . the Americans on top! . . . the planes all in formation! . . . and three hundred engines . . . *vrrroom! vrrroom!* He had civic mood on his side! He'd execrated me from the beginning, it was clear! clear! If I bashed his puss in for him, I'd be the one to get it! . . . tell it like it is . . . let's have a rethink . . . I was the one whose blood they were out for! not him! . . . I was the one to blame for everything! better keep my trap shut! . . . the mob would've lynched me! . . . tell it like it is! rethink the matter! . . . with sangfroid! My guts they were out for, not his! . . . He was getting his rocks off! he had the right end of the stick! I was the traitor! me! . . . and so on! . . .

– Pose for me, Lili! Come pose! Take off your clothes!

Lili, I forgot to tell you, was the family name for Arlette . . . You know, we called her Lili . . . you figured it out already . . .

No big deal if she took her clothes off . . . already in tatters! . . .

He was ordering her! I watched him . . . he came up to my waist, barely . . . in his gondola there right under me . . . his puss . . . only up to my waist . . . the arrogant sonofabitch! . . .

– Go on, Lili! Go on!

She hesitated . . . and I could see that the dirty low-down whore's pig, he was hoping it would all turn nasty! . . . The pilgrims were coming trotting back in swarms . . . to start all over again! . . . still others breaking in, shoving each other in the doorway . . . pointing at me! . . .

– Go ahead, Arlette! Go ahead! Do it! Pose! You, Jules, get them outta here! Come on! No?

I could see there was going to be a riot.

– Then pass me my irons!

They were under the sofa, his irons . . . way at the back . . . I reach in and get them for him, I pass them to him . . . he takes them in his fists . . . Should've seen the pilgrims skedaddle! Go on! nosy bodies! . . . not one left! all flitted off! . . .

– Come'ere, Arlette! Come this way! . . . Sweetie! You, hook me up again!

He'd gotten unhooked again! . . . busted another buckle! . . . I redo him . . . I lace him up again . . .

– You, Arlette! this way!

In his catchall he wanted her . . . where there was gas, his Auer gas lamp[237] . . . in the old kitchen . . . He wanted her to pose on the folding bed . . . wasn't often he had them pose there . . . only when he wanted to be left completely alone, absolutely no interruptions . . . no one could see from the street . . . nothing at all . . . even when the gas was lit . . . but not

a speck of daylight, though! zero! Just the gas, that hissed! ...
it shed a green light, that gas ... blue! ... ladies' faces by gas!
their skin! their flesh! ghastly!

– Lie down, Arlette! Nice and long! ...

– Oh, come on! Green?

I can't help adding my two cents' worth! ... I don't like
seeing her green! ...

– I'm doing a synthetic version of her for you, you dope!
... What do you know about green? ain't never seen her, your
wife?

– What does he mean synthetic? what does he mean, never
seen her?

He's going too far! goddamn hunchbacked gremlin! I'm
pissed off! I'll shove his friggin' irons down his throat! I better leave them where they are ...

– Isn't it about time you got outta here? Fuck off! Get the
message? Fuck off!

Bloody tyrant! A law unto himself!

– I've got to model her, numbskull! Get the picture? First
the paste! Then the clay! It'll take an hour! since I have to
spell everything out for you. You can come back later! Go
down into the metro!

– I told you I'd do her head in ceramic for you, shithead!

– Boy, you don't give up, do you? my reply! hold on a sec
for Christsake!

– Yeah ... yeah ... yeah ... I'm tedious ... this ... that ...
I'm too abrupt, I annoy him! ...

– Go on! Keep talking! You, Lili, lie down like I told you
... you'll see the finished product when it's finally fired! After
the war!

And he stiffens up his arm out to show me how it'll be! he
shows me! "Stickin' up! Stickin' up!" Pecker rigid!

Sordid behavior.

Did it on purpose! intentional insult! Me to floor him,
that's what he wants! he's really asking for it! ...

190

– If you could just picture it finished . . . just wait till it's fired!

And he spins around in his crate! Pivots! He turns back to Lili, grabs her thighs . . . gets an armful! . . . and he paws at her, rubs her, there, lying down, spread out . . .

– You'll see in the kiln! take my word!

There he goes with his goddamn kiln again!

– I worship her! so there! I worship her! . . .

He was really asking for it now, really wanted me to break his face for him! . . . so it was love! . . . there was only the three of us left . . . just the three of us . . .

– Kraut! Kraut! he's muttering to me . . . and then louder: Kraut! Kraut!

– So I say to him, you snot nose! puddin'! cesspit! stoolie! I'll do you in!

– Go right ahead! He says back, cool as a cucumber, and he has a good look at himself in his little mirror . . . he makes little faces at himself, little frowns . . .

I don't touch him . . . keep my hands off him . . . I just stand there swaying a bit . . . I can still feel myself swaying . . . He stops making faces at himself . . . he turns around toward the folding bed . . .

– Spread them! Spread them wide! Nice and wide! There you go, kid! So I can do this modeling right!

He spreads her thighs . . . thighs nice and wide . . .

– I'll do her for you in the oven! And he starts pawing at her again, lifts her behind up, on purpose, so I can see! that he's got rights!

I'm not the kind of guy who loses it, takes dark offense at a slight! no! not easy to get my back up . . . I'm the more easygoing, accommodating kind . . . but there, he was looking for it . . . I know all about the crazy-guy stuff, the joker stuff . . . I know all about hysteria! . . . I know all about the artist! . . . they all like to play the fool! . . . play it up! . . . play it up! . . . Fine! . . . the pack are laughing their leg off! coming in their pants!

okay! soaking it all up! but him there, ole Jules, he was really pushing it with me! The jealous lunatic wanted to see how far he could go! . . . the jealous lunatic was pushing me to the limit! . . . outrageously disgusting on purpose! . . . was asking for me to do him in . . . do him in once and for all! . . .

– Okay, my wee man, let's go to it! I get a hold of his poker! I grab it good! his iron bar! . . . for poking the fire! . . . Hey, look, I was young! . . . Nowadays I wouldn't do it! . . . the piece . . . this iron! he sees it! . . . he can see me, all right! . . . I'm on top of him! . . . right on top! . . . of his head! . . . a piece of iron like that! . . . like a lance! . . .

– I dare ya! . . . he shouts!

I was going right for his kisser! . . . He sticks his schnoz up . . . opens wide his trap! . . . on purpose! . . . egging me on! . . . He's defying me! . . . I was heading for him with both hands! *Crrang!* . . . his puss all smeared! . . .

– I dare ya! Double dare!

Ole Arlette on the folding bed, naked, legs wide apart . . . she starts to laugh! Uncontrollably! . . . laughing her ass off! . . . the pair of them . . . laughing their asses off!

– Oh boy, Ferdinand! Oh boy! Haaaaa! Oh! Ah! Ah!

Oh, I'm so funny! The pair of them clucking, slapping their thighs . . . Aren't I the funny one! . . . too funny! They're choking over it! . . . I send the fire poker flying to the door! Against the hinge plate! The poker falls down! . . . bounces! Jules rolls after it! . . . he picks it up so I can start again . . . Oh, the joker! I don't want his goddamn poker! So he grabs it! And he starts to threaten me! He makes believe he's gauging my eyes out! for a laugh! a laugh! Him! down there! under me! in his gondola! He loves a farce!

Lili in laughing fits, spluttering all over the place! She can't take it any more! She's flopping all over the place like a fish! The whole folding bed is flopping!

– Okay now, scram!

They've had enough of me, the pair of them! . . . But was that some laugh! Jeez, what a laugh!

– Okay now, scram!

There he was repeating it, the legless sonofabitch! . . . sly old fucker! . . . all right! . . . all right! . . . you're right! I get the message . . . they have an understanding . . . all right! . . . all right! . . . I'm going . . . I'm going . . .

Whereupon, I leave . . .

And you know, it's from that moment on . . . from then, now that I think about it again . . . from that very moment . . . precisely . . . and then what happened later . . . everything that came after it . . . that the horrors began . . . the real horrors! . . . that we were hounded, I can safely say so wretchedly hounded, worse than animals! . . . not for a month! . . . ten months! . . . ten years! . . . just the other day the "Appeals Court"![238] . . . We've raised lots of animals, Arlette and me! strays here and there that were lost, abandoned, hounded . . . we brought home a lot of them . . . never once did we find one that had suffered what we suffered . . . It takes its toll on the character, has to . . . people can't imagine at all what it's like to have the hounds after you for ten years . . .

– Now beat it, you big fathead, hit the road!

I can still hear him.

Four times he kicked me out!

I couldn't make up my mind . . .

– I'll do her for you in clay, your senorita! lacquered! Look! . . .

He taunts me from the window . . . from his casement . . . I'm on the sidewalk . . . I can't move.

– With the tongue, hey killer! like this! With the tongue!

He's calling me killer! Me!

I knew his tongue. I knew all about it! he sticks it out for me to see again, how he can curl it up! . . . In Os . . . in Zs . . . in Vs . . . from the tip!

I don't leave . . . I just have to look at him. He draws me to him.

He gets Lili up from inside.

– Come'ere, Lili! Get a load o' him!

He wants her to come to the casement, starkers . . . she shows up . . . laughing . . . cheerful . . .

They're in cahoots! . . . okay . . . in this together! There's nobody left on the sidewalk . . . Just me there! . . . Like a big dope!

– Look at this! with the fist! the fist!

He shows me how he's gonna model her! and *smack!* right on her buttocks! her hips! . . . she laughs . . . she just laughs! and she's got powerful thighs, too, something else! . . . she could smash his snout to a pulp between them with one swift blow from the knee! *thwack!* he'd see stars! But no . . . she just laughs . . .

– Hold on a minute, come back! she's gonna pose . . . he wants me to watch her pose . . . again! . . . this could go on forever! . . . he wants me to go back inside . . . he's having fun . . . such a way to treat me! . . . they're both having fun! . . . the pair of them! . . . but now there're people in the avenue . . . at the end . . . on top of the Agil Impasse . . . and then there weren't any more! . . . now it's cops! Bet your ass I go back inside! . . . here I am inside again! He closes the shutters . . . well, tries to . . . they don't stay shut! . . . in the back he wants to work . . . in the back! . . . where the gas is still on! We gotta hurry! . . . the cops! . . . the Civil Defense! . . . everything's gotta be shut!

– Go to the back! The back! Lie down! . . .

And there she is again under the gaslight . . . thighs open . . . the tits . . . throat . . . shoulders . . . it's all green . . . blue . . . and a little pink . . . flesh.

– You get the idea?

– She looks green to me.

So I say, how does he want to do her? green? gray?

– You don't like her this way, heh? Admit it, go ahead! . . .

– Uh, well . . .

– With you it's bleeding beef is all you want! . . . or geraniums! . . . I'm sure you just love geraniums! . . . You like flowers, don't you? roses? You don't like roses? . . .

194

He catches me off guard . . . How do I know? . . . I don't know! . . . my artistic tastes! . . . I don't like green, that's all there is to it! . . .

– Geraniums? I mumble . . . geraniums? . . . He dives under the folding bed and fiddles around . . . full of watercolors under the folding bed . . . he takes out a gouache, a red one . . . a flower . . . an azalea, I think, yeah, an azalea . . .

– Here, a present!

He's never given me a present before . . .

– Go on, take it, killer!

What is he talking about, killer? That I wanted to kill him? What the fuck did that have to do with it?

– Go on, out of here! Go on, killer! Leave us in peace!

That's it! He's giving me the boot again!

– Roll 'er up! Roll 'er up!

– Roll what?

– The gouache! your gouache, God damm it! and the right way!

Apparently there's a right way . . .

– Here! A little statue! . . .

He goes fiddling around again and brings back a statuette . . . another thing from under the folding bed! . . . He's stuffing me with gifts! . . .

– Scram!

My two hands are full.

– Trot yourself off!

I don't leave . . . I'm at the door . . . at the other door . . . I'm on the sidewalk . . .

– What?

– Move it! Move it! the cops! Jerk! the cops are coming! an air raid!

I didn't hear the sirens . . . at least not well enough . . . I look up . . . He tells me there's an air raid . . . I don't see any airplanes . . . Yes, one stream! Ah, yes! A stream! . . . a giant V . . . but I didn't hear the sirens . . .

– Move your ass, you schnook! Move it!

With the buzzing in my ears, I had my doubts . . . He was sending me to the metro. I always mistrust sirens . . . always . . . I get confused . . . the avenue was empty, that's for sure . . . no more cops! . . . Absolutely nobody! . . . Maybe it was an alert after all? . . . but there were alerts all the time! . . . sirens . . . cat screechings in the sky! . . . I had my own noises! my own high-flying meowings! . . . blasting in both ears at once sometimes! high-pitched mewlings! . . . not only just sometimes . . . it could be for hours on end! . . . right in my ears! . . . All the same . . . all the same . . . "To the metro! Get to the shelter!" . . . I steel myself . . . one step . . . another . . . I stagger . . . I let go of the watercolor, there . . . the present . . . "To the metro!" I drop the little statue . . . I reel . . . one step . . . another . . . I get a hold of myself! . . . and *bleuuu!* I puke! . . . It comes over me right there . . . not twenty meters from his door . . . the sidewalk's all I see . . . and then nothing at all . . . I'm puking all over the sidewalk . . . on all fours! . . . crawling . . . it's the gutter I want to get to . . . because it's the alert! Am I buzzing or am I sirening? . . . It's an air raid! . . . I'm vomiting like a drunk, me! I know it! and I don't drink! Never! Never anything! It's the dizziness! The watercolor can go fuck itself! I'll cross over! I'll cross over all the same! To the shelter over there! . . . to the vault! . . . Sirens or no sirens! . . . Yes, I'm vomiting . . . but the sirens? following the bank . . . the edge . . . listen! . . . the gutter! . . . A gutter can be enormous sometimes! . . . It's a chasm . . . a chasm that swells up . . . and recedes . . . that swells up and calms down again! . . . it makes you dizzy! . . . the Eiffel Tower that you'd think was a gutter! . . . way in the distance a little hole, it's a sewer! . . . and then huge, gigantic! . . . the immensity of it! . . . all of Paris . . . the sewer . . . at the bottom of the sewer! . . . I'm sure of it! . . . I clutch on, hold fast . . . a thousand little lights! . . . seeing stars! . . . the sewer's edge! . . . bravo! . . . I haven't been sucked into the sewer! . . . no, I haven't! I haven't been sucked into the precipice! Bravo! . . . I'm puking . . . I'm puking into it! I'm buzzing! . . . I'm so dizzy! But I won't give in to it! Menière's syndrome, it's called! . . . the houses are spinning! and then! . . . they lift off! they lift right off! Holy smoke! the buildings in the air! "Menière! Menière!" the sidewalks are really getting a kick out of this one! . . . I hear you laughing . . . No! no! no! If I just steel myself I'll be able to cross!

You jokers won't get me! I'm floating! Floating! and the song! . . . I hear you laughing! You'd like the notes? The notes are in my head, too! I'll write them for you, transcribe them! . . . You'll go get yourself a piano . . . they still have pianos . . . don't take Jules's! Don't go to Jules's place! . . . it's off key, Jules's piano! Don't go there! me, I crawl, I puke, fine! . . . but everything is off key at Jules's place! . . . I'll play you the right note! the right one! and then another! and there's your song![239]

be gone with the wind

You'll manage to find yourself a piano! With one finger you'll play! . . . They're not all dead, the pianos! Some sounds still exist! the "mi"! the "re" . . . you don't need a bugle! F sharp! There are some noises that are finished . . . but a piano! one finger! another! there are noises that no longer exist! . . . but the piano! F sharp and G! . . . there, that's in the key of G, what I'm doing for you now! Just watch! One finger! One finger! Go on! Go ahead! I'm listening to you from here where I am! Bravo! Bravo! Oh, but you cut a lovely figure! Look at yourself in a mirror! a little round one, you know the kind? Ha! Like Jules's! like Jules has! . . . Oh, but I'm an agreeable sort, too! . . .

All this is good for a laugh, but nobody wants to take my place at the bottom of the hole! . . . they leave me here to rot, my admirers! . . . songs or no songs! . . . All in it together! . . . The behind full of pus, blind, deaf! . . . hateful – fans, enemies, what's the difference? All they want is to see the beast in the bullring brought down! . . . the traitor, the purveyor of death, the Judas-in-Chief: me! . . . I've seen them all with their fangs out! Enemies, their mugs shouting for blood! The bloodbath snouts on them! And craven whores, their cracks bloody from coming! I've seen it all! Yet another example: the grand jury! last Thursday! Okay, so they engrave their names in gold in the granite walls of the Sainte Chapelle! for the edification of the poor slobs who are too generous, too hot blooded, too simple minded for what they'll be put through in any epoch you can name when they fly to the cannon's call, to the clarion call, to the sacrifice! . . . Go ahead, engrave another stone, fine, for those who'll have sold Odes to both sides, who'll have had the entire Ultimate Court on their knees! That's the lesson history teaches! Their back-and-forthing won't have been wasted! . . . the way the volunteers are treated, the enlisted men in two wars who jumped into the fire a hundred times so that the Harlot of a Nation would look altogether more noble than some piddling bunch of sellout crackpot veteran-fuckers! Seventy-five percent hero and the Ultimate Court is gonna break your heart on you! wipe your thing with your amnesty! As soon as the clarion calls the wounded from both wars, the 75 percent of 1914, you'll see what fun the sly bastards have! The Builders' great big climax![240] They don't talk about that in *Readers Digest!* But I, who'll last longer than any of them, I'll have them gold-inscribed in the marble! Fans, dupes, enemies! No one is offering to take my place in the clink! I can just go rot there! they all agree! Ass full of pus, no more teeth, blind, deaf! the beast slaughtered in the ring is all they want! To see the traitor, purveyor of death, the Judas-in-Chief impaled and then sliced up into slivers! Of course, they won't admit it, they're too yellow bellied! I want their names, their promotions, their rank and serial number, I want to know who's protecting them, how much they got for it, and just how sadistic they had to be to get where they are, put it all in gold letters, right in the granite, in Sainte Chapelle! The way they treat their heroes, the hatred they invest in them! such revenge! They who are laden down with revenue and gold! The weak excite them!

They want them to howl! I'm howling! I'm ranting! frail! I'll
howl in the Sainte Chapelle! Martin Ciborium, he isn't howling! He gets all his Gram and Brome fees without any need to
howl! He delivers engines without howling, he doesn't feel
the slightest bit of shame! Only pride! The Ultimate Court
doesn't dither, either, it breaks her 1914 heroes on the rack
without batting an eyelash! Those who amassed millions
during the occupation, they're not howling, either! They're
just waiting for the other war, the next one! They got chin-
chilla cloaks! already! They look way up their rectums, they
get together in the club especially to compare each other's
wads! "You bleeding there? You're not bleeding?" Everything's all set for the next war! Their contacts, their man-
dates, the representatives they're paying off, their carte
blanche from the High Court! Their helicopters! Their
Odes! They're running the show, they've won, they're handing out the sentences. Me, they took everything from! my
shirt! my hide! my years! . . . my manhood! I can't get it up any
more! . . . all that's left is the pellagra!
   – You'll pay for everybody, that's what they said!
   Who everybody? What everything?
   France is full of secrets . . . secrets in the mails . . . I never
could open my mail . . . Madame Toiselle, my concierge,
would open it for me, but she was soon sickened by it . . .
when people send you news it always stinks of phoniness,
hanky panky, crime . . . Oh, and especially friendly letters,
honey coated, loyal . . . friendly letters drive me crazy . . . they
arrive via the police precinct. Madame Toiselle opened them
for months on end . . . I used to say to her, "Just show me the
'death announcements' – the little coffins!" It got so tedious,
the "death announcements" and "little coffins"! the number
of people who took that to heart and paid the ultimate price
. . . I've been told that even today there are people who have
screaming panic attacks over it! from telegrams! from little
coffins! that they find them in the metro, all huddled up . . .
people obsessed! So go howl, you pansies! Down boy! Now

Artron, he never howled! He's got a goddamn poker up his ass! All the howling he knows about is in plays! He picks up a few bucks informing! He's one cute cookie! Howl, you pansies, while you're swooning! Don't be embarrassed! Howling is the animal's cry, the cry of life! Fuck all your middle-class reticence! You'll cry out when you give birth! even louder when you croak! and you'll still never measure up, with all your swooning, your juicy come-cries, to the hero that they're beating to a pulp, that they're purposely leaving to rot on a cross who only wanted his country to survive! That has extraordinary value! You can't buy that at the Auction Rooms! You gotta be the Judas-in-Chief, the shame of Montmartre like me, the exterminator of Paris, to know the secret of hatred! All the repudiations! I wrote what had to be written, I gave all I could! youth, blood, voice-poems! more than all the faggoty bars! than all the pecker and syrup teasings at the theaters! than all the magazines of every stripe! than the Courts that are grinding me, killing me! that are just waiting for the next war so they can really have the ultimate come this time, so the "Builders" can really shaft it to them again! Ah, bring on the cancer! may cancer eat out their rectum, their lungs, their tongue! the pharynx! God, whom I look in the face, hears what I'm saying! To date I have never said "Go to it!" But regardless, the whole clique is busy judging, condemning, stealing furniture, apartments! The proof! I have no hide left! I have no shirts left! I have no teeth left! But I have little tunes that I remember

my mother!

One little second of pleasure, a whole life of pain . . . my mother knew nothing of the pleasures of a good roll in the hay . . . she missed out on all that . . . like me, her son . . . a lifetime of sacrifice! . . . the woman who can grunt and rave in the throes of a deep fuck can die happy . . . Oh, but, the ass stuck, me, the one despised by all, I'm going to avenge them all, I'm going to write their historic names in engraved gold, in the Sainte Chapelle! . . . such is the power of the so enfeebled poet! so enfeebled! the most feeble of them all! Take my word, all you Hercules in judge's robes! I'll make you write your names in gold! They refused me my amnesty . . . decided I hadn't suffered, hadn't suffered enough, spat up enough blood! . . . this is between God and me! . . . I have the medal, I have the replica! The medal conferred by Joffre, November 1914! . . . example under fire![241] The other night the guard came in and got me up to sign my appeal . . . a Baltavian document . . . what could I do? . . . Was I going to quibble over a paragraph? . . . I'd get his billy club right in the kisser! I saw what a cudgel could do in Africa! I don't care for the cudgel! I prefer cannibalism! . . . I saw women, their thighs eaten by the pimps who loved them . . . I never ate anyone's thighs, myself . . . instinct, guardian spirit, who knows? . . . Jules, him, he ate thighs . . . I was saying that my concierge for a long time would read my letters and then she got tired of it . . . she just kept the "death announcements" for me . . . the most bitter poisons . . . You get tired very fast of poisons, nastiness, being clobbered! Just look at the Rack! . . . the guys on the rack have stopped howling! . . . The only thing that keeps me going is digitalis, my systole is shot! . . . *blah!* . . . *baaa!* . . . *blah!* . . . *boo!*

> *Must we tell our friend?*
> *Every party ends? . . .*
> *To hell with your kind*
> *Be gone with the wind!*
> *Farewell, dead leaves!*

I might not even have enough time left to write all that I owe to Lili, the angel she's been for me . . . I tell you everything so all hashed up . . . I should reread everything! you think! . . . digitalis the only thing that keeps me going . . . the Ultimate Court judges are holding my hourglass in their hands! . . .

they're saying: "Dirty stooge! Another month gone! And he's still not dead! Sonofabitch!"

They get all surprised . . . They get all indignant! That's what they think of me! But me, I'll write their names in the Sainte Chapelle! their names in gold! it is thusly forever, for all! . . . they'll be caught up with eventually . . . people perpetually wallow in blood . . . they can never climax strong enough . . . they need the Circus, athletes, big muscles that get torn out! . . . I'll explain all this to you later if the pellagra doesn't kill me first . . .

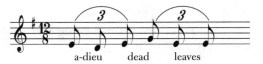

a-dieu   dead   leaves

Maybe I could get around on canes . . . tottering and shaking . . . I'm used to it . . . I'd puke outside in the gutter . . .

– So who's gonna finish him off? We've already stolen everything from him! Plagiarized him! Repudiated him! . . . Cut off his water tap and see what happens!

They cut it off on me! . . . I live without drinking . . . without doing caca . . . without urinating . . . Twenty-one days, I know . . . my ass stuck to the stool . . . by the scabs! . . . once out, if I get out, I'll have a petition passed around to you, you'll support me for life! I don't want to do a frigging thing any more! . . . neither does Bébert, or Cabbage Head, or Ninive the other cat, or Bessy the dog[242] . . . except maybe a little neighborhood doctoring? maybe! . . . just to treat a rheumatism here and there? . . .

My wife came to see me here the first few months, and then they put an end to that.

– He's not eating enough! Is what they told her . . . He's not doing his caca! . . .

That was the jailers' excuse! . . .

One enema every two weeks, boiling hot . . . there's your remedy!

Remorse will kill you.

She takes care of everything, Arlette, takes up my defense by telephone, by the bouquets that she's going to give as gifts . . . She turns the Court's hourglass over the moment I'm about to kick the calendar . . .

– He'll never snuff it!

I live only through her . . . my body's shot! . . . the soul, too, almost . . . The world has been too cruel. There's no shortage of people to skin you alive! I've known some terrible beings . . .

Ole Jules, tyrant that he was! I told you about it! . . . but I've seen him at the end of his tether . . . I could have gouged out his eyes when he was pawing Arlette, naked . . . I'll fight back, I'll make him bleed! would that he offered me up his eyes so I could gouge them out for him! . . . he taunted me on purpose from his cart . . . you can talk about a dirty old man . . . I'd like to drive his poker right into him . . . *Crrang!* Right in the eyeballs! He called me a Kraut on purpose in front of those people, and the concierge! I should've finished him off! . . . At least there'd be a reason for being in prison . . . If I reread all the pages as they've asked me to do I would find secret thoughts . . . Oh, you wouldn't do much with them! . . . you've got no rhythm in you! the human soul is full of ill-distilled poisons! . . . whence all these unclean thoughts . . . I devoted myself body and soul to saving your cherished lives! I never robbed a soul! . . . I never deceived anyone! I've never even taken a tip! . . . to show you, the gouaches, the statuettes . . . into the gutter! . . . all of it!

– Pose, Arlette! Pose for him! Go ahead! Nude!

I encouraged her . . . I can still hear myself . . .

She was kind of beautiful naked . . . even all green under the gaslight . . . she asked my permission . . . it was funny, asking permission . . . for her body! . . . I, who'd never refused her anything . . . who'd forbidden her nothing . . .

– Pose for him, Lili!

She wanted to hear me say it . . . she was sexual . . . theater

people are always sexual . . . that doesn't prevent feelings . . .
the proof? . . . a thousand proofs! . . .

– Go ahead! Go ahead! Pose for him!

I remember very well, I insisted . . . there, on the folding
bed . . . what she could offer by way of curvature, by way of
lines! . . . those long, muscular legs! those fruits of grace and
exercise . . .

– I'll do one just for you! for your eyes only!

A ceramic figurine of Arlette.

– Whenever you get back!

Now he was talking about once I was gone . . . that's what
he meant . . . he'd keep Arlette . . . perhaps it would have been
better that way . . . I wonder about that . . . She would not have
had so many woes had she stayed there shacked up with Jules
. . . she'd have been protected! And how, was he protected,
ole Jules! a goddamn pope! at least four networks! He'd help
them out a bit here and there . . . and the tables were turning!

It's cowardly, here as I think about it in the hole, not to take
on the mob on your own! everyone against you alone! the
whole pack! I blame myself for it, I blame myself for it to the
marrow! I love her, Lili, I love her like no one else, but I've
broken her . . . She's done astonishing things for me, astonishingly devoted, I didn't deserve it! coming here to the back
end of beyond in the clink here to bring a little bit of pastry,
one little orange she managed to find, what she didn't risk!
It's life itself a bit of orange juice when you weigh no more
than thirty kilos! . . . I'm throwing this all at you like that,
without thinking! I'm not sure I haven't already said it above
around page 212! . . . Here, I'll give you a hug, you'll manage!
. . . I have so many things to tell you that I'd have to live 120
years and never stop writing, to lay the groundwork . . . 200
years to get the ball rolling . . . and you wouldn't understand
everything! . . . even if the Grand Jury had me arrested and
incarcerated in the Citadel, had me garroted and disembow-
eled . . . even here on Baltavian soil! . . . I wouldn't edit it out!
I'll glorify their names in gold! The Underling from the Em-

bassy, too! And the Minister! Senatus Populusque Faggot! I have my reasons! Here in my novel, too, I glorify them! I never stop! I reflect with my ear always cocked, glued against the marble, I hear everything! I rehash memories in my head . . . how that piss-ridden legless Jules seduced Arlette . . . the coffee had something to do with it! no doubt about it! even if they had me garroted now, I'd say: it was the coffee! He had mocha coffee you can't even find any more! a real Arabian filter . . . once I left, should've seen how the mocha went to their heads! and the kirsch! she didn't even drink, so you can imagine! he forced her! I'm sure of it! he got her all worked up! she caved in! any other time, I wouldn't have given a fuck, but what would the villagers say in times like these? I told you, the two avenues, the fourteen streets, the twenty-two lanes! So poisonous that two drops was enough to kill the whole neighborhood! The worst goddamn village in the world when it came to the ferocity of the gossip! nothing like it anywhere in the universe! tongues like nowhere else! Ole Arlette posing starkers, thrown on her back on the folding bed! pussy wide open! . . . and I'm supposed to be the pimp! and the watercolors – in payment for her thighs and her hole! Where could I go? . . . I keep thinking about that . . . they were in it together . . . here's to nature! . . . agreed! . . . he's the natural-born pimp, sees everything come up roses and dough! me, I don't even see it comin'! . . .

– He sells his sweetheart's charms! He sells military secrets! For heaven's sake! of course! He sells his Lili's calves! He sells her angelic smiles! . . . He gets money from all sides! He sells the names of patriots . . . The Shame of Montmartre and of the Nation: Ferdinand!

The waffling waves from Westminster got it right, all right! . . . All you had to do was listen at the windows! . . . what was being bellowed out from the radios on the ground floors! . . . there was no more hangable hoodlum than myself, 14 avenue Gaveneau, seventh floor! . . . the proof, they sold everything off on me! the furniture, the apartment, the linens, the blankets! . . . Seven manuscripts! And they've promised to take everything else: confiscated *aeternam!* my affections . . . works! . . . my cats even! It was already being proclaimed, gibberished, crackled about! The whole BBC! from La Fourche to the North Station . . . to the point where Rommel's news came after my shenanigans![243] The Unspeakable Céline! The worst kind of dunghill Kraut character you can dream up! You know because the Great Purification Brigade, they came up as soon as Arlette and me left, 22 March![244] They chucked out my blind mother, they burglarized everything, burned seventeen manuscripts, they sold our sheets at the Flea Market, they didn't know what to do with *Guignol's Band* . . . *Krogold* either . . . or *Casse-Pipe* . . . They put some of it in storage, but since they couldn't pay for it, it was sold on the sly at the Salle Drouout.[245] I know all about their funny business . . . There are families of Purifiers who're still full of my bric-a-brac! . . . I can't go tell the Grand Jury, "You're protecting pirates!" . . . They'd slap me with another fine for calumny and the rest, me who still has so many others to pay! to two, three, four Republics! I won't buy back so much as a folding bed! . . . And my mother's inheritance! They chucked her out! Chucked out my mother before she died! Oh, but I'm very careful! I don't go complaining just any old where! You'll say, "you're so undone, why don't you just finish yourself off?" . . . Fine! . . . When I finish myself off I'm gonna say to you: it's for the animals, that's why, not men! like Cabbage Head and Nana and Sarah, my cat that left one night and that we never saw again, like the farm horses, and our friends the animals who have suffered a thousand times just like men! rabbits, owls, blackbirds! who spent so many winters with us! in the back of beyond! . . . death will be a blessing to me . . . I will have given my heart to everyone . . . It'll be over and done with, no more you, or your attachments, or your lies! . . . no more Aunt Estreme! Clemence! the brutal Toto, either! . . . Over and done with! They'll no longer be dancing in my walls! . . . the banshee will no longer be bashing his skull in

206

. . . I do not want my death to be caused by men, they lie too much! not from them would I get eternal rest!

I've got others to tell you about, other stories that are far more heart rending, with words and music . . . very well thought out . . . when you've bought *Fable!* . . . not the whole thing at once! you'll have to wait! gluttons! your heads are far too flimsy . . . your little foreheads are too low . . . first of all there's the dreadful way you read . . . you don't even retain one word out of twenty . . . you stare off into the distance, tired out . . . you're not an artist like Jules . . . him, he retained what he saw! the proof, Arlette's thighs, her knockers, her backside, the sloping lines of her haunches . . . those convulsions of a lioness . . . even the goddamn shithead of a malevolent stump that he was, I'd rather have lent Arlette to him than to Ciborium of the Academy! And I find you have another terrible fault: innate avarice . . . you pass on books to your friends . . . you totally spoliate poets, they can go drop dead! . . . Oh, I already feel like dying . . . but not for you! I want to for Bébert, Cabbage Head, Valby, wild cats, and for Sarah, my sacred little she-cat and for the farm animals . . . My style rubs you the wrong way? And my pellagra and my scrotum, which is peeling, going gangrene on me? do you think you'll live forever? Ah, I can picture you having a good look up your asshole! . . . I disgust you? I'm too beastly? . . . maybe you go in for a bit of modeling like Jules? Would I know? Will I ever know? Maybe you're on to the gypsum of the Impasse Trainee? . . . Jules's secret vein . . . that you also want Lili spread out under the green Auer gas lamp? . . . If you went under that light you'd be finished! . . . An old gal, a young one, you in the middle! . . . some kind of black Hercules with a hard-on! . . . That's the fatal blow to any inspiration! Lulli, Couperin, worked that way![246] but you know little about clay! even less about gypsum sandstone! . . . you, you'll wind up drinking infusions, sarsaparilla or flower-mix . . . with 1 percent digitalis . . . the usual concoctions . . . in a well-ordered death!

Me, I know Jules's vein! I saw Auntie Estreme there, Ciborium, and little Leo! . . . I saw Clemence, too! . . . I hightailed it out there with the notes.

be gone with the wind

You're gonna have to make a quick getaway, too! . . .
I'll give you all the music, couplets and refrains.

You'll see how it is they dance!
You'll see the lovely audience!
At the great cemetery of the Good Children!

You'll be a bit shamefaced at first . . . your right leg up in the air! . . . then one day! . . . It'd be like a "Lancers Waltz" . . . I'm not giving you the music right away! You'd think you could do anything then! You'd send back the wheelbarrow for me, the bike. You'd send me back flat on my ass again! "Ciborium, Larengon! Go to it!" is what you'd say! On the road again! Archères! Leeks! No way! if you could sculpt Arlette maybe it'd be different! okay then! now you're talkin'! But take a look at yourself in the mirror! the same as Jules! look at the sight of you! you don't look to me like an amputated hero! you don't come across like a hero at all! no! there's no more "War of '14," don't even mention it any more! I already gave you the key! "G major!" what are you waiting for? If I spoiled you, you'd only badmouth me! worse than ole Jules! you'd stick long needles into me! you'd bribe Bébert away from me with a steak! He'd gouge out my eyes! . . . the titmouse also! who's a lot sharper than he looks, and Lili's robin red-breast who comes to see us each morning . . . Oh, I'm humbled before *sol! mi!* . . . *sol!* . . . *sol!* . . . you're humbled before nothing! naturally! spoiled is what you are! you badmouth heroes! prisoners! the dying! no, I won't give you my sayings! all my sayings! there'd be no holding you back! . . . I used to accompany Jules with my left hand . . . I told you . . . it was usually with my left hand! . . . him playing the bugle to perfection! . . . I told you all about it . . . if I'd have been able to play with both hands he'd have hated me even more! . . . him, he could fiddle around with both hands! Boy, could he knead the ladies with those! . . .

– Leave! is what he says to me! Get outta here! Three's a crowd!

I'm recapitulating . . . condensing . . . it's the *Readers Digest* style . . . people only have time to read thirty pages . . . apparently! . . . maximum! . . . that's all they have time for! they horse around for sixteen hours out of twenty-four, they sleep, they copulate the rest, where would they find the time to read a hundred pages? oh, do caca, I forgot! as well! and the cancer they're looking up their ass for, their head upside down, the acrobats! "Dear hole! Dear hole!" and those who onanize themselves to boot! while imagining themselves fondling big bawdy babes! they're ruining their circulation! hours on end! in the darkness of movie houses! going broke on getting their goddamn pants laundered! over the ghosts of vampires, dead these twenty years! who come out of the cozy lair soaking wet, haggard! on the bus going home they don't know where the hell they are!

Me, I'm going to restore Art to its rightful place for you! I warned you above! not everything just for Jules! and his customers! his models, I'd do them all pink! his models! no more greens! no more yellows! Jules, his models! his pee pee all over his goddamn gondola-crate!

– My stumps are killing me today! Ha! Ha! and he'd pinch them, purposely! so the girls would finger them on him . . .

His shutters never closed right . . . never really shut . . . just so the Peeping Toms could ogle a bit inside . . . complicated business, pretty girls and cheap thrills . . . why do they come back? . . . badly joined shutters help! . . . he wanted them that way . . . took balls!

– Don't go up to Ferdine's place up there! Don't go up to

his place, my little lambs! He'll whip you! He'll gobble you up! He's an ogre! . . .

I never whipped anybody! He's the one who was spanking everybody and her aunt!

I'm going over all the bad things, all the damage he did to me . . . So let me sum up this first tome for you, a few words, a bit of music . . . If my poor old head is nodding, if I teeter and I vomit, it's not by choice, believe me! it's that I'm honest to goodness tired from too much remembering your thises and your thats . . . that it's all well and good and nice to say *Fable,* but the thises and the thats! the gas bill! the telephone! If I were independently wealthy I wouldn't write another word! . . . I wouldn't even bother saving money any more! . . . no more villa in Saint-Malo! as soon as I got there, my two maids, my doors, a soon as I bought my two bikes, can you imagine the remarks! The "NRFers" plague me,[247] they want three . . . four tomes! and tunes! out of my poor chipped noggin! what's more, they want a *Readers Digest!* . . . a sizzling *Constellation!*[248] . . . five hundred pages shrunk to thirty lines.

– Cut *Journey* down to twenty words for me! . . . with pictures!

I abbreviate everything! Cut everything down to size! Goddamn crime! You gotta be a Vauvenargues, a La Bruyère, your fans want twenty-five lines and a pinup and nylon stockings! flesh colored! That's their taste for you!

Arlette could help me out a little! I'm just a poor lyric poet, but damn it, a comic one! The way this century has treated me! I've got time to think about Jules again, but if I told you everything about him, the Grand Jury would take advantage, they'd turn my hourglass back over.

– The rest of us are already sky high! Montmartre is about to go up in flames! mines everywhere! . . . From Batignolles to Dufayel!

That's what Jules says, anyway . . .

He knew everything, foresaw it all . . . he had some incred-

ible contacts . . . the Grand Jury under his boot! One word
from ole Jules and they let me out . . . same goes for here,
where I am now . . . they send back the wheelbarrow! . . . ten
of 'em, fifteen, they jostle me off again! . . . beyond Archères!
either that or they bash my skull in! Here in my hole! between
two and three o'clock! They take advantage of visiting hours!
that's what they did to the nut job in 116 . . . I saw him the next
day on his stretcher . . . a stretcher covered in beige canvas
. . . They were taking him off to the morgue . . . he was a mystic, the guy in 116, he used to offer up his sufferings to heaven
. . . the more sufferings he had the more he got his rocks off!
They gave him a bellyful of it, all right! . . . For me it would be
another kind of torture. I'm much more of a wanted man than
the mystic! . . . I'll never see Auntie Estreme again, nor Clemence nor the valiant Toto! . . . the banshee will not perforate
the wall on me! If he knocked it down once and for all I could
finish my work! . . . but he'll never perforate anything at all.

I put him to shame in the infirmary.

– Eh, go on, you just scraped yourself, you loafer!

I take a look at his scab for him . . .

Seven poems I lost! seven! up there in the garbage, Gaveneau! . . . seven poems that soared, that set your soul sailing,
that would have raised men to the heavens, a century! but no,
there you go! iconoclastic fury! the Ultimate Court and its
hourglass! Seven invaluable poems! I can't complain too
much! I don't dare! In case Auntie Estreme hears me complaining and Clemence and the little Toto! and they figure
out how to get their revenge!

But excuse me! There's fight in me yet!

I'll get you in my sights!
Two big black holes!

I'm talking to Jules here.

your foul soul up the hole!
Will take flight!

You'll see the heavenly choirs!
How they dance upon the spires!
In the great cemetery of the Good Children!

I tone all this down somewhat . . . moderating . . .

– Do a short version, dance to the *Readers Digest* tune!
drop your head in your hands!

The "NRFers" make me laugh! The internships question?
a hundred words? nothing left out?

The Yanks are shamefully behind the times! Two hundred
years behind, the simpletons! lying spewers of gobbledygook!

Two . . . three hundred years, we're ahead of them! us! it's
laughable! We have La Bruyère on our side! The match is
won! the culture match! Why should I waste my strength, my
talents?

But I'd have more fun without the ass glued, without gangrene or scabs! I'd be as visionary as a pope! I tell you! I tell
you! If I didn't have the bowels all tied up in knots by dried
up turds, dysentery! If my hearing wasn't deafened by the
hordes of express trains! Ah, would I be happy! beatifically!
But I've already grumbled a thousand times . . . I'll grumble
some more! I grumble about everything! . . . I grumble that
you were going off to war that I can't stop you and that you
come back covered in shit, ridiculous, without weapons,
without a flag, and that you rob me to boot and that you
chuck me into prison and have me carried off in a wheelbarrow to the mud flats of Achères to wind up in the first flush of
leeks! . . .

Is that chivalrous behavior? . . . I showed you Roland . . .
Pépin the Short . . . Bayard! . . . that's enough! . . . you retained
nothing whatsoever! . . . the leeks . . . the wheelbarrow! . . .
there! . . . If they come back to get me I'll refuse! . . . I won't
leave ever again, I'll hold on tight! . . . I'll bash my own skull
in! I'm capable of it! . . . I'm not like the banshee! . . .

I've been subjected to every kind of provocation!

I've had to deal with Louis XV at the cell window, who invites me to fondle him . . . I will not fondle him!

– You handsome prisoner, I could really go for you!

He lusts after me, he eyeballs me!

– Lewd impostor of a black pig of an Underling, leave me alone!

I'm sick, my head is throbbing like a drum, pealing like a bell, but I haven't lost any of my marbles!

– Long live Colonel Des Entrayes! Be stalwart, men!

My mind is like a flag of seamless muslin! it's not some lewd sonofabitch who'll get the better of me! or a Lartron, either! or a Ciborium! same goes for Gram and Brôme and the weathervanes! . . . Lauriac either, or the funny-hat brigade! Stainless is what I am! I can't even tell you the indecency, the lewd outrageousness of their Odes! If only the truth were told! What Jules did is child's play in comparison! And he, don't forget, took my Lili on me! he fondled her upside down inside out! . . . and was pawing at her on me so that I should watch everything! under the Auer gas lamp! on absolute purpose! drooling at the mouth! didn't want me to leave until I saw that they were in cahoots! . . . And he promised me her in the kiln to boot! in his oven!

If they leave me in the clink much longer, these Hourglass potentates, people'll say: But that's not him! . . . that can't be Ferdinand! . . . wouldn't recognize him! Half of my bowels are in a knot, that's true! I've practically got half a buttock gone and a little piece of hip . . . falling apart! what's it to you? I'll make a formal complaint to the Foreign Office, I'll not mention anyone by name, but they know me . . . they'll summon me to the Courthouse . . . I won't be able to see anything . . . Arlette will recognize me . . . she alone . . . not the others! . . . that would be awful! . . . They'd start torturing me again! . . . wheelbarrow and away with you! . . .

Think about Ciborium! Larangon! Auntie Estreme! Little Leo and the Underling! I'll pretend I'm somebody else! I'll

213

have amnesia, I'll be a dribbling idiot, I'll be infantile! . . . and ole Jules, who cut me so deeply, who's still whistling all through my walls . . . on purpose he's whistling my little ritornello . . .

a-dieu   dead   leaves

These days I can only retrospect in fits and starts . . . the noises in my ears are too intense . . . aside from the howlings from the dank cells! I'm floundering along with my stool on the tiles . . . I can no longer use my bunk . . . I stretch out on the tiles . . . my ass still stuck to the stool . . . that's all the repose I get . . . I listen, take the floor's heartbeat, I hear everything! the whole prison! . . . on the bunk it's too painful . . . my right arm hurts too much . . . I need vitamins, at least 125 grams a day! as well as the enemas! . . . from irritation and turning over my skin is coming off in strips . . . There are others, of course! . . . Lots of others! . . . I'm just a small-fry martyr . . . Arlette has suffered more than I have . . . and Cabbage Head! and what about the farm animals? . . . Humans have it good! Oh yes, indeed! I could sell you whistlings, strident coarse ones through the walls that would saw your bulb in two! the bulb of your brain I'm talking about! Jeez! I hold mine, head between two hands . . . the parietals . . . the occiput . . . my whole think-box is oscillating, swimming . . . it's not a respiratory problem . . . I have no difficulty breathing . . . it's the brain, the drumming inside there! . . . clarions! trumpets! and four locomotives! *Choo! Choo!* . . . the pellagra is tearing my ass to shreds . . . tearing it off, I tell you! . . .

– Serves him right! No torture is excruciating enough for him! He asked for it!

You're like the Ultimate Court! *Dura lex!* Here, other whistlings now that I think about it . . . the guards! . . . Another roundup so they can give you some welcome punishment! . . . Their fists right in your kisser! . . . *"Oouuch! Oouuch!"* Two trucks screech to a halt on the gravel . . . it's a roundup,

214

all right! . . . It must be past midnight . . . they're gonna rumble! . . . Me, I hear it all, with one ear stuck to the ground, like this . . . like my stool is stuck to my ass, jeez, it won't let go! I can't tell you, the scabs! It must be past midnight . . . The trucks screech to a halt on the gravel . . . with the other ear I hear outside . . . I hear! . . . I hear the sirens in the port! . . . And the owls in the cemetery . . . I'm not going in for romantic effects here . . . they're dying in the cells, I tell you! We'll see the bodies tomorrow, the bodies covered over, their shapes . . . while they're bringing them out to the morgue . . . We won't see their faces . . . as long as they got holes punched in them . . . it's the guards who lay them . . . especially the women that they force into the game . . . I found out all about it, only natural . . . tourists don't get to see these things . . . tourists don't get to see anything . . . believe anything . . . think anything . . . They get out of their cars, they have a drink, they get back in again . . . "Good day, gentlemen!" The dying women that they rape, enchained, ligated, the tourists don't ever get to see them! . . . All the same it's been happening for three thousand years of History! . . . Tourists only see Paradise! . . .

   – Sir, was it beautiful in paradise?

   – Oh yes! I'll go back!

Those who aren't killed during the rumble, who've had their meat stripped off their bones but whose hearts have held out, they have to go and have a wee wash. Cleanliness must reclaim its rights! In cold water, a jet of ice-cold water! so you get a new lease on life! . . . the hounds outside howl! the whole pack! of course! because they're going at it again with the billy clubs! There's a whole lot of staggering going on under cold water! the dogs are barking again! I'm not talking about the little cells. There they kill themselves ever so quietly . . . they open up their veins . . . they just about let out a sigh, they're dead, nobody knows . . . only again the next day the canvas is spread on top of them . . . the autopsy shroud . . . but there's background martyrs! The abortionist

215

in 115, for example! . . . such bellowings that she outbellows the whole pack of dogs . . . and the she-spy in 312! so the guards charge! open up their doors again! club them till they scream, gasp, go quiet . . . *thud! thud!* no problem hearing the bludgeons! . . . their thoraxes! their thighs! me, I hear fine, I'm taking the floor's heartbeat! Resounding! My whole ear on the ground, I hear it all . . . I can't stretch out on the bunk, I told you . . . I drop down just like that! stool adhesive to the ass! . . . I tear my scabs off as I get up when they sound the whistle that it's daybreak . . . well, about five o'clock. . . . What bothers me aside from my noises is maybe even more my bowels, my ten- to twelve-day constipation . . . such heavy intestinal lumber . . . They give me an enema of boiling water and fifteen phials of "DD extract." And then they bring me back down into the hole . . . If I didn't ask them for my enema I'd die of an obstruction, of a volvulus![249] . . . Then what? You'd never get my little air! *Mi! do! do! sol!* or anything at all! not Leo, and not Auntie Estreme, either!

Even if the banshee blasted down my wall! I'd meet him again in the infirmary! I'd always meet up with him somewhere! I always do! He's used to the way I treat him!

– Goddamn good-for-nothing, you're perturbing me! You chase away my Muses! You Destroyer of the Arts! You Hun!

– Shake me up! he says.

– I don't shake anybody up! You're like Louis XV, that black Underling! lust after everything on legs!

What's more, he defecates as he pleases, the banshee! He stinks up the infirmary! great big greasy perfectly shaped stools! you can imagine me with my amoebic dysentery, I'd have a thousand times a thousand reasons to be jealous! . . . stools like that! I could also be jealous of Jules, who pisses all over his crate whenever he pleases! Me here, my stool up the ass, it's not easy to urinate! Not at all, I can assure you! You go try! And I'm not jealous! and he made Arlette come on me, I wasn't there but I'm sure of it! . . . I'd rather not look into it! The poor little darling love who's suffering! suffered enough

216

from my turpitudes, a thousand more than I have! my idiotic patriotic escapades!

They were in it together, Jules and her! It was agreed ... A certain complicity ... There was an esthetic side to it, the clay ... there was this whole plastic side to it ... molding! ... molding was the thing! ... there was some other understanding, too, but what? ... I recapitulate ... his vein ... his lode! ... the Traînée Impasse ... I've got to situate everything right for you! ... to recapitulate! ... so you don't regret spending your forty bucks! and the last pages summed up! the last thirty!

Must we tell our friends
Every party ends?
Mi! re! mi! sol! mi!

In G! The whole thing in G!

He still hasn't got it going again, his pottery kiln! but I've got all the *mi! re! sol!* that I want! Oh, but you need the words! You're right!

Be gone with the wind!

That's alive!

It's not just Jules who's jealous of my visions, the others are, too! the other cells! they all want just one thing, that I drop dead! ... that they remain! and to shine again! and a kiln, too! Such ardor for that! Ah! if they only knew Lili! the muscles! the harmony! and her nether regions! and her smile! nobody shines the way she does!

I'm aching all over, you hear! ... I hear the convicts being beaten! I hear the owls hooting! I hear the sirens in the port! but I remain stoical, harmonious, pleasant ... I know a thing or two! ... I'm remembering it all, he's got friends in high places! I think about Jules, I think about Lili . . . what I regret here flat out on the floor listening to the stone is not to have seen enough! . . . if I'd really insisted he'd have done it all in front of me, I'd have strangled him afterward!

It's the genius of his hands! . . . He had the hands that could knead them, but had I grabbed him by the neck, I'd have punctured his glottis for him! I had him where I needed him for that! And be proud of it! proud of it, I tell you! But I don't have strangler hands . . . I couldn't have done it if I tried . . . *whack!* the screams! My hands are made for work! . . . an idiot's hands . . . if I'd laid them on him for real! if I'd gone at it with my two arms, would I have strangled him perhaps? . . . I'd have gotten his glottis! . . . they would have come, all right, the pair of them . . . They were asking for it . . . they wanted to finish off . . . they'd provoked me enough! . . . I'd have gouged his eyes out for him! after strangling him! He'd wronged me enough! . . . on purpose, her there naked under the gas lamp . . . Would I have gouged out his eyes? That's the story . . . the situation! . . .

be gone with the wind

It's the way he fondled her I can't get over . . . That's what it was . . . the way he fondled her! . . . I was really worked up! . . . Yup . . . really excited! . . . a regular John! . . . life goes on . . . blood flows . . . you get carried away . . .

Notes

INTRODUCTION

1. George Orwell, *In Front of Your Nose, 1945–1950*, vol. 4 of *The Collected Essays, Journalism, and Letters of George Orwell* (Middlesex: Penguin Books, 1970), 243.
2. Orwell, *In Front of Your Nose*, 261.

FABLE FOR ANOTHER TIME

1. Fernand de Brinon (1885–1947) was a journalist and politician who became Vichy's "ambassador" and then "delegate general" to Paris. Céline solicited his help during the war, once on behalf of his patients in Bezons and once in 1943 to ask for a pardon for a young Breton whom the Germans condemned to death and then shot.
2. During the Franco-Prussian War (1870–71) the Montrouge Fortress was one of the places most heroically defended despite the ferocious onslaught of the Prussians in Châtillon. It was almost entirely destroyed and later rebuilt. In 1944–45 it was the site of the executions of some of the most notorious collaborators.
3. During the war, Radio Brazzaville was one of the most important stations of the Free French. The French colony in the Congo had rallied to General de Gaulle's cause by August 1940.
4. Bezons is the Paris suburb where Céline practiced medicine from December 1940 until his departure for Germany in June 1944.
5. Céline is referring to collaborators.
6. The battle of Stalingrad, 1942–43, where the German army was finally repulsed, is widely considered to be the turning point in World War II.
7. St. Genevieve (422–500 A.D.) is the patron saint of Paris. She is credited with predicting the invasion of the Huns and with warding off Attila's attack on the city.
8. In 613, Queen Brunehilda was dragged to her death by galloping horses. Her picture was commonplace in schoolchildren's history books.
9. Probably a fictionalized reference to a liquidation of Dr. Des-

touches's office after his failure to set himself up in private practice in the wealthy suburb of Saint-Germain.

10. The Cour des Miracles was an area of old Paris between the rue Réamur and the rue Caire that in the Middle Ages was a meeting point for the city's low life, who would vie with each other for predominance.

11. This book contains only one long "chapter." Céline was referring to the different stories he would relate about his wartime experiences, which he conceived of as chapters in one great book, but which eventually became five books.

12. "Ulysses" will soon be given his real name, Bébert.

13. On 21 February 1950 (not 23 February), Céline was sentenced *in absentia* to the confiscation of half his worldly goods, present and future.

14. These are spas for the cure of respiratory diseases and rheumatism.

15. "Magog" is a reference to the prince "Gog" of the Apocalypse of Ezekiel, from the country of Magog, who was supposed to have threatened the Israelites when he led a coalition of peoples of the north against them. Christian exegetes have depicted him, however, as an Asian invader. Céline mentions elsewhere having seen reproductions of figurines representing him.

16. Landru was a famous criminal in the early 1920s.

17. La Villette is a working-class suburb of Paris known at the time for its meatpacking industry.

18. Dr. Petiot was an infamous serial killer during World War II.

19. Otto Abetz (1903–58) was the German "ambassador" to Paris during the occupation.

20. Campéador is a reference to Corneille's *Le Cid,* whose subtitle was *Le Campéador.*

21. Céline's wife, Lucette Almansor.

22. The writer Marcel Aimé, a faithful old friend.

23. Henri Mahé, an old friend of Céline, was a painter and scene decorator who lived on a barge on the Seine.

24. Reference to the Alfred de Vigny poem "La Mort du loup" in which a wolf "Closing his great eyes, dies without uttering a cry."

25. This passage, as well as referring to the de Vigny poem "Le Cor," is also a sort of preface to others later on dealing with characters from the *Song of Roland.*

26. Céline chooses the Palais de Chaillot for this bloody scene because it housed the National People's Theatre.

27. The *Vermot Almanac* annually published mild puns and pleasantries since its creation in 1886.

28. A literary reference to Pascal, who in his "Memorial" recalls a moment of mystic union with God with the words "Joye Joye Joye pleurs de Joye."

29. *Ausweiss,* a German word for a travel permit, was in common usage in France during the war. The permit was a necessary commodity for almost all travel and a great bone of contention, subject to favoritism.

30. A "lightening cart" is equipped to transport drinks.

31. The Hotel Majestic on avenue Kléber housed the German propaganda and censorship offices.

32. "The question" is in English in the original. Céline knew English quite well and euphonically associates the BBC, which broadcast French resistance messages throughout France, and Hamlet's "the question." Words in English in the original French text are indicated in italics.

33. Robert Denoël was shot dead on the boulevard des Invalides on 2 December 1945. He was Céline's publisher and had been indicted for publishing his anti-Semitic pamphlets during the war. The crime was never solved.

34. In the arrest warrant of 19 April 1945, Céline was accused of crimes listed under Article 75, paragraph 5 of the penal code, which inculpates "Any French citizen who in time of war, corresponds with a foreign power or with its agents, with a view toward favoring this power's undertakings against France." Subsequently, however, the indictment was made under Article 83, paragraph 4 of the code, which merely inculpates acts that "might be harmful to national defense," a lesser charge.

35. Guy Girard de Charbonnières (1907–90). While he headed the French Embassy in Copenhagen, he did receive the title of ambassador. Although he had been a member of the French Foreign Ministry in the Vichy government, he joined forces with the Free French in 1942. De Charbonnières was tireless in his efforts to extradite Céline.

36. *Fable* was written at the time of the Korean War.

37. Villa Saïd in the sixteenth arrondissement served in 1944 as a prison and the seat of a tribunal processing war criminals.

38. Buchenwald.

39. The Germans won a victory at Charleroi in Belgium, 21–23 August 1914.

40. St. Martin is considered to have introduced Christianity to the Gauls in the fourth century A.D.

41. La Porte Saint-Martin area of Paris was well known as a place of prostitution.

42. A pseudonym for the chain restaurants called Dupont-Cyrano that were popular between the two world wars, one of which was at the place Blanche.

43. "Croutons" refers to a certain sexual perversion indulged in by "soupeurs" involving bread and urine in Paris's public urinals.

44. Medieval undertakers would apparently bite the toes of the deceased to make sure they were dead, from whence comes the slang name for an undertaker as a "croque-mort" or "deadman-biter."

45. A reference to a sentimental nineteenth-century song from a popular play called *Risette* in which a baby girl is born to poor parents who see the sunny sky from a leaky roof and laugh despite their poverty.

46. Jean-Paul Sartre.

47. Céline's Aunt Amélie, his father's sister, was affectionately portrayed in *Death on the Installment Plan* as Tante Hélène. Mr. Verdot was her friend and protector in old age. She died in 1950, while this book was being written.

48. These four town names correspond to the four main stages of Céline's stay in Germany, which he wrote about in the German Trilogy, *Castle to Castle, North,* and *Rigodoon*: Baden-Baden, Sigmaringen (seat of Petain's government in exile), Neurupin, and Rostock. He disguises the first two so as not to arouse passions, but he leaves undisguised the latter two, as they were less well known and less controversial.

49. This sentence refers to three characters in Bizet's *Carmen*.

50. Céline transforms ss into AA and Auschwitz into Augsbourg. Odin was a Scandinavian divinity of war.

51. Courbevoie is the town outside Paris where Céline was born.

52. Dietrich von Choltitz, commander of the German garrison in

224

Paris in August 1944, was supposed for a time to have "saved Paris" by refusing to obey one of Hitler's commands, but this story has been refuted.

53. A pun on Pétain's name, "Putain" means whore.

54. Céline was kept for a while on death row in the Vestre Faengsel prison in Copenhagen, place of his Danish captivity.

55. Satory, near Versailles, was in 1871 a place where leaders of the Paris Commune were imprisoned and executed. At the la Roquette prison in Paris, the Communards had executed several hostages on 24 May 1871. During the siege of Paris, Gambetta flew away (7 October 1870) in an air balloon from the place Saint-Pierre-de-Montmartre to Tours, where he proceeded to organize the resistance. Cadoudal was a hero of the royalist counterrevolution in the Vendée war and later against first consul Bonaparte. Sarah Bernhardt continued to act even after she'd lost a leg, in 1915.

56. Emile Loubet was president of the Republic from 1899 to 1906, well before Hitler came to power. Gallieni died in 1916. The odes referred to are those of Paul Claudel, to which Céline returns often.

57. Although Céline did not retain shrapnel in the head or have a trepanation, as he often claimed in his novels, he did suffer from chronic buzzing in the ear and painful whistling due to wounds inflicted in World War I.

58. With the exception of Jean Jaurès, all the persons listed here spent time in prison, some after military defeats, others on political or moral grounds. Jean Henri de Latude (1725–1805) spent thirty-five years in prison (despite numerous escapes) after being implicated in plots against Madame de Pompadour, official mistress of King Louis XV. After his memoirs were published in the nineteenth century he became something of a symbol of the detainee. "Mr. Braguet" is probably "Monsieur Capet," name given to King Louis XVI when he was imprisoned in the Temple.

59. The author mockingly attributes a speech defect as a sign of effeminacy to a man who tries to sound like a military man but who is not.

60. André Chenier was a poet during the revolution who wrote some verses about the cries of a female fellow prisoner. The woman escaped execution, but Chenier didn't.

61. "Screw" is British slang for prison guard.

62. The castles of Vincennes and Mont Saint-Michel both served as prisons at various times. Creusot, in the Saône-et-Loire region, was a steel-manufacturing center at the time.

63. Admiral Leahy was American ambassador to the Vichy government from November 1940 to June 1942.

64. In French "Petit-Suisse" is a brand of soft cheese much cherished by children. Here the pun is probably a reference to the fact that as a favor, Pierre Laval appointed the writer Paul Morand ambassador to Switzerland when things were not going well for the Vichy government. Céline often pointed out that he received no such favors.

65. The Wooden Bridge in Argenteuil often fell victim to war. Madame Tabouis was a well-known radio journalist. Admiral Darlan was minister of the marine when the French fleet was bombarded at Mers-el-Kébir on 3 July 1940 and chief of land, sea and air forces in November 1942 when the French fleet was scuttled in Toulon. The scuttling of the fleet in Toulon is referred to again later.

66. Names of manuscripts, which got lost at the time of Céline's flight from Paris.

67. Perhaps an oblique reference to the marquis de Sade, who spent many years in prisons, including the Bastille, around the time of the French Revolution.

68. General Maurice Gamelin (1872–1958) was in charge of the French land forces at the beginning of World War II. His error in not accurately predicting the Germans' attack made him one of the people responsible for France's early defeat in May 1940.

69. René Mayer (1895–1972), Fourth Republic politician, was a member of the Ministry of Justice located at the place Vendôme at the time of Céline's imprisonment.

70. The Rue du Repos is one of the streets that go along Père-Lachaise, a landmark Paris cemetery where many notables are buried and where Céline's parents are also buried. He wanted his final resting place there as well but knew his wish would not be granted. He's buried in the Meudon cemetery outside of Paris.

71. Céline's only child, Colette, had five children and lived in Neuilly, on the outskirts of Paris near the Bois de Boulogne.

72. Max Revol, (1894–1967) a friend of Céline, was a dancer and singer who excelled in burlesque shows.

73. Bécon is Bezons.

74. The European was a café turned music hall in the "Europe" section of Paris.

75. Bezons is situated in the Argenteuil Township. During the bombing of Paris this area saw many casualties.

76. French prison where many Jews, resisters, and then collaborators were kept.

77. Pseudonym for Dachau.

78. A probable reference here to Klarskovgaard, the village on the Baltic where Céline spent the years subsequent to his imprisonment. The novel was commenced in prison and reworked in Klarskovgaard.

79. Reference to Bikini Island in Micronesia, where the Americans tested the nuclear bomb in 1946. This passage, representing the words of a sycophantic journalist commiserating with the author on his plight, is a key one. It is the point in the novel where the French language is most atomized and fragmented.

80. Jules Moch was a socialist politician under the Fourth Republic.

81. The writer Robert Brasillach was condemned to death and executed as a Nazi collaborator on 6 February 1945.

82. Reference to Suzanne Abetz, wife of the German ambassador to France during the occupation. A Frenchwoman, she knew Céline but had no apparent role in trying to get him amnestied.

83. Pierre Laval, prime minister in the Vichy government, met Céline in Sigmaringen, but there's no proof that he was ever Céline's patient.

84. Céline's mother did not die on a public bench, but at her brother's home, rue des Martyrs.

85. A further reference to Roger Vailland, who in January 1950 wrote an article titled "We'd No Longer Spare Céline" in *La Tribune des nations*. In it he told of how during the war, the resistance group to which he belonged used to meet in the apartment below Céline's. He said that they had debated killing him but had spared his life because he'd written *Journey to the End of the Night*. "Old Maid" is a take-off on *Le Grand Jeu (The Big Game)*, a surrealist magazine Vailland had helped launch before the war.

86. G. Lenotre (1857–1935), specialist of the "petite histoire" (anecdotes about the past), whom Céline refers to often.

87. Even into the twentieth century it was common among the

middle classes to send their babies to wet nurses for nursing until the age of two or three. Céline was no exception to this practice.

88. The Bickford cordon was a safety mechanism used in explosives.

89. Gen Paul, a Montmartre painter and close friend of Céline who was already mentioned and will remain a prominent figure in the novel. He lost a leg in World War I.

90. Cardinal Dubois was not Louis XV's minister but that of the regent Philippe d'Orléans. Dubois is associated with France's colonial development through the Compagnie d'Occident and the Compagnie des Indes, both set up during his ministry.

91. Reference to the Ministry of Foreign Affairs, Quay d'Orsay, which through its representative in Denmark, Guy Girard de Charbonnières, was insisting on Céline's extradition.

92. A biblical reference to "Vade retro Satanas," meaning "Get behind me, Satan."

93. André Marie (1897–1974) was a politician under the Fourth Republic. As justice minister in 1949, he was compromised for having classified documents pertaining to economic collaboration in the building of the Atlantic Wall. He had written the librettos for comic operas before the war. "Weathervane" was a common expression after the war to describe those who, without having evinced any hostility to the Nazis, declared themselves resisters at the time of the liberation.

94. This new nickname given to René Mayer could be an allusion to the fact that he was in January 1948 the minister of finance who withdrew from circulation the five-thousand-franc bank notes in an antifraud drive.

95. Cardinal La Balue was imprisoned for eleven years by Louis XI. Legend has it that he was kept in a cage where he could neither stand nor lie down, which contributed to his becoming a symbol, with Latude, of all detainees. Names of others follow.

96. Blanqui was imprisoned in Mont Saint-Michel between 1840 and 1844.

97. Armand Barbès (1809–70), a republican who opposed the July Monarchy and was far-left deputy during the Republic, was again arrested and sentenced to life imprisonment after the events of 15 May 1848.

98. The name given to King Louis XVI by the revolutionaries while he was imprisoned in the Temple.

99. When this novel was being finished Pablo Picasso did a famous drawing of the Dove of Peace for the Communist movement. The drawing recalled the Bible story of the dove that appeared after the deluge. The ark is mentioned a few lines above, and the image of "the flood without an ark" will become a frequent one in the second of the *Fable* novels.

100. In October 1914 Celine was hit by a bullet in the right arm, which after numerous operations left some paralysis in the forearm.

101. George Montandon (1879–1944) was a Swiss medical doctor who developed racist theories and became a friend of Céline. During the war Montandon played a despicable role for the Commission on Jewish Affairs, performing physical exams to determine "Jewishness," which meant a death sentence for many people. Unlike Céline, he remained in Paris and was wounded in an attack. He was brought to Germany, where he died.

102. The juxtaposition of the names Descartes and Kruschen was done in jest. Descartes held the art of medicine in high regard, and Kruschen was something of a charlatan, the inventor of the popular "Kruschen Salts" widely used before World War II.

103. Remire is Dr. Andre Jacquot (1898–1970), who practiced medicine in Sigmaringen with Céline and testified on his behalf after the war.

104. An obscure reference to a Revolutionary-period musician.

105. These are one and the same. Papus was the pseudonym of a Dr. Encausse (1865–1916), a famous Belle Epoque practitioner of the occult.

106. A Parisian master printer who lived near Céline in the 1930s.

107. An obscure reference to another mystical figure popular at the time, Joséphin "Sâr" Péladan, whose books Delâtre printed.

108. At the time Roger Vailland was a member of the French Communist Party.

109. In a 1950 survey in the newspaper *Le Figaro*, in which writers and critics were asked to designate "the twelve French novels of the first half of the century," neither *Journey to the End of the Night* nor *Death on the Installment Plan* was mentioned. But the year before, the readers of *Carrefour* mentioned Céline as seventh (out of twelve) living writers who would still be read by the end of the century. In 1990 another survey asked the same question and Céline was listed second, behind Marcel Proust.

110. André Tailhefer was a Clichy surgeon with whom Céline maintained friendly relations until the end of his life.

111. Théophile Briant (1891–1956), poet and writer, friend of Céline's whom he met in 1937 and saw at Saint-Malo. He founded a poetry journal called *Le Goéland*, or *The Seagull*, which Céline later satirizes as "the Albatross." "La Douane" is probably a reference to the Saint-Malo ramparts tower called "Bidouane."

112. References to places in Saint-Malo, the Breton port city that Céline often visited on vacation.

113. Turn-of-the century chorus girls who raised their skirts high enough to show their black stockings and white shifts.

114. Passage Choiseul, where Céline grew up, boasted of an excellent pastry shop, Charvin's at number eleven, and the bookstore Lemere at number twenty-three. Céline's mother's shop, which featured "genuine lace" and "curiosities," was at number sixty-four.

115. Famous gypsy violinist who became the symbol of the seducer in the late nineteenth century thanks to his running off with the rich American Clara Ward, through marriage the princess of Chimay.

116. La Chaussée is the area of Saint-Malo where Céline lived.

117. Dorgeres and Lantelme were two famous actresses at the turn of the century. The latter's death by drowning on her honeymoon was a great scandal at the time. The reference to a jury is not explained. La Cerisaye is a reference to Bishop Des Laurents (1713–1785), the next-to-the-last bishop of Saint-Malo. Returning from a meeting in Paris, he was overcome with emotion on arrival in Saint-Malo and cried out, "At long last, I see my dear Saint-Malo again" as he died.

118. Reference to Maria Le Bannier, whom Céline knew in Rennes through his father-in-law, Athanase Follet, whose mistress she was.

119. Theodore Botrel's *La Paimpolaise* dates from 1896 and was first staged by Félix Mayol, noted Parisian songster. Fragson (1869–1913) was a famous music-hall and café circuit singer.

120. The *Terreneuva* was a fishing boat that caught cod off the coast of Newfoundland.

121. René Chateaubriand (1768–1848), a French writer of the Romantic period, was born in Saint-Malo.

122. Céline spent his summer holidays in Saint-Malo from 1941

to 1943 and was there again in February 1944, thus during the time when the German occupying forces sent out air-raid warnings.

123. André Dézarrois, public official, museum curator, and friend of Céline who lent him his apartment in Saint-Malo in the summer of 1941 and 1943.

124. Reference to the engineer Fritz Todt, whom Hitler made responsible for road links in Germany and then for construction wherever the Germans went. Todt thus employed Frenchmen forced into labor on Hitler's public works.

125. He is fantasizing about being freed by Mayer.

126. The architect Yves Hémard bought a house that Céline had wished to buy. Hémard turned it into a corsair museum-cum-café, but it was totally destroyed by the Allied bombings in August 1944.

127. Robert Surcouf (1773–1827), born in Saint-Malo, became a corsair and wealthy ship builder.

128. Guillotin was the eponymous promoter of the guillotine.

129. The Comet, the first jet plane to carry passengers, had its first test flight in October 1949.

130. Paul Claudel (1868–1955), noted author and Nazi sympathizer, who was a member of the Board of Directors of the Gnome and Rhône Company, which made airplane parts and worked for Germany during the war. The company was therefore nationalized in 1945. The trial of its directors later resulted in their acquital. The mocking pseudonym of "Ciborium" is due to Claudel's Catholicism.

131. The *Nationalsozialistisches Kraftfahrer-Korps*, a motorized unit.

132. Another code word for Jews.

133. Joan of Arc (1412–31) was burnt at the stake in Rouen.

134. Reference to Paul Claudel's 1943 hit play *The Satin Slipper*. The "odes" refer to the fact that Claudel had written poems first to Maréchal Pétain, then to DeGaulle.

135. Sacha Guitry, who had been an open supporter of collaboration during the war, and who got off relatively lightly after the war, serving only two months in prison.

136. Philippe Pétain and André Maurois. In his memoirs, Maurois notes that he'd frequented Pétain before the war in the French Information Office in the United States.

137. Reference to François Mauriac, who'd demonstrated more

sympathetic interest in Céline than most of his fellow writers, but who refused to help Céline at the moment of his trial in France in 1950. After the war, he continued to write for *Le Figaro*, becoming a spokesman for the Resistance fighters' point of view.

138. Pétain was serving his sentence at the time on the Isle of Yeu.

139. Paul Lévy, owner of the weekly *"Aux écoutes"* and defender of Céline while he was in Denmark.

140. From 1944 to 1954 the high chancellor of the Legion of Honor was General Bloch-Dassault, brother of the industrialist Marcel Dassault.

141. The concierge of Céline's building.

142. Sigmaringen, seat of Pétain's government in exile.

143. Goering had two sisters, both of whom were doctor's wives. It is not known whether one of them ever came to visit Céline in his room at Sigmaringen.

144. Buchenwald.

145. The existence of places of prostitution in Nazi concentration camps has been attested to.

146. Dachau.

147. Sergeant Bobillot was an important figure for Céline. A hero of the conquest of Tonkin, he died at the age of thirty-five after participating in an attack against the Chinese and destroying their mines. A statue was raised to him in 1888 at the intersection of the boulevards Voltaire and Richard-Lenoir. The two soldiers mentioned after him, Savorgnan de Brazza and Jules Chanoine, fought in France's colonial wars but did not hold as much fascination for Céline as did Bobillot.

148. Kribi is a Cameroonian name. Bikobimbo (Bikimimbo in *Journey to the End of the Night*) was the trading company office that Louis Destouches managed in Cameroon in 1916–17.

149. Darius is Hitler. Céline is referring here to ex-Nazi supporters turned resisters.

150. The Knights Templar was a religious and military order founded in Jerusalem in 1119 that became quite wealthy as the bankers to the papacy and numerous princes. They suffered persecution and were disbanded by Clement V in 1312.

151. From the German word for newspaper. Although Céline refused to write for any collaborationist publications during the war,

232

he did address many letters to periodicals and fellow journalists that were published.

152. Dr. Follet was Louis Destouches's professor at Rennes University, where he did his medical degree, as well as his father-in-law. The others were all physicians and teachers of note.

153. One of the Chatelet Theater's greatest prewar successes was the five-act play *Michel Strogoff* by A. Dennery and Jules Verne.

154. On a number of occasions in his novels, especially *Death on the Installment Plan,* Céline goes on about noodles. He had to eat them often because according to his mother they were one of the few foods whose odor did not seep into her laces.

155. Courtial is the name given in *Death on the Installment Plan* to Raoul Marquis, a publisher-inventor who greatly influenced the young Destouches. Elizabeth Craig was the American dancer with whom Céline lived while writing *Journey,* and to whom it was dedicated. Edith Follet was Céline's second wife, daughter of Dr. Follet, and Janine refers to his first wife, Suzanne, whom Destouches married in London in 1916. This was a very short lived marriage, which in any case was never registered in France.

156. Roman purification ceremony.

157. Céline often refers to St. Vincent at this time for many reasons: he had been a prisoner, he lived in Clichy, he'd been a chaplain of galley ships, and he was founder of a lay order of sisters who looked after the poor.

158. Céline was fond of the word "enthusiasm" and liked to remind people that it came from the Greek, meaning "God in us." He felt that enthusiasm was akin to madness.

159. Noé is a village in the Haute-Garonne where a camp was set up in 1939 that quickly became a gathering point of foreign Jews being deported to Germany. It was a place where particularly the old and the infirm were received. After the liberation, it became an internment camp for collaborators.

160. A reference to "the Lord's Prayer" or the "Our Father," in which God is asked to "forgive us our trespasses as we forgive those who trespass against us."

161. Possibly a reference to Anne Frank, whose diary appeared in French in 1950 to much acclaim.

162. Cécile Sorel (1873–1966), superstar of Parisian theaters, from the Comédie-Française to the Casino de Paris. Having left the

stage in 1933, she converted to Catholicism and joined the Third Order of St. Francis, becoming Sister St.-Cécile. A volume of her memoirs appeared in 1949.

163. A reference to the charity ball of the "Little White Beds," founded in 1921 by the owner of the *L'Intransigeant.*

164. Céline sometimes situates an area for recovering drowned bodies at Moulinaux, and there was a morgue located at the quai de la Rapée.

165. Guillaume Dupuytren (1777–1835) was a surgeon specializing in pathological anatomy. A museum of anatomical curiosities was named after him.

166. Until the Second World War, Paris bus routes were indicated by letters.

167. "Blond" lace is made on a spindle with untreated, natural-colored silk.

168. A reference to Victor Hugo's "Le roi s'amuse," but it is not clear why.

169. Already in "Bagatelles pour un massacre," Céline had begun to ridicule Marcel Proust by deforming his name to Prout-Proust. ("Prou" is also the onomatopoetic expression of the sound of breaking wind.)

170. Reference to Lucien Rebatet (1903–72), journalist for *Je Suis Partout,* a collaborationist publication, and author of the pamphlet *Les Décombres.* He was condemned to death on 23 November 1946 but had his sentence commuted in April 1947. He was freed in July 1952, just when Céline was finishing *Fable.* "Robignol" is also a French slang word for testicle.

171. *Reader's Digest* began publishing a French edition in 1947.

172. Bishop Pierre Cauchon (1371–1442) presided over Joan of Arc's trial.

173. In the Apocalypse.

174. From Moliére's *George Dandin,* act 1 scene 7, "You asked for it, you asked for it, George Dandin."

175. "Without counting the months at the breast" (infancy) is a French expression used in derision to describe people who want to appear younger than they are.

176. Paraphrased from Corneille's *Le Cid.*

177. Madame Voilier, associate of Robert Denoël, was put in charge of the publishing company after his death.

234

178. Céline's wife, Lucette, was detained eleven days before being freed.

179. A famous old department store in the center of Paris.

180. Céline's early manuscripts were written in ink. This novel was the only one written in pencil, presumably because he was denied the use of pens in prison. His last manuscripts were written in ballpoint pen.

181. Aristide Bruant, a Montmartre songster.

182. The Vascons were named in *La Grande Encyclopédie,* which Céline had at his disposal at Klarskovgaard, as the Basque mountain people who attacked Roland in the "Chanson de Roland."

183. From Alfred Vigny's "The Horn."

184. Beers, Suez, and Saint-Gobain were stock market shareholdings.

185. Reference to the caps and uniform worn by the one hundred members of the French Academy.

186. Clementine is a character in the song "Settling Scores" that Céline had copyrighted in March 1937.

187. Achères is a suburb of Paris noted for its use of sewage for the cultivation of marshy vegetables. This passage is reminiscent of other scenes throughout Céline's work in which something like malaria-induced hallucinations are recounted as fact.

188. Reference to Jean-Paul Sartre and the poet Louis Aragon.

189. Where the Ministry of War was situated.

190. During the state visit of French president Vincent Auriol to Washington DC in 1951, there was an accident involving a car in his motorcade in which the chauffeur was killed and a number of passengers injured.

191. Sartre wrote in "Reflections of the Jewish Question" that Céline had been in the pay of the Nazis. This accusation more than anything else infuriated him.

192. Karl Heinrich von Stupnagel (1886–1944) was commander of the German occupying forces from 1942 to 1944. The premiere of *Satin Slipper* by Paul Claudel was held on 26 November 1943 at the Comédie Française. It was a cultural highlight of Paris under the occupation, much heralded by Germans and French alike.

193. Tarnier is the name of the maternity ward where Céline did an obstetric internship from October to December 1922. There he met the Doctors Brindeau (who would become director of his doc-

toral thesis on the Hungarian doctor Semmelweis and his studies of the relationship between hygiene and postpartum maternal death) and Lantuéjoul, with whom Céline remained on good enough terms for the former to attest on his behalf at his trial.

194. Céline, while living in Cameroon, was preoccupied with the problem of cannibalism. In *Journey to the End of the Night* he makes numerous references to it as well.

195. The "Picot bed" was a metal folding bed that won prizes at the World Fairs of 1878 and 1889 and that has constantly been in use by the French army ever since.

196. Charleroi, the Marne, and Saint-Gond were three battles that took place at the beginning of World War I, when Céline was a young cavalryman.

197. The "pip-cell" was a Danish slang word used to describe the "secure" cell where prisoners were mistreated and tortured.

198. In Napoleonic times, some Grand Army prisoners were held in old ships in many English ports, including Portsmouth. Sanitary conditions were shockingly bad.

199. Two sections of Napoleon's army that fought courageously in the Napoleonic Wars.

200. Whereas the Cuirassiers were part of the Heavy Cavalry, the Hussars were members of the Light Cavalry.

201. The Invalides Veteran's Center contains a military museum that carries all the uniforms of the French armies.

202. The "Bats" were a punishment battalion sent to Africa. The reference to "crummy pictures" is obscure. Bringing together the mannequins of the Invalides Museum and the Grévin wax museum perhaps suggests that we should understand the "crummy pictures" to be those from Epinal, a town in eastern France famous for its production of cheap and popular prints.

203. This imagined ghostly unit of the army, the "First Specters," will be referred to again. It seems to represent for the author one of the few groups to which he can still belong.

204. At first the author seems to be defending himself, but he slips into a fantasy of defending the reader in front of a military tribunal of the "First Specters."

205. A reference to the One-Two-Two, a well-known house of prostitution on the rue de Provence.

206. Céline knew about Louis Aragon's *Ballad of the Man who Sang During Torture* from a performance given by the Compagnie Renaud-Barrault in Copenhagen in October 1945.

207. A military parade on 14 July 1913 at Longchamp.

208. The viewing parade of 14 July 1913 saw the launching of the dirigible the "Commandant-Contelle."

209. The "Sabre-et-Meuse" is a military march dating from 1871. The "Sidi-Brahim" is a charge composed in honor of the African Chasseurs to commemorate one of their military exploits. The Marsouins were the navy infantry troops.

210. Raymond Poincaré was president of the French Republic from 1913 to 1920.

211. "Do you see them?"—the first words to a song entitled "The Dream Passes" (1906) in which members of Napoleon's army appear to a young soldier.

212. Names of three military bases in Paris.

213. Radios used to broadcast the time from a "talking clock" at the foot of the Eiffel Tower.

214. Short for "hypochondria," in former times the name of an illness. It seems to be used here as an exclamation.

215. Rio Tinto was a company quoted on the stock exchange.

216. Apparently a reference to the *Cote Desfossés,* a newspaper giving listings of stock quotes.

217. The Paris courts are surrounded by high ironwork gates.

218. Fauldès was the victim, and not the perpetrator, of a famous murder in 1817, which gave rise to a popular song.

219. Céline was sued in June 1939 for anti-Semitic remarks in "École des cadavres."

220. Dictionary publisher.

221. Charles de Gaulle, Mao Tse Tung, Joseph Stalin.

222. No longer a word in common use in French.

223. Pierre Laval and François Mauriac are here taken as witnesses to the torments of dying, the former because he was executed after trying to poison himself, and the latter in recognition of his articles defending those sentenced to death for war crimes after World War II.

224. A reference to Saint Louis's anti-Semitic exhortations: "As for laymen, when they hear [Jews] speak ill of the Christian

faith, they should defend it in no other way than by the sword, they should drive it into the belly of their adversary as deeply as it will go."

225. The silent film star Lila Lee. The "vamp Daisy" cannot be identified.

226. Alexander Bogomoletz (1881–1946) was a Russian biologist who invented a serum used in surgery thought for a while to be a rejuvenating agent.

227. People without legs used to navigate around on their fists, using irons for support.

228. Reference to Paco Durio, a celebrated Montmartre ceramist, friend of Gauguin, and neighbor of Céline, who, according to him, had the last kiln in Montmartre but lacked fuel for it during the First World War. He died in 1939 shortly after being evicted from the Maquis, referred to later in the text.

229. Céline's two transatlantic journeys in 1934 and 1937 were made on the *Champlain* and the *Liberté*.

230. The Maquis, at the northern side of the Montmartre hill, was at the turn of the century a sort of territory unto itself, inhabited by artists and marginal types. It progressively got torn down and replaced by the new buildings on avenue Junot, rue Girardon, and rue Saint-Dereure.

231. Gen Paul did a lot of reproductions of Spanish paintings.

232. Reference to different grades in the Legion of Honor.

233. The rue Taitbout was known for its antique shops and rue La Boétie for its art galleries.

234. Félix Ziem was a Montmartre artist who had a studio in the neighborhood. There's a street named after him in Montmartre.

235. *Le Petit Duc* and *La Périchole* were nineteenth-century operettas.

236. There was an important battle in Lô, department seat of la Manche, in June 1944.

237. Auer gas lamps were a common household item in France at the turn of the century.

238. On 6 December 1951, the Appeals Court rejected "in the interests of the law" the amnesty that Céline had been granted in April. It was a bitter blow to him.

239. This music-score fragment was inserted into the typed

manuscript by ball-point pen, apparently in Céline's writing.

240. The builders of the Atlantic Wall, the Nazis' defense against the Allied invasion.

241. On 25 November 1914, Louis Destouches was awarded a military medal with the following citation: "In liaison with an infantry regiment and his brigade, volunteered to carry under heavy fire an order that the infantry liaison agents hesitated to transmit. Carried this order and was seriously wounded during the mission."

242. Pets Céline had in Denmark, Bébert and Bessie the dog were brought back to France; the others mentioned here were not.

243. Field Marshall Erwin Rommel, Nazi Germany's leading general, was forced to commit suicide in October 1944 after being linked to the military plot against Hitler.

244. The actual date of the Destouches's departure from Paris was 17 June 1944.

245. Yvon Morandat, who occupied Céline's apartment after his departure, put his furniture in storage. When Céline returned to France in 1951 Morandat offered to have the furniture returned to Céline as long as he paid the storage expenses. Céline refused, and the furniture was sold.

246. Apparently this is not so. The seventeenth-century musician J. B. Lully was not at all a ladies' man, and neither was Couperin.

247. The "NRF" (from *La Nouvelle Revue Française*) is the great French publishing house with whom Céline had a long and tumultuous relationship.

248. *Constellation*, started in 1948, was a French imitation of *Readers Digest.*

249. Volvulus is a medical term for a bending of the intestine that causes a blockage.